F
EYR

Eyre, David, 1941-

Float.

$19.95

	DATE		

6/91

© THE BAKER & TAYLOR CO.

FLOAT

New York   Toronto   Auckland

Doubleday   London   Sydney

DAVID EYRE

FLOAT

PUBLISHED BY DOUBLEDAY
a division of Bantam Doubleday Dell Publishing Group, Inc.
666 Fifth Avenue, New York, New York 10103

DOUBLEDAY and the portrayal of an anchor with a dolphin are
trademarks of Doubleday, a division of Bantam Doubleday Dell
Publishing Group, Inc.

DESIGNED BY ANNE LING

Library of Congress Cataloging-in-Publication Data

Eyre, David, 1941–
   Float / by David Eyre
      p.   cm.
   1. Vietnamese Conflict, 1961–1975—Fiction.   I. Title.
PS3555.Y67F55   1990
813′.54—dc20   89–77768
                                                                CIP

ISBN 0-385-26685-5
Copyright © 1990 by David Eyre
All Rights Reserved
Printed in the United States of America
November 1990
FIRST EDITION
BVG

FLOAT

1

PART

1 "Mr. Dubecheck, sir? The gook just threw up."

"Really?"

"Really."

Lieutenant (junior grade) J. P. Dubecheck, USNR, can understand that. The gook is sick for a very good reason.

Dubecheck yawns with utter fatigue. Another day and it is starting with a quiet little muffled cough of rose-gray in the eastern sky. Technically, it started hours ago, at 0000 hours, a moment in time Dubecheck will never come to grips with. It looks like it is going to be a beautiful dawn: a flamingo-pink horizon with black palm-frond silhouettes and Tarzan movie birdcalls. The agate-black river slowly turns dirty brown in the increasing light and begins to stink as the heat rises. The days are like fevers that don't break until the next dawn. Dawn flirts with you, then turns into another bitch of a day. The sky gets white, the air is white, the humidity fills one's head like smoldering kapok. It's just a shame what becomes of the dawn on the river.

Particularly for the little Asian man with his arms tied behind his back at the elbows. He has been squatting motionlessly on his haunches for five hours, his bare feet splayed out on the steel deck plates that rattle over the monotonous grind of the diesels pushing the boat hard against the brown flood tide.

"See? The gook threw up, sir."

Dubecheck looks down at the little man. Sure enough, a golf-ball-size dollop of rice sits steaming between his feet in the silent dawn chill. The man is wet and shivers like a cold bird dog. He wears black shorts and a cross on his thin bare chest. Everyone stares down at him and he stares down into the olive-drab deck plates, looking far ahead at some unpleasant visions; immobilized.

"Maybe he's hurt?"

Hurt? He damn well should be. He's been in a horrible accident. The operative word here is "accident." He's lucky his bowels weren't sucked out his asshole and his intestines left lingering in the river, twisting and coiling like ink in water. Hurt. Tough shit.

"Put a blanket around him and dry his goddamn head off."

Dubecheck looks down at the top of the man's wet black head. Who *is* this guy? *Why* is this guy? The closest Dubecheck will ever get to him is the little ball of rice. He moves the rice out from between the man's feet with the toe of his combat boot, drags it across the deck and sweeps it overboard where it disappears into the silky brown water sluicing alongside the hull. Dubecheck looks after it, where it disappeared into the rush of water, mesmerized by the wake, by the endless flow of current and water. His mind wanders again. As it has been doing more frequently of late. A reminiscence comes by and snatches his mind off; just like the current that has snatched off a balled-up cigarette pack someone has tossed overboard.

"Maybe he's hurt *bad,* though, sir." It is Seaman McDowell speaking at Dubecheck's shoulder as he stands looking off the port bow into the hypnotic flow of the river. Dubecheck turns to see McDowell's highly magnified soft, empty, eighteen-year-old eyes look up at him from behind his large circular glasses. McDowell has a large round gentle face that belies the fact he is, by all weights and measures, stupid. But, to Dubecheck, at least he is not cruel. He is not necessarily kind either, but Dubecheck is generally touched by the tender concern McDowell can affect when he is not gleefully partaking in creating the explosive havoc he is on occasion told to wreak. As if to emphasize that faint trait of compassion, he is holding a New Testament the size of a deck of cards in his hand where a gun should be, since, as Dubecheck recalls, he told McDowell to guard the prisoner, a simple task at worst. The *prisoner*. At least, Dubecheck feels, he takes them.

"Didn't I tell you to guard the prisoner?"

"I did. . . . I mean, instead of standing there pointing a gun at him all day, I decided to tie him to a stanchion."

"Yeah . . . how?" Dubecheck glances over to see the man tethered like a duck.

"I looped some line around his neck with a bowline. He moves, he's tits up." McDowell scratches the side of his nose with the New Testament. "Besides, so I got a gun on him? He tries to jump, I can't shoot 'im. Could you . . . sir?"

McDowell talks in a lulling singsong which makes everything he says make sense. Dubecheck wonders who all these people around him are. Four months ago he didn't know a one of them. Now they're more important to him than his mother. He wonders why McDowell isn't doing something. That's what his leading petty officer, Scoog, is for. To make sure these enlisted men have something to do, to have this postpubescent in front of him polishing something or at least pretending to be available and alert.

"No, *I* couldn't shoot him, McDowell. Why couldn't *you* shoot him?" Dubecheck looks over toward the prisoner. The blanket has slipped off him and he blinks like a stunned bird.

"Because that would be murder, sir. I've figured it all out. I can *kill* people, sir, but I can't *murder* them." McDowell is dead serious. He starts to pick his eyetooth with the corner of his New Testament, going for a small piece of turkey, stuck like a torn tan flag. He's been into the C rats, which reminds Dubecheck that he too is hungry.

"Well . . . you hit it there, sailor. Go get me some C rats with the peaches and pound cake, honey." Dubecheck pinches McDowell on the cheek and heads toward the wheelhouse. He stops over the prisoner and shouts back to McDowell, "See if the gook'll eat somethin'."

Dubecheck squats down on his cracking knees and lifts the prisoner's chin up with his forefinger. Just the right amount of belligerent tension in the fellow's neck to let one know where he stands. His eyes meet Dubecheck's. They are bright and dark brown with a certain deadness in them that Dubecheck has found in the eyes of those who do not mind killing other people for a cause. He will not blink as Dubecheck holds his chin up. Dubecheck drops his finger, undoes the bowline at the nape of the prisoner's neck and tosses the bitter end across the deck.

He picks up the gray blanket and puts it over the man's shoulders. A low grumble comes from the man's whippet-thin chest and he starts to cough violently. Dubecheck wonders whether the guy will die on the spot here. And if he does will he boot him overboard like a dollop of rice? And he wonders how the little fart is still alive anyway . . . after surfacing like a skinned otter, stunned, after a small barrage of concussion grenades had him bobbing on the river under the naked flare light like a . . . survivor. They pulled him from the river by his white shirt back, soggy human flotsam. Now he spits in Dubecheck's face. Mister Tough Guy. Dubecheck is so tired, he wipes the spittle from his cheek with the back of his fist, thinking he should tee this guy's head up like a golf ball and drive it into the river with the stock of the M-60 he sees leaning against the wheelhouse like a baseball bat. But things might be worse for this guy if he lives to talk to his countrymen. By the Chicom Tokarev pistol that was hanging around his neck on a wrist loop, Dubecheck figures this fellow for a heavy-duty cadre. And if he does live, he is in such a world of shit that Dubecheck could feel as sorry for him as he thinks he already does. So he just spits back into his face and gets up and walks around into the wheelhouse.

This is a funny boat, Dubecheck thinks as he stands looking forward. There's an 81mm mortar up front below the fo'c'sle where in better times the fishing gear might be stowed. Built upon the hull of a pleasure cruiser, a perfectly nice boat, which the Navy turned into something meant to go in harm's way. Painting it olive drab and camouflage. Mounting .50-cal here and there. Armor plate. Heavy diesel and twin screws. Antennas bristle from the top of the wheelhouse next to the radar, whip antennas sway like electric saplings. The radio, the size of an accordion, whispers with white noise amplified in a cone over the monotonous grind of the diesels.

There was an unexpected flap last night and now Dubecheck's got a souvenir squatting on the deck: a living, breathing, soggy number with a name he probably can't pronounce.

Problems *do* come up that one is never trained for. Dubecheck does not want to kill this guy, although he is sure a few of his comrades last night *were* killed.

He will turn this fellow over and he will be interrogated and it won't be nice and by the looks of this guy he won't crack and they'll tear at him and pull on him and pound on him and then they'll probably kill him.

Sisler is at the helm, reeking of Mateus. Sisler is twenty-eight but he doesn't look it. He looks forty-nine. Gray bags hang under his eyes like puffy hammocks. And his eyes roll around in a constant pink wash and his jowls droop, though his face is a thin one. His jowls droop under the weight of the perpetual five o'clock shadow that gives him the appearance of a chimney sweep.

The graveyard shift doesn't flatter him. He's driving home after a hard night at the office. Dubecheck thinks on that. They're all just-coming-home-after-the-night-shift. Commuters.

Although they've been up for at least twenty hours, Dubecheck realizes he hasn't said good morning to Sisler. He has been talking to him off and on for hours in grunts and nods and sign language. An overwhelming urge to be civil wells up in Dubecheck.

"Good morning, Sisler."

"Good morning, Mr. Dubecheck."

Sisler turns to Dubecheck, both hands on the wheel, standing there like an elevator operator, his sweat-stained combat fatigue blouse open down his chest. Dubecheck pokes his index finger into the black wiry mess on Sisler's chest and taps it. He looks him in the eye. He utters a confidence.

"We can change the world."

Sisler laughs and looks back out onto the river. Bow wind musses his black hair. Dubecheck turns and peers down into the thick rubber cone the size of a small dunce cap that fits over the cathode ray tube of the pie-faced radar. *Cathode ray tube.* It makes him feel like Buck Rogers as he mumbles the words to himself and watches the thin sweep swish around and around, making silent chartreuse explosions about the contours of land abutting the river. Just another strange-colored planet. A radar sweep is not a good thing to watch if one is tired. But it is a good thing to watch if one is bored. One can count to infinity if one wishes, each revolution hypnotically stabbing your brain with the repetitious, brutal bludgeoning of time. All of a sudden, Dubecheck can't dock this boat soon enough. He pulls his head up, a black raccoon stain around his eyes that will soon fade into a sweaty grime. He sees the RPMs straining at 1800 and reckons they may be making eight knots at best against the solemn brown waters of the Mekong River Delta, a huge, indifferent pulsing vein on the planet that ebbs and flows to the incessant rhythms of the South China Sea and the moon. He hops out of the wheelhouse wondering where his pound cake and peaches are. They are sitting like a couple of olive-drab hockey pucks on the deck next to the prisoner's feet. McDowell is trying to spoon-feed the guy some ham and motherfuckers from another can, but the guy won't have it. He's pursing his lips and shaking his head like a two-year-old.

"McDowell, those things'd kill that guy." Dice-size chunks of industrial-strength ham and khaki-colored lima beans mired in a cloudy urine-colored sauce.

"They're *my* favorite." McDowell seems hurt. As if he slaved over a hot stove all day. Dubecheck bends down and picks up his pound cake and peaches and leaps up on the flat mini-helo deck and decides to ignore this ship of fools for as long as possible, perhaps do a little sight-seeing. The natives are beginning to come out on the river in their sampans. The river is closed for the night so the morning brings a rush hour of commerce just like in the real world. Each sampan has a little yellow and red flag snapping smartly from either the stern or amidships. The flag shows the boat owner's loyalty to the Republic. Everyone appears loyal this morning. It looks at times like the world's largest yacht club: yellow and red burgees fluttering from each craft as the little two-cycle Briggs and Stratton outboards putta-putta the sampans up and down the river. Briggs and Stratton must have gotten here right after Stanley and Livingstone, Dubecheck thinks.

He sits on the deck and opens his tins of food. He tosses an empty can into the river where it sinks like a rock. Littering in the Orient. *Loitering* in the Orient. The bright egg-yolk-colored peaches slide sweetly around in his mouth, the puck of pound cake, possibly baked in 1954, crumbles between his thumb and forefinger. The crumbs slough down into the peach juice. He drinks the mushy mixture down and tosses the can at a little sampan going the other way. A small kid makes a grab for it, misses, laughs and waves. Now this is living. He lights a C rat Pall Mall and sucks in enough sweet nicotine and tar to swell his chest in a cancerous pride and exhales with a delighted sigh. The tobacco fumes comingle with, then overcome the gusts of diesel and sweet mixed octanes of fifty-to-one fumes that now lie on the river's surface like a morning mist.

Sampans come racing out onto the big river from small canals the size of back alleys, a few inches of freeboard separate the choppy wakes of other boats from their huge wicker loads of fruit, vegetables, documents, spies . . . chickens and ducks in small bamboo prisons.

For a moment the sun feels pleasant. Dubecheck lies down and lets the warmth play on his face, feeling as drowsy as if lying on a wooden dock during some idyllic summer vacation by the side of some mythical lake. He's at camp. We've all just come back from a field trip. Boatswain Sisler is at the helm. McDowell is carrying on some missionary work astern with the Abo we found bobbing in the river. Hatch and Scoog are asleep below, heads on their flak-jacket pillows, snoring softly. Zeller and Saltinovitch, last seen poking about in the large carton of C rations, yawning, scratching their nuts and wiping the fatigue from their eyes. A shot goes off on shore.

It is close. Another shot pops off farther inland. Warning shots. Ridiculous. They couldn't be for Dubecheck and his crew. If anybody looks like they've got the off duty sign up, they do. Dubecheck gets up and squints inland, knowing he'll see nothing but what his imagination and conjecture will tell him. The VC warning system. A little old white-goateed man, trembling, firing an ancient carbine into the air. One shot and then he runs and shakily hides the weapon in the bunker beneath the wood pallet in his sister's hooch. Then, somewhere, two young men will run wildly to a spider hole, a narrow dark tunnel dug beneath a stump. They hide in the dirt warren, paralyzed like rabbits, their hearts pounding from their crotches to their throats. Too scared to breathe. One shot. That's enough to bring in a rain of fire, some desultory shit storm, if the wrong people have nothing to do. Sure enough, there must be some jumpy American unit in there, beyond the shoreline and the first paddies, back behind the tree line a half mile away. Some contact might have been made. One shot can be contact. Some jumpy patrol leader is taking no chances and has called in some Air, because an F-4 Phantom jet comes streaking down the river, its bright silver fuselage glistening lethally in the sun, its engine roaring over a deafening subsonic whine. It banks sharply and descends like a goddamn steel hawk; the heat from its exhaust slams down on Dubecheck in a rolling gust of kerosene stench. It slants down, angling unerringly in a lock-on dive. Oooops. He dropped something. Say, you a . . . The F-4 pulls up sharply in a near vertical ascent, flashing like the blade of a knife in the sunlight, twisting as it climbs in a bit of show biz for the boys on earth. A muffled WHUMP arrives at the river after a large, black, greasy fireball has roiled upward a good ways behind the tree line. Napalm. That's it. Probably, previously, a small collection of thatched huts were in a dirt clearing. Now the structures are crackling quietly in flame. The dust, ringing reverberation of shock wave, hangs suspended in the scorched air. Then everything falls down like a dead moth. And everything is dead and real quiet for a while and all you can hear is fire crackling. Jesus.

The F-4 is now just a shiny speck on the horizon. The pilot is on his way back to Bihn Thuy with another combat sortie under his belt. Drinks at the O Club.

Dubecheck is aware of someone next to him. It is Hatch, the tall, gangling obligatory country boy every squad in the American military seems to have. He whistles through his teeth at the dirty black cloud that is still rising. He hands Dubecheck a pair of binoculars. Dubecheck twists and focuses and strains to see across the dry, diked flat behind the scraggly trees into the base of dissipating smoke. Nothing but . . . but what looks like a large scorched pig that wiggles along on its side like a beached fish. Dubecheck hardly imagines he can hear its faint bleating from this far away. A dirty white water buffalo lumbering through some black smoke, dragging an unmanned wooden plow behind it. He takes down the glasses. The oddly innocuous sound of small arms chatter comes wafting across the landscape. It loses its menace over the distance. Little strings of firecrackers popping off impotently in the dirt. A small skirmish of no significance. Over before it really started. Daytime in the Delta. Small pustules of violence on a drab, pockmarked, premonsoon plain, leaving scabs and scorched scars in the dirt. And after the small automatic weapons stop chattering, not long after the crackling fires are out, the birds will take wing again. In the new silence they'll start to chirp again; giving the "all clear." It is all so weirdly disjointed. Nothing *seems* to connect. There-are-long-stretches-of-hot-boredom-eating-at-vigilance-and-sanity-like-flies-on-shit.

Dubecheck looks back to the prisoner. He is still staring down into space with equanimity. Maybe. Dubecheck admires the prisoner's detachment, if that's what it is. It could be shock. Catatonic anxiety.

Prisoners of war do act a little differently. They always walk around in a daze: lollygagging, confused, looking like they've just landed on another unpleasant planet. Due in part, in all probability, to the fact that they are surrounded by people who don't share their same grave appraisal of the situation. Adding to their confusion is the fact that there usually is a language barrier. But there is no communication problem. Shut up! Sit down! Hands up! Eyes ahead! Universal commands that get across readily regardless of race, color and creed. Dubecheck feels there is a dollop of DNA in the chromosomes and genes of Homo sapiens whose genetic message is: how to act upon being captured by the many foes you are likely to encounter in your life.

He could let the gook go. That thought always crosses his mind. Just kidding . . . You can go now. He'd wish the same on himself. Uh . . . do unto others. Hey, Sisler! Close the bank, you hear now? We gonna let off ol' Nguyen here. Right now! And zoom! There he goes. Flashing off like an unhooked, released little trout, white shirttails flying, zigzagging through the short palms, leaping the wrist-thick vines, bounding, boing-boing. Gone. And then . . . and *then* some-dark-night, huddled, scared, confused by the stupid noise, trying frantically to unjam his goddamn, motherfucking, cocksucking M-16, a gook leaps down upon Dubecheck and raises up his tomahawk and's about to bring it down through Dubecheck's sinus when . . . he *stops!* The tomahawk freezes at apogee and the gook gasps, "Rootenant!" . . . He looks around conspiratorially, a descending flare light flickers against his face like a scout's at fireside. "Rootenant Dip Shit!"

"No. It's Dubecheck. Lieutenant Dubecheck!"

"Shhhh." Dirty, sweaty hand across the mouth. "Yes. Yes. Dip Shit. I know. I no kill. I go now. You okay GI." He runs off in a low crouch, then turns and flashes a smile. AK-47 in one hand, tomahawk in the other. A tomahawk? Then he disappears into the one million living silhouettes of a jungle at night, taking his friends with him.

Uhn-hunh. Sure. Dubecheck has already called ahead. There'll be some people to meet the passenger at the dock. He's informed the base commander's nineteen-year-old, going-on-fifty, yeoman petty officer. He will take care of protocol and make the little decisions that will have a lot to do with this guy's future. Better the yeoman second class than the lieutenant commander. The lieutenant commander is a soft, gentle sort who has taken to bed and looks like he intends to remain there for the duration of his tour. The bed belongs to a chubby little Dragon Lady sort of woman who calls herself Madame Phong.

Dubecheck envisions it. Lieutenant Commander ("Tuta" in the local vernacular) C. B. Foote, abed with his demons and the seal-shaped body of his moon-faced mistress Phong. He recalls the time he thought he had enough of an emergency on his hands that he should convey it to the base commander by word. Feeling somewhat hesitant about barging into the Phong residence at 0200 hours, he tiptoed up and peered in through an unshuttered window and saw the softly snoring custard-colored heap of Madame Phong giving off a faint glow in the near dark room. A naked Tuta was kicking fitfully at the twisted sheets about his ankles as he tried to sleep in the muggy heat. The almost unfurnished room had an aura of a darkened laboratory, or worse, a morgue, a cubicle of white tiles casting a muted moonlight. The leaves outside rustled and their shadows played faintly on the walls and ceiling like moths. Tuta's eyes opened wide and he stared at the ceiling. Dubecheck hissed and Tuta sat bolt upright and froze.

"It's me," Dubecheck whispered.

"Jesus Christ the Lord," Tuta whispered back. "Who's you?" He got up and came to the window where he and Dubecheck carried on a whispered conversation, up on their tiptoes through the bars like plotting prisoners.

"I thought that was it, man. Murdered in my bed. Hacked, bludgeoned, whatever. It's bound to happen, Lieutenant. Bound to happen." Flickering leaf shadows mottled Tuta's round, gnomon-nosed face. His eyes had the odd walleyed look of a man who's supposed to have his glasses on.

"I'll bet you're wondering what I'm thinking. Right? Well, I'll tell you, man. Triumphs do not occupy the mind in these mean lonely hours. It's the humiliations, the failures, failures real and imagined." Tuta spoke in a conspiratorial rush, looking about as if they might be overheard by the guards. "Relentless Nada convenes, Lieutenant, at all sober reflections upon one's life such as those that occur in the dark before the dawn. You can look it up. Right?"

"I guess so."

"Bank on it, Bunky. I'm gonna die from lung cancer. I've gotta stop smoking too goddamn much. Two packs last night. My liver aches, or maybe it's my kidney. There's a dull pain in here somewhere, somewhere deep in my dark viscera. Do you know what it looks like? What it looks like inside? Like worms? It must be dark and hot in there. Perfect environment to breed and sustain disease. I'm a grown man and I don't know what the inside of my body looks like. At least I know it's called 'viscera.' Smart guy. I'm thirty-eight and every organ and limb pains."

"Pain is nature's way of letting your body know something is fucked up." Dubecheck remembers that from Mrs. Kraftenberg, fifth grade.

"No shit, Dubecheck? That's good. Every pain and ache is a signal that the end is at hand, that your body is beginning its inexorable march toward a painful, lingering, filthy disease in earnest. Lungs, liver, kidneys, bowels, glands, lymph nodes, arteries . . . each goddamn born-to-fail component just waiting for a cancer or to have a shiv rammed through it while you're bending over to pick up the Sunday newspaper off your own goddamn front porch. Hey! Hey! I gotta get ahold of myself!"

"Yeah. Do that. I gotta go now." Dubecheck forgot what he had come to say and figured it didn't make much difference under the circumstances anyway.

Madame Phong snorted and rolled over in her sleep; her hand reached out next to her as she groped for her chubby buddy.

Tuta looked back over his shoulder at the sound. He and Dubecheck watched her hand blindly search the empty bed, Dubecheck feeling oddly silly, like he was watching a bizarre variation of pin the tail on the donkey.

"Pretty nice stuff, huh?" Tuta seemed truly proud. "She's my mistress. Everybody above full lieutenant has a mistress. Below that they have whores. Hey? You got a smoke?"

"Yeah, sure." Dubecheck popped out a Pall Mall through the wrought-iron bars and Tuta took it. It was as if that was the whole purpose of Dubecheck's two-in-the-morning visit.

"It's rumored she has connections." Tuta turned and tiptoed back toward the narrow little bed as if he were sneaking up on it.

Dubecheck reflects back on that interlude. No, he doesn't think he'll burden the base commander with the situation now at hand. Tuta has his own problems.

o   o   o

Dubecheck sits down on the deck across from the prisoner, out of spitting distance, offers him a Pall Mall knowing he probably only smokes Salems like the rest of the citizens of this menthol-starved nation. Could there be a menthol deficiency in the air of Asia? All things are possible on the planet.

McDowell sits down next to Dubecheck. For a long time, his mouth dully agape, he stares at the prisoner as if he is watching TV. Dubecheck snaps his fingers in front of the young man's trancelike gaze.

"Well, McDowell? What do you *see* here?"

Up comes the New Testament to the eyes and . . . No. It's a camera instead. McDowell focuses in on the top of the prisoner's bowed head. The prisoner didn't respond to Dubecheck asking him if he wanted a cigarette and now someone's going to ask him if he wants his picture taken. And this will be the easy part of his day.

"Set it for less than infinity." Dubecheck looks at McDowell with a cocked head.

"I *know*, sir." McDowell's forefinger and thumb move as subtly on the f-stop as if he was cracking a safe. "Can you get him to look up, sir?"

All of a sudden Dubecheck realizes how he dislikes McDowell, but he also realizes it will pass. Yesterday it was Hatch who repelled him. The day before it was Scoog *and* Sisler when they were drunk and friendly and fawning upon him with the obsequious, bootlicking, transparent frankness enlisted men have around officers as drunk as they are. But he hates McDowell more often lately. It comes from the *cleanliness* of the fellow. He reminds Dubecheck of someone who would be secretary or treasurer of his sophomore class . . . a good grocery clerk. Life would be nothing more than just taking care of business, albeit business would be taken care of well. Neatly and *cleanly.* Give him a dozen ill-kempt Sislers, nay, a gross of Scoogs, but save him from Larry McDowell and his friends with their Plymouth Belvederes and souvenir ashtrays from the Black Hills of South Dakota.

"Yeah, I bet I could get him to look up, McDowell." Dubecheck shakes up another Eisenhower Administration Pall Mall, lights it and waits for Seaman McDowell to get the picture.

"Sir?" McDowell holds the Asahi Pentax up to his eye, elbows out like wings, his tongue curled upward in concentration. "I'm ready, sir."

Dubecheck quells the urge to grind his cigarette out on the kid's temple. He points with it instead. *"He* isn't, though."

McDowell petulantly shows Dubecheck that he knows more about the workings of the world than Dubecheck does. "Well, you can make him, sir."

"I've got a better idea. Gimme your camera."

McDowell hands it over, eyes curious and wide behind his rimless glasses. Dubecheck wonders at what point McDowell, or anyone else who's supposed to take orders, would refuse an order from him. He wonders at what point he, Dark Singer, might refuse. "Move next to him."

Dubecheck frames them together in the viewfinder. Oddly enough, the prisoner has brought his head up and is looking thoughtfully into the lens. His face is softened by the minute mesh of the viewfinder. In frame, a little wand flickers up and down as the two subjects brighten and darken and lighten beneath a dappled pass of mottled clouds scudding overhead. McDowell is blinking thoughtfully, his arm is around the prisoner's shoulder as if posing for a picture with his dog, and the prisoner is looking toward the camera with the dead look the totally confused have. The composition of the two together is so overwhelmingly ridiculous, Dubecheck is mesmerized. Of the two subjects, it is the prisoner who stares back at him like his own self. This is a picture of McDowell at camp. Where in God's name is this picture ever going to hang? The prisoner's face seems to soften the longer Dubecheck holds him and the other fellow in pose. As the dark spaniel eyes of the man widen, Dubecheck realizes he no longer has a thing against this man. He has become a *man,* as Dubecheck always knew he would, back when this man was nothing more than a dull embryonic blip on a radarscope. Back when he had reached the farthest perimeter of some ill-defined patrol he undertook. Back before this man existed, before he was hurt, bobbing in the black water, ducking beneath the surface, swimming desperately while a bright white searchlight flashed back and forth across the river surface like slow lightning. And he has to be hurt. His men were tossing concussion grenades at him like a bunch of kids throwing rocks at a bobbing beer can. If the asshole is not plugged or welded shut, the submarine shock wave can suck out the bowel in a flash, leaving one attached to a floating umbilicus of intestines.

And the whole incident all started at exactly 0000 hours; as if the thing was to have a legitimate beginning, middle and end of its very own that was supposed to mean something. But that doesn't happen much. Really.

2 0000 hours. But never for long. It was as dark as a closet. No moon and a low invisible blanket of cloud. And no night light from all-night drugstores, doughnut shops or night owl cafés. The country was shut down for the night and out on the river, twenty klicks down from the base, inside a vast blackness, Dubecheck and his crew drifted toward the sea, pulled smoothly by a strong ebb tide. It was still and windless, the sense of solitude overwhelming. All Dubecheck heard was the cotton-soft idling of the diesels, the bubbling gurgle of water playing astern as Sisler made slight rudder changes on the current.

Down below there were a few muffled coughs from men wishing they could smoke.

In the black Dubecheck was blind, navigating solely by radar. The only sense that confirmed they were on the river at all was the knowledge that the boat was still floating. Dubecheck peered down the rubber cone over the radar to see if they were still in the middle of the river.

The gain was set so the revolving wand was only thread thin and . . . *bing* . . . what's this? The wand was lashing up against a blip on the river with each circular sweep. A fuzzy green neon blip the size of a grain of rice that glowed, faded, then brightened as the sweep lashed against it like a whip. What *was* this? Nobody was supposed to be out here.

He flicked the scale from five-mile rings to a one-mile ring and Christ! It was at one half mile, one thousand yards and closing. The sweep lashed against the now pea-size blip and the blip faded less easily. It left a faint glow at ten o'clock on the scope. A large log? But it appeared to be moving port to starboard, relatively fast, heading for the south bank five hundred yards to starboard. Now it had stopped. Maybe.

The pistons in the diesels knocked slowly and quietly in the cylinders.

"Back down," Dubecheck whispered. He looked fruitlessly downriver into the blackness, then slammed his eyes back to the rubber, adrenalin rushing fast, constricting his throat. The diesels revved slightly and the boat drifted broadside, resisting the pull of the tide. The backwash of the prop churned the water with a hiss. "Just keep stern way so we can maneuver." At this rate they'd drift down on the blip at roughly six knots . . . they'd close on it in less than five minutes. *Close* it, they'd ram it.

"Hey! Down below." Dubecheck whispered hoarsely over the

increased grind. The water percolated astern and the boat surged on a strong ribbon of current and seemed to lose control as it broached on the flat surface and began to revolve like a leaf on an eddy. The compass spun like a roulette wheel and if things didn't shape up fast, Dubecheck foresaw vertigo and they'd collide with the target like a pinwheel. The engines revved and Sisler spun the helm, trying to find a spot on the compass where the rudder could purchase some water and find the boat a course.

There was a bustling below, some clumping and banging in darkness so thick that night vision was worthless.

"Quiet down there!"

"I'm one-eighty out but I can hold it on course."

"Good. Hold it here. Yeah, we got something. Get ready." Diesel fumes from the exhaust curled back upward into the wheelhouse. Much longer at this position and Dubecheck felt they'd get sick. He heard Scoog's bare feet slap on the decks below and whispered, "Okay, assholes, turn to. On the double."

The blip was just sitting there less than six hundred yards away, dead astern. The heavy cocking of .50-caliber machine guns sounded like snapping big branches, metal rang against metal.

"Scoog! Load a starshell." Dubecheck heard the crew mumbling sleepily, trying to find out from Scoog what was going on. Dubecheck wished he knew himself. It was too large for a recon sampan. It could be a whole platoon of bozos out there, ready to hit the other side and tippy toe around in the night and raise cain. But *was* it moving? Dubecheck *thought* it was but maybe he imagined it. The eyes played tricks out there more than they leveled with you. If it was moving and at the speed he thought, it had to be outboard propelled and with the noise they couldn't have heard him then. In the murk they sure as hell couldn't see him. And they couldn't smell him. The few light puffs of breeze that wafted upriver would push the diesel fumes the other way; besides, they were close to the water and the river smelled very musty, overpoweringly so, like a muggy backwater slough of liquid mold.

"Bring the bow around as slowly as you can. When we catch the current just keep on one-two-zero. Gun it if we have to. If they go, I bet they cross south. Keep right of one-two-zero all the time, man."

Dubecheck felt his heart thumping in a huge circle around his lungs; it also seemed to weigh a lot. The fuzzy caterpillar shape glowed on the radarscope, and inside that glow Dubecheck conjured up a reality of a different dimension: to engage or not to engage . . . and if to engage . . . why? Why? Because it was his fucking job.

It could be a provincial reconnaissance unit. A bunch of PRU pirates led by some AID cum CIA alphabetical acronymic maniac like Snazzy Fesler. But they would have *told* Dubecheck that; but then again he wouldn't bet on it. There were too many other diversions to keep staff et al from being totally consumed with coordinating what the poor bug-eyed jerks out tromping around in the dark with loaded guns and tight assholes were doing for a living.

Two hundred yards. He heard and felt his heart beating in his head. And *they* stopped. And they were stopped because they were *frozen* and they were probably tasting copper pennies and breathing softly through their mouths and quickly licking their dry lips because they knew that someone else knew they were there and they weren't supposed to be there. It was extraordinarily crowded out on the river.

"Come around starboard." Why? Why not just go home?

Sisler spun the helm, the port bow caught the current and the boat fell away from course and bore down on the reciprocal.

"I'll need power, sir." Sisler's voice quavered some.

"Use it." The diesels clattered as the boat surged down on the target like a breaker. Dubecheck's palms were sticky wet and his heart pounded as if he'd been running. He reached in a dark corner of the wheelhouse and blindly groped for his M-16. It had a little handle on the top like a fucking briefcase. Time to go to work. It not only looked like a toy but felt like one. It seemed so ineffectually light, but it felt better in his hands than sweat did.

"All stop!"

Sisler backed down hard. The blip was gone, it disappeared into the center. They were *all* in the center. The deck vibrated and rattled, steel clanked against steel. It sounded like a million nails raining upon a tin roof. The water churned and frothed astern. They had arrived like garbage men at dawn. Dubecheck reached over his head, fumbling for the spotlight switch. He'd blown it. They'd arrived like a reeling, stumbling drunk somersaulting down the stairs. Dubecheck needed light. If just for a moment.

"Grab the flare pistol!" Goddamnit! Why didn't he already have it? He heard Sisler clumsily groping in the box for it, muttering, swearing. The boat began to spin slowly like a . . . like a bottle . . . spin the bottle . . . sixth grade, and it slowed on a girl named Marilyn who wore braces and her breath smelled like a tin can and what *was* this! Why does the mind *do* that? The spotlight was angled up into the universe and the beam was swallowed up by the darkness above. Jesus fucking terrific! Why not have a neon sign on the boat instead? EAT! SHOOT HERE! Dubecheck twisted the handle back and forth, up and down, trying to find the river surface. The sampan was huge! The light locked on. One, two, three, four, no . . . five or six white shirts dove overboard and disappeared beneath the surface.

"Flare!"

The flare whooshed up out of the pistol. It arced and ignited in a matchstick-yellow flame, hissed, then spread a soft candlelight upon the river, making it the color of light mud. The sampan appeared to be empty, bobbing and rocking from the hasty abandonment. It was less than a hundred and fifty feet away.

"Hose it down!"

The two port-side .50s opened up with an awesome barking, shooting out slugs the size of small thick cigars that hit the river with slaps. The tracers painted thin red lines into the surface, then dreamily ricocheted up into the darkness and faded to nothingness. Foot-high geysers curtained the sampan's hull at waterline.

"Scoog! Scoog! Light!"

The flare slowly descended, flickering, sputtering out, spreading licks of orange light over the now dark brown surface.

The hollow thunk of Scoog's starshell left the mortar tube with a ringing clang. It was quiet. The stinging sour smell of cordite hung in the air like pollen. The small flare hit the river with a hiss. The starshell burst high overhead, illuminating a huge expanse of water with a brilliant white light. The river appeared a flat, khaki-colored plain rimmed by a black nothingness . . . a huge, dirty tan disc.

"There!"

A head, then two heads, like bobbing black balls, broke the surface seventy yards away. The heads ducked back under the surface as the pulsing high light cast unearthly colors, a cone slowly descending from what seemed like outer space . . . fluorescence . . . the *cathode rays* had come alive and they were all made of flesh and bone and blood and breath and steel and fire and fear and the eternally unnerving sound of screaming human beings.

"There! There! Over there!" An M-16 ran out a quick dozen and the bumblebee-size zingers nicked at the river like it was pavement and skipped off somewhere into the darkness.

Dubecheck pointed toward where the last head ducked under and Sisler moved the boat toward the small watery swirl. As the starshell lost its brilliance, a dirty dusk started to settle.

"Pop out another one!" Two heads broke the surface a hundred yards astern, then submerged. They were dispersing with great effectiveness, but it looked like every man for himself. The second starshell popped like a flashbulb high in the sky and the great tan plain was bright again. The guys were so close, their mouths could be seen gaping wide, sucking in oxygen, then snapping shut, puffed-cheeked, before they dipped beneath the surface. Another person surfaced and began to breaststroke toward the shoreline, lunging up out of the water, straining to break the surface as if he were swimming through glue. Dubecheck fired his M-16, putting a spray of innocuous full auto across the swimmer's bow, cutting off his line to the shore, wondering why he just didn't waste the guy. . . . *Because.* . . . Because Dubecheck is a bad killer. Because he can kill *somebody,* but he can't *murder* anyone . . . and this was all just a real bad unnecessary dream . . . a loud, really bizarre *movie,* and maybe, just maybe, it was all unreal because the light was white and the water was mud and the tracers careened off dreamily and pinwheeled, no, cartwheeled off into the void and it was all like a big noisy kaleidoscope and the pieces shifted and slammed together with a horseshoe ring-clang-ring of .50-cal cocking, recoiling, banging and a small waterfall of brass raining on the steel decks like pissed rivets and the snap, crackle, pop of 5.67mm and the wheezing grind of diesels and people shouting, ". . . there! where? where? there! where! there! . . ."

A metronomic clatter of .50-cal beside Dubecheck's ear snatched him from a fog. Tracers still sketched wild red scratches against the night, one could watch them forever. Another burst across the man's line of flight did not dissuade him. How could you kill someone *swimming* through the water? All Judeo-Christian ethics and an Anglo-Saxon sense of fair play dictate that you wait until the fellow hits the beach and gets up, stands erect . . . like a man, and *then,* and not before, shoot him in the back before he becomes a moving target. Why didn't he stop? He could've hit the guy by *accident.* That was now the problem, avoid all accidents. The boat closed the bank rapidly and there could be a lot of the wrong people there. The man closest to shore bobbed beneath the surface, then popped up again. He must have been breathing on fear, for he couldn't have had enough oxygen in his lungs to blow out a match. The descending starshell dimmed and the scene began to fade from streetlamp fluorescence to moonlight white.

The hull of the boat shuddered and rang as two concussion grenades exploded like tiny depth charges out toward where two swimmers were seen to dive. It was getting darker and the boat was too close to shore to pop another starshell. The object now was to prevent this guy from reaching shore and to *not* kill him. Dube- check had no idea where this decision had come from; but acted on it nevertheless.

"Cease fire! Cease fire!" The scattered crackling M-16s came to a ragged halt. A few more rounds popped off. Dubecheck had found that it is as hard to get people to stop shooting as it is to get guys to stop tossing around the football so you can choose up sides. "Cease fire, goddamnit! Scoog! Shoot the next son of a bitch that pops one off!" "Yo!" It was probably Scoog plinking into the river anyway. Scoog shouted, "Goddamnit! You heard 'im! Cease fucking fire, you cocksucking sons a . . ."

"Scoog! Shut up!" Dubecheck turned and backhanded Sisler's shoulder with a slap. "Back down! You're gonna run this thing up on the bank!"

Sure enough, the boat was being drawn toward the shoreline as if they were drifting down on a waterfall; a swift eddy of current began to twist the boat and send it sideways toward the bank. Where jagged trees skeined with vines loomed up suddenly like huge ragged spiderwebs, the macabre struggling vegetation growing up out of the damage of defoliation, very eerie, and then it was black again and night vision was shot and the rot on the land could be smelled.

"Pop another flare!" Dubecheck whispered hoarsely as if someone ashore could eavesdrop. He slammed his head down on the rubber cone. The blip was gone. He switched scale. The blip had drifted off and was far downriver. Dubecheck came out of the wheelhouse and leapt up on the deck as if space would help him get his bearings. He didn't know where any of those people were. The pistol flare shoosed out of the wheelhouse and popped open low in the sky like a campfire. He stood up on the deck like a tin can on a fence post with no more than ten lousy little baby bullets in his M-16, wondering what insanity this was, caught up in an adrenalin flush in an incident that was, on its own, crashing recklessly out of control.

"Whadda we doin', sir?" Scoog actually reached up and tugged at Dubecheck's trousers.

"Good goddamn question, Scoog. Just be ready to hose down the shore."

There were two of them, up for air less than fifty feet away. And then, oddly enough, they seemed very dangerous. They'd strung

Dubecheck and his crew out to where fear and real danger reached out and touched them like the overhanging boughs from the scraggly trees ashore that brushed the hull with scrapes like fingernails down a blackboard. Dubecheck's throat was thick and his body rippled in short spasms. His hands were ice cold. He could *hear* those men gasping and choking on the water and saw their thousand-pound arms flapping against the water like useless paddles. Dubecheck dropped and pressed himself onto the deck. He fired off a short burst over their heads. A guttural babble of M-60 streamed out from below and one head disappeared at the waterline, extinguished in the dark like the light. The boat broached, bow out toward the river, and Dubecheck saw Sisler's broad back to the beach, the stern opening on the wheelhouse and a thousand shapes moving ashore. He jumped down and moved into the wheelhouse and emptied his clip at a jagged black tangle astern.

"We're stuck!" Sisler shouted windedly, as if he'd been trying to pull the boat off the shore by hand. The diesels revved wildly. The ebb tide was flowing so fast that the wake dropped by the second. The stern was sinking, the props digging themselves into mud like spinning wheels. The noise was awesome in the surrounding nothingness as the boat bawled like a cow mired in mud.

"Everybody forward!" Dubecheck heard the clatter of feet moving toward the bow, ammo boxes being dragged forward. The urgency of the moment was not lost on anyone. It would be a long, God-awful night sitting in a boat high and dry, not breathing, your eyes bugging out like gargoyles, doing isometrics with your sphincter, thinking that this was all some terrible mistake, you really needn't be here, and wondering how many of those people got away and how many saw this hulk settle into this black tar pit.

Sisler rammed forward on one screw, then another, alternating, trying to get the stern to waddle up and out, to get up off its ass and stand up and walk away. The port screw caught a bit and the hull lurched to starboard an inch. Sisler drove on the starboard and the boat inched to port. Dubecheck looked astern, just waiting for the beach to erupt in a noisy curtain of green tracers or worse, the horrible chilling hiss of B-70 RPGs. A certain calmness overcame him and he turned back to Sisler and calmly said, "Get the fucking boat off the beach."

The hull shuddered as the stern wiggled and fishtailed into deeper water. The boat glided off into the dark comfort of the river. "Nice work, buddy." He could feel his body then and was chilled. Apparent wind hit his sweat-drenched body like a cool breeze and he shuddered. He flicked on the spotlight and flashed it across the water. Ninety feet away someone slowly trod water with agonizing effort. They eased up toward the person. His face was grayish yellow in the fading cone of light. His lids were half closed. He appeared drugged. The men ran from starboard to port and peered out at the enemy.

"Pull alongside, I'll get him." Dubecheck pulled his 9mm automatic from the baggy pocket on his thigh as he crawled on his hands and knees along the gunwale. The man's white shirt glowed dully in the dark. Dubecheck pointed the pistol at the man's head as it lolled around on his neck. It would be so easy. An insignificant crack in the vast emptiness of this insignificant night. The man's eyes were glazed as he looked into the ugly iris-size muzzle of Dubecheck's piece. Dubecheck flicked off the safety with his thumb. It would be easy, but not for him. He could kill people but he couldn't murder them. He reached out and grabbed the back of the man's shirt and pulled him up against the hull.

"Bear a hand." The man's chest was a bellows; he felt the man's heart thumping wildly against his fist, thinking how easily hearts can be made to stop. Scoog and McDowell reached down and gaffed him up with their hands; he came aboard like a slender fish. Dubecheck dragged him down the gunwale by a dangling, limp arm and left him lying spread on the deck in front of the wheelhouse. The man's stomach sucked in and out and he moaned. Then he began to vomit and cough. His shorts were halfway down the fish-belly-white mounds of his tiny ass. Water spread around him like he was melting in the dark.

Dubecheck looked up to see the crew staring down at the man as his body arched and strained with dry heaves. His insides could be pudding. He arched high again and Dubecheck stomped down hard with his bare foot on the man's forearm: a Tokarev pistol was looped around the man's wrist by a thong attached to the bottom of the grip. A Chinese-made, or "Chicom" in the parlance, little number chock-full of 7.63 by 25mm bullets cranked out by the Czechoslovakian arsenal in Prague. Only VC officers or cadre carried those things, or so the legend went. Or NVA. This guy was the real thing. The thing you read about in the newspapers and heard about on TV and talked about at Counter-Insurgency School.

Dubecheck took the weapon off the man's wrist. The man breathed slowly, savoring oxygen, coming back to the real world, the one he fought so hard to stay in. He stared down into the wet steel deck inches from his eyes as if having mixed feelings about it.

Dubecheck sat him up against the front of the wheelhouse like a broken puppet. He didn't weigh more than a hundred and ten pounds. Dubecheck peered into the prisoner's face with a flashlight, looking at him with the goonlike curiosity one feels around a celebrity. The face was thin and hard; a bronze color began to flush back to it. His black hair drained down his cheeks and his breath smelled sour. I have met the enemy and his breath stinks. Dubecheck rose up and told Scoog to tie the man up and Sisler to take them all home.

The engines ground as the hull surged into a fresh dawn breeze.

The enemy turned out to be another human being. Just as Dubecheck had suspected. He'd heard them before, their weapons firing, he'd seen the garbage and wreckage they'd left behind. He'd seen them dead, their carcasses lying around in black pajamas, the pajamas caked with dry red mud, pale purple bloodstains on their hands. There were four or five and now they were gone and Dubecheck felt drained, depressed and foolish, and wondered just exactly why they all went through this, why they did it. It was just like real life and in real life you don't *have* to do all the things you think you have to do . . . you can fake 'em, fake 'em real well as a matter of fact.

Dubecheck looked down on the radar and flicked it to ten miles. The algae-green fingers of two islands glowed on the scope, indicating they'd drifted west several kilometers since this flap commenced.

His body started to shake from release. The sweep searched for the blip that might be the sampan, but it was gone and not worth the search. It was probably just a deadhead by then, bow up, bobbing out there in the dark. The sampan had been killed. The thought brought Dubecheck back to the realities of his job. There would have to be a report. A SITREP or a SPOTREP, a summary of the situation. This one would be an exercise in imagination . . . it would be terse. Sometimes they were fun though. Terse reports reflected a certain macho reserve that went over well in the military. "Sighted sub, sank same." Clever. The *sine qua non*, the world heavyweight champion of SPOTREPs. Pass off all incidents as if they were mere irritants in the larger-scheme-of-things. Well, come to think of it, that's all they were. "Sighted sampan, created navigational hazard." Dubecheck mused a moment as he stared up at a small break in the clouds. A star shone at him. He was willingly doing all this. He wondered what had brought this about. Maybe he'd ask Norman the NILO when they were high and they could pretend their answers made sense. Would this SPOTREP be confidential or secret? Was this event a secret? One hoped not. Too many people already knew about it. He'd make it confidential though. Dubecheck couldn't even recall if there was a message that could just be sent without a classification. The fucking lunch menu could be top secret if someone wanted it to be.

Ah, now he remembered. It was supposed to be secret if somebody was killed. Yeah. That was it. And secret messages went out on green paper, or did they go out on pink? Or yellow? Color-coded claptrap. Fabrications that taxed the brain. He'd seen so many lies typed out that he had difficulty believing anything, and that was an uneasy state of affairs. In fact he'd typed out some lies himself, so there you go, and people had read them, believed them, initialed them and filed them right on down the line. But was anybody killed? One would think a few of those oriental chaps might have bought the farm. Might have become KIAs. Killed In Action. Some dude's obituary, an American acronym typed out on a four-inch by eight-inch piece of newsprint with the significance of a snowflake in a blizzard. No. No KIA on this SPOTREP. They all got away, which was neither good nor bad. They swam to shore and bounded into the bush like coyotes. Except for one. He shivered on the deck and stared at molecules, probably thoughtfully analyzing his karma, which had turned as sour as his breath. Dubecheck should have had McDowell photograph him, then Dubecheck could point to the photo and say, "This is forlorn." The prisoner squatted, elbows behind his back, his face as empty as if it were made of wax, as empty as his knowledge of the future. What did a guy draw on then?

Dubecheck felt . . . felt sorry for him. The feeling came so easily, it must be right. And he had more in bond with the man on the deck than with the people he turned the man over to, stronger than his bond with the White Mice, stronger than the ones with the loud, red-faced, dice-cup-thumping senior officers, stronger than with the President of the U. S. of A., and stronger than with his coterie of well-scrubbed, bright, witty, intelligent, arrogant, cocksure team player assholes running the war. The guys who always needed to win at gin and tennis. Oblah-dee, oblah-dah. And the guy on the deck had notches, more than likely, on his gun and baby blood on his hands. We're all as vicious as we can be as we drive around through the stars in a brand-new late twentieth-century karma. And that guy's karma check was as irrefutable as Dubecheck's law: someone's bad luck is your good karma. And vice versa.

3 Camaraderie. No other word for it. They're in the next room on the other side of a thick, dirty white plaster partition talking idly, a few men and a few near men with large Adam's apples and pimples sitting in various stages of undress in the wet heat, toying with their dog tags, picking their toes and smoking cigarettes. They sit on their dirty mattresses on their bunks with their legs folded beneath them like Cub Scouts. Mosquito netting hangs like bunting from the racks. They chatter in the soft easy manner of men with no particular place to go and nothing particular to do. Chattering quietly like monkeys at ease in a jungle clearing. For a moment their talk is about women.

There is silence, a scratch of a match, a nail clipper clicking.

Lieutenant (jg) Dubecheck, alone on the other side of the partition, sitting at a small desk, stops writing and leans back to eavesdrop. He taps his pencil against his nose and stares up past the broken fan into the high white ceiling and thinks upon the rising coil of smoke snaking out of the Pall Mall that smolders in his ashtray. Watching the smoke as it mingles at the ceiling with that of Gunner's Mate First Class Rodney Scoog's Lucky Strike.

He visualizes Scoog on the other side of the partition: sitting on the edge of his broken bunk in olive-drab boxer shorts, his penis peeking out, his condom-white torso blotched with rosettes of acne; cigarette between his yellow fingers, holding court before the affable, semicretinous gaggle of sailors who comprise Dubecheck's command.

It is in inane lucid moments such as these that Dubecheck often finds himself legitimately wondering how he got here, floundering in the invisible currents of chance.

A professor named Teague sure helped. An insufferable poseur, Teague would stroll before Dubecheck and his classmates like a foppish, chalk-dusted boulevardier, as if born with a pipe in his mouth and reasonableness in his demeanor. In the vast desert of Dubecheck's undergraduate daze, Teague stood out. He would walk casually about the room, the wooden floor creaking beneath his chukka boots, pausing to punctuate his prattle by sucking on his pipe and brushing imaginary lint off his tweed jacket. On occasion he would go to the window and gaze out, mellifluously prating, soothed by the sound of his own voice, perhaps gazing at the huge chunks of words coming from his mouth, big soap bubbles of words floating out on the hot air, then popping into nothingness: "emanate . . . dichotomous . . . manifestations emanating from socioeconomic . . . a deferential dialectic . . ." And Dubecheck and his mates sat, like twits, writing all that drivel down. It came to Dubecheck's attention one glorious day that everyone's purpose would be much better served if the professor had inserted, in place of every word of mellifluous weight, the word "cheese." It was a growing awareness of such reasonableness that started Dubecheck on his thousand-step journey to the deck of a boat pushing water up a dirty river in Southeast Asia.

And so it came to pass that, prior to the final examination for this fellow, rather than study, Dubecheck played pool and drank beer with some honest ne'er-do-wells like himself, then moseyed into the examination full of bright ideas and an empty blue book. As he wrote circles around the question, cautiously sniffed at it, picked it up and turned it in his hand like a chimp perusing a ball, he was hit by the sudden type of brilliant flash only mystics and drinkers can have. At every point in a sentence where a meaningful word would normally belong, he inserted the name of a cheese instead. Brie was the first to go down. Limburger, Swiss, Stilton and Cheddar followed in rapid order. Gorgonzola seemed to deserve an exclamation mark after it, such was the force it conveyed to him. Cheese words came tumbling out of his pen like boulders in the avalanche of sentences that began to fill his blue book. He was the first to finish the examination and walked out of the room to the awestruck gawkings of his classmates. He had completed the final in fifteen minutes.

To his surprise, he received an F. The letter was written on the inside cover of the blue book and took up the whole page. Scribbled below like a hasty afterthought were the words "Come see me."

Associate Professor Edwin Teague sat at his cluttered desk in his cluttered little office. His graduate assistant sat in a straight-backed chair in the corner, hands folded on his lap, peering at Dubecheck from behind glasses reflecting the glare of a fluorescent tube flickering in its death throes.

Teague shuffled papers on his desk in a long contrived effort to ignore Dubecheck's presence, then turned and looked at him thoughtfully, his head cocked in an affectation of "wry amusement." He sucked on his unlit pipe and tried not to blink.

"I make it a point to review all A's and F's my assistant awards my students. An F such as this one, on the final examination, compels me to try and, um, let us say convey a . . . umm, a sense of . . . well, the seriousness of the nature of this . . . this . . . ." Teague rolled up the blue book and began to drum it on his knee in hopes of finding some words. He dumped it off on Dubecheck.

"Is there anything *you* have to say about this?" Dubecheck looked down at the floor, wondering how they put the designs in linoleum, and listened to the assistant snuff snot up into his sinus. Then he shrugged contritely and shook his head. No, he had nothing to say. Teague read from the blue book, after clearing his throat. " 'The Austrian chancellor, Monterey Jack, was equally concerned about the European balance of power. The Congress of Vienna, assembled in Gouda in 1814, led to the formation of an alliance between Stilton, Chilton and Brie. Forces led by Count Gorgonzola eventually carried the day. Soon came the Treaty of Port Salut . . .' Ha-ha. F. Do you think it is funny now, Mr. Dubecheck?" Puff, puff, puff. "I find an F a serious thing, Mr. Dubecheck. . . . I happen to find it a very serious thing." Teague swiveled in his chair and stared at Dubecheck.

As a matter of fact, yes, Dubecheck still thought it funny, but preferred to keep the thought to himself and preferred to carry on his half of the conversation within his own head. Serious? How serious? As serious as the clutch going out on his car? As serious as his father's cancer? As serious as his aching lust for the scrubbed pink, fluffy blonde, rose-scented snatch who sat three rows in front of him in this aimless, inane class he elected to take in order to fulfill requirements leading to . . . to what? He had pretty much had it with all this idiocy geared to keep him off the streets, out of the menial job market and out of the Army. And he had pretty much had it with all the Edwin Teagues he'd run up against since he was five.

Did-he-have-anything-to-say? Where would he start? They hadn't taught him to answer the way he wanted to. So he taught himself and he chose here not to answer.

"You're a senior, Dubecheck. I've checked your transcript and an F from me does not allow you to graduate this spring. I have no particular desire to see you *not* graduate, nor do I have any particular desire to see you graduate. But you'd find some small course soon enough and graduate eventually. *I'll* not fail you. In the end, you'll fail yourself." Professor Teague leaned back magnanimously in his chair. It squeaked as he swiveled to and fro. He puffed on his dead pipe and looked over the rim of his glasses at Dubecheck, who showed no emotion as Teague's words rolled around in his head like bilge water.

"This doesn't seem to particularly please you." He rocked forward in his chair and withdrew his pipe from his mouth. He tapped the pipe bowl into his palm and looked toward his assistant. "He's not pleased, Mr. Treadwell."

Treadwell, not sure of what to do, responded with a contemptuous snort. Dubecheck looked toward Treadwell's white neon eyes and said, "I am overcome with gratitude, Professor Teague." Since Dubecheck didn't know exactly how he meant that, Teague didn't know exactly how to take it. Dubecheck turned to see Teague's eyes narrow, his noblesse oblige wobble on its knees as if it had been hit with a right cross. Teague spoke with a little less patronizing wind in his sails.

"Students like you cause me pain, Mr. Dubecheck. The waste, the indifference, the immaturity . . . and yes . . . sheer ignorance. And it hurts me. It hurts me very much."

So Dubecheck graduated and a college degree enabled John Paul Dubecheck to become, after a brief stint elsewhere, a commissioned officer in the United States Navy.

The brief stint elsewhere was the U. S. Navy's Officer Candidate School in Newport, Rhode Island, where during a period of roughly one hundred and twenty days white guys with college degrees found themselves transformed from young civilians into young commissioned officers. Ensigns, to be exact, to swell the ranks demanded by the spot of bother in Southeast Asia.

Dubecheck was about to be drafted into the Army, whisked off to Fort Ord, California, and a two-year tour as a GI when some vet on a bar stool told him he might as well be an officer because they got paid more and it looked good on your résumé if you were ever thinking of having one.

So Dubecheck took a half day's worth of written examinations and, while a chief in dress blues graded them, sat in the hot Navy recruiting office that had posters on the wall that made the Navy look like an exotic travel bureau: smiling sailors against a backdrop of picture postcard ports of call. He was the only civilian in the fluorescent-lit room. A first class yeoman and a second class petty officer sat at their desks like a couple of secretaries talking about the Stanley Cup hockey finals. Outside it was raining and gray and Dubecheck felt as silly as a person interviewing for a job he didn't really need, let alone want.

Then he went into a small bare room with the chief, who closed the door behind them for privacy. This was to be the "oral interview." It consisted of one question. "Do you drink?" Dubecheck said, yeah, he did, and the chief told him to have his sweet ass on the doorstep the next morning at 0800 hours sharp to be sworn in. And after he was duly sworn in, he found himself out on the sidewalk with a playing-card deck of the International Code of Signals. He was told to memorize them before reporting to OCS three months later.

The four months at OCS were sort of like summer camp combined with the petty hazing of a boys' club. Long hours of "academics," a modicum of the usual chicken shit and marching. Lots of marching. Lots of early eighteenth-century close order drill with old M-1 Garand rifles.

His company was very bad at marching. They came in last every week at the Saturday pass-in-review competition.

Preparing to column-left, moving into an eighty-man synchronized left turn preparatory to bearing down upon the reviewing stand where El Commandante and his minions stood, the bickering inside the slowly wheeling mass of young men was intense. Lots of sniping and bitching as upper classmen and true believers whispered hoarsely, "Dress it up! Dress it up!" "Watch your hands! Watch the swing!" "Not so fast! Slow down! Pick it up!" There was near fucking hysteria inside that clumsy, khaki-colored chorus line mincing around a ninety-degree turn just before they'd begin to kick out and stride as one, a small batch of boys as symmetrical as a tennis-court-size cornfield, bearing down for their big moment—a full-on precision-swivel "Eyes right!" salute to the commandant, who stood on a raised platform with his right hand welded to his brow in a perpetual salute as company after company, sixteen of them, passed in review. It was a rush.

His company always graded out last. Some guy, two in, third row from the back, would have his dick hanging out or somebody's World War I puttee would slip down around his ankle like a bag lady's nylon stocking. Serious business. The company officers, student and cadre, would fret. So they'd have the company practice marching hour after hour in one of the parking lots. Right oblique, left oblique, column this, column that.

Looking back upon the marching, his puttees, his toy soldier schoolboy patrol bandolier, his unloaded gun, he figures it was as good a training as any.

O   O   O

Dubecheck rocks forward and the chair scrapes the tile floor. The soft babble in the next room washes over him like Muzak. They're talking about cars as well as fucking now and they will continue to do so until they get hungry. He shuts their voices out and tries to concentrate upon his menial task. Is it a SITREP or a CASREP? It is a CASREP, a Casualty Report on an inanimate object. But he can't concentrate. He is just aware of staring at his name on the envelope of a letter sent to him by a woman presuming to be his girlfriend. *His name.* Like his great naval predecessor, Jones, Dubecheck's name, like so many other things, starts out with such great promise and ends with a shrug. John Paul . . . Dubecheck. Lt. (jg) John Paul Dubecheck. His name shimmers up from the pink envelope like a mirage through the heat. Sweat trickles down from his armpits in droplets that must be wiped or slapped away like irritating flies. The heavy perfume from the envelope wafts up and mingles with the pervading stench around him; the odors begin to rise up from the street below as the midmorning sun cooks up a stinking stew of shit, urine, diesel, dust and rotten garbage. It makes the air as thick as hot fog. Dubecheck feels he could drag his fingernails across his skin and the smell would cake under his nails in a gray-green film.

It is already so hot and humid, his cheeks and ears are beginning to burn. He gets up and walks out to the veranda and looks down through wrought-iron curlicues at the huge pile of garbage the gooks are amassing in the narrow dirt street three stories below.

The pile has been there as long as he can remember. It is beginning to have some curious architectural and geological characteristics Dubecheck finds interesting. The chief architect seems to be an ancient crone in a white tunic and baggy black silk pants. She is now struggling barefoot across the chuckholed street with a bucket of slop hanging from her right fist. As she approaches the pile she gives herself a running start and with an underhanded pitch, as if quenching a fire, flies the slop up toward the summit that towers over her head. The garbage arcs near the summit, then slides down the sides and builds upon the perfect cone that now takes up half the street, leaving it wide enough for only one cyclo or a Jeep driven by a drunk. The street doesn't lead to much anyway. It dead-ends fifty feet to the left in a small lot full of weeds, empty oil drums, a brier patch of rusty concertina wire and, today, a woman kneeling next to some dead soldier's coffin. Her head is buried in her forearms resting atop the coffin, which, draped in the yellow and red flag of the Republic, looks like a big, bright box of firecrackers. Her tiny fists pound the coffin slowly. She's exhausted. Earlier she had been thumping the coffin like a tympanist, wailing and moaning and crying and carrying on, but the guy still wouldn't come out of the box.

The woman had awakened Dubecheck a little after dawn and now he feels as exhausted as the woman looks. Two spindly old men in baggy blue shorts and dirty T-shirts stand off from her at a discreet distance. One impatiently rocks the handles of a big wood wheelbarrow back and forth, dumping loads of air. The other is lighting a cigarette from the butt of one his partner has just finished. Soon they will go over and load the coffin on their wheelbarrow, wheel it along the path through the weeds, around a pile of oil drums, and stuff it into the stucco charnelhouse that sits just out of sight. Then they'll burn the box. That's what else is in the vacant lot: a small mom and pop crematorium the size of a large doghouse. These are small people. Dubecheck wants to be gone before they kindle today's fire.

The men go over to the woman and the guy with the cigarette clenched between his teeth gently tugs at the woman's shoulder. That sets her off and she wails and falls back, swaying around on her knees like a flowing sea plant. Down below, the old crone arcs another bucket of garbage up toward the summit.

The keening, nerve-wracking wail of the woman at dawn has now, at midmorning, become nothing more than another dissonant decibel in the growing city sounds of the provincial capital of the Southeast Asian outpost. Traffic is picking up on Tu Do Street fifty feet to Dubecheck's right. From the third-story balcony of the old, crumbling windowless French hotel the Navy has commandeered for its warriors, Dubecheck gazes out over the tile-roofed, three-clumped textures of Dong My. He hears the goose-call honkings of tiny cars, bicycles ringing and an occasional truck accelerating slowly, then shifting under a heavy load. The sound of hammers pounding comes from across the street where a two-story building is cocooned in a bamboo scaffolding. A half dozen men in blue shorts and sleeveless T-shirts swing and leap about the scaffolding like zoo monkeys, laughing and pounding: repairing mortar damage. Next door, behind wild shrubbery and a caved-in stucco wall, sits the one-story French provincial library with a hole in its dull red tiled roof the size of a piano. The windows are boarded up with faded wood. Dying oriental ivy clings to the decaying yellow plaster walls like desiccated snakes. A few nameless pink blossoms on the thin vine, imitating bougainvillea, climb up over the hulk of an old rusted Renault that lies on its side in the cracked concrete court-yard of the library. Tufts of grass grow up through the cement. A couple of pigeons waddle across the courtyard, seemingly unaware that the library is closed forever.

Dubecheck turns to see the brightly shrouded coffin being wheeled with great effort along the path and the woman watching after, biting her fist. The woman watches the coffin, he watches her . . . who watches him? His *superiors*, that's who. He must inform them of a situation. He sighs and rubs the back of his neck and looks up into the white sky. CASREP.

He turns back toward his room, dragging his left foot like a clubfoot. The strap on his shower shoe is broken and to drag his foot along is the only way the thin rubber sole will stay on. He will never fix it.

His room. Home. A ten-by-ten cubicle with white plaster walls and two bunk beds with rumpled green poncho liners atop their sagging springs. A few pairs of combat boots grow out of a pile of damp combat fatigues curled up on the floor like sleeping dogs. There is a junior high school PE-type locker full of nothing but wire hangers and a burp gun painted white leans in a corner. He doesn't know whether the gun works. It came with the place. Spiders live in it. A large rectangular mirror on one wall with a diagonal crack through it enables Dubecheck to reflect upon and confirm his creep-ing schizophrenia. There is a wooden table with a fourth leg bal-anced on a sock which keeps it from wobbling when Dubecheck or his comrade, Lieutenant (jg) Michael Recore, does the insidiously aggravating paperwork that falls to junior officers of minuscule command.

A naked light bulb hangs from the high ceiling next to the four-bladed fan that has been immobilized by heat and humidity. The wall down the center of the third floor, for some odd reason, comes some twenty inches short of the ceiling and over this barrier flows the flood of information coming from his "men" in the adjacent room. Above the ceiling is the flat roof of the old hotel. The roof is all that separates Dubecheck from the 122mm mortars that occasionally sail into town.

Dubecheck sits down to finish his task. The casualty report. A minor carburetion problem exists in the engine of one of the small boats in the jury-rigged fleet he commands. The boat will not run. The last time he saw it, two waving legs stuck up out of the hull and a muffled voice was swearing. Socket wrenches, box wrenches, screwdrivers, gaskets and oily rags lay on the deck among nuts, bolts and washers. There was a greasy, clinking, thumping surgery going on down below and the doctor was carrying on a filthy one-way conversation with the patient. The problem could be any number of things, but Dubecheck chose the carburetor to be the problem. The words "carburetion problem" please him and seem to suffice.

The list of information addressees he must include in his CAS-REP never ceases to amaze him. On occasion he even allows himself to believe the absurd notion that the Chief of Naval Operations (CNO), the Commander-in-Chief Naval Operations Pacific Fleet (CINCPAC), the Commander-in-Chief Naval Operations Atlantic Fleet (CINCLANT), the Commander Naval Forces Vietnam (COMNAVFORV), and lesser luminaries like the commanders of the United States Navy's First, Seventh and Amphibious fleets of the Pacific Ocean might even read his "confidential" CASREPS. He imagines a staff officer, an aide-de-camp with ringlets of gold braid flopping against his right shoulder, rushing into the half-acre office of the CNO breathlessly shouting, "Good God, Admiral! It's Dubecheck's carburetor!"

The admiral quickly snatches off his glasses and chews the stems thoughtfully before rising to pace back and forth in the two-inch nap of the wall-to-wall carpet. The carpet has a seal of the United States of America the size of a small corral woven into its center. There the admiral stands wringing his hands, chewing his lower lip. A patch of ribbons the size of a Gideon Bible heaves over his left breast.

"Good God is right! The carburetor must be fixed!"

"Yes, Admiral."

"It's essential!"

"Yes, Admiral." The aide-de-camp begins to write rapidly on a clipboard for fear of looking as if the import of the moment is lost on him. He writes: "Got-to-be-fixed."

Dubecheck wishes to assuage them. Cool palms held up in the air. Not to worry, Admiral. Young Dubecheck has a man on it *right now.* An eighteen-year-old petty officer third named Julian Salti-novitch who's got gonorrhea and a way with the perversities of the internal combustion engine.

Dubecheck can feel the sigh of relief drift in on a cool breeze all the way from Washington. The admiral goes back to his desk and returns to his paperwork. Just as Dubecheck does, sitting in his duck-shit-green shorts over ten thousand miles away. Ten thousand miles. Funny, but it seems farther.

Then again, he doesn't have to send the CASREP at all. But he decides to cover himself. That particular piece of equipment will be legally "down" in case one of those incompetent intelligence officers is lingering about down the street with some inane "intell" from their semi-cagey triple agent, Phu, whose life and modus operandi consist of hedging his many bets. That is a wise course in this partic-ular theater of operations, especially for him, but intelligence from Phu is a contradiction in terms. It sometimes gets the wrong people upset. Dubecheck tries to avoid becoming upset at all costs and finds the effort all-consuming.

He gets scant relief knowing there are officers of commensurate rank, even officers of greatly superior rank, who would jump at the chance to be clear, concise, cogent, witty and, at the bottom line, indicate their existence somewhere out there on the outer links of the vast chain of command via message traffic of confidential im-port. And perhaps slip in an eight-by-twelve glossy of themselves while they're at it. But they're doomed to labor away ingloriously, at the mercy of their senior officers, who became senior by publiciz-ing their own triumphs while heroically overcoming the well-publi-cized failures and shortcomings of their peers and juniors. Dube-check is allowed in on the tangled snarl of bureaucratic message traffic because he has found himself, after all the cards were dealt, a commander of a task element, the last official door on the left along a long hallway called a task force.

The task force is headed by a Very Important Grown-up of flag rank and he has a three-digit number identifying him and his task. The task force is broken down into task "units" headed by men of lesser rank and given the three-digit task force number plus a deci-mal point and another numerical digit to identify them and their subtask.

Task units are further broken down into task elements headed by relatively junior officers, and they are given the three-digit num-ber identifying the task force plus a decimal point and another digit identifying the task unit plus another decimal point and numerical digit identifying the element of that particular unit of the task force. The resulting number identifying one's place in the task's chain of command could conceivably look like this: CTE 123.4.5.

The elemental aspect of Dubecheck's command is to help deny insurgents the use of the watery maze of canals, creeks, streams, sloughs and rivers that crisscross, bisect, twist and tangle in an utterly confusing labyrinth upon a two-province stretch of the Mekong Delta plain.

Dubecheck commands his own little three-boat navy. He is as semiautonomous as, perhaps, a regional sales manager for a very large concern. His own task element number identifies him as surely as a fingerprint and he has a snazzy code name that correlates with his billet. He is on the tip of the big toe of American foreign policy. A Yankee Doodle Dandy.

Dubecheck finishes off the CASREP quickly, failing to proofread it, allowing for some flunky up the line to discover procedural errors. Once, having worked writing messages for a pompous fart of a full commander, Dubecheck learned to leave a few errors in message wording. That gives one's superior a minor, authoritative egostroking foray into the clumsy but well-meaning efforts of his flunky. It also maintains the fragile ecosystem of rank, jealousy, envy, fear and pride. It also, in this case, spreads the war effort around, since he is aware so many of his comrades in arms have so little to do.

He fills in the To: ———— and the From: ————. From: DARK SINGER. That's him. Spiffy. DARK SINGER. Which one? Al Jolson? Ray Charles? Sammy Davis, Jr.? He hopes not. Maybe Aretha Franklin with a little luck. DARK SINGER. Jesus. Today it should be DIP SHIT. He scribbles in DARK SINGER, smiling, thinking of his opposite number: some poor Russian son of a bitch somewhere in the bowels of Soviet intelligence. A huge vodka hangover pounds in his head like an anvil chorus as he wearily adds DARK SINGER into his phone-book-size directory of United States Military Monikers. The monikers stay the same, only the running dogs like Dubecheck slip in and out of them with maddening frequency. According to his scratch wall convict calendar, Dubecheck will shed the snakeskin of DARK SINGER in ninety-two days. Then he will slither away, leaving the mantle to his relief, as aptly named a thing as does exist.

He flips the rough draft of the CASREP aside and finds himself looking into the beady bird-bright eyes of the Secretary of Defense on the front page of *Stars and Stripes*. The Secretary of Defense of the United States of America is pointing at a bar graph on an easel. It seems to Dubecheck he has seen this sight many times before: the guy pointing to graphs with a long baton, conducting the war, pointing to bar graphs, line graphs, circle graphs, numbered graphs, all upon that ubiquitous easel . . . graphs without smudges, graphs done where neatness counts, graphs like in books, large cardboard graphs that would be better used for college card stunts. In the foreground one can see the backs of the heads of apparently attentive grown-ups. Apparently believing the man.

It strikes Dubecheck that the guy is the perfect-looking type of man to be pointing to a graph and having faith in it. Glasses like clear neat circles give his somewhat puglike face an owlish countenance. He has a spit shine shave and his hair is drawn back flat atop his head as smoothly caked as shoe polish and cleaved down the middle to give, one imagines, his dome symmetry and order.

In this particular photo on the front page of *Stars and Stripes* the graph is unreadable: it's just a mass of dark and light grays, telephoto dots, and more than likely just as meaningful.

"Scoog!" Dubecheck shouts up over the partition. "Yo!" echoes back. Dubecheck has lost confidence in his Secretary of Defense. Ever since the man recommended bulldozing a ten-mile-wide swath across the nation of Vietnam and putting up an electric fence to keep the NVA from infiltrating down into the south. Even the eight-year-old pimp down on Tu Do Street knows the NVA comes circling down through Laos and soft-shoes across the Cambodian border through the Parrot's Beak. Besides, who was going to string all that wire? The Wichita Lineman will. Somewhere, slowly approaching, Glen Campbell's crooning voice over the Armed Forces Radio Network tells him so . . . "And I want you more than need you, and I need you for all time."

"Wouldn't ya like to muss up his hair?" It's Scoog bending over Dubecheck's shoulder, looking at the photo. His dog tags tinkle quietly over the thumb-size tattoo of a bumblebee upon his pale hairless sternum. He holds a transistor radio in his left hand and in his shorts and shower shoes looks like he's headed for the beach. True, every hair on the Secretary of Defense's head seems to have an assigned place from which deviation is unimaginable—and the guy has no daily chance of having a bullet smash through such meticulous filigree. But Dubecheck doesn't wish that upon him, nor anyone else, for that matter. He would not be opposed, however, as the man sits at his breakfast table shaking out his Sugar Pops, to having a decomposed rat fall out instead.

Dubecheck tosses the paper aside and leans back in his chair. "Shut off the radio, Scoog."

"Yessir."

Scoog pulls a cigarette from behind his ear and reaches down on the desk for some matches, pausing to shift gears as smoothly as an automatic transmission from brash, ranking petty officer to deferential, subservient enlisted man in the presence of an officer. He's also a bit uncertain as to whether his remark about the Secretary of Defense was out of line. You never can tell, because . . . An enlisted man never knows about an officer, because they're . . . different. And, to Scoog, Dubecheck is especially different. It is difficult to figure out when he is serious or if he ever *is* serious. Scoog, in his nine years in the Navy, has run through a lot of junior officers and most have been easy to scam. You let them talk, then go do it the way you want to, the way it's been done for two thousand years. But this officer is strange. He's a likable one, which snarls up all of Scoog's instincts, emotions and better judgment like a pile of conjugating worms in his brain. He lights his Lucky Strike and hesitates to toss the match on the floor.

Dubecheck hands Scoog the rough draft of the CASREP. "Have someone take this down to COM, sailor."

Scoog takes it, more comfortable now that he's been told what to do. "Yessir. You puttin' the little itty bitty boat down then."

"That's what it says, and that's confidential poop, Scoog. You gotta *con-feedential* clearance, pal?"

"Everybody does, sir. This whole war is confidential." Scoog traipses out of the room, leaving a cloud of smoke that hangs, lighter than air.

Dubecheck's eyes feel like they're rolling in sockets of sand. He feels like he hasn't slept in weeks. He puts his head down on his arms and thinks of this day upon which he has found himself cast away, but he's too tired to sleep. He gets up and walks out onto the balcony and yawns. Thin parallel clouds bisect the pale blue sky high above. Specifically, about thirty-two thousand feet above; up where the B-52s, quiet and nearly invisible at the ends of their contrails, head back to Thailand, Guam or L.A. International, wherever they come from, after another tough day at the office, another no-sweat southern milk run wherein bombardiers release batches of seven-hundred-and-fifty-pound bombs from the bellies of lumbering, kerosene-belching airplanes. The bombs fall lazily, like black logs through the snappy sixty-degree-below-zero clear blue, fade to dots, then disappear as they hurtle down into the heat and haze six miles below, down on the planet Earth . . . where they EXPLODE.

Somehow the name "Seven-Hundred-and-Fifty-Pound Bomb" doesn't do the apparatus justice. On detonation, it puts a crater in the earth the size of a baseball diamond, as deep as a summer-camp lake. They drop them in bunches, like bananas, sixty-seven of them a load. They moonscape the hard, dry, premonsoon land, pockmark the planet like a pox, and during the monsoon the craters fill up with water, and from the air, from horizon to horizon, the country looks like the Land O' Lakes.

They drop the big bombs on "suspected enemy concentrations," utilizing what is termed "the element of surprise." Dubecheck imagines the surprise: sitting on the warm dirt, back against a rough palm, the sunlight red and pleasant against closed eyes, taking a break, the smell of cigarette smoke on a light breeze that crackles the palm fronds sending shadows swaying to and fro upon the pungent, freshly tilled earth while upstairs, roughly thirty-two thousand feet upstairs, an unseen hand quits scratching the crotch that owns it and presses a button and it's "Bombs away, boys," as emotionally said as "You have reached a disconnected number; please check to see if . . ." and the plane lurches slightly as it responds to the drop in ballast, a slight banking away from course, subtle G-force building throughout the U-turn . . . goin' home. Imagine.

Down below you scan the soft cotton hedgerow of cloud puffing pleasantly up above the horizon, hear birds chirp, watch a water buffalo stare off, deep in cow thought as it chews its cud; switch and snap its tail among the platoon of flies patrolling above its bony rump and . . . SURPRISE! Very big surprise. First, the mind-fucking sound of a freight train rumbling down some tracks in . . . *in the* SKY? Trains in the fucking SKY? Then catatonic, thermodynamic detonations whose shock wave alone rips the feathers off birds a par five away. Denuded, incinerated, scorched. Hundreds of them scattered all over the black, brush-cut earth like burned baked potatoes. And that water buffalo is just flat gone. It went to heaven in a handbasket. . . .

Dubecheck watches the clotted contrails high above unravel, then disappear. The B-52s subliminally annoy him. There are these *people* flying them on round-trip journeys of a thousand or more miles, like dump truck drivers, each one dumping five dozen half-acre shit storms of searing hot chunks of steel, hurricane of bird shot, a maelstrom of jagged blood-dripping jaws, magma-gushing steel in volcanic fury cooking flesh, bodies curling up like caterpillars under the torch, roaring like ten thousand Niagaras, chainsaws through baby tummies. Bummer.

From a distance, at night, the B-52 explosions set the horizon rippling with a nervous-looking dance of summer lightning. The muffled sounds follow, long after, clumping overhead through the air like some drunken flamenco. They are called "conventional warheads." Sounds nearly harmless. Well, how about a conventional seven-hundred-and-fifty-pound warhead dropped on second base at Chavez Ravine during a Dodger-Red game some nice balmy night? That would send the folks on the home front crawling and stumbling toward the jammed exits, bleeding from the ears, dragging their gushing stumps over the peanut shells and hot dog wrappers, their eyes as big as baseballs wondering, *What the fuck?*

"The element of surprise. Can't beat it."

That's what Captain What's-his-name from Kankakee, Illinois, says here in his interview with the *Stars and Stripes* (Asian Edition). Dubecheck holds the paper in his hands and looks down at the photo of the smiling, bland face of Capt. J. R. Wilson, Jr., USAF, 29, Kankakee. Land of a thousand smiles. Quite a grin here. Makes Bert Parks look positively grim. Captain J. R. Teeth, who can hardly wait to get out of the United States Air Force and into United Airlines. Out of the Air Force blue and into the United chocolate-pudding brown. Well, there you go. That's how those fucking bus drivers of the friendly skies apprentice. By bombing people. Go visit Aunt Edna and Uncle Verle via the Friendly Skies, you got a killer at the helm. Hell, Aunt Edna herself puts the fuses in the seven-hundred-and-fifty-pounders down at the plant. No shit. Somebody's got to do it. Dubecheck feels nostril exhaust on his bare shoulder.

"Give me the gun, monsieur."

It's Norman Dupree, the nearly normal NILO doing his Inspector Clouseau. Sneaking around.

"I don't have it and don't ask me again. I dropped it into what our Army colleagues call the 'blue feature,' even though they're all brown."

"That's a lie. Why do you lie to me? That's all everybody does to me. Right to my fucking face. Like I was a, a, a . . . bovine animal. I'm a Naval intelligence liaison officer, as I recall, and . . ."

Dubecheck flicks a large prehistoric-looking insect off Dupree's shoulder with his finger, then takes a pack of Pall Malls out of Dupree's blouse pocket.

"Go on. Don't stop this petty tirade on my account."

"You expect me to believe you tossed a Czech pistol into the reevar. Har-har mighty, ye be full of sheeit. Har, har, har and avast." Dupree hunches around in a circle like a crab nailed to the floor. "Har-har-har."

"Are you drunk already?"

"Man, I wish. Colonel Minh wants the gat, Comrade. I don't know why, but he's holding his breath and rolling around on the floor and kicking his feet, he wants it so bad, so cough it up so we don't have an international incident on our hands."

"I'm already deeply involved in an international incident."

"That's cute. That's really cute and clever. Come on. Do I have to whine? I will if I have to. Look, I'll *buy* you a gun. A John Wayne commemorative model. I've got the money. The poor fuck you dragged in last night is heavy cadre. He's NVA. He's a feather in Minh's cap. In *your* cap. We'll have a party. By the way, there *is* a party today and you and your Cro-Magnon roomie are invited. Feathers in our cap. We'll look like a tribe of fucking Comanches. You can be Cochise. Give me the gun."

"I dropped it into the wa-wa, Norman. It was an accident. Or was it? Did it happen . . . or didn't it? It's all such a . . . such a dream to me now."

Dupree sighs, rubbing the side of his big French beak of a nose, an appendage of such aquiline disproportion, it seems to pull his face down in a perennial hangdog expression of deep sadness, weariness and woe. He has his reasons.

"A fucking loaf of bread and a quart of milk." According to Dupree, that is why he's in the Navy, in the war and out of his mind.

"I was a scion, Dubecheck." It was said over drinks in the O Club one morose and maudlin night. "A scion of a prominent family. As in 'Scion of Prominent Family Held on Charge of Negligent Homicide.' Newspaper headline stuff. Not just a rich kid, mind you, but a scion. *Town and Country* takes pictures of me taking a shit. I'm in that league that goes way beyond money. Let me see . . . I mean, *Napoleon* owed us money . . . like we were the brokers for the fucking Louisiana Purchase. American aristocracy, man. Sons of the Profits. Stolen property, filthy lucre washed by six generations, wealth you can trace back to the cave ladies. This is me, suh. Southern scion. My father had—shit, still has—congressmen around the house like toy poodles in a trailer park, all curled up on his lap, their little pink tongues panting. I digress or whatever . . . but there I was, all tuxed up, toilet paper heiress on one arm, vaginal douche heiress on the other . . . a fucking loaf of bread and a quart of milk." Dupree closes his eyes and emits a strangled whine, then tosses back another half jelly jar of Johnnie Walker Black.

"I thought we had servants for that shit, nappy-headed old gents of the colored persuasion with merely one name . . . Jodhpur, Reginald . . . Armageddon. Well, we did, but the ingrates were out marching somewhere for their rights that day and my mother, my sainted mother, says, just like she was June fucking Cleaver or something, she says, 'Norman? Would you go to the store, please, and pick up a loaf of bread and a quart of milk?' I'd never done anything like that before in my life, nor had I ever been asked to. Till this day I still don't know what she was going to do with a loaf of bread and a quart of milk. Maybe use them in a still life. She was an avid painter, or pretended to be. She would stay in her 'studio' all day and emerge for cocktails besmudged with cadmium red or burnt sienna, reeking of Mouquin brandy and very little product . . . but I assented. In fact I was rather excited about it. I even said, 'Sure, Mom!' like some cretinous kid on TV. Sincere, helpful, Boy Scoutish. I was getting into it. Boy . . . did I never get into it."

Dupree and Dubecheck sat alone in the tiny dark O Club, beneath the eye of an eavesdropping dart board, both staring down into a tire-size table with two dozen wet glass rings staring back up at them. A nearly empty bottle of Johnnie Walker Black stood before Dupree's face like a microphone. Dupree resummoned the reminiscence after a long pause punctuated by the gnawing of a rat inside the plywood walls.

"I'm twenty-two at the time, off on my first errand ever of any magnitude for Momser, suffused with family pride and fresh-faced eagerness. It was like I was standing above myself, out of body, watching this nice kid hop into the seat of his brand-new Corvette, a gift from my father for finishing somewhere in the bottom third of my class. Was I drunk? A battery of lawyers for the paltry sum of the President of the United States's yearly salary would contend otherwise."

"Were you?"

"I was whatever two and a half bottles of Boone's Farm does to you."

"What flavor?"

"Strawberry Hill."

"Ah . . . then you were just fucked up."

"As opposed to drunk. Right. Right there. But how do you explain that to them? I can see a man like you, Dubecheck, would understand, but them? No way, José."

Dupree emptied the last of the scotch into his jelly jar and swirled it around.

"She's walking down the sidewalk in white slacks and a red halter top, all nineteen years of her, with her hair hanging down to here, thick and brown, swishing back and forth over her world-class ass. The Stones were playing. Not too loud. Just right. 'Brown Sugar.' It was a setup, looking back. I cruise alongside, top down. Up till now all she ever had for me were those three little words."

"I love you?"

Dupree slowly shook his head. "No. 'Leave me alone.' But that day . . . I say to her, 'Hey, like a lift? I'm just going down to the store to get my mom a loaf of bread and a quart of milk.' Proud of myself. She gets in. I'm in love. Her pretty sandaled foot tapping the floorboard, her thigh flexing in its tight white sheath and her eyes wide and bright brown, her tongue poking out the corner of her mouth while Mick chomps on the mike. 'Brown Sugar, how can you look so good?' and she says, 'This is bitchin'. How fast does it go?' . . . Before I knew it I was red-lined, counting speedo error, doing, I figured, a legit one hundred twenty on a residential street." Dupree paused and squinted off into the bull's-eye. "With a cul-de-sac that mysteriously appeared at the end of it. I went through someone's living room, according to those who profess to know those things after the fact, at approximately one hundred and five, crushing a tricycle on the lawn before entry and taking off the top of the girl's head before exiting through the laundry room and coming to a stop against a backyard jungle gym, and me without a single scratch . . . at the wheel of a ticking wreck. 'Brown Sugar' still playing. Negligent homicide. Chick slaughter, really. Her hair hanging down over the dash like a scalp. Her last words, I'll never forget. . . . But corruption, greed and graft, as usual, prevailed. They plea-bargained a prison stretch into a stretch with Uncle, no record. I made OCS. Sick. Really disgusting. Here I am. A fucking loaf of bread and a quart of milk and that girl screaming in my ears every night. She's dead but she won't shut up."

"What an asshole. What were her last words?"

"I told you already. She said, 'This is bitchin'. How fast does it go?' . . . Think about it. It says it all, man."

Dupree now looks up at Dubecheck with his sad spaniel eyes and lights up their Pall Malls with a Bic. Dupree sighs. "So I don't give a shit. Keep the gun. A guy needs all he can get around here. Colonel Minh's asshole assistant Nguyen McNguyen also is outraged, offended and pissed off. They don't like you because you're tall, American and, if you live, get to leave."

Dubecheck sails a paper airplane he made with the *Stars and Stripes* over the balcony down into the street. Capt. J. R. Wilson, Jr., USAF, in command, his keyboard smile along the fuselage. It glides toward the old brown dog that shuffles about the open-air hotel like a drugged tortoise. The plane bounces off the dog, who looks up and, recognizing Dubecheck, enters the building where he will laboriously climb three stories, then collapse into a coma at his American friend's smelly feet. Dubecheck envies the dog. Doesn't envy the gook prisoner though.

"NVA, eh?"

"Roger that. You know, those guys that aren't really here but are just figments of your imperialist imagination. I'll bet he wishes he was just a figment about now."

Dubecheck winces. A slight pang of pity and shame commingle as he thinks of Minh and his men, who will treat the man brutally. Fucking interrogations. The gooks really get into it. Once they get going, it's like a shark frenzy, the torture biz. Christ, life's a triumph on this planet if you can avoid torture. Avoid torture and prison in this century and you break the tape in first and die with a smile on your face. It takes work, though, a dogged adherence to an ancient Zen dictum that Dubecheck finds impossible to comply with: *Avoid the authorities at all cost.*

"I feel bad about that gook."

"It's your job."

"I feel bad about my job."

"The guy's the enemy, Dubecheck. You've got to be a little more pragmatic about these things. Figure if you didn't do it, someone else would. Look at it this way . . . if they don't kill him, you probably saved his life."

Dubecheck thinks on that. Yeah, if. The gook's face is probably purply now, lumped up like cauliflower, his eyes swollen shut, slits, his eardrums numb from that shrieking, screaming simian chatter the gooks vent upon each other in their cruel frenzies. Excitable boys, like a school of noisy piranhas around a chunk of meat. Anglos interrogate with diffident calm by comparison."

"They torturing that guy now?"

"He's undergoing intensive interrogation."

Dubecheck can see Colonel Minh, Nguyen McNguyen and the

White Mice noncoms now: wiping the sweat from their pale bronze faces with white hankies, the thick sweat of fear, exertion and evil that congeals on the face like shiny scum, taking their breathers, lighting up Salems, pissed. The authorities.

"Wouldn't it be a wonderful world . . . we wake up some morning and there's no more torture because everybody's been told to tell everything they know and there is so much information that they all have to put down their truncheons and cattle prods and sort it all out and file it? The dungeons would be filled with filing cabinets instead of screaming peons. I got it!" Dubecheck writes across the air in front of him with his cigarette. "Suppose They Gave an Interrogation and Nobody Came."

"I like it. Like a poster you can put on your refrigerator."

"Right. Like 'What If They Gave a War and Nobody Came?' "

"Hey. Up on the refrigerator too. Next to 'War Is Harmful to Children and Other Living Things.' Every time you go to make yourself a salami sandwich you can remind yourself how much you dislike evil. I like it, Dubecheck."

"Except someone always comes."

"What?"

"Some side will always show up, I think. War's sorta like golf, you can play it by yourself. What do they expect that guy to tell them that they don't already know?"

"That's not the point. The point is to torture him. He's been bad. So they're engaged in the old beat-the-puppy-with-a-rolled-up-newspaper-for-pissing-on-the-rug to its logical conclusion. Besides, there's lots of people who really enjoy doing that. Personally, I abhor violence."

Dupree flicks his cigarette butt over the balcony as Dubecheck leans on the railing and looks out over the flat, double-story confusion of Dong My, rotten at the edges with collapsed shanties, kicked-in hooches and bombed-out plaster and concrete hulks with twisted tines of rebar poking up like weeds in the wreckage. "Violence makes sense. Ever hear that phrase, 'senseless violence'? I don't know what they mean by that."

The scraggly verdant vegetation at the city edge threatens to run amok and engulf the perimeter. Hedgerows, bushy trees and dead meadow, scruffy foliage and dry dikes crisscross and collide in gnarly profusion. It's dangerous out there. A little stroll in the sun could get you a .30-cal ball in the noggin, a .51-cal in the shorts, an 82mm down the throat. There's a different caliber for every fucking day of the year.

But the center holds. The streets of Dong My are busy and Tu Do, the main drag, is choked with old Peugeots and Citroëns, Vespas and Lambrettas, cyclos and Jeeps. The sound of horns bleating and beeping rises up from the two-lane street along with the exhaust and dust that silts back down upon the leaves of the huge plane trees, coating them khaki.

Schoolboys and -girls on foot weave in and out of the motor traffic in blue and white uniformed squads, swinging their briefcases and laughing. People buy things and sell things and go here and there and then back over to where they came from and across the rutted dirt street down below, and the dark patch on the dirt next to the collapsed plaster wall where the dead ten-year-old kid stood staggering as six quarts of blood gushed from the large hole torn in his side when a mortar landed in his room is no longer red but just a brown stain in the dirt. An ugly, scabrous white dog sniffs at the dark patch, then lifts its leg and pisses next to it and the piss seeps into the dust and looks the same as old blood. And farther down the street, behind the wrought-iron fence with curlicues and scrolls, under the soft mottled shade of an opulent shade tree, behind the thick white ivy-covered walls of the National Police Station, they're torturing some guy down in the basement. Dubecheck feels like he's been here forever.

Down in the basement. The plastic bag is in vogue now. Dubecheck walked in on an interrogation a few days ago in the munitions Quonset hut down by the pier when he went to pick up a box of mortars. A big, thick-armed, redheaded kid with a Kirk Douglas chin and Coke-bottle glasses whom Dubecheck had never seen before had a small, clear plastic bag over the head of a skinny gook in blue shorts and torn bloody T-shirt. He held the open end of the bag twisted in his fist at the nape of the man's neck and the man's elbows were tied together behind his back. The kid twisted the plastic in his large fist and the bag tightened over the man's face so he looked like his head was inside a tight balloon and his eyes were wild and his nose was squished, flattened to one side and his lip twisted awry, slightly parted, and as the plastic seal tightened, the forearm muscles of the kid rippled. Isometrics. The gook nervously slid his bare feet back and forth on the wood floor, slowly at first, then faster as if he was trying to run away. Two gooks in civvies, Hawaiian sport shirts hanging out of their pegged chinos, shower shoes and sunglasses, dove on the man and held his legs down while he arched and thrashed in hopelessly desperate spasms, seeking air. It was very quiet in the Quonset hut, just the sound of a muffled struggle under the naked light bulb. The man's bare heels thumped once, twice, three times on the floor, then his legs went rigid, he appeared to levitate and then collapsed as if every tendon in his body had snapped, as if he'd been shot; he lay motionless on the floor. A puddle of piss spread from his crotch along the wooden floor.

The redheaded kid quickly pulled off the plastic bag, the light from the naked bulb popped off his glasses like flashbulbs. The two civilian gooks knelt and put their ears to the man's skinny chest. One of them sat up and hit the prisoner's chest with his fist twice and shouted quickly to someone standing in the shadows. It was another gook in tiger stripes and he threw a Folger's coffee can of water into the unconscious prisoner's face. The man, as if awakening from a very deep sleep, slowly moved his lips, sputtered and fluttered his eyes. Starved for air, he began to hyperventilate.

Dubecheck saw Recore and an ARVN major standing beneath skeins of web gear hanging from some shelving at the edge of the light bulb's pale arc. Recore emerged from the shadows and sat on an empty 7.62 ammo can in front of the prisoner, who lay gasping on the floor, sucking in huge lungfuls of the hot, canvas-smelling air.

Dubecheck looked down on Recore. "What the fuck? Over."

Recore just looked up at Dubecheck with a slight, mischievous smile. "A little CO_2 for Nguyen here."

Recore is in the Phoenix Program, which means he gets to strong-arm and kill civilians, just like the VC and NVA. It also allows Recore to patronize Dubecheck because he thinks he knows more about what he is doing in the Mekong Delta than Dubecheck does. No contest there.

Mentholated smoke hung in the muggy air as one of the ninety-pounders in civvies slapped the prisoner's face back and forth and shouted at him so hard his sunglasses slipped down cattywampus on the bridge of his nose. He stopped slapping to adjust his glasses, but they kept slipping down as he slapped and he got angrier and out of rhythm and frustrated and hurled his glasses across the hut, where they ricocheted off an empty 81mm mortar crate and landed at Dubecheck's feet. Where Dubecheck slowly stepped on them and flattened them out, the dark lenses fragmenting like clamshells. He lifted his foot as if out of a pile of dog shit and looked down at the jeweled sole of his combat boot, then up at everyone in the hut. They were all staring at the mangled shades in rapt silence. Even the prisoner. He squinted up through the puffy slits of his eyes at Dubecheck, silently asking what Recore voiced.

"What the fuck did you do that for, Dubecheck?"

The gook whose glasses had been destroyed looked back and forth between Recore and Dubecheck, obviously hoping the two Americans would figure it all out before he had to say anything.

"I mean, really, John. What did you go and step on his glasses for? I mean, you deliberately stepped on his glasses."

"Jesus Christ, Recore. It's not a, a, a, a . . . *war* crime. I don't know why I did it . . . it just seemed the right thing to do at the time. You . . . you had to be there." Dubecheck tapped his temple several times. "Here. You hadda be here."

"Well . . . well, you'll have to buy him some new ones. What are you doing here anyway? The door was supposed to be locked."

"I want some mortars. They're for the war effort."

"Well, pick out your mortars and leave."

Dubecheck edged his way through the interrogators and stepped over the prisoner, sidled past the ARVN major and the gook in tiger stripes with his Folger's coffee can. He reached up and pulled down a heavy crate of 81mm mortars, feeling everyone's eyes on his back. He turned and walked back the way he had come, stepping over the prisoner, who appeared to be mumbling quietly to himself as he stared up into the ceiling.

"Not a word about this, eh, John?"

Dubecheck stood holding the ball-busting load of mortars by the crate's rope handles and looked down at Recore, who smiled up at him as if he'd been caught jacking off in a phone booth.

"Whatever you have to do." Dubecheck lugged his load toward the door. The gook of the late shades rushed to open the door for him, all the while nodding and bowing and smiling like a whore-house doorman. Go figure these people.

Dubecheck walked out into the bright sunlight and took a deep breath of humid air laced with diesel fumes. Somehow the air seemed fresher than in the Quonset hut. A bird chirped in the dusty tree he leaned against as he held the crate of mortars and thought. He thought of the fat chance that he'd buy that ninety-pounder a new pair of sunglasses. But if he did, he wondered if he'd get him an elastic strap to snap on the stems like basketball players wear so when he beat people during interrogations his shades wouldn't fall off.

He thought about the last thing he heard as the door closed behind him. "Tell him if he doesn't tell . . . we'll blow his fucking brains out." And it wasn't a TV-show actor in there who was saying that, so there was a possibility it might happen. Really. In fact,

Dubecheck recalls, they probably did blow his fucking brains out. Later that day, near dusk, he opened the door to the hut and up where the picture of a *Playboy* Playmate of the Month flapped in the breeze against the back of the door like a shiny, creased tapestry, Dubecheck noticed a few pale gray dollops stuck against Miss May's right tit. Brains. No doubt about it. The human brain has the consistency of snot. Of course he probably deserved everything he got. He probably started rocking the goddamn boat! Goddamnit-didn't-we-tell-you-not-to-rock-the-fucking-goddamn-boat! And more than once too! Sure enough, Dubecheck can see him now, in his bare feet, arms flailing, one foot on one gunwale, one on another, making the girls shriek and scream, rocking the goddamn boat back and forth, water sloshing in the bilges, fucking up the freeboard and everybody screaming, "We're all gonna sink and drown and *die!*" The prick.

For some time after that there was this kid, an oriental Alfred E. Neuman with brown almond eyes out of kilter, a gap between his front teeth and freckles flecked like fly shit across his cheekbones, who followed Dubecheck along the streets and alleys of Dong My saying, "You! Hey, you! You numbah ten GI mothafuck!"

"Who is that guy?" Dubecheck asked.

For two weeks, when their schedules coincided, Dubecheck back from an Op or the kid out marauding, the kid ran alongside Dubecheck like a dog chasing a car and screamed, "Hey, you! You! You numbah ten GI Cheap Charlie!"

"This is embarrassing."

People turned to stare at the kid, then at Dubecheck, obviously taking the kid's word for it.

Scoog, frustrated and irritated by Dubecheck's stoicism, simmered. "Mr. Dubecheck. You gotta say something, sir." Then he wheeled on the kid and screamed, "No! No! Diwi numbah one! Numbah one!"

"Fuck you, GI. Him numbah ten!" The kid sprayed spit as he wagged his finger in Scoog's face. "Numbah *fuckin'* ten Cheap Charlie!"

"Well, hell, Mr. Dubecheck . . ." and Scoog threw up his hands and gave up.

Dubecheck walked off with his angry entourage, for Alfred had picked up support, half a dozen little allies who yapped at Dubecheck's heels like hyena puppies while Alfred kept up his prepubescent nasal litany of abuse. Dubecheck winced, deep in concentration, wondering, Do I *know* this guy?

He decided to turn the question over to United States Naval intelligence. He had forgotten all about it until Dupree now brings it up.

"Remember that kid you asked me about? The one that used to terrorize you?" Dupree asks.

Dubecheck gets momentarily excited. "Is he dead? Is he? Huh? Huh? Is he dead and gone?"

"No. He's not dead, but I found out who he is."

"Really? Who is he?"

"Give me the gun."

"I'll go get it." Dubecheck turns to go and Dupree catches him by the elbow.

"No," he laughs. "You can keep it. But you owe me one."

"Who *was* he, Norman?"

"Remember the guy whose sunglasses you crushed?"

"Yeah?"

"It's his kid."

Dubecheck shakes his head. Kids. The place is crawling with them. The leading national industry: target larvae. Soldiers. The whole planet is crawling with soldiers this century. And all the kids here grow up to be on one side or another. All kids anywhere grow up to be on one side or another. Life is a matter of picking the right side. As if there's a choice. It's all just a cut of the cards. Draw high, you got it made, draw low, you're fucked. Dubecheck wonders what side he's on. What card he's cut. All the Yanks in this country are here because they either are or were professional military, black, tan, broke or curious. Dubecheck was broke and curious. Now his curiosity is aroused by the wailing conga line of woe snaking through the crowded streets down below. A harsh banging tambourine-type drum punctuates the atonal din of sorrow. There is a long file of white-shirted mourners clapping in unison as they accompany a black, gaily decorated coffin that rocks on the shoulders of six pallbearers the size of jockeys.

The procession moves like a stop and go line through a turnstile, bumping through the crowd. It momentarily halts motor traffic. Cars and trucks rev their engines as they wait for the funeral cortege to pass. A motorcycle rider racks his pipes.

"Sailed a 122 into town last night."

"Bummer."

"Fucking roulette. Come up double zero, you buy the farm."

Dubecheck shrugs. It's all a mystery to him. He wonders what it would be like to die from a mortar round, a fragment. He wonders what dying is like. He wonders if it's okay to die if it doesn't hurt. He used to get under his flimsy rack when the mortar attacks came. They usually came around three in the morning. He'd get under a spiderweb of wire covered by a poncho liner as if that might stop ten pounds of high-explosive steel from shutting out the lights forever. Now, the small, harassing, sporadic attacks might not even wake him unless they land on one of the paved streets. That tends to amplify the commotion. BRANK! Like a pistol shot in the tiled shower stall. The shrapnel scratches as it skids and ricochets across the concrete at Mach 1 seeking soft, vital organs to lodge in.

The funeral procession disappears around a corner and the traffic resumes like a noisy wave.

"Seven-year-old kid. Obviously a government sympathizer." Dupree lights another Pall Mall and shakes one out for Dubecheck. "Thanks. I can't smoke enough of these things, Norman. They keep me on an even keel." Dubecheck inhales deeply, slamming seven-hundred-degree smoke back against his epiglottis.

"Kid was lucky. Died in his sleep. Wanna go get drunk?"

"Too early to get drunk." It is, after all, the Lord's day, or at any rate he thinks so. He remembers, through the hallucination of half sleep, watching his roomie Recore meticulously comb his black hair with a wet comb, standing before the cracked mirror like some sleazy junior high stud after P.E. Then he carefully put his utility cap on his head and put a .38 Smith in the waistband of his fatigues at the small of his back and covered it with his blouse like some off-duty cop going out for Chinese. Except, Dubecheck thought, he must be going to mass. Recore is a devout Catholic and every once in a while a chaplain makes the circuit and feeds some of the boys baked Jesus and Mateus from the seminary PX for eighty cents MP a fifth.

Dubecheck envies Recore. He envies his dead solid certitude about things that help a guy anchor himself in stormy seas.

And from this certitude, an aura of confidence radiates like neon. Jesus was the only begotten Son of God and Mary-was-His-Mother-goddamnit!

God is the Father. And there's the Father, the Son and the Holy Ghost and that's a fact, Jack!

There's a heaven too, which in his case is a lock because he'd done all his first Fridays, or second Tuesdays, whatever that meant, and there was hell. Where your-ass-will-be-roasted, Jim. Eternally. Another fact is gooks wandering around during the night without a hall pass are dead meat. Fair game. And he has a commission, imprinted in clear black and white, a real standing order to hunt them down.

It is all hunting to Recore. In fact, Recore has told Dubecheck that after the war, or whenever they are done with it on a personal basis, Dubecheck should come back to New York and go hunting with him.

Guys were always telling each other they'd get together back in the States and that they'd keep in touch, but as soon as a guy left you'd never hear from or see him again. He'd vanish. They all went to the dark side of the moon or its equivalent or, more logically, the feeling was that this place was a disconnected outpost you went into, a different dimension of the real world. But it was a nice gesture to suggest.

"Yeah, John, you'd like it. New York isn't just the 'Big Apple.' Some rough country upstate. We could even go over to Maine and hunt moose." Recore held up a finger pistol and went "Pow!"

"Moose?"

"Yeah. Like one of them Budweiser horses with antlers. Moose."

"I know moose. That's like shooting a dump truck that breathes." Dubecheck had a friend who went up to British Columbia once. He sat in the woods all day next to his guide, this Indian who didn't speak a word until he raised his finger at some shadow in the trees and said, "See moose? . . . Shoot moose." Bang! Time of the guy's life.

"Well, maybe ducks then. Hose down the old flyway."

"Yeah, sure. I'll see if I can fit it in." But Dubecheck doubted it. After a guy's hunted armed Homo sapiens for a while, big game, upland birds and migratory waterfowl probably wouldn't get it up for you anymore.

Dubecheck thought of what a good killer Recore was, how he was glad he was on Recore's side and how Recore, being a good Catholic, was just right for the job because essentially his job was to send gooks to heaven.

And Recore and his men, about a dozen guys you wouldn't want to meet in a bright alley, have sent a lot of gooks to heaven lately. They are very tough guys and maybe a half a bubble off plumb too, which can come in real handy around here. For the most part they look just like every American mother's son, indistinguishable Mark I grunts. Somebody's kid out there on the cutting edge of mayhem. Officially, Dubecheck has nothing to do with them, but on occasion has found himself chatting with one or another of them at some quiet time, cruising back from an op when he or the guy may have tired of talking to those with whom he constantly lives.

One guy, Conklin, was Missouri State Class A high school 880-yard runner-up. He wanted to be a high school biology teacher. He was very interested in the human brain and when a drowsing comrade, Van Buskirk, heard that, he got up on an elbow and said, "Study this then," and flicked at Conklin some pasty-colored little dollops that were stuck on the knee of his fatigues like dead flies. Van Buskirk smiled like some kid who loves to drown ants on the playground in a Dixie cup filled from the water fountain. "That's what's left of some Nguyen's brain." Then he lay back down to snooze.

Well, if you're trying to find people who will attack people, you need these guys. And you never know where they're going to come from. Usually right next door.

Van Buskirk, in a well-controlled free-form rage at some ninety-pounder they jerked up out of a rathole, rammed his K-bar into him. The guy was being held by Van Buskirk's friend Weathersby, and the knife went right through and cut Weathersby, who hopped around shaking his bleeding hand, screaming he was going to need a tetanus shot.

Weathersby has told Dubecheck he wants to own a miniature golf course someday. Just like the one on Santa Catalina.

o   o   o

"Are you awake? I said. Do you want to go get drunk? Where y'at, ya mother?" Dupree snaps his fingers in front of Dubecheck's face.

Dubecheck yawns and shrugs. Dupree, hunched over like an old man, shuffles off muttering to himself. Dubecheck knows where he's at. Nobody else knows or cares where he is, though. He is certain of that. Maybe Lat. 10. Maybe Long. 110. That young woman who sends him letters knows he's here. Except she really doesn't know where "here" is. For all she comprehends, he's sitting at the bottom of a blue mailbox watching TV and waiting for her letter to fall into his lap. Dubecheck feels jagged. He's been tired for so long he thinks just being awake is a heightened sense of awareness. His mother would be angry with him for not getting his proper rest and he'd just as soon be with her listening to her nag than be stuck in this deadly ennui. Perfect. There you go. Senior officers, noncoms, chiefs. Who needs them? We need more mothers.

"Now you just march upstairs and clean your weapon!"

"Aw, Mom. Do I hafta?"

"Don't you 'Aw, Mom' me, young man. And finish your C rations or you don't get to go down to the whorehouse after you finish that sweep by the Cho Gao Canal. And why you feel you have to do that sweep anyway I don't know, those Viet Cong seem like nice young men to me, but I never did claim to know what makes you silly men tick. Now drop trou!"

"Aw, Mom!"

"Come on, I don't have all day. Short-arm inspection. If you've got the clap Mother must know, and honestly, son, I don't see how you can wear these fatigues, they're filthy. Just leave them here on the floor and I'll do them. What if you were to get shot and had to go to the hospital and—you aren't even *wearing* underwear." Mother's lip starts to quiver and her eyes water. Then she breaks down and begins to cry. "What happened to my little boy?"

Good fucking question, Mommy. He has less of a clue than you. But maybe not. Mommy seems to be in a daze of her own of late. Dubecheck's picture of his mother is chiseled in some mental frieze. She sits at the kitchen table, holding her coffee cup in both hands, and seems to stare down into it like a dog transfixed by a whirlpool. A constant worry crease cleaves her forehead like an exclamation mark. He hasn't the foggiest idea what grist she is silently grinding inside that head with the silver feathers at the pulsing temple. Her salt-and-pepper-colored short hair is, unlike a couple of her mutually quasi-wretched friends, mercifully without curlers. Those acquaintances, sharers of woe, bearers of news of disease and malfunctioning body parts, chroniclers of familial distress, agony, divorce, failure and death, seem to come in duos and trios and wear bathroom-pink and bile-green hair curlers at all times, as if they were directional antennae bristling to receive the latest bad news that hums in the ether like radio-static electricity. Dubecheck would see them shopping with their curlers and kerchiefs and wonder if the object was to make their hair look nice, who were they making it look nice for?

He can see them sitting in the kitchen now, the table with its plastic checkered tablecloth, the coffee cups, the lipstick stains on the golden, crushed cigarette filters in the bean bag ashtray.

Cigarettes, coffee, conversations about hysterectomies and assholes. Assholes like husbands, nephews, brothers-in-law, uncles and sons. At their age their own fathers were safe from their wrath. Daddy was, as they thought in the very beginning, after all, okay. But as for the rest, a good word about a man was about as hard to find as a good man. And there were not many good words for women who weren't in that room either. Dubecheck figured that what basically made those women tick was their dislike of the opposite sex and then, after deep thought, their own.

There was a time, as a child, through all the petty pains, fears and uncertainties, that he could find some equilibrium. It was in those large people who loomed up in his life, Mommy and Daddy, seemingly self-assured and knowing, exemplary of that magic point in your life when you got it all under control . . . the confident assumption that someday you would be "grown up" and all would finally be . . . okeydokey.

Listening to the crones around the kitchen table, Dubecheck started to get the chilling inkling that maybe you never become a "grown-up," that the term was a myth, that all the uncertainties and agonizing questions of youth remain, none of the questions can be answered, or they keep getting harder in a lifelong series of pop quizzes on subjects you've never heard about.

But maybe a little bit of God and Jesus can buck you up. That theory hung heavily in the air with the cigarette smoke.

"The answers are all there, John," said his mother as she pointed to a Bible sitting on a lamp table by the TV. She just walked into the living room one day and said that while Dubecheck was reading a copy of *Sports Illustrated* and walked right on through without another word. One of those near hallucinations one doesn't pay much attention to at the time.

Dubecheck thinks of how he loves his mother. He thinks she keeps and has kept bad company. He has seen her laugh and then catch herself, as if laughter were not allowed, and then hug him, and he has seen her slowly straighten up from a bend at the waist, as she pulled him to her warm-smelling skin for a squeeze, to rise full up as an aging woman watching her son flinch from hugs, go away, go to war, go to hell. All he has seen is that years add up on most people and make them quieter in word and deed. Drive them down into a slouch, a shuffle and then into the grave. That's reality.

As real as the pink envelope he holds in his hand from the near woman who thinks she's his "girl." He could reread the letter from the young woman, but he remembers it is full of labored inanities and small talk. Just like "real life," Dubecheck thinks. Real life, man. *The Beeg Time.*

It must be a real chore to write to him. Distance and time have shown how little he has in common with those two women who write him. Mom and Mary. Christ, how can a guy have a girl named

Mary and take her seriously? John and Mary. Jesus. The names somehow characterize the whole affair. They met at the weekly Friday night body hunts held in the "ballroom" of the Marine Corps Recruit Depot, the MCRD, in San Diego. They met in the dark. The air was dank from the body heat radiating off dancing humans. The music was loud: standard Mark I bar band, rock and roll. Dubecheck watched the lucky civilians play rock and roll and wished he was them instead of him. His mouth had a citrus pucker to it and his head ached from too few or too many gin tonics. It was a dangerous place. It was full of a lot of very lonely people a long way from home, and the urge and need to pair up was so thick and palpable it hung in the air like humidity. Consequently, a lot of hasty decisions were made there. Guys got wives out of there. Girls got husbands. Navy and Marine officers proposed to secretaries, department store clerks, typists, preschool teachers, the odd young women who did nothing. Who did they expect to meet? Trapeze artists? Brain surgeons? Movie stars?

The band was playing "A Whiter Shade of Pale" and the quasi-melancholy strain of the organ dirge drove Dubecheck over toward a fire exit to catch a cool breeze and take in the palms and the emerald beauty of floodlit grass at night. He remembers the song because he later made her promise she would never refer to it as "their song." He liked the song, but it was too long to dance to with a stranger. She was standing in the shadows along the wall by the exit in one of the small packs of women who showed up together. Duos, trios or quartets teamed up for moral support. One pretty one, or at least a semiattractive one, bonded with the physically bland, plain or downright ugly with the universal constancy of an atomic element.

Her face briefly lit up in the candlelight glow of cigarette lighter held by her friend. She leaned forward, frowning, a filter-tipped Tareyton between her pursed lips. It made her look serious, intelligent—not that intelligence was an attribute a carousing sailor demanded. To laugh at his jokes would be enough. She was pretty. She had an almond-eyed, high-cheekboned face and shoulder-length brown hair. She had a wide mouth and when she talked to her girlfriend the cigarette danced around between her lips. Unguarded, not knowing she was being watched, she had a funny "tough kid" look that was curiously alluring because she obviously wasn't too tough or she wouldn't have been there, a somewhat apprehensive-looking wallflower. She leaned against the wall in a leisurely slouch, not nearly as intense and tightly wound as her compatriots, who seemed to have much more to lose than she. It seemed that, as far as all this tribal dancing and preening went, she could take it or leave it. Maybe. She was pretty in her white short-sleeved blouse with a Chinese collar, her thin arms folded over her breast, the cigarette then clenched between her teeth like a cigar. What great things she could do with that cigarette! He loved it. They could grow old together with their cigarettes, coughing and hacking in the morning and dying of emphysema in each other's arms somewhere in the cool murky future. He realized beauty is only skin deep but skin was about all he had in mind. He was going to get to go to Southeast Asia soon anyway and saw no reason to get to know someone well enough that there'd be tears at the airport. She turned her head, eyes straight ahead toward the dance floor, and spoke into the ear of her friend, who would nod seriously, then occasionally laugh. He wanted to know what she was saying. A bad sign. He butted in, which was allowed there, and they danced slowly to "A Whiter Shade of Pale."

She was an airline stewardess, or hostess or flight attendant. She was in San Diego on a layover and one of the quietly stewing young women glowering enviously at them as they danced was her cousin.

o   o   o

They carried on their six-week affair mainly by voice, forlorn long-distance calls from pay phones at night on his part, quiet layover hotel room calls to him on her part, and the distance created an odd, depthless pining that probably would never have lasted had they been together. They never had sexual intercourse. They had passionate, hard breathing, mouth-bruising entanglements, but she would draw the line, her clothes askew, lips swollen and reddened, face mottled, eyes glazed, hair tufts wildly ascending from her head, blouse unbuttoned, brassiere twisted about her waist, her crotch sopping, smelling slightly of low tide, her breath beating like baby gull wings against his neck in hot puffs. A passionate lust distilled to purity by torturous abstinence. He didn't mind. He felt lucky as it was. He was at the awkward age where women were few and far between, so any woman was dangerously precious.

The night before he left for Asia they looked for a motel anywhere between San Francisco and Travis Air Force Base. Hundreds of square miles. He couldn't find one open. Not one. It was impossibly ridiculous: the farther out they got from the city, the more preposterously apparent it became that every motel west of Oklahoma was booked. They drove around in the dark, squinting at the bright lights of oncoming traffic in a dreary rain. The songs on the radio had a plaintive monotony to them. Dubecheck realized his whole life seemed to have a sound track to it, a pervasive Top Forty bubble-gum rock back beat for as long as he could remember. In the house, in the car, in the bar, everywhere there was canned music bleating out a plethora of ragged rhythms and drumbeats with one message . . . Love Gone Wrong. There were no swelling crescendos of lush woodwinds and violins in his life. Just a bunch of nasally screaming teenagers, peers and black people wailing and whining in the background about sex, cars and chicks. That was the good rock and roll. Well . . . it was all good. He couldn't imagine life before electric guitars and rock and roll. But that night the music, which generally drove him to dance, drink and drive a little faster, sounded to him, he thought, probably as it sounded to his parents. He turned the radio off and they drove in silence, listening to the hiss and squish of tires on the wet black streets and freeways, looking in vain for a red neon script that didn't spell "Sorry," gas glowing inside glass tubes spelling "No Vacancy." Science. It knocked him out.

They spent the nearly sleepless night uncomfortably curled up together in the back seat of her Mustang convertible. Parked by the side of a road that loud semis frequented at odd, startling times. It was miserably cold and the roof leaked and Dubecheck didn't know what to say or do and neither did she. Every attempt to convey whatever was on their minds or in their hearts came haltingly to nothing. For Dubecheck it was difficult, because he didn't really know what he felt, and every time he went to say something he realized what he was about to say sounded like lines from some movie or TV show. And that embarrassed him. It seemed there was nothing emotionally monumental in his life that hadn't been covered before by a song, a movie or a TV skit. He felt robbed, that he wasn't able to lead his own life with any originality, that it had been preempted by everyone else's as portrayed on the silver screen. How to act like a tough officer? Watch John Fucking Wayne. Everybody else seemed to. The whole military was full of caricatures. So was America. It was like he and everybody he knew in the whole United States of America had learned how to behave by watching movies. And when it came to saying something heartfelt, emotional or *real*, everything that came to mind seemed to come from the mouths and words of other men . . . movie stars, singers, soap opera eunuchs.

So his life was just an extension of an ongoing movie. The America Movie. And he was just a pissant extra in a *cast of thousands.*

They were awakened in the morning by an irate-looking Califor-
nia highway patrolman who was tapping on the window with what looked like a twelve-battery flashlight. Dubecheck felt like shit and the landscape was tan-gray and wet and flat. It had been an unpleasant night he didn't want to ever end, for he knew what the morning would be like: bright and full of no promise. The first sensation he remembered of that morning was fear. It centered in the stomach like a dull pain and moved down toward loose bowels.

The cop became pleasant when he found out Dubecheck was going to Travis Air Force Base and fly away and get out of everybody's hair. He was about Dubecheck's age and had a wistful "Better him than me" look on his face as it receded in the rear-view mirror, the guy waving good-bye like he was Dubecheck's pal. Fuck him.

They drove to Travis in silence and waited in the terminal with all the other couples and families who stood around quietly, as if struck dumb by the enormity of such a weird, nonsensical parting. Hundreds of soldiers, sailors and marines in uniform clutched their legal-size manila envelopes full of orders and endorsements in one hand, and if lucky or unlucky, depending upon choice, a loved one in the other.

He was called to board. Mary hugged him, they kissed and he flew away. . . .

But she is trying to breech this communal loneliness. Trying more than he deserves. Absence has not made his heart grow fonder. He is beginning to see the effects the siege of time and distance have upon whatever they have in common. Which is probably not much. They may just have been kidding themselves. Happens all the time. Nobody *here* has anything in common with anybody *there.* Not even language. It's twisted here. It's not even the same day there. He picks up the letter and peruses the looping curlicued writing with its irritating stupid little circles over the *i*'s and the *x*'s at the end and wonders who the fuck is this person writing this fucking weather report. ". . . cloudy, rain, rain, rain. Later in the week it stopped raining with a few bright spots in the clouds, but it was still cold." Christ, he'd harm this woman, maybe not, but maybe the brown dog at his feet, though, to be alive in a cold goddamn day for a change. Needles of freezing sleet. Six feet of snow. The works, searching for the middle.

". . . It's supposed to warm up some, but they never seem to be right or know what they're talking about."

Who doesn't. Who doesn't know what? Who knows what *who's* talking about? Who's right? What *is* right? What's this letter *about?* Is it in code? Why is somebody going through the effort to write this crap? What does it all mean?

Dubecheck feels like seventeen hits of speed have just had a head-on collision with his brain, a carload of drunk amphetamines are racing down to his nerve endings where they're going to have a party. Isn't there a party tomorrow? Didn't somebody say there's a party? How can you have a fucking party in this country? How can you have a party on this planet with everybody dying like fucking flies from one thing or another? Maybe it's a wake. One gigantic ongoing wake. Maybe she writes because she *loves* him. A nasty weapon against the fear of being totally alone, a thin rind keeping out the final terror. A shudder goes through his body as he contemplates the thought that the letters might stop coming. It happens all the time. They start balling some other guy. The letters trickle to one a week, one a month, then they stop altogether and guys go crazy. Platoons go out of commission. Cunt. They're worse than the Cong.

He reads through the young woman's letter, savoring each empty word in his mouth like hard tasteless candy, mouthing them and all the time frightened that all the words mean nothing, that she means nothing and that he means nothing. If you live anywhere but here, in Tacoma, Washington, or Moline, Illinois, you do not know this dog exists. You know of dogness, but it is all ephemeral. Dubecheck thinks it might all be ephemeral. He'll have to look up the word. The ephemerality of living objects, irrelevant but material. Like him. Tomorrow he could be out on the river, up a canal the size of a dark alley, picking his nose, and suddenly take a Chicom B-40 in the solar plexus and be gone, an unrecognizable mass of wet, red meat, shards of splintered white bone lying in a pool of urine, shit, undigested pound cake and peaches. Ragged tatters of olive-drab cloth, his "uniform" pasted to the deck with sticky blood. He wouldn't hear his shipmates vomiting, or see the flies zigzagging over the pile of viscera that used to be him. He wouldn't hear comrades wishing they could just hose him off the deck with a garden hose. They'd have to cover him with a poncho and smell him putrefy in the heat while they waited for the civilian ghouls from the United States in on the body boom to arrive and crack jokes.

"Got a Crispy Critter?"

"No."

"A floater?"

"No . . . we don't know what he is anymore."

Irrelevant is what he'd be. That dog would still be around and so would everything else except for all the other guys who died that day and it wouldn't really make any difference anywhere for long. All us dead guys. Where do we go? Up to heaven to play pool with each other and wait. And wait for what? More pool players, stupid, and while you wait for your shot you look down on the blue planet and realize your life was a short piss in the ocean. Pick one. The Atlantic, Pacific or Indian. Look down and watch the brief matinee of sorrow that attended your *demise*. Nice word for it.

The sorrow surrounding most men's demise, especially young men's, is experienced by about as many people as were elated by their birth. Dubecheck figures that group wouldn't be too large in his case. He was just another kid that got born somewhere. Mommy and Daddy were happy. Ah, Daddy. They couldn't find enough friendly help to bury Daddy, to help carry his coffin. Dubecheck felt like he was walking around trying to find a fourth for bridge with a salty ball gagging his throat. In the throat. That's where it gets you. You just get strangled and all you do is want to breathe.

To find six pallbearers was out of the question. Dubecheck's father had not been a gregarious man. There were not many family friends and they had moved a lot throughout the small towns of the Pacific Northwest where the patina of friendliness soon washes off with the interminable rains and reveals the same petty conflicts, bitterness and unshared pain that exist in all unhappy families. Dubecheck was just hoping to come up with a man for each corner of the coffin. Then they were three. After a brief, muted discussion, Uncle George and Eldon Pottinger, a gone-to-seed rummy from the VFW who wore his ludicrous garrison cap with more trinkets on it than an eight-year-old's beanie, decided John Paul should hold up the front while the two older men would hold the rear, each shouldering a corner. Now Dubecheck had a choice. He could hold the front up in his hands and walk backward, like he was moving some furniture . . . "Hold it . . . you got it now? . . . Okay. . . . Watch it here . . . watch the corner. . . . Uunnnh . . . got your end? . . . Watch it now. . . . Easy." Or he could have the heavy end dig into his shoulder, hunch over a bit, hands up steadying the sides. He'd be damned if he was going to rest it on top of his head like some Watusi with a load of wash heading to the river. He opted to have the sharp wooden bottom edge dig into his sternoclidomastoid, made it ache, made it goddamn hurt, hunched over with his rough black tie, a leftover from mandatory Army ROTC, hanging down straight as a plumb bob toward his fourteen-dollar Thom McAns trudging one ahead of the other over the gravel beginning to blotch with fat cold raindrops, and that was when Dubecheck began to cry for his father. That his dead and gray feather-light father's body, empty as a chrysalis, was being hauled around as if by a pickup crew from Bekins. And the strangled throat so thick he couldn't scream if he wanted to.

There was the flap about the headstone, haggling over models and price as if they were buying a used car.

There'll be none of that for him. He has it all planned. He's going to have his tombstone donated by Coca-Cola. Just like a mom and pop liquor store. Coke donates a sign and puts the store's name on the sign for free, then brackets the name with Cola-Cola logos and everybody's happy. Dubecheck's tombstone will have the beautiful Coca-Cola script written across the top, then his name beneath printed in dark Coca-Cola green on a field of pure Coca-Cola white. Perhaps a bumper sticker, "I'd Rather Be Sailing," slapped on beneath the date of final surprise. And stick the son of a bitch in the ground smack dab in the middle of Arlington National Cemetery among the other heroes, preferably hard by JFK's eternal flame for a little bit of the old yin and yang. And when they take the annual UPI, AP, Reuters for international yearly dissemination photograph of a platoon of Kennedy's kneeling at graveside, ostensibly praying, each one in private thought . . . my knees are cold . . . Dubecheck's headstone can be seen in the background: Drink Coca-Cola. Coke is it. John Paul Dubecheck. The Pause That Refreshes.

Dubecheck whirls and slams his forearm against the plaster jamb to his room and cracks it with a satisfying crunch. A forearm "shiver." Pure channeled violence learned on the playing fields of America. Specifically, Washington State University. How pleased and moved he was to hone his violence during those hard, cold businesslike workouts surrounded by the bleak, dead brown wheat fields of eastern Washington.

Home for the holidays, he proudly showed off his newfound athletic weapon with the unbound exuberance of the eighteen-year-old nitwit he was. He gently slammed his forearm into the door jamb leading into the kitchen and cracked it, surprising himself, shocking his mother and stunning his father into an even deeper morass of quiet confusion.

"Is that what they teach you?" His father was genuinely per-plexed. His father was a wimp. His father was brave. His father was weak. His father was strong. His father was a confusing chimerical man whipsawed by the American Dream, chewed up, spit out and beat up. He didn't have a prayer. He had the shit kicked out of him and along the way he fed and clothed his son. He was an accountant for some of the gypo logging companies that existed in the small towns of the massive dark green Cascade and Olympic mountain ranges of Washington State. Towns where most of the men, unlike his father, wore their balls on their chests like oak-leaf clusters. Loggers, truckers, mechanics, miners; they wore black Frisco jeans frayed at the cuffs to keep them from hooking deadly little snags and tripping in the deadly big forest; they wore vertical striped Hickory shirts and red galluses, silver hard hats, Cat and Stihl ball-caps, black fingernails. They chewed Copenhagen and spit it out. They spoke in gravelly voices that took years of practice to main-tain. They were soldiers fighting the vast forest and the cloud-shrouded mountains and the cold, angry, wet weather, and when they came down from the front they acted like victorious warriors. They were tough, proud survivors and took joy in daily triumphs. They took beer. Gallons of it, in smoky taverns that reeked of sawdust, bar oil, gasoline, wet, muddy clothes, and freshly felled fir trees as tall as buildings in big cities. They had Thirty-ought-sixes and Two-seventies and Thirty-forty Krags in the rifle racks of their pickups and they shot deer and elk in or out of season and Dube-check thought he liked them. They liked him. They liked him be-cause he could run and hit and on miserable wet Friday nights under the bleak yellow light of small high school football fields, with the frigid rain driving down into the torn turf and black mud, he scored touchdowns for them and, better yet, dealt out punishment and played in pain and gave their brutal lives some moments of hard beauty and sweet surcease as he flew across their hopes and kept the tenuous link to victory close at hand, tangible, delectable, always possible.

But his father wasn't one of them. He was oblivious to football, to the transitory adulation his son ingenuously basked in. Had they been remotely close at all, this emotional snub would have dismayed a more sensitive kid. Or so he thought. Dubecheck wasn't insensi-tive, he just hid from the realization that love was often impossible to make anything of if you couldn't put your finger on it.

Daddy was at war long ago. He was in "The Big One." He too got to fight the "Yellows": Tinian, Saipan, Guam, Luzon, the Marianas, around there . . . all those warm semitropical names redolent of dead gooks and palm trees and dazed Americans. Then Uncle George in Korea. An unknown malarial Grandpa vomiting to death in the Philippines. Good Eastern European men shoulder to shoulder with all the Yankee Micks, Yankee Spics, Yankee Frogs, Yankee Wops, and Yankee Krauts who so often seemed to find themselves arm in arm marching to the Orient to kill the Yellows and often die at their hands. Purple Hearts in attic trunks. More violet than purple, actually, the silk thick, the medal with the weighted heft of a man's penis.

Why didn't his father like him? Perhaps he didn't like anybody. He didn't seem to like his mother. Dubecheck couldn't imagine that urgent quivering coupling taking place between them with any degree of passion. Sperm skewering ovum in a fastidious business proposition resulting in . . . him.

Father and son spent nearly two decades incommunicado. Nearly normal. And there was an argument about America and a derogatory remark about America from his dour father, offhanded, not worth lowering the paper before his face.

"But *you're* an American." Dubecheck shouted angrily at the newsprint wall of auto ads.

His father lowered the paper. "I'm a human being."

Perhaps they were going to get into an actual conversation about "things," the world, and Dubecheck excitedly forged ahead, clumsily, like the intellectual klutz he was, stumbling over the unformed thoughts in his head. "Well, what's so good about *them?*" A non sequiter?

He didn't even know what he said. He was embarrassed and he saw his father for the first time in his memory begin to smile. He felt he was about to be laughed at and became as enraged as a frustrated mute. He fought back an overwhelming urge to cry, the awareness of the urge to cry feeding the onrush until he had to leap up and leave the room where he regained his composure with the balm of force, slamming a forearm against the doorjamb with such force, a jagged crack shot across the sheetrock like frozen lightning. He didn't know anything. He didn't know shit. He wanted to know when you'd ever know something on your own, *really*, instead of only knowing what you'd been told by older, smarter people.

"You'll have to fix that," his father said later. Calmly. Distant. Oh, drop dead. He did.

Dubecheck, whose hands were made for catching balls, not repair, taped a picture of a dog barking at a grizzly bear over the crack. He cut the picture off the cover of an old *Sports Afield* magazine found in the basement. It said, "Grizzlies—Tough Customers." The last he knew, the picture was still there. But his father's not. He's dead. And *gone*, as they say. Gone to heaven on a football scholarship.

He looks at the crack he just put in the Dong My wall. A couple of ants scurry out as if they'd been living inside the wall for years; they go in circles, confused by their freedom. Figures. He feels a strange heaving up of the past, all the little instances of his short life seem to converge and collide upon a huge groundswell of emotion. A raging mute. He remembers the first time he used his forearm shiver in a game. They were playing the Oregon State Beavers in Corvallis, Oregon, in a mistlike drizzle in the Beavers' old depression era stadium. His assignment as a flanker on this play was to fake (he was always faking something now that he thinks about it) a Z Out and crack back on the middle linebacker, a thick brutish kid who'd been touted All-American, complete with a press agent's intimidating nickname that Dubecheck can no longer recall.

The guy was an imposing-looking rectangle in his black uniform with orange numerals and powdery white lime stains. And he was a noisy fellow with one of those hoarse, clipped voices semitough nononsense guys affect in case you're in doubt about them. His face guard made him look like a muzzled circus bear, but even Dubecheck's mother would look tough with a helmet on. He ran up and down behind his teammates, slapping them on the butt and exhorting them, and they looked like they wished he'd shut up. As Dubecheck was watching him rant and rave behind his down linemen, "Come on, you cream puffs! Come on, you cream puffs!" a High School Harry chant that could cover either team, he caught the eye of a defensive tackle who had just been slapped in the ass, one of those grass-stained, sweat-shiny pack mules who get their names in the paper as often as their obituaries. The down lineman smiled, shook his head and winked conspiratorially at Dubecheck, who winked back. We're all in this together, except for the assholes, right? There it is, sucker. Then the play snapped into action with *"Eaahhhhs"* and *"Arrhhhs"* and the clack of pads.

Dubecheck sprinted out, barely ducking the flying forearm of their skinny black cornerback, a little mean shit, and faked left. The little asshole took the fake long enough for Dubecheck to duck back and cut against the flow of the play and find himself on target lock on with "Mean Gene." *That* was the linebacker's nickname. Mean Gene Gianopoulous. Mean Gene was screaming, "Pass! Pass!

Pass!" which was absurd, and he wasn't really looking where he was going because, when Dubecheck hit him with his forearm right in the face, it came as a near fatal surprise. Mean Gene went down and out. Dubecheck thought he'd killed him and just stood staring at Mean Gene while pads clacked and guys thudded windedly into heaps on the ground. Two guys spun out of the play crashed into Dubecheck and sent him sprawling on top of Mean Gene, making a sandwich of tired athletes wheezing on the cold swampy field. The whistle blew. Mean Gene's face was inches from Dubecheck's, face guard to face guard, and Dubecheck started to laugh but it was hard with five hundred pounds on top of him. Then Mean Gene opened his eyes and, with seven hundred pounds on him, croaked, "Who are you? What's so fuckin' funny?"

On the way back to the huddle a couple of Beavers slapped Dubecheck on the butt. In the huddle people scolded him with mock seriousness.

"Jesus, J.P., you shouldn't have done that."

"Yeah, wha'd ya do that for?"

"Shit. Now he's going to be *mad* at us."

For the rest of the game he was referred to as "Creamed Gene," which kept most folks, Beavers and Cougars, snickering until bone-wracking fatigue set in.

After all, except for the assholes, we're all in this together, right?

He wonders where all those O's and X's are now? Better times, those. Dubecheck laughs at the recollected "Creamed Gene."

"Tch. Tch. Tch. You're laughing out of context again, Diwi." Lieutenant Recore, hired gun, is back from mass. He walks into the room and pulls his .38 from his waistband and tosses it on his rathole of a rack. He and Dubecheck usually work at night, so the racks have the misused abnormal look of daybeds.

"I was reminiscing about my glorious but brief collegiate foot-ball career. I owe everything I am to the game. Diwi Dubecheck, warrior. Death to the yellow horde." He picks up Recore's pistol and sniffs the barrel. "Shoot anybody today?"

"Better put that down before you hurt yourself, sonny." Recore admires himself in the mirror, pleased with his custom-tailored, pegged fatigue trousers.

Dubecheck twirls the pistol on his finger like a revolver. "Hurt myself? I'm the fastest gun in town."

Recore doffs his olive-drab cap to himself. "I look pretty. You get pretty too. We've been invited to a party." Recore starts doing a soft shoe in his nonreg tennies and hums. " 'Puttin' on my top hat, puttin' on my tails . . .' "

Engaging man, Recore. The Delta sun has given him a red-chocolate tan that shows off his piano-key smile. He has a middle-weight's build. He walks with that quick, slightly bowlegged strut, swinging hands cupped halfway to fists, that so many stocky men have, as if they're always ready to crouch, freeze and pounce.

He is brave in the pure and simple sense of the word: generally fearless. He paints his face black and ocher and green and leads men through the dark swamps looking for the opposition, on his tiptoes, barefoot, through rice paddies, down trails into trouble. He has a real war wound. A bullet stain on his shoulder that looks like a pink plastic smear of Fleer's Double Bubble. It happened over a year ago one night in a kaleidoscopic matrix of green and red tracers and orange barrel flashes. He was the only person in a huge hospital ward in Japan who was there because he had been hit by an enemy bullet. That made him the object of a perverse envy. All the others were limbless or filled with garbage from booby traps, mines, mortar splinters and pointed stakes. In the pecking order of wounds they were sucking hind tit to Recore's Russian bullet.

He is the only pure killer Dubecheck has met who doesn't have a Southern accent, which for some curious reason makes him seem a bit more gentlemanly to Dubecheck's Northern sensibilities. Those Johnny Reb drawls about "hosing down gooks" strike the ear a bit hard. Although it all adds up to the same . . . carrion. Best of all might be a clipped British accent, along the lines of "potting off Jerry." Somehow killing people with a British accent seems civilized, sporting. Smashing! They'll have to try it sometime.

"What's new at Our Lady of Defoliants?" Dubecheck slips the clip out of the .38's grip and flips it up toward the ceiling and catches it.

"Same old shit."

"What do you do there anyway?"

"I listen. You listen."

Dubecheck staggers around under another high clip toss like it was a pop fly. "They say anything about me? I mean God or the angels and shit?"

"Sort of. My communion wafer had a little message on it. Sort of like a fortune cookie. Never happened to me before. It said, 'You and someone you know are going to meet two ugly Army nurses, drink whiskey and dance the bunny hop.' Fucking strange."

"Terrific. I'll assume I'm your guy. I'd like that. Just lemme practice a bit here." Dubecheck puts his hands out in front of him as if holding an imaginary waist and pistol in one hand and clip in the other, bunny-hops about the room with his feet together. "Dadun! Dadun! Dadun! Da dundily dundily dun!" He stops. "I'm ready. When you're good it comes back easy." He tosses the pistol to Recore and starts to pull on his fatigues, feeling the near euphoric rush a young man generally experiences on Friday nights. That is, if he doesn't have to work. He's been working weekends too much lately. Been working too much period. Fifty-five combat ops in the last sixty days. Time to *unwind* and hope the old springs don't go *sproing* and scatter in the dirt.

"And put on your hat. Lieutenant Kooseman said Tuta wants you to wear your hat."

"A jerk of the first magnitude, Kooseman. Tuta could care less about my hat."

"Yeah. He says at night on the streets it helps identify you as an American."

"That's a mixed blessing. What does he think I look like now? That guy just doesn't like me. What did I ever do to him besides call him a stupid shithead for a very good reason? Remember?"

"Yeah. Put on your hat."

"He almost killed us. Remember? Killed, as in untimely death. Dead. As in gone but forgotten. Him, Kooseman."

"He outranks you and he's smaller than you are. That's why he doesn't like you."

"There you go, makes the world go round."

Kooseman almost killed Recore and Dubecheck once because he had some people bomb the wrong coordinates. It was an honest mistake. This in fact would not have been an uncommon way to die in the American military. Kooseman made that honest mistake when he first arrived in country and was eager to do well.

Tuta was off puttering about somewhere and Kooseman, the new kid, was in the Comm Center where he overheard the minor skirmish Recore was involved in at the time over a net that was being monitored by a third class petty officer perusing a Sony catalogue. Kooseman decided to call in help and dialed up a couple of jet airplanes that carried more lethal ordnance than a squadron of Jimmy Stewart B-17s. Havoc, as they say, ensued. It was the last time Kooseman tried anything like that, and now it seems all he does is monitor the length of Dubecheck's hair and pull rank for the sheer perverse pleasure of it. That and lie about what Tuta says or wants done. Tuta doesn't want anything done. Tuta wants to make about as much effort on the local scene as a potted plant. The man remains somewhat of a mystery to Dubecheck, a rarely seen phantom, which suits Dubecheck just fine. The less one deals with superiors the better. Tuta has spoken to Dubecheck maybe twice. Once upon Dubecheck's arrival in country when he walked up to him and said, "Hello. Who are you?"

Dubecheck attempted to reply but Tuta walked away in mid-sentence, leaving Dubecheck standing alone in a cloud of flies.

The other time he spoke to Tuta was through the jalousies of his mistress Madame Phong's house at two in the muggy morning.

Essentially, according to Dupree, Tuta had sort of resigned from the Navy before his present tour of duty was up.

"Negats. The Navy quit him," said Recore. "They're punching his ass out. The shit for brains stacked a destroyer up against a pier in Subic when the squadron commander was aboard. He never drank, but I hear he did that night. He ended up throwing up on an admiral's wife at the Cubi Point O Club."

"That'll do it."

"Yeah. His next billet was supposed to be stacking blankets in the Aleutians but he ended up here instead."

"Does he ever talk to you?"

"No. He doesn't, which is all one could ask for in a superior."

"Really."

4   The streets of Dong My have quieted in a combination of siesta and piety. The Catholics are doing their business and the Buddhists are doing whatever they do on a sleepy Sunday ambling toward noon. A covey of monks in their tangerine-colored togas mince along in the heavy shadows of the huge trees along Tu Do, the sun glaring off their shiny bald heads, wormy veins bulging and pulsing with thoughts of nirvana and overthrowing the government.

The hungry are behind their jalousied doors and shutters eating rice, the shops are closed and barred. All the cars and motorbikes are parked, their metal ticking in the heat. A lone Jeep can be heard several blocks away accelerating, then backing off. A group of small boys have taken over an empty nameless street off Tu Do, their tiny shouts swallowed up by the heavy Sunday quiet. They have skinny brown arms and legs and distended tummies and are playing with sticks and an empty Black Label beer can with the squealing exuberance of boys who think they're onto a game never before played. Dubecheck and Recore stop to watch for a while, leaning against a big tree, smoking, loitering in the Orient.

Across the street the barber, in his sleeveless T-shirt, sits in his barber chair eating with chopsticks. His family sits in the golden shadow behind him, his eight-year-old daughter goggle-eyed, mouth agape, full of tiny pearls of rice as she spots Dubecheck. She squirms in her chair like a puppy on a tight leash. She bums cigarettes from him when she's out running amok on the streets, leading her gang of dirty-faced, thirty-pound racketeers. And there he is, easy meat, and she's boxed in by Mommy and Daddy, who don't know she smokes like a combat trooper.

In return for the cigarettes, Dubecheck gets to make scary faces at her and pretend to chase her, while she pretends to be scared and squeals around the big pile of garbage in front of the hotel, cigarette clenched between her teeth like a stogie. If the war goes on a few more years she'll get to be a whore like the other little Lolitas in the makeshift plywood bars that stand on pilings over the dirty brown canal that comes off the main river. Fuck for electric fans and antiperspirant from the Dong Tam PX.

Dubecheck waves to her. Her parents look up and nod and smile in that obsequious oriental manner Dubecheck feels is calculated to embarrass.

"This is a pretty little town," says Dubecheck.

"You can have it."

"I got it, Mofo. I got it bad. I heard the barber's VC. So what do I do? I had him shave me the other day. With a straight edge. Cheap thrills, man. What do you make of that, tough guy?"

"You're a sick kid, Dubecheck, and why am I following you?"

"I'm going to the club for an eye-opener or a nightcap, one of the two."

"The club's closed."

"It's our club; let's open it."

"Your buddy Kooseman's got the key. He's locked it on Sundays in a petty power play, if you don't recall, since you threw a chair at him."

"We'll shoot the lock off with your piece."

"Testy. Testy. Kooseman will be angry with you."

"What's he going to do? Send me to Vietnam?"

They stop before the O Club, a plywood structure the size of a large Otis elevator with a cinder block foundation sitting in a court-yard by the mess hall. The mess hall is a French provincial concrete structure with wrought-iron windows. Inside, a hooch maid sits alone at a small table in the empty room. She smokes and stares at the pack of Salems she twirls on the red and white checkered table-cloth. Flies hover over a little island of ketchup and salt and pepper in the middle of the table. The wooden fan hanging from the high ceiling slowly rotates with a tired squeak. The sight suddenly exhausts Dubecheck.

"This place is going to kill me."

"Speaking of getting killed, I read your SPOTREP. What happened last night, pal?"

"How would I know? I was there. You need an impartial observer out there to get things down. Maybe some Swiss referee in a smock carrying a clipboard. I dunno. It was noisy. You hadda be there."

"Why didn't you hose those guys down? That'd be a few less guys *I'd* have to worry about. You're on *my* side, remember? You trying to get me killed?"

"I don't know. I can't shoot people floating in the water, to tell you the truth. Maybe I should be in the Army, in the *land* war in Asia." Dubecheck feels embarrassed. Maybe he's a bad warrior. Worse, a coward, afraid to kill people who aren't specifically trying to kill him. Each outing has been a bit jumpier lately. "I got a prisoner."

"Great. We need prisoners like I need the clap."

"Maybe the Chiefs' Club is open. I want to change the subject."

The chiefs have acquisitioned a large masonry house and turned it into a casino. An eight-foot-high wrought-iron fence surrounds a lush verdant courtyard fronting the imposing ocher structure.

"And quit whining, Recore. Look at it as more gooks I've left for you."

"Yeah. There's a bright side to everything, isn't there?"

"Jesus, chiefs don't like this JO gate crashing, you know."

"Maybe no one's in there."

"They got these huge chips on their shoulders. I guess I would too if I had to spend my life saying 'sir' to a bunch of punks twice as stupid as I was."

Dubecheck and Recore enter into the deep, cool, sylvan air of the Chiefs' Club, widening their eyes to adjust to the semidarkness.

A quartet of chief petty officers sit at a round green table fingering tiny red, white and blue columns of poker chips in front of them. They look up at Dubecheck and Recore and nod curtly.

"But they won't refuse us a drink at their joint because, if anything, they understand that when a man needs a drink, by God, he should be able to have one. Especially if he outranks you."

Chiefs crack Dubecheck up. They rise to the top of the enlisted heap only to be stood upon by the lowest-ranking junior officer. The payoff is everybody pretends they, like sergeants in the Army, run the Navy. They are proud of their clubs and as military wanderers they consider a club a little bit of home away from home, home being the Navy; and, being generally affable and gregarious, or else they wouldn't have made chief, they like a guest now and then. It gives them a chance to show how well they have milked the system, the revenge against the indignities of caste.

Recore and Dubecheck hop up on a couple of stools at the end of the long mahogany bar. The place is empty, save for the four chiefs and two officers, and is as hushed as a cathedral. Fronting the five-foot-high mirrored back bar is a massive pipe-organ pyramid of booze. The tiny mosaic-tiled floor has a white marble sheen. Thick green curtains over the windows give the long, narrow high-ceilinged room the quiet light of a forest dell. An air conditioner that actually works hums softly. A line of slot machines stands along a wall like robots at attention, fruit cluster eyes staring straight ahead.

"Nice place. Wonder what the VC Chiefs' Club looks like?"

Although there are only six chiefs in Dong My, it's a club for the chiefs of the world, visiting tops and gunnys, visiting chiefs like the ones now playing seven-card high low split and drinking Bloody Marys, RivRon 15 patches on their black berets. Guys from somewhere else stopping off for a little home cooking and ammunition.

Plaques from PBR squadrons, SEAL teams, mobile support teams, intell units, any old outfit that can fire up a motto and coat of arms, are hung on the wall next to shellacked *Playboy* Playmate center folds, rosy pink Kewpie doll bimbos with tits the size of grapefruits and heaps of cotton candy hair. "Chicks worth fighting for," Recore says.

Curios from every Westpac Navy port of call furnish the room. Cheap Hong Kong tapestries of fierce-looking, sword-wielding, slant-eyed, baldheaded warriors, chartreuse and orange Japanese

dragons on black silk Chinese lanterns, red plastic Vietnamese doo-
dads, bamboo lampshades, Kaohsiung whorehouse bead curtains,
fluorescent sloe-eyed Filipinas painted on black velvet, place names
tattooed against the walls like two hundred years of salty history
reeking of rust, rain, seaweed, cordite, paint and oil, echoing with
the endless rush of water sluicing along hulls, creaking rigging, boatswain pipes, cannon fire and crying gulls: Pearl . . . Midway . . .
Wake . . . Guam . . . Yokosuka . . . Tokyo . . . Kaohsiung . . .
Keelung . . . Olongopo . . . Subic . . . Hong Kong . . . the Delta
. . . don't forget the fucking Delta.

"Hair of the dog, eh, sir?" A shiny-bald heavy-set chief talks out
of the side of his mouth at Dubecheck and Recore; the other three
chuckle as they look and sort their hands. Just a bunch of guys.
Even wars have their locker rooms.

"Roger that, Chief. How about an unrep? Four Marys around?"

"That'd be a BZ from us, sir."

The chiefs raise their red drinks as they study their cards, nod,
mumble, "Bravo Zulu" and take obligatory sips.

But the finest acquisition the chiefs have is Co Lan. She emerges
from the shadows at the end of the bar like a slender cat and
traipses on tiny slippered feet up the length of the bar, smiling
slowly at Dubecheck with her pussy-plump, pale purple lips, her
glistening plum-colored tongue tip clenched between her pearl teeth
like a hard, thimble-size nipple. She is twenty and frightens everybody. She is so beautiful, everyone is afraid to talk to her, so they
nervously joke with her in pidgin English and Vietnamese when all
they really want to do is put their heads in her lap and whimper and
smell the warmth of her faintly humming sex rhythmically droning
in the blood rush through her arteries, pulsing, diastole-systole, in
and out, thumping hotly at her pressure points, listen to her coo as
the breeze blows her jet-black, jasmine-smelling hair out behind her
like some silken pennant waving from God's own jackstaff.

"Oh, moan. It's Co Lan."

"Big deal, Dubecheck. A chick's a chick. All cats are gray in the
dark."

"How old are you?"

"Twenty-five, why?"

"You're a twenty-five-year-old Catholic guy from Rochester,
New York, right?"

"So?"

"Twenty-five-year-old Catholic guys from *anywhere* don't know shit about chicks, probably never will. So don't give me this 'Chicks are—' "

"Morning, Diwi." Co Lan lowers her eyes at Dubecheck and Recore. The light from a Tiffany bar lamp gives her slightly bowed head a golden corona. Her lithe body is laminated with a white silk ao-dai like a second skin, her bikini panties embossed beneath the tight sheath that is slit up the left leg, exposing her sunrise-colored thigh. On the street she'd wear baggy silk trousers beneath her ao-dai, but in here she's done without. The ao-dai curves from her hard rump into her tiny waist, which gently flares upward to mold a wedding-gown-white swell over her breasts, things Dubecheck imagines to be the size of major league hardballs and just a little less firm, with nipples the size of Kennedy half dollars.

"How are you too-day, Diwi?" She speaks in a nasal singsong, which seems incongruous since her nose is no more than a slight ridge lifted from between her high curved cheekbones, a ridge dwarfed by her dark, moist, cocker spaniel puppy eyes with lashes like dark awnings.

"I'm fine, thank you."

"No, he's not. He's sick because he can't fuck your brains out."

"Recore! Jesus Christ, man."

Co Lan feigns indignation and shock. She shakes her head and wags her finger at Dubecheck. "Oh, Diwi. Numbah ten, Diwi." She laughs, a tinkly wind chime, as Dubecheck feels embarrassment spread across his face like a prairie fire.

"That's not true."

Co Lan puts her hands on her hips and pouts as if affronted.

"It is too, Co Lan. All Diwi Dubecheck talks about is boom-boom. Boom-boom Co Lan, take America, have beaucoup kids. No lie."

"Fuck you, Recore."

"Hey, relax, if you're not obnoxious how they gonna know you're interested? I know chicks. We owe those guys a round, Co Lan. And my pal in harm's way here'll have . . . ?"

"A double Beefeater martini up, no olives." Dubecheck sulks into the bar top.

"Hey-hey. The guy's gonna play hardball. I like it. Draw two, wonder snatch."

"Jesus, Recore. Can't you be nice. I mean, would you talk to a woman in the States like that?"

"There are no women in the States like that." They watch Co Lan gracefully walk down the bar, as fluid as tall grass in the wind.

Women like that, Dubecheck thinks. If you are lucky you might make love to them and you feel the wondrous luxury of something beyond sheer sex, where the silken feel of cool molten skin slides like life's water over your rotten little soul and you realize that this is worthy of deserving men. Take your tongue and place it on the tongue-tip-wide crease at the base of her spine and drag it upward over the hard little lumps of her xylophone, across the salty dew, the crevice sheathing the primordial power driving the electric pudding, taut, bending like a compound bow ready to unleash an arrow that impales your heart, or more likely your nuts. . . . Teeth gnashing as she thrashes, fistfuls of her voluminous hair in your hot hands, black corn silk flowing through your fingers like cold blood.

"What are you thinking about?"

"Why?"

"You're staring into the bar like there is something in there of interest."

"I was thinking about death, or maybe Indiana, about GI life insurance. All kinds of things."

"Buy the drinks."

Co Lan sets two martinis before them and Dubecheck pays with a piece of funny money with the picture of a fluffy blonde in a 1940s hairdo. Co Lan places her hand on top of his for a brief birdlike instant, drops her eyes and walks down and begins to make Bloody Marys.

"Chicks are fucked, Dubecheck."

"Really?"

"Yeah. She touches your hand, I see it. But she's shacked up with some Trun Wi in the United States Army. He gives her all his salary. He crawls one mile over broken glass just to smell her shit."

"Co Lan doesn't shit."

"I catch your drift, but what can I say?" Recore takes a small sip of martini. "Jesus, this is lethal!"

"It gets easier." Dubecheck takes a mouthful of cold gin that nails his palate like anesthetic.

"Like chicks in America. Between tours I'm out with a chick and she hears I've been in the war . . . the one on TV." Recore sips. "More than one chick, to tell the truth. They all want to know one and only one thing: 'Did you kill anybody?' I wonder why they want to know that? They must sort of get off on it. Like they're around something evil, so they get a rush they don't have to pay for. You tell 'em you've killed somebody and they feel sorry for *you*. It is truly weird, but American chicks are really stupid, so it isn't too weird when you think about it. They feel sorry for *you*. Notice they don't feel sorry for the guy you offed."

"Sometimes I feel sorry for the guys that get offed."

"Feel sorry for the guy you brought in alive. The White Mice are doing a number on him. He hasn't said a thing."

"What's to say? 'I'm sorry?' Christ, I should have shot him."

"Now you got it. They went through his wallet. He's from Hanoi. Picture of his wife and kids and some letters from home. Little tiny things, those letters, like they've got mailmen about two feet high." Recore laughs and the chiefs look up from their cards for an instant.

Co Lan sits on a bar stool in a narrow cone of sunlight down the bar and reads her romance comic book. She chews her lush lips and swings one of her pretty feet over the fulcrum of her partly naked thigh. She arches her neck back and shakes her hair and goes back to her story. When Dubecheck was a kid he saw a tomcat hop a female cat between the garbage cans in the back of a supermarket where he stacked bottles. The dirty orange tomcat had his teeth sunk into the nape of the black and white female's neck and covered her and they seemed frozen, as if they were stuffed, but they'd blink and growl and it was hard to tell who made what sound, and the sounds were like they were in pain or, he'd later learn, ecstasy. And sitting on top of the garbage cans were three other cats who watched what was going on, motionless voyeurs giving him only the briefest glance, licking their tight little cat lips. Dubecheck threw an empty Nesbitt's bottle at the voyeurs and they just sort of ducked, so he sat on a crate and watched with the cats, just like another dumb animal, intently contemplating the lovers. He wants to gently sink his teeth upon the warm salty nape of Co Lan's long neck, like a panting lion with a mouthful of gazelle.

Recore tosses down his martini. "Little mailmen. I oughta be on 'Laugh-In.' Nice-lookin' chick, too."

"Who?"

"The gook's. The pictures with the letters."

"What did the letters say?"

"I don't know. The gooks were reading them and giggling."

Dubecheck washes his martini around in his mouth and swallows. "Sometimes I wish we were fighting asshole Nazis, dirty Japs; I wish there were front lines and rear lines and you knew where in the hell you were and who the hell to kill and maim and cripple. That is what we do, isn't it? The old bottom line."

"Bottom line. Dead bodies. Dead 'little people.' If they're dead they're VC."

"Like General Duntley. He claims the 9th Division killed twenty-five thousand VC last year, with tears rolling down his face at the change of command, he's so proud. I guess a psychopath is as good as anyone else for a commanding general."

"Actually, the best. Soldiers are supposed to kill people. It's in the contract, in the boilerplate, been in there for a long time."

"Like maybe *France.*" Dubecheck holds the empty martini glass to his eye. "And we'd come rolling into a little French village on a tank and these French babes in these tight flower print dresses would come running up to us, their high heels clacking over the cobblestones, tossing roses at us, shoving wine bottles into our faces, and we'd guzzle the wine and it would run down our chins and those beautiful French babes would hop on our laps and we could feel their soft asses spread on our thighs and smell their perfumed hair and hear them laugh and dead Nazis would be stacked alongside the road like cordwood and accordions would play—"

"France. I like it, Dubecheck, all the way up to the accordions. Let's go. We can get drunker than this."

o   o   o

The Strip is a lumpy, chuckholed narrow street paralleling the brown, alley-wide slough that comes off the river. Stilts and pilings coming up out of the slough brace up ramshackle shops, cheap eateries and several hastily fabricated little dives for the Yankees to get drunk in and meet the ladies: child-faced teenage whores who look as if they were made up by drunken morticians, with thick mascara, blue and white eye shadow and pink lipstick framing smiles that reveal teeth as rotten as the building's foundations.

The whores sit on sailors' laps, stolen fatigue caps on at jaunty little angles. They wear miniskirts and nervously swing their bare and dirty feet as they chew gum, drink Coca-Cola from red plastic glasses and hit people in mock anger, looking as if they are doing eight things at once to the din of rock and roll 45s.

With a couple of PBR squadrons in town today, the dives are packed. The local units are standing down waiting for some make-work assignments, so the Strip is boiling like a cheap carnie.

Dubecheck ducks into Phu's Cocktail Lounge, wincing from the heat and raucous din. Phu's is packed with about forty sailors in Delta-drab fatigues, each one screaming his lungs out to be heard in unintelligible, meaningless conversations. A pall of cigarette smoke hangs in the air like ground fog. Dubecheck spots his crew sitting at the prime table by a glassless window overlooking the slough and across to the shanties on the other side. They wave wildly at Dubecheck, as if they were proud of their drunkenness. They sit with a couple of PBR sailors who wear little whores on their laps. The girls wear the sailors' black berets and laugh all the time as if everything was funny. Dubecheck eases his way through the screaming throng, past the DJ, a small barefoot boy in shorts and a sleeveless T-shirt who stands by a portable record player and a stack of red vinyl 45s from Taiwan. Two sailors are screaming at him. "Rolling Stones, you little shit!"

"Maybe it's Lolling Stones!"

"Yeah," laughing maniacally, "yeah. The *Lolling* Stones. Play some Lolling Stones."

The little DJ just shakes his head and stares down into the floor, twitching like a cornered rabbit.

"Little *asshole*. Little motherfucker. *Soc mau* you, little dinky *dau* shit."

They laugh and walk away as the kid looks after them, then turns to watch the record go round and round on the little portable. The Beatles are singing "You Better Run for Your Life" in a language the kid can't understand.

Dubecheck arrives at Scoog's table. Hatch, Saltinovitch, Sisler, McDowell, and the two PBR sailors and the girls sit looking up at him, glazed-eyed, sweat-greased, and grinning like gargoyles. The light green oilcloth atop the rickety table is puddled with lakes of Coca-Cola and nickel-size lumps of ice, an ashtray overflows with butts, everyone looks like they're smoking four cigarettes at once.

"Lemme buy a drink, sir!" Scoog shouts to be heard. He holds up a red plastic glass and Coke sloshes out of it. "Hey, Debbie! Get your ass over here. We got ourselves an officer!"

"No, thanks, Scoog." He recalls that the only cocktail sold at Phu's Lounge is rum and Coke. He looks around. Eleven-thirty in the morning and it's like goddamn New Year's Eve. The town will be up for grabs by dusk. Dubecheck looks out the window at a bouquet of garbage floating down the mud-colored slough. A cloud of fat black flies zigzags over Scoog's small table as if it were a rectangular sheet of shit. He feels he's inside some noisy internal combustion engine and forgets why he is here. The needle scratches loudly off the record, a girl shrieks and a roar of male laughter bounces off the pale green plywood walls.

"Don't go pussy on us now, sir." Scoog shouts as his voice is drowned out under a babbling wash of jabber; something about drinking him under the table and getting him laid or blowed. "No shit. One buck PC. It'll knock your socks off. . . . She takes out her false teeth . . . no shit, she's a fucking millionaire . . . unbelievable, sir!"

"Get the little boat fixed!" Dubecheck shouts to Scoog. "We're going out Tuesday night. You and me! No-frills op. You and me. So get it right."

A nauseated look comes across Scoog's face and he sobers for a nanosecond. He nods down into the table until his petulant reverie is broken by the sound of busted glass and a table scraping across the floor. Scoog leaps up.

"And no goddamn fights! Any of our guys get in a fight, tell 'em I'll kick his ass." Dubecheck edges his way out of the dive, getting a gauntlet of dirty looks from everyone as if he were trying to crash a line.

He pops out onto the street, straddles the paper-clogged swamp of the gutter and looks back into Phu's Cocktail Lounge. Brownwater sailors swarming inside like olive-drab maggots. Compared to Phu's, the ninety-five heat and humidity outside feels like a breath of fresh air. Camaraderie. Can't beat it. Duress, ennui and frustrations don't have a prayer against it. Dubecheck looks in at the false bluster, bravado and drunken swaggering. Fucking teenagers, teenagers with tattoos who should be back home doing something else: working at the Dairy Queen, pumping Exxon, jacking off, mowing lawns, falling asleep in class, taking shit from Dad. But instead they're doing something else, being assholes.

Recore splashes up alongside Dubecheck in his platoon's Jeep, a bent stolen number they got up in Saigon months ago. They shot off the lock around the steering column and raced it out of town, put three bullet holes through the front window, changed the paint numbers and service branch on the outside, deliberately ran the right front fender into a palm tree and had a Seabee create a card file on it for all the preventive maintenance performed during the last three years. Recore sits at the wheel smiling with pride of ownership. Dubecheck hops in and the Jeep races down the shade-dappled street and comes to a roundabout that doubles as a patriotic plaza where a bronze statue of a soldier stands atop a large concrete pedestal. He thrusts his bayonet in textbook style but somewhere along the line his head has been blown off and he has been whitewashed with pigeon shit. The dead tan grass at the foot of the pedestal is littered with paper as if the statue had walked through a ticker tape parade of garbage. Dusty bits of paper fly up in the Jeep's wake like confetti. Along the road loose pyramids of brick rubble spill out of some bombed-out structures. Two laughing little boys chase a skinny brown dog over the brick hills.

At the edge of town Dubecheck sniffs up the stale, pervasive claustrophobic stench of the city, a living stench that marches up through the nose, up into the brain where it spreads like an indelible stain . . . brackish water, dust, diesel, rot, urine, especially urine, right out there in front holding the guidon, and you can't wash the stink off because it's in the water.

Dubecheck remembers the small, smooth ice cubes in Phu's Cocktail Lounge and wonders why the ice cubes in Asia, from Kaohsiung to Bangkok, don't seem to be cold, they just seem like big wet cough drops that pick up the flavor of whatever sauce they float in. And the ice cubes smell and everything you drink and breathe stinks and it comes out in your sweat and your shit. It just doesn't smell *right*.

The Jeep cuts back down a narrow dirt street lined with bamboo and skimpy stick fences that sag in the heat in front of small, bare dirt yards surrounding little adobe-looking houses. Chickens squawk angrily out of the way, a half dozen kids chase after the Jeep, laughing and waving as it stops for a huge tethered sow lying on its side in the middle of the street, bloated and panting, encrusted with dry mud, ten thousand flies hovering over its slimy snout and around its anus. The pig won't move even though Recore is honking the horn. The kids, in dirty shoes, bottomless and barefoot, hold their sides as they laugh hysterically and point at the huge porker. The pig's ears occasionally ripple as if coursed by an electric current; other than that, she continues to snooze.

Recore looks around with bemused trepidation, as if this might be some bizarre ambush perpetrated by Walt Disney. He pulls out his .38 and pumps a round into the dirt a foot from the pig's snout.

"Jesus Christ, you scared the shit outta me, Recore!"

The kids shriek and jump back at the sound, then continue to point and laugh as an old purple-mouthed crone comes hobbling out of a hut wielding a big stick. She heads for the pig and the Jeep.

"Good. The proper authorities seem to have been alerted," says Recore. He sticks his .38 back into his pants and looks up to smile just as the old woman steps forward, club cocked, and driving off her back foot like Babe Ruth with a knobby Louisville Slugger, lashes out at Recore's head.

"Jesus!" Recore shouts. His hands slam over his head in a helmet of fingers and get smashed by the big stick. He scrambles up to get out of the way of the blows bouncing down off his head and shoulders but his trouser cuff is caught on the gearshift and he is trapped in the Jeep and the kids are screaming in delirium and falling to the ground and hitting it with their fists, tears rolling down their faces.

"Do something, Dubecheck! Goddamnit, make her stop it! Goddamn it! Ow! Ow! Jesus Christ!"

But Dubecheck can't help because he is laughing so hard he can't breathe and rolls out of the Jeep. The old woman grunts with exertion, purple betel juice seeping down the vertical crevices beneath her mouth to her chin; she drools and grunts as she flails away at Recore, who looks up at Dubecheck, forlorn, resigned to his thrashing, yet struggling away from his hiding screaming, "All right! Okay! Enough already for Christ's sake!"

Oddly enough, the old woman stops. The laughter stops. The pig has gotten up on all fours and walked around to see what all the commotion is about. She brings her flies with her and they buzz in the humid silence.

Recore slowly sits back up in the driver's seat. The hushed wide-eyed kids, expecting the worst, look from Dubecheck to Recore to the old woman and back as if trying to light their eyes upon the safest spot. The only sounds heard are the muted clucks of the chickens and the old woman's heavy breathing. Recore rolls his head around on his neck to check for malfunctions and nerve damage and, finding none, smooths his hair back with his hands, puts on his utility cap, puts his hands on the wheel, stares straight ahead and quietly asks, "Is the pig out of the way?"

Dubecheck hops back into the Jeep and nods. The Jeep pulls out under the sunlight that flickers through the leaves of the three-story trees. Dubecheck looks out to the side, biting his tongue; he hears what sounds like the front of Recore's face explode and turns to see snot flying from Recore's nose, a pent-up burst of spray from his mouth. Recore pulls the Jeep over. He slides down into his seat, shuts his eyes and begins to laugh in hysterical huge gasping cries. Dubecheck joins him and they laugh until their jaws and heads ache, till their eyes feel cold, drained of tears, sniffling, hiccuping and then running off into another uncontrollable riff of belly-ripping laughter, pounding the dashboard in hopes that might help stem the tide of hysteria, shaking their heads in dismay at something.

Dubecheck finally whimpers to a halt as he stares up into the blue sky over the dusty treetops. Even the blue sky seems dirty, bleached and drained of life. He feels a huge sudden urge to go away; he looks into the rear-view mirror and wipes tear stains from his face. The word "ridiculous" enters his mind. He wonders if any of this means anything. Or worse, what if it did?

5 The party is U.S. military Mark I macho: charcoal-grilled meat and copious quantities of canned beer tasting like something made in chem lab. As Dubecheck sips, a strong whiff cons his taste buds into thinking, Formaldehyde. He washes the swill around in his mouth like sour Alka-Seltzer, then swallows it in good faith—that it will hold up its end of the bargain and get him drunk.

He surveys the roster of guests, thirty or so officers and noncoms he has never seen before. But that's not unusual. Strange guys seem to be wandering all over Southeast Asia like dazed tourists. Go around any corner and there they are: Yanks in olive-drab fatigues with a can of beer in one hand and a cigarette in the other, laughing too loud, as if the forced volume will help them get a joke they don't quite fathom. "Poltroons" is the word, Dubecheck thinks. Just like me. A posturing poltroon with a cigar clenched in his teeth to make him feel like he deserves the sweaty balls between his legs.

There are some Army types standing in little knots of three, four or five, in each one the senior man holding forth like some raconteur while his JOs and noncoms hang on each word like they really give a shit. Cigar smoke hangs in the air of the enclosed patio like fog. A couple of gooks dart in and out of the mist like wraiths bearing paper plates, napkins, sacks of potato chips, jars of mustard and ketchup, then disappear into a forest of tall Americans. Dubecheck thinks they wouldn't be called ketchup and mustard, though. They'd be called: Condiments, U.S. Government Mark I and Mark II.

The Army guys wear the sleeves of their fatigue blouses rolled up over their biceps in a thick band. Come to think of it, everyone

who doesn't cut them off does. Even foreign correspondents. Dubecheck thought he saw one when he arrived. They stand out in a
crowd like a jive-ass pimp at a wedding, 35mm SLR amulets hanging around their necks, pockets bristling with pencils and tape re-
corders, shades, Cool-Rays, man, real cowboys, war junkies, mustaches and long hair and playing chicken with the whole gig like it's
just one big goddamn game, the only game in town really. But all
these long-sleeved fatigue blouses rolled up. Someone's made a killing on all the cloth they don't need that's balled up around all these
biceps. If Dubecheck knows his military, all the short-sleeved
blouses are stocked in a mile-long Alaskan warehouse.

Dubecheck looks out the large wrought-iron gate closing the
revelers off from the natives. Across the dirt street a semicircular
mob of kids jump up and down as they point and shout excitedly at
arriving Jeeps like a crowd at a Hollywood premiere. The war is an
endless child's garden of diversion. Here, real life is better than TV.
Dubecheck figures that's one difference between East and West. No
way is real life better than TV in the West.

"Cocktails for Thieu?" Dupree soft-shoes up holding a clear
pint bottle in his hand.

"Ha-ha, Dupree. Funny. How long do you think you can go
through life with a lampshade on your head? Think about it. These
are trying times. They give men sober thoughts and pause."

"Really?"

Dubecheck looks at Recore, who arrives with five cans of
Hamm's in his hands.

"Well, I got a million of them. Stop me if you've heard this one."

"I've heard it."

"Listen up, Recore. You should broaden your mind . . . with
humor. Some humor to balance your homicidal tendencies."

"*Tendencies?*" Dubecheck takes two beers from Recore.

"Dubecheck. Don't drink that shit. Have some of *this* shit."
Dupree holds out his pint.

"Warm gin. My favorite. You really shouldn't have, Norman."
He takes it.

"You're going to need it." Dupree rolls his eyes and Dubecheck
follows his gaze to see four women standing in a huddle under the
shade of a dusty tree in the far corner of the patio. They look about
with an air of conspiracy, plotting, like cheerleaders at a letter
men's picnic.

"Oh, no."

"Oh, yes. Nurse Anastasion. She's been glaring at you since you got here."

"I gotta get outta here."

Recore grabs Dubecheck by the arm and holds him back.

"For us, Dubecheck. Do it for us. Of all the American males in the Orient, it is you for whom she pines."

"Yeah. You gotta let her have her way with you, Dubecheck, then you can tell us about it. That's the least you can do. I'll put you in for a Bronze Star."

"Norman, Jesus."

Dubecheck peeks over Recore's head at Anastasion, who nails him with her black eyes. Nurse Anastasion loves misery and for some unfathomable reason has picked upon Dubecheck to share her woe. She is not unpleasant to look at. She is tall and angular with the aura of a demented voodoo priestess. At least he thinks she's angular if that means bony and made of planes the light hits like crystal and gunmetal. As a civilian American nurse in the Provincial Hospital she can wear any uniform she wishes, and today, fresh from the morning shift, she wears a baggy sea-green polyester shift with a slightly bloodstained lace camisole over it, which makes her look like a transvestite. Combat boots adorn her splayed feet. Her nails are polished red, but she bites them constantly like some cornered rat chewing its paw; her eyes, brightened by an inner fever, gaze out with the ten-thousand-yard stare of those who have seen too much of the wrong things. It is what she might see in Dubecheck that worries him. What she sees *inside*, as if tea leaves and tarot cards are churning around within him like a soggy, shuffling kaleidoscope that only she can read.

She has always gone out of her way to let Dubecheck know she is morally superior to him—and everybody else for that matter. She doesn't have a job so much as she's serving some sort of penance. A lapsed Catholic angry at God because of the things He allows to happen, which Dubecheck always thought silly. None of this shit is God's fault. Even God can't bat five hundred.

Good sound theology he never forgot. But shit like that is hard to explain to Catholics. At least Catholic chicks like Anastasion.

Once he asked her on a "date" and to everybody's amazement she accepted. The boys at the O Club had been talking about her, and Dubecheck said she couldn't be that bad, but she was. He took her to a little café hanging over the canal that had Christmas tree lights strung all over and they flashed and reflected off the pungent slough like a silent fireworks display. The café had red checked tablecloths. The salt was in little open dishes and had the consistency of wet sand and sat next to little bottles of Nuocmam, sauce, which was the national condiment made from rotted fish.

"We're the only white people here," she said.

Dubecheck looked about and, except for the four waiters standing at parade rest at the four corners, they were the only people around, period.

They ate something that looked like a run-over duck and as Dubecheck picked at it in silence he felt that Anastasion didn't even look "white" herself. She looked like some crazed bright-eyed Arab, what with her black bed-sheet dress and old-lady-gone-to-mass scarf over her head. The rumor that she ate opium like it was cheese dip seemed believable.

Dubecheck tried to initiate some conversation, the basics, like since both of them were from America maybe they knew some of the same people. They didn't and Dubecheck suspected they never would. Then she opened up. She had one of those chips on her shoulder that people who were shit on in high school seemed to carry forever, people from back East who sort of felt they weren't as good as some other people, like people with *money* and *family*.

She came from some shitty old wiped-out shoe factory town back in that gray, dirty brick jumble Dubecheck imagined the whole northeastern United States to be, except for the places where the pretty autumn leaves fell. He'd never been there, but he'd met enough people from there and they all walked around like they had a corncob up their ass. But what did he know? What he didn't know was what a "guinea" was.

"It means an Italian?"

"Where I come from," she said, and she said it in that sullen huff, the way she said everything.

As a kid Dubecheck had known a few Italian kids. Their parents made them learn the accordion and their grandmothers made ravioli for Christmas and Thanksgiving. They were called "wops." Big deal.

She graduated from a Catholic nursing school and came out with a starched white hat and got into a 1960 Ford Falcon with another graduate; they headed west together until Reno, Nevada, where her friend stayed to become one of those chicks who deliver keno slips to people who are too lazy to get off their bar stools and walk over and get their own.

Anastasion ended up on a Trailways bus to San Francisco and volunteered to help miserable people in Asia, and the insufferable pain of others became the emotional foundation of her insufferable self-righteousness.

She never asked a thing about Dubecheck and after dinner she got up and shook his hand. Her fingers were cold and limp and she walked out and he was left in the empty restaurant with the four waiters, who stood quietly holding their towels in their hands pretending some other people might come.

He heard later she thought he was a conceited asshole. She gave him the creeps.

Who doesn't give him the creeps? He gives himself the creeps.

Every face is a gargoyle. A Halloween party starring that clown and his snake, the little SEAL sailor with a teenage boa constrictor draped around his shoulders. Later he'll put that mottled, oily, thigh-thick serpent in a cage with a chicken and everyone will watch the chicken die and be devoured. Everybody will go quiet, like they're watching a porn flick, then start making humorous cracks when the chicken gets the picture and starts shitting the stinking fear out of its body, fidgeting, thinking, OhmyfuckinggodI-can'tgetouttahere. And that huge python mouth goes over the feathers and just sort of sucks the thing down in gradual increments, blinking slowly, bored, taking lunch. Dupree says it gives him a hard-on. It gives Dubecheck the creeps. What doesn't give him the creeps? He wonders where he *belongs?* Where does a guy anchor his ass nowadays in this storm? He catches Anastasion's eye. She looks at him like she's squinting through a sandstorm. She is not the girl next door, she's the girl from outer space, and things are going badly enough for Dubecheck that he sure doesn't need someone to go through psychotherapy with.

He eases his way over toward the U. S. Army guys. He'll let the cavalry save him, maybe that swell-looking guy with the starched fatigues and yellow ascot, West Point and Benning written all over him, spit-shine shave and salt and pepper skullcap haircut and Foster Grants. He'll sidle up to that guy and pretend to bask in his shared wisdom and glory with the two blond, Nazi frat-brother-looking lieutenants rocking on their heels in front of him. They hang on his every word as he holds his can of Hamm's with a napkin around it as if he was at a cocktail party on the third floor of the Pentagon E-ring. As Dubecheck gets closer he sees the little threaded Aztec-looking birds sewn into the lapels of his tailored fatigues and realizes he is in the awesome presence of a full chicken colonel, RA. A Regular, by God. In the mighty six-foot-four shadow he casts, two little ARVN majors stand, ascots around their necks like little oriental cowboys, their shades, darkly concealing their obviously contemptuous thoughts. Our counterparts, with their trousers creased and bloused over their shined combat boots, and they too holding their Hamm's beer cans wrapped in napkins and not drinking. Decorum. Just like their *adviser*. "I advise you to look like me." Our Vietnamese counterparts, Dubecheck thinks. Decorum. *Dulce est decorum morte pro patria.* Something like that. If he throws up today, please God let it be on these guys. Hit the bird kern with the first salvo and pick up the counterparts with fire for effect. Hit 'em with some body-temp condiments and pea-size shots of Hormel wienies right in the chest, then slide down on the old hands and knees right in front of them and heave out the old high test on the black Kiwi-smelling toes of their jungle boots. Give 'em a good Zolotone shine.

He slides in behind the colonel, putting him between himself and Nurse Anastasion's radar. He smells the colonel's Mennen Skin Bracer. The Army must bring the stuff in by the tanker load. . . . Mark I or Mark II . . . Old Spice or Mennen. Whole fucking divisions smell the same. On a hot day you can smell a battalion at muster for miles. The 115th Old Spice. A long and glorious tradition. The man's deep voice resonates in his chest. Dubecheck can't understand what he's saying but recognizes it as one of those voices the guy must practice in the bathroom. His back is as stiff as if he had a piece of rebar in it and he carries himself like one of those assholes who'd call in Willie Peter on his own position if he thought he might be overrun. On *his own* position. He may not be talking for the other guys, who'd rather not be fried with phosphorus. But what the hell. The world seems to figure they need men who presume to speak for everyone else as if somebody has to speak up for the stupid mutes.

Humidity and heat really can dial up the Mennen Skin Bracer. Dubecheck feels he is about to gag on the cloying perfume. Christ, there's even a dried white dot of Gillette Foamy in the guy's ear. It all brings Dubecheck back. Locker rooms, the barracks. They all smell like shaving cream and soggy towels, the blast of a guy's toothpaste breath as he sneezes in your face and farts rip the air like a ragged concert of French horns. Ah, the barracks in the morning: guys hawking up lugies, snot smashing into urinals, gas ricocheting around toilet bowls, spit hitting porcelain, coiled pubic hairs drifting like goose down to paste themselves on toilet rims, soapsuds evaporating to a wet gray paste of dead skin cells and dirt and gumming up the drains, whiskers dusting sink basins like soot, pin dots of toothpaste speckling the mirrors where guys check themselves out, slap on the Old Spice, slick back the hair, give themselves a grin and think women like them. Regulars, by God!

The hairs on the back of the colonel's neck rise up a bit. Not bad. The guy must have Dubecheck in his range. He can't be all bad, he's a big guy. Most big guys in the world are all right. He spots a couple of big guys, Army captains, across the court who are really pounding down the beer as they eye the blind date ugly trio huddled around Anastasion.

You run into a *mean* big guy, you got trouble, though, because a mean big guy is really an asshole, as opposed to a little mean asshole who can't do as much damage. The guys across the courtyard look mean. They're thick and beefy and red and look nervous in their bodies and are to be avoided unless one feels perverse . . . like Dubecheck.

So far, size has been good to Dubecheck. The extra size he has carried isn't really good for much but it usually buys a second or two while someone else thinks twice about giving him the same shit they'd normally have given a smaller person. Dubecheck's eyes meet those of one of the captains across the way. Red pig eyes. He holds the gaze for an instant. Big guys really get the willies when their bluff is called because big guys know how much damage can be done. Rooms get broken, walls crack, the air is charged with everybody's undivided attention. The eyes of the big captain across the way begin to dart back and forth as if he has a battery of lawyers in his head, covering the microphone and bombarding his brain with options, positions and other bits of conflicting advice. He's confused. The old Do-I-*know*-this-guy? bell is going off like an alarm clock in his sleepy-time Hamm's head. Dubecheck wonders why they are looking at each other. The hackles go up on the back of his neck, a bad sign. Dubecheck is starting to believe more in the animal side of him and less in the Cro-Magnon. So what? They've merged into an indiscernible mass. Dubecheck puts the colonel's head in front of the captain's oddly manic gaze. The colonel's head is becoming a big pal of Dubecheck's. Twice it's jammed incoming radar. He wishes he could take it with him wherever he goes, pluck it off from its stem and stick it in his bowling bag and use it now and then to hide himself from people looking for him. The colonel's flunkies are nervously beginning to notice Dubecheck, as if he were a doddering, drooling uncle at the reception, so he decides to go over and look at the chicken staring out of its little wire cage. It regards Dubecheck for a beady-eyed instant, dismisses him with the air of a bird that knows this guy can't fill in the blanks and pecks the steel floor at its feet as if that might materialize some food.

The sailor with the boa constrictor wrapped around his chest like a bandolier is getting drunker and laughing a lot, which is bad news for the chicken. Dubecheck feels a perverse pride that he knows more than the chicken does about the scheme of things, the near future so to speak. But not much more. Life is just flat glacial, a wall of ice the size of a century has relentlessly ground down through his head, turning his brain into a jagged mass of peaks and valleys and fucking rubble. That's how he sees it in there . . . rocks of various size, dates (1492, 1776, 7 December 1941, the numerically dated and codified history of the world).

The two large Army captains have moved in on Anastasion and her puffy-faced, pool-hall-pallored friends, Army nurses with the skin tone of the freshly dead, a cadaverous luster from standing under fluorescent lights all day, scrubbing blood off their skin and drinking till they pass out into the healing grasp of oblivion. Fucking saints that look like Poppin' Fresh in olive drab. He has always been curious why ugly women always seem to want to help the lame and the halt and realizes it is because nobody else will. The ugly, the lame and the halt and this chicken. Dubecheck wonders if he should help it escape. Fuck it. They'd just find another one. Christ, who dealt this hand?

Somebody has turned up the volume of the party. Uniformed Americans are still coming through the large gate and the courtyard is taking on the appearance of a well-crashed lawn party. Voices are rising and people are laughing loudly. The chicken looks around like it's trying to get the joke. Dubecheck kneels behind the cage to look at the party from the chicken's point of view, out through the wire squares breaking the party into a Sunday comic strip, slipping from one page to the next. Dupree's gin sits burning atop the closed entrance to Dubecheck's stomach like a charcoal briquette.

"They've all got Social Security numbers and service numbers. My service number is 793819."

The chicken regards him with a cocked head and blinks at him.

"We're all numbered; they're used to identify us. Each one of us is like a snowflake. Not one of us is alike. Amazing. In a whole blizzard, not one snowflake is alike. 'Prove it,' you say? Well, not one of our fingerprints is alike. You figure that means anything? It must mean something . . . then again, why should it?" He kills the can and the beer foams in his mouth like carbonated vomit. He spits it out onto the brick patio and watches a platoon of ants race for a nearby crack like someone has called Willie Peter in on them.

Dubecheck feels very comfortable. There is a big white ivy-covered wall behind him and to his left, and his right flank is covered by a phalanx of garbage cans. The caged chicken guards him from the front but not too well, for its rapt attention is upon Dubecheck, who talks to it. "I'm in exile, trapped in Southeast Asia. A prisoner of war. A trustee. I can't leave if I wanted to . . . honest to God."

"Praise be to God, Jesus, Joseph and Mary. Purrrraise God." Heavy coughing follows this shout. From behind the garbage cans on his flank the chicken looks confused, as if watching a ventriloquist for the first time.

"Puuuraise the Lord God." A garbage can moves noisily across the bricks and exposes a bleary-eyed middle-aged man who rolls up onto his hands and knees and sniffs at Dubecheck, blinking in the sunlight like a hung-over dog.

"The Lord is king." The man clears his throat and spits into the bricks and wipes his mouth with the end of a white silk scarf draped over his neck. His fatigues are stained with polka dots of dampness in various stages of dryness. His breath smells of sweet whiskey and sour rot. He dabs his face with the scarf and groans. "Talk about assholes. Then talk about your Abraham." The plump man rolls over on his ass with the labored clumsiness of a fighter trying to beat the count. He gives up and leans his back against the ivy-covered wall next to Dubecheck and sighs so deeply, Dubecheck expects a death rattle at the end.

The man has a soft fleshiness about him, a sheen of grease and sweat on a pink face peppered with pockmarks like a pumice stone. A bulbous nose sets off bright, beady brown eyes that peek out at something he alone can see and his slack lips look as if they're willing to smile. The man has crosses sewn into his collar. Chaplain, U. S. Navy. Commander. Very heavy. He looks to Dubecheck, then looks at the chicken and speaks quietly, directing his remarks to the bird.

"Abraham the Asshole would have killed his son. He would have thrust a dagger into his breast and twisted it and ripped it around and ground his son's heart into hamburger because somebody purporting to be the Lord commanded him to. Do you think the guy might say, 'Hey, wait a minute . . .'? Yeah? But not Abraham. He was a good Jew. He was just following orders. I submit he was just another gutless asshole. But what do I know?" He regards Dubecheck and whispers, "Praise God, purraise the Lord, my son." He fishes in his fatigue blouse and pulls out a pint bottle of Jack Daniels, unscrews its top and hands the half-full bottle to Dubecheck. "Don't look confused. I know you aren't my son. I don't have a son. I've got four daughters. There isn't a raised toilet seat in the house."

Dubecheck takes the pint and takes a tiny swallow. It's as hot as tea. "Thank you, Commander." He hands it back.

"Call me Chaps, call me Padre. I command nothing. . . . 'The way of man is froward and strange.' Proverbs 21:8. This your chicken?"

"I don't know. I've been thinking about it."

"It's a helluva chicken." He pokes Dubecheck in the chest with his finger. " 'The imagination of man's heart is evil from his youth.' Genesis 8:21. Say, you don't mind if I'm drunk, do you?"

Dubecheck crouches farther down behind the cage and sits Indian style as he spots Nurse Anastasion wandering through the crowd like Lady Macbeth, oblivious to the troops watching her as if she was as nuts as she appears to be, wandering about as if she is searching for something. It's a little early, but she must be getting ready for her speech.

The Army captains are laughing so hard their faces are purple and they're stomping their feet and gasping for breath and spitting their drinks out. Always a good sign, spillage. One can't help but smile. Maybe they're okay. Maybe everybody is okay. Maybe it really is a wonderful world full of wonderful people. Maybe this party will really pick up. Comrades with their arms over each other's shoulders singing in drunken three-part harmony. "Auld Lang Syne," "Don't Sit Under the Apple Tree," "The Name Game," now with an F very plain.

"I ask you a question and you keep a civil tongue. Wise counsel indeed. Me, what do I know? 'The Lord is a man of war.' Exodus 15:3. So I'm a Lutheran. You, Lieutenant, you don't look like a Lutheran. You look like yourself and a remarkable resemblance at that. I'd know you anywhere and you oughtta bring Christ into your life or, if you'd rather, have another drink. Six o' one, half dozen of the other." He tosses the pint to Dubecheck, who holds the bottle to his eye and squints through the whiskey at the scene before him, turning it into a watery, amber-colored painting of people he could do without and happily never see again and he realizes nobody is minding the store.

There seems to be a tacit understanding among the myriad military of greater Dong My to knock off for the day. Maybe it's an order. "Seriously, guys," says the Great Comedian in charge of all of this, God knows his name, "is it really necessary to go outta your *way* to *prosecute* the war? Hey, knock off. Take five. *Relax.* You've been too hard on yourself. Just rip this day out of the history books. Who's gonna miss it anyway? Some kid down the road? Some kid sitting at his desk in U.S. history with a hard-on, picking his nose and trying to stay awake while looking at a black and white two-by-three-inch photo of some troop firing a hooch in a war that covers two pages of a dirty dog-eared text with 'Fuck gooks' and 'Harvey Poll sucks Dick' scrawled in the margin? Yeah, you got it. Knock *off!*"

Dubecheck likes the plan. Knock off for the day and start backsliding. The next thing you know, you've knocked off for a week and you're ready to say, "Fuck it," for the whole gig. Then maybe you got Charlie knocking off for the day. Come back to the ville and see his kid for the first time in ten years. Take him fishing, sit on the bank and dangle their slender brown legs in the cold brown water and listen to the transistor. Chew some Wrigley's Doublemint, working the jaws flashing the happy white teeth. Mamma-san ducks the smoke chasing her from the roasting pig in the pit and the family laughs because the smoke always wins. Someone will say in Vietnamese, "Smoke follows beauty," and everyone will laugh. Hard-breasted maidens daintily scatter flower petals in the meadows, hopping piles of buffalo plop in dainty leaps. Grandma wipes pineapple juice from her mouth with the back of her wormy-veined hand, grinning, hacking apart the rich yellow fruit with a cleaver; Grandpa puffs his pipe. The fine white hairs on his chin sway in the breeze like dangling dry moss. Bicycles glide along the tops of the dikes and the slim girls sit sidesaddle as their beaux pump along, the skirts of their ao-dais flying out like Superman's cape as they laugh and twirl parasols in their dainty, white-gloved hands and the chaplain throws up at Dubecheck's feet, his hand pressed down upon Dubecheck's shoulder as he leans on him for support.

"Reeeeeeearrrgghhhhhh." Then he spits down on Dubecheck's boot tops for a moment, clearing a bad taste from his mouth. "Whew! That's better. Jesus, what a relief. You know how it is, just before you blow your tubes, ya think you're gonna die. Christ, ya *wanna* die, but the big fella upstairs says, 'Call for Ralph! Ralph it up.' And sho'nuff. You follow the call of the Lord and *purge* the body, cast off that vile curse of demon rum. *Wrestle* that John Barleycorn to the ground and stomp his ass and teach 'em the fear of God and Jesus, goddamnit!"

"Is this man all right?" The shadow of the colonel falls across the chicken cage. Dubecheck looks up to see the concerned yet accusatory face of the man himself, flanked by his JOs, their faces reflecting a lesser chagrin, proportionate to their rank.

Dubecheck looks at the chaplain and shrugs. He likes the cut of the fellow's jib and has developed an immediate fondness for the man, but feels no urge to defend or explain him.

"He's a chaplain."

"I can see that. Is he all right?"

"He's throwing up. Other than that, I don't know, sir. His conversation's sharp."

"I've got a mind like a steel trap. Whatever that means."

"I'm talking to the lieutenant."

"Good. He'll do all my talking for me." The chaplain belches dryly and stares at the ground, still leaning on Dubecheck. The two lieutenants are looking at Dubecheck as if he was a bad smell. Come to think of it, he does smell. He smells like a rancid jockstrap because the last warm shower he's had in two weeks has been under a premonsoon squall. And now he smells a bit of vomit. He looks down to see a green pea poised on the scuffed toe of his combat boot, compliments of the Lutheran leaning on him, breathing hard as if he were exhausted.

"You men get to your feet."

"Call me a cab and you've got a deal."

"You're a cab." One of the lieutenants tries to make a joke and the two Vietnamese counterparts, up on their tiptoes trying to see, chuckle until the colonel ices the lieutenant with an 0-6 glare, does an actual parade-ground about-face and looks down to one of the lieutenants.

"Take care of that man. He's a disgrace." He strides off as if he had a regiment behind him; his knees, dipping at each stride, give him the goofy lope of a world-class nerd and blow his bearing all to hell. Dubecheck thinks he'll never make brigadier for that, but tough shit. From what he's beginning to figure, life's cruel.

"Disgrace my ass. What's that schmuck know from disgraces?"

The two Vietnamese counterparts nod and smile in feigned deference and maybe admiration. The gook guys whom Dubecheck has drunk whiskey with chug it like spring water on a hot day, then fall down and sleep. That's what it's for, isn't it?

The lieutenant reaches down to help up the chaplain.

"Unhand me. Let *him!* The guy next to me. The *Navy* guy. He's been through thick and thin with me. Thick and thin. He's been like a son to me. My son." He gives Dubecheck a smarmy grin and a clap on the back.

"Whatever you say, Padre," says the lieutenant.

"Padre? Do I look like a padre to you?" He struggles to his feet, using Dubecheck for support, and goes nose to nose with the pained-looking lieutenant. "Do I look like I'm wandering around in a burlap sack going, *'Dominus vobiscum'?* Do I? Do I, sir? Take another gander. I'm a chaplain in the U. S. Navy. I've had Marines *default* right in my arms. Praise Jesus, fuck the Lord and have 'em strike my ass down if I haven't had more goddamn teenage offal fuck up my slacks than the next guy and I've got enough rank to make a sandwich out of you and"—he points to one of the Vietnamese majors—"and, and *Cato* there. Padre my pink Dakota ass." He begins to brush himself off with the dignity of the affronted.

"Yes, sir. I just thought we'd . . ."

"Learn to mind your own business. You'll go far, my son." The chaplain gives a slapdash salute intended to dismiss.

The two lieutenants and the Vietnamese majors look to Dubecheck, who shrugs. They back off muttering something about "Dinky Dow mutherfuckers" and, drawn by the gravitational pull of rank, meander toward the sulking colonel, who glowers by the beer bin across the courtyard.

"I admire the way you hung in there with me, Lieutenant. When the going got tough blah, blah, blah and abracadabra. Christ can use soldiers like you. A Christian soldier. Damnedest oxymoron I ever heard. Where's the whiskey?"

"It's gone, Your Grace. I finished it when you were . . . a . . . berating the dashing young cavalry officer."

"Your Grace, I like that. I like that a lot. But this means we need more whiskey. Not necessarily that kind. That stuff kinda acts up on me."

"Where do we get it around here on Sunday?"

"Where do we get it? Good Lord, man. Don't be so stupid. I wonder about you sometimes. I buy it. I buy it in a PX with hard-earned Yankee dollars. I'm a war profiteer." He reaches into his pocket and pulls out a wad of scrip the size of a baseball. "Here, you handle the money. I'll drive. Come on."

Dubecheck turns and sees who he thought he smelled. Nurse Anastasion, reeking of Betadine, dry blood, denatured alcohol and Hamm's beer. She stands blocking his way.

"Hello, Lieutenant Dubecheck."

"Hello, Nurse Anastasion." Dubecheck has always been curious as to why, at first, they are always so formal with each other. However, it invariably disintegrates into something Dubecheck can neither control nor explain. He brings himself to look into her tawny, nearly thirty-year-old face, the skin drawn drum tight over her cheekbones, her naturally mauve-colored lips beginning to twitch. He realizes he doesn't have much time.

"Excuse me, Nurse Anastasion, but get out of my way. You're blocking my way and I know what you're up to, so please knock it off because I don't need you to—"

"You're scum, Dubecheck. A moral eunuch."

"I know it. Can I go now?" He looks over her shoulder. Those who know her are moseying toward the confrontation with the bemused demeanor of a cheerful lynch mob. Dupree and Recore are in the forefront with smug looks on their faces.

"You know this gal, buddy?"

"Yes, sir, Chaplain. Not well, but I know her. Nurse Anastasion, Chaplain Whatshisname."

"Just another scum-sucking son of a bitch too, Dubecheck. You all are."

"This I know and you've made that clear in the past. I'm no better now than I was . . ."

"You make me sick." She is getting louder and a few heads turn.

"Get it over with then."

"This is very interesting." The chaplain strokes his chin and purses his lips.

"No, it's not interesting at all. It's abuse pure and simple. This woman singles me out for—"

"The snake! The snake!" An Army guy Dubecheck has never seen before is running around the patio like a delirious courier, the drink in his hand sloshing out. A line of Army guys, infantry badges sewn into their fatigues, cigars in their mouths, swagger about like they all think they're Chesty Puller and shuffle in noisy commotion toward a corner of the courtyard.

One of the messmates runs over and takes the chicken out of the cage and walks toward the gathering, holding the squabbling bird before him with stiff arms as it drips droppings across the ground.

"What's up? I sense something ominous. I can feel it. I'm good at that." The chaplain clutches Dubecheck's biceps.

"They're going to feed the snake."

"Snake? What snake?" The chaplain lumbers toward the crowd.

Dubecheck follows and stands at the back of a semicircle of men craning their necks toward a coffin-size wire cage where a boa constrictor lies thickly coiled upon itself, greasy gray with bright dark oval spots, its flat anvil head as big as a huge fist and its tongue flicking out like electricity.

The chicken holder shows the chicken the snake, but the chicken has long since got the picture; it is motionless in the man's hands, its shiny eyes dart as tears of whitish shit now fall from its bottom like droplets from a melting icicle.

"Hey! Watch my boots, chicken!"

Everybody laughs.

"Somebody open the cage."

Somebody does and the man tosses the desperately squawking chicken into the cage. It freezes in a corner and falls as silent as the rest of the courtyard. Dubecheck hears a car horn honk in the distance.

The snake stirs, its dull eyes having caught a glimmer of something. Its tiny nostrils pulse. Its tongue flicks.

"He's got it." Someone coughs quietly. The crowd is silent, save for an occasional cough, a few lame cracks, attempts at levity.

The snake shifts, the top coil tumbles down and the second coil unfolds as the snake unwinds slowly like a stiff hawser toward the frozen bird. The chicken shuffles its feet for a moment and lets out a choked, barely audible cawk. The fat, heavy snake, as thick as a man's thigh, raises its head a bit, sniffing, sensing as it drags itself effortlessly toward the chicken, rustling quietly through the torn newspapers at the bottom of the cage. The snake stops, its head inches from the terror-struck bird. Then, quicker than can be seen, its jaws are spread and its huge mouth has engulfed the bird. Its throat works, undulating as the chicken slowly descends, head first, its feet dangling out of the snake's mouth. They quiver, become rigid, then go limp. The chicken protrudes half out of the mouth for a while, motionless, wedged between the gaping jaws like a feather duster. Then the throat starts working again and the chicken disappears by degrees.

"Jesus," someone says quietly.

"No shit."

The crowd breaks up, quietly mulling what they've just seen before the babbling slowly starts up again.

"That was *gross!*" It's Anastasion. Right at Dubecheck's side. "You're all a bunch of barbarians. Every one of you. You know what stunt one of your barbarians pulled last week?" A few flecks of saliva bubble and fade on her lips. It appears to Dubecheck she is going to start up on him early today.

"Come on, Anastasion. Please."

Dupree comes up. "Hey, Anastasion, you're not on yet. Did you see that, Dubecheck? That snake chug that chicken? Man, that was lewd."

"You're sick, Dupree."

"Lieutenant Dupree to you, Nurse."

"You're all barbarians!" Heads turn and Recore seems to slink off in the distance.

"Recore! You oughtta hear this too. All of you guys. You know what happened here?"

"Where?"

"Right *here.*"

"Is she creating a scene?" the chaplain turns to inquire of Dupree.

"Last week one of you . . . someone stuck a bayonet up a woman's vagina. Real neat! A bayonet up a woman's vagina. Real neat! Trying to get her to talk. An enemy woman. A sharp knife up her vagina!"

"Bayonets aren't that sharp," someone shouts.

"Barbarians! Filthy barbarians! She was in the hospital for fifty stitches and she escaped. She could barely walk! Filthy goddamn barbarians!" Her shrill, hate-filled voice echoes off the flat white walls of the courtyard as the crowd, drinks in hand, gazes at her with the curious detachment of people forced to watch a home movie at a picnic. Some look a bit hurt and those who don't know her and her routine seem confused, wondering what a bayonet up a VC's vagina has to do with them. *They* didn't do it. They've all got airtight alibis. Most of them don't even own a bayonet, much less think about using one.

"Macho Wonder Bread killers raining rot on the earth, spilling blood so you can soak it up and use it to paste ribbons on your goddamn tin soldier uniforms." She shrieks and ululates, sending a covey of birds out of the large dusty tree in the courtyard.

Her body shimmies and she scrunches her eyes shut and begins knocking her knees together as she screams. "You love it! You're sick, you're drunken slime, dirty goddamn grave makers and baby buriers." Spittle flies from her mouth as she sinks to her knees before the awestruck crowd in the silent courtyard. Dubecheck looks out into the street and sees that the boisterous party voyeurs have also become silently transfixed.

Anastasion begins to hyperventilate and pound her fist on the bricks. She emits a long, low drone that is broken by the staccato clicking of the war correspondent's cameras. He's shooting Anastasion with a variety of lenses at a variety of angles as if she were a fashion model rending a bloodstained camisole from her body. She balls up the torn garment and holds it into the air; while the photog, one eye closed, mouth twisted open, gets right in her face. He ducks back just in time to avoid her snatching out for a dangling camera. She sinks to the pavement, lies out forward like a swan, a prima ballerina in an exaggerated bow. From behind, Dubecheck and the chaplain see her in a fetal crouch.

"Nice ass," whispers the chaplain.

Anastasion begins to whimper and sniffle as she rocks her forehead back and forth over the gritty bricks, pretty much indicating she is done for the day. In the silence there are a few muffled coughs.

Dupree puts his hands on his hips, then strokes his chin as if deep in thought. Gazing down upon Anastasion, he turns to the assemblage horseshoed behind him.

"All in all, not a *bad* performance. Though I've seen her better. Her work has a certain panache to it. This display, although showing a certain lack of restraint, indicates a maturity and command heretofore missing in her earlier work. I look forward to her efforts in the future. We may be in the presence of, if not genius, a consummate professional. I'll give her an eight. Do I hear more, or is eight it?"

Numbers shout out, making the courtyard ring like a commodities pit. Nurse Anastasion's friends go to help her, glowering at Dubecheck as if he had just beaten her down into the dirt. Dupree comes over and bends down and pats Anastasion on the back.

"Seven. That's all I could get for you. Seven."

The foreign correspondent stands looking down on Anastasion like he's waiting for her to regain her composure so he can get a release. The party has gone back to normal; the buzzy cacophony of prattle and laughter fills the muggy air like a resonance.

Nurse Anastasion gets to her feet, walks over to the shade by the three ugly stepsisters. Her face is soft and puffy from tears and fatigue. She looks over her shoulder at Dubecheck.

"Man, that was a piece of work. She do that often?" The correspondent takes another shot with his Asahi Pentax.

"When she can," says Dupree, emptying a tiny drop from his upside-down gin bottle.

"Damn fine girl. Nice ass too." The chaplain squints toward Anastasion.

"Yeah. She wants to give it to *him,* but he won't have any of it."

"This guy? This guy next to me? My son?" The chaplain thumbs toward Dubecheck. Dupree nods. "My son, the stupid kid. He's a stupid kid. What's his name?"

"Dubecheck. John Paul."

"He took all my money. I don't have any money. I don't have a drink either."

"How about a Hamm's?"

"A Hamm's? A Hamm's *beer?* Bears. That's what bears drink, isn't it? Those Hamm's bears. Do I look like a bear? Nooooo. Purraissse Jesus, we're not bears. Let's get a Jeep, my son." He puts his arm around Dubecheck and pulls him toward the large wrought-iron gate.

Dubecheck is nearly out the gate when he feels the pitty-pat of little fists thumping on his back. Nurse Anastasion grunts with the effort. She leaps up and locks her legs around his waist and her arms around his neck. She begins to shriek as the chaplain and Dupree try to peel her off.

The chaplain stops and calmly strokes his chin.

"Why is she doing this to this guy?"

"Why are you doing this to me?" Dubecheck shouts. He writhes and shakes, clawing wildly and futilely at the growth on his back. Finally he stops and stands panting. His hands hang down at his sides and Anastasion remains wrapped around him like a hundred-and-twenty-pound rucksack. He turns toward the courtyard and sees Recore laughing so hard he must lean against a wall for support.

"I think she likes you."

"Yeah, well, I don't care. And I don't think it's very funny, Dupree. This woman is sick! Sick with a capital K, man. Anastasion? You hear me?" Dubecheck tries to twist his head around to speak to her. "I'm going with the chaplain here, so de-tach. Jesus!"

"Purraise Jesus! Bring her along, my son. She's on you like a limpet and I don't have all day." He pulls Dubecheck by the arm and out the gate with his burden as the partygoers hoot behind them.

6 Out on the dirt street Dubecheck and the chaplain bump around in a maze of a dozen or so Jeeps metallically ticking in the heat of the day. A crowd of small children stand bothering the lone sentry guarding the vehicles, a skinny Adam's-apple-bobbing sailor with a pink tapioca complexion who stands reading a *Playboy*. His M-16 leans against one of the Jeeps he's protecting. The sailor looks up and blinks dully, then comes to a lethargic semblance of attention. He gropes for his gun and stuffs the *Playboy* down his pants while he looks at Anastasion and tries to salute. Dubecheck feels like he's in a strange used car lot.

"Pick a Jeep. Puuuurrraise Jesus we're not bears. Any one with a key. Any one. Can bears drive? Hell no. Bears can't drive. Thank the Lord God we're not bears!" The chaplain crosses himself and puts on a pair of glasses he has snatched from his breast pocket. "I'm looking for one honest man and a Jeep some fool's left the keys in."

The burden of Anastasion, whose hot breath is tickling Dubecheck's ear, is getting oppressive.

"Get off me or sit on my head or shoulders. Just move, for Christ's sake, you're killing me."

"For Christ's sake it is then. Any one with a key." The chaplain meanders quickly through the Jeeps like a fat olive-drab rat in a maze. "You got a gun, Lieutenant? I'm taking a short cut. We may need a gun. Unless you got Christ. If you've got Christ, all we need's a key."

Dubecheck looks around at all the kids swarming through the parked Jeeps, giggling and pointing at him. It seems the kids are always pointing and laughing at him like he was in some ongoing traveling minstrel show, or a cartoon that has spilled off the screen and he can't get back on, so he is forced to play out this joke and meander around through this childish giggling audience while they point and laugh at him. The sentry swats at them as if they were flies with his rolled-up *Playboy* magazine and shouts at them to "Didi!"

Anastasion climbs up and straddles Dubecheck's shoulders and nearly blindfolds him with her hands. He likes a fun party as well as the next guy but between the drunken chaplain and Anastasion, whom he has managed to avoid for weeks, he has to really consider what he is doing. Anastasion has picked on him out of some perverse whim he's not happy with. It's not that it's been intense and they've had ample time to date. He has seen two white ladies in all the time he's been in Asia, at least until today. Now there're four of them, including Anastasion, wandering around. Four nurses and that short, dark, furtive, surly-looking little woman whom he thought he saw darting about with the war correspondent like a ferret in a henhouse. The chicken!

Dubecheck looks back into the courtyard and sees the sailor with the boa constrictor around his neck dramatically pretending to sneak up on the chicken cage with a gang of laughing idiots around him. Somebody has put a cigarette between the slit of the snake's mouth, and owing to the tacky slime of its skin, the cigarette stays, making the snake look ludicrously sinister. A cartoon snake. And he's a cartoon man. They clamber up on the bars until an American kid with the rank of captain in the U. S. Army sprays them with a shook-up can of Hamm's.

"Sick," says Anastasion.

"Who?"

"You!"

"Well, God bless us, one and all, then. Get in this Jeep, lady. There's a key right here." The chaplain points.

Anastasion gives Dubecheck a nudge, as if he were a horse, and he climbs into the Jeep with her on his shoulders and sits heavily.

"Sailor! Move that Jeep in front of us." The chaplain starts the rig and revs the perky Willys engine wildly. It's a beat-up convertible. A U. S. Army one. Pretty soon it appears it will be a stolen one, too. The sailor laboriously pushes the blocking Jeep out of the way just as the chaplain pops the clutch and the vehicle lurches and jerks along, lashing Anastasion back and forth on Dubecheck's shoulders.

The chaplain grinds the manual transmission through three gears and is soon going zero, according to the broken speedometer, but at least forty-five by Dubecheck's reckoning. The chaplain's white scarf flies out behind him in the wind. His glasses, circular panes of a blurry translucence with the opacity of glass brick, slide down the bridge of his nose, rendering him, from what Dubecheck figures is the prescription, virtually blind. The trees lining the narrow potholed road flash by in a dirty green blur, giving the impression they are hurtling through a bumpy tunnel. The chaplain brakes and the Jeep drifts through a macadam corner, tires chirping, until it hits a chuckhole, bringing Anastasion down into Dubecheck's lap, then bursts out into the bright white sky glare of the roundabout, where the headless bronze soldier stabs blindly up and out toward unseen galaxies.

Two young Vietnamese men on Vespas are driven into a ditch and fall off with exaggerated drama and, finding no audience save a receding rear-view mirror, get up and angrily hoist the finger.

"Missed. Purrraise Jesus. Purrr-raise the Lord."

"Where we all goin'?" Anastasion sounds like she's been picked up at the drive-in by Zeke and Deke.

"The seminary!" She has squeezed herself between the chaplain and Dubecheck and straddles the gearshift, her bloodstained green nylon skirt hiked some way up over her dirty kneecaps. One arm over the chaplain's shoulder, the other over Dubecheck's. Buddies. The smooth arcs of her lightly bouncing calves curve into the tops of her combat boots. Her thighs, covered by the wretched-looking fabric, seem more perfectly turned than if they had been exposed. Her half-naked legs, covered with a curly dark down of tiny black hairs, spread slightly as her feet splay. They seem like the stems of a beautiful olive-hued wishbone ready to snap, wet and hairy at the apex.

Dubecheck feels a subtle shifting of the ballast in his scrotum and squirms on the hard coiled springs of the busted seat beneath his ass. Out of the corner of his eye he sees her worm-thick artery pulsing beneath the sheath of skin tightly wrapping her neck.

He turns his face toward her. She turns toward him, her soft lips looking as if they might curve into a smile. He smiles at her, an "All is forgiven" twisted protrusion of the lower lip.

"Fuck off, Dubecheck."

"What?"

"The seminary," the chaplain shouts. "Listen up, shit for brains. It's just out of town. The United States Army has a liquor store and communications center out there."

"I know that." Dubecheck sulks and looks out the passenger side of the Jeep.

"You can get measured for a Hong Kong suit while you're at it!" He laughs as if that were an uproarious concept.

Dubecheck already has. He and Recore went out one day when the tailors from Sang Woo of Hong Kong were there taking orders. A couple of short, stubby, pasty-looking Chinese guys with measuring tapes around their necks and chalk stubs in their powdery white fingertips. They had several huge catalogs with swatches in them, four-inch-by-four-inch squares of every imaginable fabric on the planet. He remembers perusing some neon-looking colors with silver threads coursing through them. The fabric leapt off the page into his eyes with dazzling ugliness.

"No, no, no, no." One Chinese guy wagged his finger and laughed at Dubecheck, showing a full boat of gold and enamel on the lower gum and above. "That for Amelican niggah. Ha-ha-ha-ha-ha. Niggah swatches. Niggah cloth. No, no, no." The guy laughed and ran off a rapid litany of diphthongs, grunts, whines and snapped bowstrings to his partner, who laughed as he ran his measuring tape up and down Recore's torso. Recore's arms raised up inside a demo suit coat, standing like a scarecrow, the sweat still drying on him from a dawn ambush three hours before, when he hosed down a brace of gooks caught on a trail, two skinny barefoot geeks in short pants, whistling, each tossing a hand grenade up and down in his hand like a baseball. Recore being measured for one of the four variations of charcoal-gray suits he was ordering because he thought he was going to be a banker when he grew up and got back to America.

"How do I look? I don't know if I'm getting a French, Italian or American cut here."

"Maybe Norwegian. Who gives a shit?"

"Clothes make the man, Dubecheck. Get serious, pal. You'll never get a suit of this quality for this price in America."

Dubecheck figured what the hell. Get a business suit. He had the vague supposition that that's what he was supposed to do if he survived this and got home. You grow up and go into business. Get a job. If you got your shit together when you get a job you get to wear a suit. Ain't that America? Be a right proper Yankee professional in *uniform*, a tailored suit that meant you were *Mr.* Jack Shit. Dubecheck doesn't have a clue what he's supposed to be or do, but by God he might as well do it with a business suit on and get some fucking respect. Call *me* shit for brains? Well, it's gonna be *Mr.* Jack Shit for Brains with his custom business suit from Sang Woo Tailors of Hong Fucking Kong—but doing what?

All he knows for sure is that he doesn't want to do *this* anymore. Maybe, with luck, this clown driving will roll this Jeep and he can spend the duration of his tour in some naval hospital in Japan watching "Father Knows Best" and "American Bandstand," play gin rummy and scam a Purple Heart for his DD 214 and résumé. A Purple Heart in his file and on his chest to help him get a job. Looks good on the record even though it merely proves your ability to be in the wrong place at the right time. Like now, in Asia, adrift.

Anastasion's bare thighs and calves jiggle as the Jeep bounces along the road that in the distance appears to be blocked.

If her calves were jiggling, what must her breasts be doing? He's

never given her breasts much thought. In the few times he's seen
her she's always been bound about with an assortment of rags and
cloth that has made her chest an indifferent matter. He turns his
head and stares at her chest, a mere foot away, burrows in with his
beadies, pretending to be Superman with his X-ray vision quite
obvious, because he doesn't give a damn anymore. Been shoved
around enough, by golly, so no more Mr. Nice Guy; just swivel the
old head and take a gander at her rack.

To his eye . . . Anastasion's milk glands are . . . average.
Whatever that means. The apex of her breasts seems to be nothing
more and nothing less than a slight elevation a palm's width below
her collarbone; this, beneath tawny skin exposed by the scoop neck
of her shift, looks eerily skeletal, brittle, as if she could be easily
shattered.

An MP is now peering down into the stopped Jeep from behind
his mirrored sunglasses, allows Dubecheck to watch a split-screen
movie of himself in their reflection. The MP's black helmet gleams
with the sheen of a billiard ball. His .45 creaks in its leather holster
as he leans down to speak. A billy club the size of a Little League
baseball bat hangs down his thigh. Another MP sits in a Jeep across
the road, picking his teeth with a .223 bullet like a bored Southern
sheriff. Two twenty-year-old cops.

"How do, Sheriff. Puurrraise Jesus."

The MP salutes. "Vehicle registration checkpoint, sir. May I see
your papers, please?"

"Papers? Papers? What is this? I don't know where the good
Lord put those papers, son. Take a look, Lieutenant, in that glove
box there." The chaplain revs the Jeep impatiently.

Dubecheck rummages in the map compartment and finds nothing but crushed Pall Mall and Camel packages, balled up, flattened
and coated with dust. They want papers to prove the right people
are driving the right Jeep, since Jeeps are being stolen by Americans
from Americans in a disorganized crime wave of huge proportions.

"Well, there you have it, my son. Yes, we have no papers." The
chaplain salutes and pops the clutch, and the Jeep shudders forward. The engine stops. The MP in the Jeep stops picking his teeth
and leans forward.

"Sir, you can't go. I have to see those papers. Orders."

"Say what?"

"I have to see those papers or the Jeep she's illegal, sir. Impound
it and file—"

"Look, Sergeant *Preston,* or whatever your name is. What in

Christ's name, purraise the Lord, is an illegal Jeep? And what are you doing in the middle of the road on an insufferably hot day, flagging down three fellow Americans, when you should be flagging down our little nut-colored comrades who are flying about the roads on their little Wop motor scooters. Flag *them* down for Christ's sake. Purraise Jesus the Lord, they're flying around these roads like drunken trapeze artists!"

Dubecheck watches this movie upon the tiny twin screens of the MP's shades. Amazed. He wonders where the chaplain gets his energy.

"Sir?"

The other MP climbs out of his Jeep, transfixed, absently toying with his .223 bullet across his mouth like a lipstick.

Anastasion lights up a Lucky Strike with a four-inch whoosh from her Bic and stares coolly out the cracked, bug-splattered windshield as if she were bored, picking tobacco off her tongue with her thumb and little finger. There is a long quiet pause while the chaplain gets his wind.

"Sir? I just need your cooperation."

"You don't need my cooperation. You need papers. That's what you said, isn't it? Didn't he say he needed papers? Didn't he? Papers?" He looks to Anastasion, who nods. "Papers? We don't need no *stinkin'* papers! Do we?" He looks to Dubecheck for confirmation.

"Yeah. We do. Where have you been? You need papers for everything." Dubecheck closes his eyes and leans back, wishing he could go to sleep and wake up in his bed, somewhere back near the age of eight.

"Well, Mr. Lieutenant Know-it-all. We don't have any fornicating papers, do we? So what are we going to do? Sit here in God's screaming furnace till we're coddled? I think not." He starts the Jeep. The MP looks confused. He looks to his partner, then back at Dubecheck. He puts his hand on the handle of his automatic and the other on the knob of his billy club as if drawing comfort and knowledge from them. Dubecheck gets out of the Jeep and walks over to the second MP. The other MP follows. Dubecheck decides to try reason.

"We're going three klicks down the road. We're coming right back. We're going to be gone five American minutes."

"But, sir. I can't do that, sir. You know that."

"I know we can tap this bullshit back over the net all day,

Sergeant. We need some whiskey, and there's going to be hell to pay if we can't get up the road and bring back some hooch."

Dubecheck looks across the road and thinks he sees the chaplain begin to twitch. The man's nearly verifiable insanity, compounded by booze, heat and regulations, looks as if it might cause a terminal short circuit. Arteries and veins pulse on his scalp, his knuckles are white on the steering wheel, a ribbon of drool glistens off his chin in the sun. Anastasion tucks wisps of her sweaty hair behind her ears while looking in the rear-view mirror, cigarette clenched between her pursed lips. Dubecheck's new friends. Suddenly he loves them, family. A benign sense of concern for their well-being for all time suffuses him like a soft benevolent seizure.

He turns to the MPs who, with lip-chewing consternation, are churning all the combinations and permutations of the situation over and around in their police heads. They've been told they are the equivalent of generals when it comes to enforcing he law. They believe that. They are licking their lips in anticipation of busting a full commander and a jg thrown in for the hell of it. The only sand in the Vaseline is that the old perp is a man of God. Both of them reek to high heaven and are disgusting. Dubecheck peers through the mirrored glasses into the cop's brain and sees a file cabinet of regulations, statutes, missives, memos, tips and Dick Tracy crime-stopper hints tip over and crash to the floor of the kid's brainpan as he frantically tries to find the proper directive in time to arrest everybody in sight.

The MPs continue to lick their lips like a couple of frustrated German shepherds. Dubecheck is surprised they aren't whimpering, as if straining on some invisible leash. The only thing keeping them back is the cop's genetic respect for authority, no matter how much in disarray.

"Well, what in Christ's name is going on? Do we carry this thing on our backs or she illegal just goin' thataway?" the chaplain chirps up brightly. "Or is it legal in reverse? Or better yet"—the chaplain climbs out of the Jeep—"you guys drive it." He slaps the tall MP on the back. "That touches all the bases, eh? Puurraise Jesus, praise Willie Mays!" The chaplain walks about, looking up and down the road as if waiting his turn to speak again, an observer, content to spend the rest of his life here, debating options and nuances. Nurse Anastasion seems to be watching, with the total absorption of a cat, the aimless meandering of a fly on the windshield. A small crowd of children have appeared out of nowhere, like ants at a picnic, and stand watching with tentative smiles, ready to break into laughter since the Americans always seem to do something silly.

"Maybe you could find the papers back where you came from."

"I—the none of us can drive this Jeep! It stops here. It's an illegal Jeep and I'll be damned and roast in hell and piss on the grave of Hosea, Peter, Paul and Mickey if I'll let you break a 'reg.' You're made of stern stuff, Sarge, and I'll not be the cretinous fool to cross the strong arm of the law. We'll take the bus. When's the bus come?" The chaplain stands in the middle of the road, his hand bridged over his eyes, and swivels back and forth in search.

"What bus?" says the tall MP.

"What bus *indeed!*" He sticks his finger in the MP's chest. *"Now* you're getting the big picture." He climbs back into the Jeep and reaches over Anastasion and pulls Dubecheck into the other seat. "Well! We got no stinkin' papers! We're obviously Chinese spies and I don't like the look of things. This shrewd sleuth here has us in a box canyon. There's only one thing to do. Make a run for it. Sergeant, you do good work. Praise the Lord, praise Jesus and Avois." The chaplain chirps the tires and speeds off.

Dubecheck hears the MPs scream, "Halt! Halt!" over the whine of the accelerating engine. He turns to see the tall MP reach for his .45 with one hand, flapping dust from his face with the other. His deputy runs for their Jeep.

"They're going for their weapons!" Dubecheck notices the kids stagger around and laugh. They weren't let down. The American cartoon never stops.

The Jeep fishtails down the narrow road. Dubecheck puts his hands over his head as he hears two shots boom into the air and turns to see the kids scatter and point in hysterics as the tall MP clambers into the Simonized Jeep. Their Jeep curves around in hot pursuit, its huge whip antenna waving wildly in the air.

"He's right on us." Dubecheck glances at the chaplain, scrunched down in his seat, peering through the steering wheel. At least I'm junior man, Dubecheck thinks; the whole terrible misunderstanding will be handled out of court. He'll hang on the coattails of this drunken Lutheran screaming "WEE-haww!" Anastasion looks to Dubecheck, shrugs and tries to light a Lucky with the butt of another as the Jeep lurches, pitches and yaws, weaving wildly through a covey of cyclists who dive toward the roadside ditch, abandoning the white ducks hanging upside down from the handlebars by their tied feet. They squawk hysterically as the bikes crash to the pavement, where the bug-eyed ducks frantically flap their wings. Dubecheck cannot help but wonder what the ducks are thinking. He's given up on the chaplain.

The Jeep begins to drift sideways through a slight turn, then leaves the road and speeds through two empty hooches and heads toward a water buffalo the size of a dumpster before veering off and bouncing over into a dry rice paddy.

"Goddamnit! Stop this thing, you jerk!" Dubecheck shouts.

The chaplain shouts back. "A jerk? They called Christ a jerk! All great men have been called jerks one time or another. Puuuraise Jesus, purraise jerks!"

The Jeep goes into a dusty slide as the chaplain guns the throttle, the tires spin in the dirt, catch, and the Jeep heads off toward a scraggly thicket bounding from hard hillock to hillock, slamming down into the crumbling ruts of the scrubby field, mowing down the thicket as saplings and twigs lash Dubecheck's face. Anastasion's head flops on his lap as she clutches his knees with her arms. The Jeep smashes through a pale green curtain of bamboo and vine, emerging from the other side trailing vegetation like crepe. It goes up a slight incline and down over the dike, slanting, tilting, slipping down and miring itself, bogging itself down into some thick black loam at an impossible cant, wheels spinning, spitting mud, the engine revving at top end, the whistling tires eating deep down into the mud.

"Kill it!" Dubecheck reaches over, turns off the ignition and hops out and staggers around dizzily as if alighting from some carnival ride. He looks at the Jeep tilted into the mud, nearly standing snout down, marveling how easily the chaplain achieved the difficult: getting a four-wheel-drive vehicle stuck.

"Well. We lost them, by God. Jumpin' Jehoshophat and Joltin' Joe DiMaggio, we sure did."

Anastasion jumps out of the Jeep and starts brushing her clothes off as if she thought they were nice. Dubecheck's scalp tingles as he gets the picture. The road is barely visible about four hundred yards in the distance behind a scraggly tree line. There are no other humans, no birds, no beasts. Just the humm of seven thousand unseen insects, and the Jeep's hot engine ticking like a huge clock.

"Adios, Padre. I'm getting out of here—I'm running out of here, and I'd advise you to come along too." Dubecheck grabs Anastasion by the hand and tugs her along.

"But the car?"

"Do you know where we are?" Dubecheck's head nearly rotates around on his neck as he constantly scans his position. "Jesus!"

"I'm staying by this Jeep. Help me get it out."

"Blow it out your ass, Chaps. We're in a world of shit and I'm going to didi. Come on, Anastasion."

The chaplain blinks in confusion.

"Do you understand? This is Indian country. This is not where the party is."

Anastasion sits down in the dirt and lights up a Lucky Strike and watches the chaplain go to the rear of the Jeep and try to pull it down. The Jeep is up to its hubs in the front. Astern, only one rear wheel barely touches the ground. The chaplain grunts. Nothing. Dubecheck scans the horizon: tree lines, hedges and dikes shimmer in the heat. The heavy quiet amplifies the chaplain's labored breath.

"I think you should help." The chaplain sounds petulant.

"You'll need a tank to get that out. Let's go back and steal one of those. Now."

Movement. Oh shit, yeah. Two, three hundred yards away. Surreptitious movement. The chaplain blithely circles the Jeep as if it were stuck on a back road in Kansas. Dubecheck moves over and roughly pulls him down into the soft earth with a thud. They land next to Anastasion.

"Come on, Commander. Forget the Jeep," Dubecheck whispers hoarsely. "The both of you just start doing what I tell you." He snatches the cigarette out of Anastasion's mouth, grinds it out in the dirt and waves a white cloud of smoke away with his hand.

"Hey?"

"Hey, just shut up. You've been real quiet for a while and it's been wonderful." Dubecheck feels his heart pounding, a pin cushion tingling in his gut. It is much too quiet. The road, a quarter of a mile away, looks as if it's in the next province. This is no place to be out walking alone, especially with these two alarm clocks dangling around his neck. He wishes he was as drunk as the chaplain, but even the chaplain, sobering slightly from the exertion, seems to be getting the possibly grim picture.

"Are we going to die, Dubecheck?"

"Shut up, Anastasion. Maybe *you* will. I'm not." He peeks up over the dike after rubbing his face with dirt to cut the glare.

"Wow. That was clever . . . seriously."

Dizzy bitch thinks it's a game. An eerie finality hovers over Dubecheck. The event now has a life of its own as indifferent to him as the bleached blue sky. Fear has his nerve ends groping like tentacles. Shit, as usual, is about to hit the fan.

Little man, so spick and span,
Where were you when the shit hit the fan?

**F
L
O
A
T**

Where and when was it that he first heard that one? Fourth grade; he walked down a hill carrying a wooden pole with a red STOP flag on it. Second lieutenant in the schoolboy patrol. Wet pavements, cold squishy shoes and a runny nose in the raw wind. If he'd stayed, he figures he'd be general by now. He should have stayed in the fourth grade and the schoolboy patrol. He was happy there. Paradise lost. And how did he get from there to here? He wants to know the *reasons*, why things get out of control. He doesn't *care* that they're out of control, that's bound to happen. He just wants to know why. He wants to see the map—see its red and blue arteries, serpentine labyrinths of lies, culs-de-sac, box canyons, washouts, bridges, roundabouts, detours and dead ends. See where the graveyards are.

Dubecheck rolls over, gets to his hands and knees and drags the chaplain along like a sack of coal.

"Keep down, Anastasion." He peeks over the dry dike again and glimpses what he thinks is a crouching runner, a glint of sunlight flashing off something. Birds are being driven ahead of *something* several hundred yards across the lime-yellow rice paddy; they leap-frog in little coveys from one small tree to another. Shadows dart in the deep shade of the palm grove. A motorbike can be heard puttering and missing far away on the main road. The sound fades and takes Dubecheck's heart with it. He has never felt so alone, and perhaps the time has come to just get up and walk away. Get up, start walking and never stop, walk all the way to the sea, then walk on the water and walk for a long time, way out beyond the range of birds, walk across the huge gray swells undulating upon the liquid desert, walk home to where it rains and snows and the smell of fir and pine hang in the sharp clear air and a guy can shiver from the cold instead of fear. Dubecheck clenches his quivering jaw and tugs at the sweat-soaked uniform of the chaplain. Dead grasses hiss at ground level as a breeze puffs hotly.

PLAT! PLAT! Fisssst. Fissst. They've opened up. The ragged crack of many rifles lags behind the bullets that have hit the dike or sped by. Dubecheck pulls the chaplain down and flattens against the warm, soft earth. A flood of fear cascades through his body, and precipitously he begins to teeter on the familiar edge between terror and insanity. A dam breaks and adrenalin surges, racing toward his fingertips. Anastasion blinks down into the dirt with a curiously creased brow; Dubecheck feels paralyzed. He knows he must move, but where to? He's pinned down like a moth in a box. Maybe he's already dead.

Fissst! Fissst! Fisssst! Plitttt. Plittttt. Firecracker reports follow, singly and in threes. Some discipline out there, which is bad news. Although the sharp caplike pops sound like M-16s, there's also the brute crack of heavier AK beating the air. They're right on target, whoever they are. VC with M-16s. The thought sickens Dubecheck.

"What is it? Who is it?" The chaplain sounds flustered, confused, as if he just woke up. He gets up on an elbow and Dubecheck knocks him backward with his palm.

"Keep your head down."

"Going to die. Going, going, soon to be gone." Anastasion rolls over on her back and shakes out a Lucky Strike and lights up.

She smiles nervously, more like a twitch of the lips, and tosses one over to within Dubecheck's reach. "The last one." She balls up the pack, the cellophane crackles, and she tosses it over the dike. "Bad manners."

"It's so hot." The chaplain's voice sounds small and tired, as if someone had ripped out his wires. His conversation is punctuated by little strings of ladyfingers going off in the distance, accompanied by bee farts of lead tunneling the air.

"War is always in the most miserable weather. It's either too goddamn hot or too goddamn cold. Too wet or too dry."

There is an odd pause in the fire. Dubecheck leans over and hands the cigarette back to Anastasion. His hand is shaking. He has no weapon to steady it and it feels icy like his feet. His face feels flushed and hot. Maybe he's embarrassed. Parts of his body are either too goddamn hot or too goddamn cold.

"Korea. Now that was cold. Black fingers and feet, black and purple. You could snap off some fool's toes like you were shuckin' summertime peas, and the toes, they'd lay in the bloody snow like . . . burnt caterpillars . . . and the spotlights, at night, huge searchlights, like a Hollywood premiere, would shine against the brown ridge, making it look like some dead flesh, and the Chinese troops would be swarming on them like a billion lice on the belly of a sick dog. And their bugles would play. Make the hackles go up on the back of your neck. Never could figure how so many men could die. The gun barrels would melt and warp from the firing. So many dead Chinese, piling up like snowdrifts in the searchlights while the guns and rifles roared and smoke hung in the air like a pall of fog

and the smoke froze and stank. . . . Jesus, it-is-hot . . . maybe
we should go."

Dubecheck can't feel most of his body. It couldn't go anywhere
now. The firing starts up again in earnest. The dirt on the other side
and on top of the dike churns up in a raging fusillade. Dubecheck
slithers farther down into the warm dirt; "groveling" is the word, he
thinks. His lips press to the earth. Kiss it good-bye enters his mind.
His mind is a jangle of conjectures, bad answers and apprehensions.
A little ant scurries beneath his eyes, mechanically negotiating a
minute vista of hills and gullies. The ant is carrying the body part of
what appears to have been another ant. The ant fights against a
headwind emanating from Dubecheck's nostrils. Perhaps, if I hold
my breath, Dubecheck thinks, and make the ant's passage easier,
God will notice my benevolence to living things and God, in His
almighty benevolence, will spare my life. Allow him to get captured
instead. No way. He'll run for it first. He'll not have his cock and
balls sliced off and stuffed in his mouth, his skin peeled from his
body, spend a lifetime in a bamboo cage at eighty-two pounds. He'll
run first and be shot in the back and it will all just go black. He will
be gone and God's heart won't have missed a beat. And he knows
how it will be because he has dreamed it . . . his getting-dead
dream, where he is running and *they* are shouting for him to stop,
and he keeps running, waiting for it, feeling his scalp tingle orgas-
mically in anticipation, and it comes like a sharp blow to the back,
thump, right between the shoulder blades, a hot fist, and he tumbles
forward in slow motion and things (the light of this day on earth)
slowly fade to black while he has time to ask himself, So this is it?
. . . It isn't bad at all.

That's it, he'll run for it, feel the wind in his face and then . . .
then what? Turn around and get shot in the face, which he imagines
to be something like getting a crowbar rammed up your nostrils;
shot as he turns back to get his friends. He could get away but for
them. He will stay here and die because he cannot abandon his dear,
dear friends. Utter nonsense. You run, you get cut down. They're
shooting at you, man. It's always the same when the bullets blip by
and the dreamy, distant cracks get muffled by the puffy clouds
stacked on the horizon. It never seems real at first, they're just fake
clouds on a fake horizon with a fake backdrop of fake trees, and it is
so quiet and dead between the crackling of *small arms* and you
never see anyone and it's all so unreal because it is such an incredibly odd thing to do in Technicolor, it is business more suited to

grainy black and white, an intense dream moving in and out of your mind like a curtain in a soft breeze. Until it gets noisy.

Somebody is on rock 'n' roll, a run of full AK auto smashes the sky like an air hammer and the air above Dubecheck is whipped and torn with dissonant whines, howls and momentary moanings. They are getting closer and louder and he can hear them shouting in that frenetic, chilling, nearly alien-sounding chatter. A quick look up and he sees some of them in their black pajamas and the sight stuns him like a blast of heat.

"Jesus Christ! Stop! Stop it! Stop it! Cease fire!" The chaplain screams into the dirt in front of his face.

The initial surge of adrenalin has run its course through Dubecheck's blood. His temples pound and a sort of catatonic numbness pervades. Will it hurt when the bullets drive into him like nasty nails? Will they surrender? Yeah. Of course. Sure. To run, if given the chance, is suicide. He has an inexplicable urge to get back to the Jeep, crawl back to the Jeep, as if that would help. Maybe he's supposed to die in a car. *Do* something, Dubecheck. He wonders how guys sat out sustained artillery barrages. They didn't. They went nuts like some of the strained, twisty-faced clowns he knew that hung out in taverns with VA checks from WWII and Korea, guys who floated around and washed up on the shore like bottles with unreadable notes inside.

He rolls over and feels his heart pounding against the earth and recalls a friend's admonition about that: "You'll be the first one to feel it stop that way." A huge dollop of sweat hangs from the tip of his nose. He becomes curious: how long will it hang there? What makes the flies buzz so? Everything is important and begs an answer that begets a question.

"I can't move. I . . . can't move." The chaplain speaks wonderingly.

"So? There's nowhere to go. Nowhere." Anastasion sounds entranced.

Dubecheck twists around and rolls over and lies on his back. "What do you mean, you can't move?"

"Doesn't matter. Like she says. No place to go." There is a lull in the firing. Dubecheck stares up into the sky, waiting for the dead dream to come. A couple of huge cumulus billow up like cauliflowers. The gauzy curtain blows in, bearing sounds: scattered pops like sparks from a fireplace. The dream-distant crack of rifles, so distant they must be meant for someone else.

Hey, you must be mistaken. Are you shooting at me? Are you

sure this is not just some lousy mistake? It is a lousy mistake, but it's lousy true and he is sad, not so much that it is true, but that it is sordid and lousy. He is not real afraid of dying because he's young and because you never really believe you're going to die when you're young, right up until the second it's a lock. But it is lousy, sordid and small though. It's so, so, so . . . so what? It's happened to a lotta guys lately, in his lifetime. The Deuce, Korea, the fucking Nam. In his lifetime . . . which looks like it's going to top end after two dozen laps around the sun, no more, no less.

"I can't move."

"Just shut up, okay?" An impatient, quiet anger enters his mind. When he thinks about it, maybe this guy's killed him.

"Maybe he's hit, asshole."

"Are you hit?"

"Who is it?"

"No. You hit?"

"I don't know who it is. Who is it?" The chaplain pulls out a handkerchief and wipes his sweaty face. Looks like a guy pulling weeds.

What is the quiet about? A time out. Intermission maybe. Give Dubecheck time to clear out all the rubbish in his soul, clean it up because God's coming to visit. And kill him while He's at it. There's a few short bursts of guys clearing their clips. Which only means they're going to put full ones back in their place. The sound is closer and Dubecheck thinks he can hear music, hurried shouting and some laughter.

Yes, Mrs. Dubecheck. He was killed in action by the 215th VC Comedians, bandoliers draped across their chests like grins.

"Gooks," the chaplain sighs. "I've spent the good part of my life administering to the spiritual needs of white men, brown men and black men fighting yellow men. God, there's a lot of them. Speaking of God. 'The Lord is a man of war.' Exodus 15:3. And stop me if you've heard this one—'The imagination of man's heart is evil from his youth.' Genesis 8:21. I've got a million of 'em. How about my favorite, 'The way of man is froward and strange.' Proverbs 21:8. This is a sore test, this earth, Lieutenant . . . do you have a name, Lieutenant?"

"Douchebag. Lieutenant (jg) Douchebag."

Dubecheck wonders how Nurse Anastasion can be such a caustic, vindictive ass at such a moment.

Dubecheck is thinking why he should answer the chaplain when he hears jangling ammo cans moving up less than fifty yards away, maybe the sound of bare feet slapping some buffalo wallow, some winded breathing. There is something sickening about cowering in the dry mud. Like standing in front of a firing squad with your pants down around your ankles, your dick shriveled up to the size of a peanut. Dubecheck draws little furrows in the dirt with his fingertips. Dark mud below smells strong and the heat lies on him like a warm blanket. A withering burst of automatic weapons fire pounds into the dike; a grenade explodes above it. The pressure wave cleaves Dubecheck's head, then slams it back together again with a crack that empties his ears, then refills them with a huge humming, ringing dissonance. Shrapnel sneezes through the air and flings itself into the dirt. The chaplain cringes fetally, his arms wrapped over his head. His mouth is wide open but Dubecheck can't hear him scream because an AK going off about twenty feet away sounds like rocks raining on a tin roof. Then it is quiet. Dubecheck squeezes his head to press out the pain. The stench of black powder peppers the air. Anastasion sounds like a strangled chicken and the chaplain gurgles, moans, then gasps and goes silent as if he is holding his breath.

Dubecheck feels two bodies slam down into the opposite side of the dike. A muffled tinny transistor plays "Strawberry Fields Forever." Two male voices converse in a hushed whisper, then begin to giggle. An AK is cocked, the bolt slams shut with a metallic crack.

Dubecheck wants to say, "Don't shoot," but his throat is too dry and tight. He hears the faint chatter of other voices shouting in the distance and the Beatles harmonizing about a place that sounds like a fine place to be, but a place he will never see. He turns his head to the chaplain, whose face has a green honeydew-melon tinge to it. Dubecheck is about to shout when sputtering fuzzy static breaks squelch on the other side of the dike.

"Do you dildos have contact? Over."

One of the voices keys his handset and speaks in Vietnamese. A radio voice interrupts.

"Hey, speak English, damnit, I got a hangover."

Dubecheck crawls to the top of the dike and peers down at two Vietnamese in black pajamas. One smokes a Salem and holds the transistor to his ear while the other holds a PRC 10 handset to his ear.

"Hey! Gimme that, goddamnit!" Dubecheck screams down at the startled young men. Their mouths fall open as Dubecheck scrambles down the side of the dike and snatches the handset from the RO.

"Snazzy, you son of a bitch, get your ass over here so I can kill you!" Dubecheck fumes for a moment, then, ever thoughtful of proper radio procedure, adds, "Over."

"Hey, who's that? Who be bangin' my brain with the bad rap? Huh?"

"It's me, Dark Singer, asshole!"

"Dube? Hey, Dubie baby. What the fuck, over?"

"Snazzy, you opened up on us. I think we need a dust-off, you—you moron." Dubecheck tosses the handset to the puzzled RO and scrambles back over the dike.

The chaplain rolls his head to and fro, moaning in agony. Anastasion pulls a handful of hypodermic needles out of one of her pockets and fills one from a vial of Mark I government issue morphine and rolls the chaplain's forearm over.

"What the hell you doin', Anastasion?"

"Morphine. I give everybody morphine. People like it. *You* want some? *I'd* like some." She looks up at Dubecheck. "Hey, if God didn't want us to have morphine He wouldn't have given us veins." The needle pops the chaplain's pasty forearm, drawing a bead of blood.

"What's his problem? You want a dust-off? Huh? Huh? Answer me!"

"He's got no problem now."

Anastasion removes the needle, tosses the syringe over her shoulder and dabs a teardrop of blood from his forearm with the tip of his dirty white scarf.

"There! You'll be *real fine* any second now." She pats his forehead.

Dubecheck thinks he recognizes the kid who had the handset. Nguyen something, with pockmarks like rain in the dust all over his face. Last seen wildly waving a pistol around at a poker game in a cardboard barroom down by the canal, guys scrambling from the room on all fours, drinks knocked over, the usual shouting, swearing and screaming. The guy murdered a Chinese chick in Cholon, but his dad was a newspaper editor or a judge, so now he's here instead of there. Nguyen the PRU, sort of out on work release. Like the rest of his mates.

Dubecheck can see a squad of black pajama-clad PRUs running across the paddy like a soccer team. The squat body of Snazzy, the CIA adviser to this provincial reconnaissance unit of bandits, pimps, thieves and muggers emptied from the jails of Saigon, lumbers in the rear. He feels like he should call somebody on the phone but has no idea whom, so he just stands on top of the dike with a handset in his hand and watches people in black pajamas carrying guns run toward him while the Beatles sing they want to take him down to some Strawberry Fields. Which would be fine with me, just get me out of here.

The kid with the transistor nods and smiles. "Beatles? You like? Numbah One." Dubecheck nods. He feels none of the normal exhilaration of being shot at and missed. That halfway into the second glass of champagne buzz that hums through the body after you're verified live once again.

The motley platoon of PRUs stops in a semicircle and stares at him, curious, but more than likely disappointed they can't hose down Homo sapiens. By the time Snazzy comes staggering into the assemblage, Dubecheck is no longer incensed.

"Hello, Snazzy. Nice to see you."

The pale, plump Snazzy stands wheezing. He pulls off his glasses and cleans them with the tail of his black pajamas, looking like some chubby hardware clerk who's been chasing shoplifters.

He squints up at Dubecheck, puts on his glasses and scratches at his crotch. "What are you doing here?"

"Drunk driving. Get this Jeep out of the muck back here."

"We lost three guys out here the other day. As in dead. And yeah, so we're a little quick with the gats. Live and learn, learn and live. You're in a free-fire zone, buddy, and it's a slow day. Makes you a lucky sailor. Who's the dust-off?"

Dubecheck gets up and motions Snazzy to follow.

"Get their Jeep out." He waves and a dozen PRUs head over the dike. "We were going for whiskey. There's a party. What are you doin' out here on a make-work when there's a party? You aren't in the Army."

"I need some ops for my budget. What the fuck is this, Dubecheck? Who's the bag lady and Jesus Christ? You tryin' to tell me we clipped a *commander?*"

Snazzy leans down and checks the chaplain's vital signs. "Where's he hit?" He frisks the chaplain. "Where's he hit? Where's he hit?" He rolls him over. "I can't get a dust-off with a Prick 10. We're in bumfuck Egypt for radio range. Who's the chick and why's she staring into space? Hey, what's the matter with this guy? Dubecheck, I don't get this!"

The chaplain's tongue starts to push out of his mouth like a purple hard-boiled egg. He sounds like he is strangling.

"Hey, Anastasion! Get over here!"

She crawls over on her hands and knees and looks down.

"Oh-oh."

"What's this oh-oh shit, Petunia? This guy's like going into grand mal."

"Oh-oh. I mean like oh-oh. He's going to die, I think, unless I do something."

Snazzy screws up his face in sheer puzzlement. "What the fuck? Who *is* this?" The PRU with the transistor comes up. Janis Joplin is in a plaintive hoarse wail about love gone wrong.

"You lost three guys here? Shouldn't you set up a perimeter or something?"

"Don't tell me how to do my job. Hey, Tran!" Snazzy shouts to a tall lanky PRU. "Set up a perimeter. And turn that shit off." The other PRU turns off the transistor and tells him the Jeep is out.

"You got a knife?"

Snazzy hands her a K-bar.

"A smaller one. I think I gotta give this guy a trach."

"Oh. Oh well, why didn't you say so? *What the fuck, Dubecheck!* You're gonna get me involved in an 0-5's throat slashing? I am not here. You've never seen me and I don't believe this."

"I don't either." Somehow, a vague feeling that he is going to get court-martialed comes over Dubecheck. Years in Portsmouth behind granite, pounding rock, singing spirituals.

"We better do something soon or he's going to die. He's reacting to the morphine, I think." Anastasion pokes him.

"Morphine? Who is this woman? Dr. Doom? Look, honey, you better save this guy's life or we're all in a world of shit."

The chaplain is turning a nasty-looking color. Whiskey, Dubecheck thinks. It does it all the time. The stuff is fun but it can blow up in your face now and then. Anastasion stands holding the huge knife.

"Use the *point* of it if that's all we got. The guy's going under."

"Gimme my Bic." Dubecheck picks it off the ground and hands it to her. She blackens the tip of the six-inch K-bar blade with flame, blows on it, wipes it on her skirt and says, "Hold him down." The chaplain's eyes are rolling around in their sockets. He can probably *hear* all this.

"You still drunk Anastasion?"

"Yeah, thank God. I couldn't do this sober."

"I think I'm going to be sick."

The PRUs who haven't set up a perimeter sit on the dike like snickering bleacher bums and watch the operation and try to look up Anastasion's skirt.

Anastasion puts the tip of the knife near the middle of the chaplain's clavicle below the wattles of his throat. She bites her lower lip, inhales and cuts through the epidermis. A line of purplish blood appears, crests at the surface of the slice, then cascades out.

"Shit!"

"Shit! Whaddya mean, shit!"

"I can't see it. Help me find it."

"Find what?"

"His trachea, asshole. It'll like a—a—sort of like a chicken's leg."

"A fucking drumstick?"

"No. A *real leg*. Like the part you don't eat and it walks on. Bands. You know, like between the feathers and its foot. Like there!"

There is a brief glimpse of a pink vertical cord between Anastasion's blood-drenched fingers. "Gotcha!" She holds the slippery trachea in a finger weave and sticks the knife tip into it, slits it and gives a twist.

"Oh, *man* . . . I need a tube of something. Quick."

The chaplain's face is almost blue, eyes half-lidded slits.

Snazzy and Dubecheck stand up, frantically looking around. Dubecheck grabs the knife from Anastasion and runs toward a little copse of bamboo. He hacks off several lengths and runs back to Anastasion with them.

She inserts a foot-long hollow length of bamboo into the chaplain's trachea. Air surges into his lungs in a whistle.

"Hey! Carve some notches in it, see what he can play." Snazzy chuckles and slaps Dubecheck on the back, greatly relieved. "Let's get this sucker home. School's out."

They drape the chaplain across the back of the Jeep like a dead bear, his bamboo tube flicking back and forth metronomically. Anastasion squats over him to ease the ride as Dubecheck drives off with Snazzy seated beside him holding a PRC 10 on his lap. Snazzy turns around in his seat and shakes his head at the sight. Dubecheck checks out the chaplain too. The bamboo tube still has a little leaf on it. It trembles like a quaking aspen, vibrations from Snazzy's hysterically silent laughter. "Another day, another dollar."

The main road is empty save for an animal that looks something like a horse drawing a cart full of pineapples and a guy in a white shirt walking his bicycle alongside. The chaplain seems all right except that he may have gone completely insane. His eyes have a wild, cornered-mongrel cast to them.

7 Snazzy calls in a dust-off. They got within range for the little PRC 10 to transmit to some Americans and rendezvous at the seminary, where they hope by then to have their stories straight.

Dubecheck looks back to the distant tree line from where they came. It looks quiet and dreamy. It doesn't look like much of a place at all, flat olive-drab paddies stretched out to the horizon, where dark-bottomed cumulus hint of the coming monsoon. He feels baffled and vaguely frightened by some constant, curious tension fed by sadness so pervasive it's chronic, inescapable. It's like he's at the end of a long shuffling line passing through nowhere, trudging under the sky, waiting for something big and heavy to fall from it.

Snazzy radios to his PRUs and tells his man to have them hump it to the road. He gets out of the Jeep.

"Assholes. They're really assholes, Dubecheck. But gimme a coupla divisions of those guys and it's hot dogs in Hanoi by Christmas. Since I'm not with 'em they're probably Cong now, so I better rendezvous ASAP. Cheerio." He walks off singing "White Christmas."

Dubecheck watches Snazzy waddle after his troops and wonders what makes guys like him not only tick but constantly explode. The guy's got a death fix. He looks like a pharmacist in some sleepy rural town, but he's as lethal as a fucking puff adder. Funny about guys like that. The most efficient, ruthless killers Dubecheck has ever seen are like that. Nondescript guys. Whatever that means. Guys you don't notice right off the bat: the five-nine postman, the skinny guy who wraps the cheese at the A & P, the chubby little bus driver with thick corrective lenses sitting behind the wheel of the crosstown, the pint-size swarthy guy who just came out from beneath your car on a dolly, a greasy beanie on his head, holding the throw-out bearing of your car in his hands like a time bomb.

And Snazzy, a.k.a. Leonard Russell Fesler, is one of them. Little guys who look like . . . well, they look like nothing because no one *sees* them until it's too late.

Snazzy hangs out in an old stucco building on a dirt street where everybody pretends to really care about all the potted vegetable plants they're growing. He's supposed to be an agricultural expert helping peasants. A Purdue Boilermaker trying to bring technology to the rice paddies, a conduit for better living through chemistry.

"Dubecheck. There's a place in the New World for you." Snazzy tells Dubecheck that all the time. Snazzy says that to people he likes and, according to Dupree, he has only told Dubecheck, Recore and Tuta there's a place for them in the New World. Dupree can't hide his disappointment that Snazzy hasn't said there's a place in the New World for him. He says Snazzy is just a petty bourgeois.

Recore said if Snazzy was just a petty bourgeois he'd be a banker somewhere in Yonkers and call himself L. Russell Fesler instead of a hard-ass little son of a bitch called Snazzy.

One day when Dubecheck visited Snazzy and watched him pretend to be interested in the horticultural aspects of the stucco building they ended up listening to some of Snazzy's opera records. They sat in his office, which consisted of a cot, a swivel chair, a filing cabinet full of ammunition, maps, hand grenades (smoke and percussion), a slide rule, a Jacuzzi pump, several copies of *The American Horticulturist*, a clip from a 9mm weapon, a screwdriver and a torn newspaper photo of the 1954 Odessa, Texas, High School football team.

Dubecheck didn't know opera from incoming, but the lush roller-coaster harmonies of many female voices and the hearty male lead singing like a large Italian bird caught his ear.

"Nice tunes there, Snazzy."

"You bet. There really is a place for you in the New World, Dubecheck. Mascagni. *Cavalleria Rusticana.* The guy had one shot. He took it. Bull's-eye."

"You in this picture?" Dubecheck held up the worn photo of the Odessa High School football team.

"You bet. Number 52. We Feslers come from a long line of centers. We have a great rivalry with Midland. We beat 'em at football and they beat us at golf."

Snazzy was a Texan before he was a Purdue Boilermaker. Dubecheck couldn't help it, but he'd never met a Texan he didn't like; they were all full of genial shit and didn't care whether you knew it or not.

"Life isn't serious, Dubecheck. Until it gets serious," Snazzy told him once.

"Snazzy, can I ask you a question?"

"No."

"Why do you do the things you do?"

"I could say 'What are you talking about?' but I know exactly what you're talking about and I'll try and answer you, because there's a place for me in the New World too. I like guns. And because my wife is a Lutheran and a pall of insufferable melancholia hangs over my little white brick bungalow in Falls Church, Virginia.

Other than that, I don't think I can get too specific. There is the gratification of wandering around thinking you're doing something vital. I really don't have beaucoup brains, Dube, but I don't shoot at Communists. These guys aren't Communists. They're criminals. Someday folks are going to figure that out. By then I'll be dead."

Snazzy reached up and took the newsprint photo from Dubecheck's hand and looked at it for a long time, as if it were some strange hieroglyphic. Then he balled it up and threw it in a dark corner as the opera ended. They sat and listened to the needle hiccup on the final groove for a long time.

o   o   o

Dubecheck pulls off the road into the seminary, a low cluster of rambling gray plaster buildings with red tile roofs. Huge antennae and wires bristle upward. It used to be an old Catholic seminary but the U. S. Army moved in and made it into a communications center and shopping mall. Topheavy in officers and noncoms sitting on their asses turning knobs and dials. It is set in a clearing of red dirt surrounded by a billowing double perimeter of barbed wire as bushy as tumbleweed. A huge generator drones constantly.

Two Vietnamese sit in the shade of a sandbagged bunker at the gate, carbines slung over their shoulders, Salems dangling from their lips. They laboriously get to their feet and salute lethargically as the Jeep rolls through the gate. Dubecheck parks in the "No Parking, Staff Only" space in front of the Quonset hut PX where a slant of shade can cool the chaplain. The place looks deserted but in the intense midafternoon heat everyone will be inside hugging the air conditioners that rattle at the windows.

"Shall we get him inside?"

"Nah. They'll be here any second." The chaplain's mouth works like a fish as he stares unblinkingly up into the sky. Anastasion leans against the Jeep and absently strokes his forehead with her slender bloodstained fingers, staring off and combing her hair with the fingers of her other hand. In the distance the chatter of an approaching helo begins to drown out the clatter of the air conditioners. "It's either too hot or too cold, too quiet or too noisy."

The Huey descends upon the helo pad, a flat square of concrete set in the red dirt with a white circle painted on it. Dubecheck backs up the Jeep as close as he can get. The rotors whistle and whine and toss dust in the air. The wind blows the bamboo out of the chaplain's trachea and rolls it across the ground. Dubecheck jumps from the Jeep and chases after it. He stomps on it with his foot, picks it up and runs back to the Jeep, shouting at the Medivacs in the din that the chaplain can't breathe. They carry the chaplain to the helo and hoist him inside. Dubecheck duck-waddles under the whirling blades and tosses in the bamboo. The chaplain's head flops to the side as the medics begin to work on him.

The helo lifts, dips its nose and leaves in a noisy rhythmic clatter and Dubecheck watches after it, squinting through the dust until the noise fades to a chuff-chuff-chuff-chuff soon overcome by the rattling clatter of overworked air conditioners.

Fear. The face of fear everywhere. The war isn't the problem. It's the whole scheme of things. And in taking stock of the whole scheme of things, Dubecheck realizes he doesn't get it and is inclined to think he never will.

He sticks his hands in his pockets and pulls out a clammy wad of military scrip the size of a rotten baseball.

He walks over to where Anastasion sits on a painted white rock and sits down in the dirt next to her. She has cadged a couple of Salems from the sentry and hands one to Dubecheck.

"I wonder what that was all about?" he says.

"What?"

"Was any of that supposed to mean something? Is there any lesson to be drawn from this?"

"Drive safely."

"Why did you give him morphine? Was he hit? He didn't look—"

"He sprained his ankle, I think."

"Say, you're real good for a nurse. Now he's got a trachcotomy and might die."

"What can I say? Modern medicine is essentially just in its infancy."

"You think maybe you could have killed him?"

Anastasion shrugs. "This is the Orient, Dubecheck. Life is cheap." She pauses, then smiles with some hesitation and awkwardness, like someone with bad teeth. "He'll be okay." She has a bad smile.

"How about me? Will I be okay?"

"No way. You're gonna die."

"Yeah, well, not in my lifetime. You're a dizzy cupcake, you know that, Anastasion? I'm sorry to say that but . . ."

Dubecheck gets up and heads toward the PX with the big wad that, in the day's excitement, has fallen into his hands.

As PXs go, this is small, the size of a mom and pop grocery, but it will be, nevertheless, to Dubecheck's mind, wonderful.

GIs work for a company store full of more things to buy than one could possibly need and never as much as one wants.

Dubecheck enters the air-conditioned cornucopia. It appears empty except for two young Vietnamese COs standing at their cash registers in red checkered smocks and smoking Salems. They give him a cursory glance and continue to singsong with each other, nervously picking their nails.

The merchandise is laid out with the geometric linear precision of a military cemetery. Generals come in and inspect these places so the toothpaste better be standing like a row of spit-shined privates. A battalion of deodorant sticks stands by a regiment of products from the Land of the Rising Sun, giving a sharp "Eyes right!" to the discerning consumer.

"For every bullet America makes, Japan makes a transistor": Dupree's law. Items for sale: A wall of radios, AM and FM, to tune in Johnny Grant on Armed Forces Radio as he interviews starlets to keep up the morale of the boys. Over the magic of radio he will ask them to describe the length of their legs and the heft of their mammaries, the color of their hair and the knickknacks in their heads. There are banks of stereos, stacked in shiny black plastic display: Sanyo, Sony, Pioneer, speakers as large as refrigerators, pre-amps, amps, knobs, toggles, gauges, dials, tape decks, reel to reel, spools on which to play the Shirelles. And cameras stacked like dominoes: Yashica, Asahi Pentax, Mayima-Sekor, Canon, telephoto, zoom, fish-eye and wide-angle lenses so you can take a picture of a whole ditchful of dead VC for your scrapbook, dead gooks with cigarette butts stuck in their mouths for comic relief, pictures of you and your buddies with your arms draped over each other's shoulders, grinning into the glass, thinner than you'll ever be again in your life, young and lean, standing in churned-up red muck, trees sheared off in the background, jagged, standing in a forest hit by a thousand bolts of Dupont lightning, a cigarette dangling from every mouth in sight, bought from the PX where the pretty, colorful cartons are stacked as high as the eye down to a vanishing point of perspective along aisles so clean you could eat off them. Pall Malls, Lucky Strikes, Camels, Chesterfields, Marlboros, none of that "low tar and nicotine smoking is hazardous to your health" shit either. Just cartons of the real stuff stacked as neatly as the thousands of shiny aluminum coffins Dubecheck stumbled upon in a huge hangar at Travis AFB.

It's a wonderful PX. And around the corner from the cigarettes is the cornerstone, the linchpin, the glory of the system—the Alcoholic Beverage Section. Cases of beer are stacked to the ceiling; only the curved roof of the Quonset hut keeps them from reaching to God in heaven. Thousands of bottles of *beverage,* polished glass gleaming, labels like artwork, stand locked at attention begging a snappy salute. Crack troops: General Black Jack Daniels, Corporal Johnnie Walker, Mr. Jim Beam, Señor Jose Cuervo, scout, a knife between his teeth deep behind enemy lines. There's the Beefeater and the deep forest-green presence of Tanqueray, its squat Churchillian aura carrying the whole weight of the British Empire on its rounded shoulders. Flagons of Mateus, Drambuie and Grand Marnier are stacked, in pyramids of promise, proclaiming, "We are here to help you." Just like the taut, plump cellophane sacks near bursting with air and Corn Curls, Cheese Puffs, pork rinds, potato chips, Cornnuts, pretzels and peanuts.

There are virgin cartons of Baby Ruths, Snickers, Butterfingers, Mounds, Hersheys plain and with almonds packed tightly together, colorful clones, the wrappers still connected so you have to tear them off from each other like an endless skein of free tickets. Happy candy. Cases of chewing gum, brought across the vast Pacific on an armada of freighters from Wrigley's factory, beg to refresh you. So familiar, so comforting, all these little dingers from "home," from America, where you know they are still churning out the manna in little snappy shiny packets of clean, wholesome, government-inspected treats to drink, suck, chew and inhale all the days of heaven.

And around the corner there's a brilliant aisle-length mural, a mosaic of Gleem and Crest boxes, bright blue and red on a field as white as a million American teeth. And nobody can smile so, or has so much to smile about, and does so with such glaring, dazzling porcelain panache. Chompers. Dubecheck grits, then grinds his teeth at this fortress of tubed paste in Pavlovian response. He looks around to see he is alone in the cool, glenlike atmosphere of the softly humming room. He pulls a box of toothpaste, the cornerstone, out of a wall of Crest and fifty more follow, crashing quietly to the floor. He steps on some boxes and feels the firm, smooth, turgid tubes give under his weight as he treads through a pile, feeling the cartons crush and the paste pressure blow off caps and burst seams. It feels good. He feels quietly possessed.

What appear to be eight thousand canisters of Right Guard deodorant stand next to a thick wall of Dial, Palmolive and Ivory soap. He swipes his hand at the shiny gold bricks of Dial soap and the bars come tumbling down in a muffled avalanche at his feet. He kicks a few bars down the aisle like pucks. He turns four cans of deodorant upside down. He removes the lids from a can of Foamy and a can of Rise and has a Southeast Asia aerosol can research and development test, pressing the buttons of each and watching the white foam come out over his hands like thick white lava and ooze down off the shelf and drip down onto the floor in soft dollops. The cans hiss and gurgle, soap squiggling out like perfumed serpents.

He has a headache now and pulls a bottle of aspirin off the shelf and takes two, crunches them between his teeth, tasting their sour, astringent bite, then pours the rest of them on the floor and grinds them into powder under his boot heel and he doesn't know why.

He buys three fifths of Jack Daniel's and a carton of Luckys, goes outside and is blasted by the boiler-room heat and bright glare of white sky.

"You're kinda sick, Dubecheck. I like that in a guy." Anastasion accepts the carton of Luckys from Dubecheck. He sits down next to her on a rock painted white. No one is in sight.

"Why's that?"

"I just watched that toothpaste caper. I decided to leave before I saw something really heinous."

"What can I say? Someone has to do it." He has no idea what overcame him. He feels it must be related to the headache. A disease. Maybe Tuta will know what it might be. Anastasion lights two Lucky Strikes and hands one to Dubecheck.

"Were you scared?"

"About the toothpaste?"

"No. Out there in the woods with the bullets."

"Yeah. I was. I'm scared all the time. It's the only constant in my life these days."

"You been shot at a lot?"

Dubecheck shrugs. "I don't count the times anymore. I wish they'd stop shooting at me, but I've only myself to blame. It's a rotten neighborhood. The worst part is meandering around waiting for it. Sometimes it's a relief when the shooting starts, though. It's sort of a diversion from your fear, which is really hard on your stomach. But after a while enough is enough. If it gets too bad we try and leave, though. Or call up airplane guys. Thunder gods. They are wrathful gods."

"What are you *doing* here?" Anastasion squints up at Dubecheck through the smoke of her Lucky. Dubecheck moans and sighs simultaneously.

"What kind of stupid fuck question is that supposed to be? Maybe it's because I'm a young man and young men get to be soldiers on this planet. I have studied this and found it to be true. You can look it up. Thermopylae, Gallipoli, Valley Fucking Forge, Chickamauga, Château-Thierry, Stalingrad, Hue. It's a constant. There is a need for pissants like me. It's *our job*. Besides, I took the pledge of allegiance. And, being a boy of my word . . . ."

"I pledge allegiance to the flag of the United States of America and to the Republic for Richard Stands?"

"Yeah. That's the one. I put my hand over my heart, too." Every weekday morning, and the flag hung down limp on the pole in the corner, gold tassels, and the rain beat on the windows and the radiators hissed and clanked and the room smelled like erasers and chalk and everybody chanted. It was like a chant, wasn't it? He always wondered why they did it every morning, though. He figured once was enough. He wasn't going to change his mind during the night. "There wasn't any other country I was interested in and there weren't any interested in me. I mean, guys wouldn't go 'Pssssst. Hey, kid. C'mere!' and step out from behind a tree in a trench coat and shades and say, 'Bolivia. You wanna pledge allegiance to Bolivia, kid?' No. No way did that happen. Now I can't even remember the pledge of allegiance, but I took the sucker. Eight hundred times, easy." The thought seems to clear up things. Dubecheck smiles. "That's why I'm here."

"Don't you dislike dirty Commies?"

"To tell the truth, I've a vague dislike for them, I suppose. That's natural. You know, the pledge of allegiance reminded me a lot of 'Now I lay me down to sleep.' The old pledge in the morning and the 'Now I lay me's' every night. And the one that got me about that was the 'If I should die before I wake' bit. It seemed there was something illogical or irrelevant there. But you know, looking back, they seem to have worked. Here I am. Not dead, wide awake and loyal. Jesus, I hate that sound."

The muffled, staccato beat of a helicopter rises in the distance and grows in volume as it approaches.

"I take it you're not a career man."

"Now it's my career. I'd hate to think of this as my hobby, so I figure I'll stay in this poor country until they say I can go. I'd like to leave and do something else but who knows? Time flies. This'll all be nothing but a fond memory, just like the past is supposed to be."

He puts out the Lucky in the dirt. "You know, we gotta hop this Huey, because we sure as shit aren't going to drive that Jeep back through that roadblock."

The helicopter's explosive clatter fills the air as it descends onto the little pad in a noisy dust storm. It bounces twice off its sled runners and settles down. Dubecheck covers his eyes with his fore-arm and listens to the slowing blades slash the air with a whistle letting a gust of dust pass, then lowers his arm and squints. A U. S. Army officer climbs out. He carries a briefcase, looking (except for the pistol on his hip) like a commuting businessman. An ARVN officer hops out behind him and they both crouch beneath the blur of the blade and duck-waddle out so it won't decapitate them. Then a woman tumbles out, landing on her face on the concrete. An ARVN soldier hops out behind her and butts her in the back with his M-16. Her arms are pinned behind her and her hands are bound at the wrists with green tape. She is barefoot and wears baggy black pants caked with dried mud and a dirty white tunic. Her face is puffed and swollen violet about her eyes. She walks on her knees from under the blade that droops to a halt. Dubecheck gets up to watch.

The woman gets to her feet and stares through him so vacantly, he turns to see what might be behind him. The ARVN shoves her forward with his rifle butt and she stumbles, catches herself and, sullenly affronted, walks toward a bunker. She is pushed to the ground. She shakes her head to get the hair out of her face, blinks dully and frowns as if she is trying to remember something. Her mouth is set in a straight line. She rolls up on her knees, then squats on her calloused feet and stares straight ahead.

The two sentries from the sandbag bunker go over to look down and giggle at her with her ARVN guard. Dubecheck wonders what she would look like in Saigon: white gloves on her hands, holding a parasol, wearing a white silk ao-dai as she sits sidesaddle on the back of her guy's Vespa. Going to the movies. But she apparently chose to go into politics. Dubecheck hears the word "cadre" from one of the gooks hovering over her like a skinny vulture.

Dubecheck walks toward the helo to ask for a lift. In the dark shadow of the doorway he sees the gunner take off his helmet, wipe his brow, then reach down to the floor and tug at something. He heaves with both hands and pulls the body of a small Vietnamese male to the doorway. It wears blue shorts and a torn white T-shirt. It is so thin and tightly muscled it looks like a skinned animal.

The door gunner shouts, "Hey, Nguyens!" and waves the sentries over.

The gunner shoves the body out with his foot. It hangs up at the edge of the doorway, then falls, almost as if in slow motion, into an awkward heap onto the heli pad. The welts of the gunner's boots have put a precise dirt pattern on the T-shirt.

The two sentries each take an arm and drag the body over the concrete and across the dirt. The dead man's heels furrow up a soft rooster tail of red dust. His head is ballooned out on one side like a pink melon. The bullet hole would be on the other side then. Dubecheck looks to see the woman watch the transit of the corpse with apparent indifference. Then she looks down at her feet and begins to chew her lower lip. Anastasion turns her back to the whole affair and, elbow in palm, starts to blow perfect smoke ring after smoke ring out toward the empty road—something Dubecheck finds oddly endearing.

"What's all that about?"

The gunner lights up a Camel and shrugs. "I dunno. I just work here."

"Me and the nurse over there need a quick hop to Dong My. There's a bottle of Jack in it."

"Ask him." The gunner nods toward the pilot, who has just fired up a Winston. The pilot, a skinny, bleary-eyed young black guy, nods that it's okay with him.

Dubecheck tosses a fifth of Jack Daniel's to the gunner. "Just honk when you're ready." He walks toward Anastasion and notices the prisoner has attracted some sightseers. Three pasty-faced GIs have meandered outside from their radio sets to check her out. They squat before her. One talks to her and looks up at the Vietnamese, who laugh and nod vigorously at whatever the GI is saying. In the shade, twenty feet away, the body draws a curious crowd of flies.

A heavy-set Baby Huey-type GI with a red face reaches out and puts his large hand over the woman's left breast while his buddies snigger. A big dark circle of sweat fills up the back of his fatigues. Dubecheck doesn't like any of them. Rear Area Mother Fuckers. REMFs who go home and invariably play the heavy Vietnam vet bit with each other over pretzels and beer.

"Hey. Nice little titties there, mama-san. . . . That feel pretty good? Hmmmm?"

The woman looks down at the ground, then off through a gap between the young men circled around her.

"Hey, troop."

The GI looks up at Dubecheck. His face is already blotched and sweaty as if he's not used to being outside. The start of a half-ass black mustache dirties his upper lip.

"Yeah?"

"It's 'Yes, sir,' sonny. Get your fat hand off her tit."

The GI stops his kneading but leaves his hand on her breast. Dubecheck realizes he wears nothing on his fatigues to indicate he's an officer. He could be a garbage man for all they know. But he's a large garbage man.

"Whoah the fuck ah you?" His eyes dart to the other two GIs and the three Vietnamese troops for some sort of confirmation.

"You don't have a need to know, so take your hand off her before I break it off." Smoke coils up from every cigarette held between each soldier's fingers.

The GI slowly takes his hand off and wipes it on his fat thigh, staring at Dubecheck. He slowly rises. The Vietnamese look confused. The other two GIs suck on their cigarettes, waiting for the big guy to do something. They are skinny, half-bent-looking young men with vapid faces and dull eyes. Dubecheck sees them in maroon polyester slacks with white belts and checked sport coats somewhere down the road, VFW beanies on their heads and a belly full of bourbon talking about how they won the war. And the big kid, big and beefy and loud, maybe post commander with a cigar in his mouth and a quiet, mousy wife worried about his drinking. Fucking Americans are starting to get on Dubecheck's nerves.

Another one of them comes banging out of a Quonset hut across the enclave. It is the officer with the briefcase. He looks efficient, doing a double-time swagger toward them, while his ARVN counterpart tries to keep up. Dubecheck figures they probably just stopped to take a piss, but they're acting like they just called the President on the phone and he wants to see them. Right *now*. The briefcase is a nice touch. It's probably full of dirty underwear and a couple of *Playboy* magazines.

Everyone salutes the American major and his counterpart. The American nods to his diminutive clone, who then chatters to his troop, who then yank the woman to her feet by the crook of her arm and lead her stumbling sideways toward the helo. The major salutes the motley assemblage about him and strides off toward the helo, leaving them all to carry on whatever it is he thinks enlisted men carry on. Dubecheck goes to get Anastasion.

"Hey, *asshole*. Where you think—?"

Dubecheck whirls and buries his fist into Baby Huey's solar plexus all the way up to his wrist and walks away, not bothering to look back, knowing the guy is probably on his knees wondering if he'll ever breathe again while his buddies gawk at him, no help at all, maybe bending down to his wild-eyed face to say, "Hey, Wendell. You okay?"

Good thing he's leaving, Dubecheck thinks. In the New World it doesn't do for officers to go around hitting enlisted men. They've got a strong union, and it's not too good to turn your back on them. Respect for authority is not what it used to be. He glances over his shoulder and is pleased to see Baby Huey heaving up some of his Mark I government issued five-thousand-calorie lunch, in yet another daily waste of the taxpayers' money.

o   o   o

She can't be too old. About the age of the girl back home who thinks she loves him, the age of a coed. He wonders if this one even knows what a "coed" is. Freckles of dried blood dot her tunic. She stares down into the deck plates of the helo, which has shot up ten stories like some noisy clattering elevator with the walls kicked out. It heels over and down. Out the hatch past the door gunner Dubecheck sees the tiny, meaningless figures of people in the clearing below. He just hit one of the tiny, soon-to-vanish figures in the stomach; the figure is still on the ground inside a circle of tiny figures that will diminish in size until they no longer exist to him.

There it is, another interlude in the day scattered out on the ground with the rest of them and he couldn't put them together if he tried.

The door gunner speaks soundlessly into his microphone. It curves out of his football helmet like half a face guard. He lights a cigarette from the butt of another and tosses the butt out the door, then, for some inexplicable reason, smiles and gives Dubecheck the thumbs-up sign. These guys who fly are always giving the thumbs-up sign and it can mean anything. He seems to wait for Dubecheck to do it back but, getting no response, winks at Anastasion, then gets grim behind his weapon like he was standing a tight watch, cigarette clenched between his teeth, eyes squinting in the wind. Fucking movie star.

Everybody is smoking except the American major and the prisoner. The major has that "I've only two percent body fat" chiseled gristle look to him, so of course he wouldn't smoke. He probably runs forty-six miles a day back at Sill or Benning and won't allow smoking in his office but realizes if he said anything about it here he'd be thrown out of the helicopter.

Dubecheck wouldn't want to be stuck in an elevator with this crew. Anastasion is starting to make little cautious forays that indicate she might want to be his friend. The ARVN troop is a slug. He sits swaying, his eyes closed, using his M-16 as a staff to balance him in his sleep like some Mexican shepherd on a bus. The American major has opened his briefcase and is perusing a green piece of paper in some horseshit display of cost-efficiency time management. A green sheet is usually "Confidential," which is about one step below what you can read in the local newspapers. It's too noisy to talk but he probably figures he's too important to just look out the window at the pretty aerial view, so he furrows his brow, deep in thought over a toilet paper requisition. The ARVN major doesn't begin to have anything real to do either, so he reads the fine print on his pack of Salems. All Dubecheck can see of the pilot is the back of his bubble helmet, as though they're being flown by a robot. The passengers, like silent strangers on a bus, sway as if they were going over a bumpy road, smoke and stare into their own strange thoughts.

Her high cheekbones are purple and swollen. Probably from fists thudding into them with the sound of a club smashing cabbage. Dubecheck wonders what it could possibly be that has gotten her into so much trouble. There are women her age back home whose only problem this moment is that they don't know what to wear today.

The VC chick gingerly licks at her swollen lower lip where it's been split. She's the second small frightened individual with its arms pinned behind its back he's seen this day. Right close up, where he could smell them and their warm stoic terror. The vibration of the helicopter is moving Dubecheck's foot toward hers. He lets it come to a stop against hers. She slowly draws her bare, dust-mottled foot away but his foot, riding the cavitation, seems to follow. He stops his foot. She has nowhere left to hide hers. He can't take his eyes off her: the tiny mole on her neck beside a narrow blue blush of vein, the dusty gray pallor of her face, the purplish puff of her pouty, split lip, the straggly black hair that hangs down her back and veils her right eye. He reaches out and places two fingers on the top of her bowed head. He looks up to see everyone curiously watching him. Startled, she looks up and for an instant her eyes meet Dubecheck's. They are black, ineffably sad, yet coldly indifferent.

She blinks as he moves the strands of hair from her face with his fingertips and loops them over her ear. He hears the sound of tape ripped off a roll. The ARVN major leans out and pulls a green adhesive blindfold across her eyes and secures it with several quick turns about her skull. He tears off the tape and tosses the roll to the deck. Then shakes out a Salem. Dubecheck looks at everyone watching him and thinks, somewhat irrelevantly, the girl-woman will never see him again.

8 He wishes it were night already, anything to indicate the day might show some signs of ending. He cannot shake Anastasion, who has been tailing him at a discreet five-foot distance, smoking, saying nothing, asking for nothing and behaving, in general, like a dutiful peasant wife.

He has meandered in from the Dong My helo pad to the party, a leisurely two-mile urban stroll.

Just outside the gates, before he enters, he sees Tuta in dark sunglasses, crouched behind a parked Jeep waving wildly. Dubecheck goes over.

"Is there anybody there I should know about?"

"Who should you know about, sir?"

"Movers and shakers! Movers and shakers. Has anybody asked about me?"

"I don't know, sir. I haven't been there in a while."

Tuta thinks on that a moment and chews his lips. "Thanks. You're Dubecheck, right?"

"Yes, sir."

"Well, don't you say a word of this. You haven't seen me. You don't know me."

"Right."

"I'll remember this. I never forget any kindness. They're not that common in this world of pissants, grovelers and the high and mighty. And I could go on. Believe me."

And Lieutenant Commander C. B. "Tuta" Foote trots off down

the dusty vacant street without a look back, with the clumsy, knee-buckling stride of an exhausted man who doesn't like to run.

Dubecheck finds the party to be a noisy din of blithering idiots. The snake appears to be in a deep sleep with a lump in its throat.

Dubecheck's in a wired, trancelike state compounded by the fact that he has nowhere to go and, like his comrades, chugging and shouting and screaming and laughing in the courtyard littered with paper plates smeared with grease, red and yellow stains, crushed beer cans and cigarette butts, he has nothing to do. They are all in a formless exile. They cannot go anywhere except heavily armed and in harm's way, pleading self-defense.

Dubecheck scans the gathering of the clans. Army, Navy, theirs and ours, and the CIA. Snazzy has shown up with two other spooks under the cover of the AID and everyone pretends they're being covert so as not to hurt their feelings. But Snazzy is drunk and is blowing his cover, an acidic pH soil factor farmer complaining about what lousy shots his PRUs are. An American officer is loudly whining about a fucking gook artillery unit that was having lunch and wouldn't stop to lay down a barrage. A constant low-level mewling about the fucking goddamn gooks permeates the tropical air. It's like a convention of contractors talking shop, complaining about the lousy help these days. They've got the war parceled out to the different trades, each one more fucked than the other. Dubecheck feels he could just as well be in Akron, Ohio, at the Ramada Inn. Same guys, different clothes. At least they're not maudlin yet. That comes later. It must have something to do with the moon and the tides, the declination of the sun. The watery eyes and the stiff-upper-lip business only start going down during what would normally be dinnertime. But since most of them have been drinking all day and through dinner, they'll start crying instead of eating. Basic chemistry at work.

Dubecheck too has found himself at it more than once; they all sing the blues, sorrow emanating from a gravity of thought that comes out in hushed, forthright tones, as if the words were written on the bottom of the drinks they stare into. The troops will get maudlin and that's followed, on the lower levels, by fights in the EM enclaves. And after all the crying and fighting and carrying on, the blubbering forgiveness, it all ends, with everyone drowning in a mawkish camaraderie as thick as their heads, followed by the sweet oblivion of sleep and the next exciting event of life—morning.

"Where the hell you been?" Dupree comes up and whispers to Dubecheck. "They're coming tonight." It is Dupree's running gag.

Week in and week out Saigon sends down some hot intelligence indicating that Dong My is going to be attacked in force by the enemy. This information is partly based upon the lies and complete fabrications of Lieutenant Dupree's intelligence reports. He obfuscates the obvious and freights the obscure with irrelevant data, pandering to the paranoia of those who think things around here tend to fall into patterns. His reports are generally false and he has correctly assumed that it makes no difference, since nothing is ever acted upon in logical sequence anyway. The reports sound and look beautiful and are highly thought of where it counts—in Saigon, and eventually in the Defense Department and in what is referred to as the "intelligence community," a gathering of people Dubecheck has found to be nothing more than military astrologers.

"You're drunk, Dupree. There's nothing more disgusting when you're sober than loud, laughing, obnoxious drunks. Who are all these people anyway?"

"Hey, man. Comrades in arms. This is your life. Enjoy. The fruit of America. Her sons. It's kind of surly in here, though." The scene before them looks as disorganized as a Greyhound bus depot.

People are meandering around in various degrees of drunkenness, vaguely dazed, trying to drag out an event that has lingered on long after it's over. Guys wander about trying to find something new, the smiles on their faces more like grimaces, as if they are beginning to realize they didn't have as much fun as they thought they did and now they feel hot, sluggish and aggravated.

Two Vietnamese busboys with push brooms sweep up noisy rolling cans and paper plates as dusk begins to shade the day like a cloud crossing the sun.

Dubecheck stands holding the fifths of Jack Daniel's at his side like two bowling pins. Dupree pulls one away from him. "You better hide this stuff or some of these guys will tear you to shreds."

Anastasion, appearing quietly at his side, pulls the other bottle from his hand, unscrews the top, takes a pull and hands it out to him, then slides the flat of her palm up and down against his crotch like some Wanchai Hong Kong whore. He buckles back reflexively and looks at her, somewhat shocked. It's just not something an American girl does. In public. But this is not *public*. It is one of the strangest places on the planet these days and he feels an uncontrollable pulsing in his crotch. She is not someone he'd have thought of romantically. All he can think of is Co Lan, but he realizes that maybe he *can* think of Co Lan. Gazing into Anastasion's face, a face that normally would not get a second look, he begins to see a subtle shifting of her angular, somewhat twisted features, which look as if they had been drawn with a blunt black crayon. He takes a long pull of Jack Daniel's and blinks in the perverse wish that upon opening his eyes she will look more like Co Lan. But she doesn't. She does look better, however. As the burning whiskey lands on the top of his stomach and sends hot flashes outward, she begins to look quite nice after all and presently, groping, he finds his hand in hers; two sweaty palms and ten gritty fingers gnarled together in a clammy grasp that feels good. He can't remember the last time he held another human being's hand, although he's not certain of the wisdom of holding hers.

He won't be mean to her, he's afraid to. He figures one doesn't kick someone in the face who's looking for a little compassion, no matter the inconvenience. He doesn't know the origin of this ethic, but it goes back a long way. Back to when he believed God was watching him from high above, up above the stacked cumulus, up where the B-52s now fly through the invisible. The Lord God he said "Now I lay me down to sleep" to, big guy, maybe looking somewhat like Leonardo da Vinci or the old guy that blew the wind on the map inside the cover of the huge dictionary he sat on when they tried to make him learn piano. God watched everything you did and took into account what you did right and what you did wrong and *you* knew what was right and what was wrong, and if you did wrong you got a queasy feeling in your stomach and you didn't feel good. Like the time he tried to be nice to a kid who had polio and no friends. Other kids would tease the kid with polio, because his legs were funny-looking; he swung them around beneath his hips like his pants legs were empty, using his crutches for limbs. And when he tried to be nice to the kid, they began to tease him too, and he realized it was easier to join the others, but he knew it was wrong and he felt sick. Then the kid with polio drowned when he fell into the Hamma Hamma River the next summer on a Scout trip and they didn't find his body for three days and when they finally did, it only had one shoe on it. A U.S. Ked he never really walked in. And Dubecheck felt sicker when he heard that the kid had drowned, the sole of the shoe barely scuffed, bound about a bloated baby-size child's foot. To tell the truth, Dubecheck realizes, he still feels sick about it. He did wrong and not only did God know, *he* knew. He knew as much as God did. Logic. You can't beat it.

He gives Anastasion's hand a little squeeze. She stands next to him as quietly grateful as an ugly blind date, and he feels he is standing right where he should be, among the crippled and ugly. It's easy, there's so many of them; and he realizes he doesn't know any pretty people and that is because he's beginning to feel there just aren't that many. Odds. You can't beat them either.

9 She takes off her clothes and delicately hangs them up, as if they were nice, on hangers in a little plywood closet at the end of the small rectangular room. There's a sink and above it a cracked mirror. (Is there a mirror for miles not cracked from some shock wave or another, seven years' bad luck to run concurrently forever in this country?) A mattress lies on the floor, a green blanket piled in the center. There is a shelf in the closet holding towels and a large box of Kotex Super sanitary pads. Industrial-strength sanitary pads. Dubecheck wonders if the ability or need to wear them is in itself a sign of strength of some kind. God bless great big America. A land of Wheaties, Breakfast of Champions, Kotex Super Maxi Pads, giant economy size blue Cheer, the new improved Pontiac. Longer, Lower, Wider. Maybe he'll have his coffin done by General Motors. Purchase the New! Longer! Lower! Wider! Deadboy Mark II. Maybe some louvres and pinstripes on it by Kustom Koffins, of Van Nuys, California. Real class.

Anastasion's hovel is the end of a narrow corridor in the provincial hospital. The smells of formaldehyde and medicinal astringents clash over a cloying, humid, coppery smell that Dubecheck recognizes as blood. Someone is moaning in the room next door. He sounds like some outboard motor droning far offshore. The hallways and corridors leading to her yellow-walled cell were littered with maimed, like the back alleys of some battlefield. Except there were no soldiers, just old men and old women and young women and babies and children with bloody white balls of bandages over the stumps of their little limb sticks. And some people looking like they were sleeping but, more than likely, dead.

There was a baby with a burn-blistered face, her little lips swollen the size of plums, unable to scream for the pain, so she just shuddered, her wide catatonic eyes glistening. Dubecheck stepped over her mother, who was trying to rock her, but it was too crowded to move. So the mother just closed her eyes and bit her lip white.

Across the hall from Anastasion's room is a closet with brooms and mops in it. A mop sits in a bucket of gray stinking water and cramped into the closet was a person sitting down, with a white bandage wrapped around its whole head, tapping a bare foot to a tune of pain, a mummy head. Anastasion called him the "Human Cotton Swab." She pulled Dubecheck into her room.

Now undressed, she turns to him, her breasts like two poached eggs with purplish yolks. He likes her back better. Hard trapezius narrowing to her waist. She runs her fingers through her hair and sighs and looks at Dubecheck. "Well, take your clothes off." She seems surprised he's not naked. He can hear a baby screaming outside, a sound that drills a nerve in his head. She slides her panties down over her hips and steps out of them and stands flat-footed, hands on her bony hips, as if awaiting a physical. She goes to a small table in the corner and lights a stubby candle and turns out the electric light. The candlelight reminds Dubecheck of the color of Co Lan's skin. Anastasion wraps her arms around his waist and puts her head against his chest. Her hair smells like rice paddy dirt and cigarette smoke and her back is hot and tacky from the heat and sweat. He must be far worse. She clumsily tries to unbutton his trousers, as if using the wrong hand, trying to be somewhat romantic, then giving in, falling to her knees to pull at the buttons, and suddenly puts her hot mouth over the bud of his penis, sliding her hands up and down his thighs, whimpering, her brow creased with concern as his penis stays like a flaccid lime in her hard-working mouth. He wants her to stop and the baby to stop screaming and the man next door to stop moaning, moaning louder and louder as if in competition with the baby to see who can best share their pain with that indifferent groaning mob hunched up in the corridor like a bunch of wounded stranded on a train.

He stops her hands, she spits out his penis. She gets up and walks across the cracked linoleum to the little table and lights a cigarette. Her magnified shadow wavers on the wall.

Dubecheck stands with his pants down around his combat boots. For some reason he realizes next week will be his sixth year out of high school. He looks behind her on the table at a framed photo of two dowdy, middle-aged Americans. A lobotomized-look-ing man and a woman, differentiated only by their haircuts. He with a cropped brush cut and she with a nondescript gray hash from the local Kut 'n' Kurl. They seem to be staring at him from behind their horn-rimmed glasses, a faint embarrassed look upon their faces, curious as to why their baby daughter has a young man in her room with his pants down around his ankles, but somehow confident she has a good, fundamental, logical reason for it, as sound and prudent as the polyester pant suits that upholster their egg-shaped bodies.

"The folks?"

"Yeah. Why don't you pull up your pants? You look ridiculous."

"Not right now. It's cooler this way. And I am ridiculous."

She crosses to the mattress, smooths the blanket out and lies down on her back.

"Hey, a . . . a . . . Anastasion. I'm sorry but . . ."

"Forget it."

"Well . . . well, no, I won't, but see . . . I gotta get *outta* here. No wonder you're nuts."

The din outside seems to have fallen into a Gregorian chant of some kind.

"What are they saying out there? Can you understand all that?"

"Ouch."

"What?"

"They're essentially saying 'Ouch' and variations on that. Something routine and terrible must have happened a little while ago, but it's my day off and there's very little I can do to alleviate their pain and suffering except maybe to fuck. But that appears to be out of the question right now."

"Yeah. It does, doesn't it? Say, you want me to lay down next to you or something? Maybe like just . . . hug?"

"That won't get it." She grinds her cigarette out on the floor.

"Oh. Oh. Well, a . . . in that case." He pulls up his pants and buttons them. A shriek goes up outside the door, followed by a long ululating duet.

"Jesus!" Dubecheck's startled by the volume.

"Somebody probably just didi'd right in somebody's arms. You wanna shoot some smack, Dubecheck? Get it on for your Yankee merit badge? Hey, wait. Don't go. Sit down and watch. Help me." Anastasion raises her knees and buries her fingers in the shadow between her thighs. Her index finger wiggles rapidly as if she's scratching a persistent itch. "Come on, Dubecheck, watch! Watch me!"

The wailing outside gets louder. The moaning chant behind it grows in volume, feeding upon itself. The baby screams louder in the contagious din and the man next door starts to pound on the wall, probably with his head, Dubecheck thinks as he snatches open the door and runs out, Anastasion screaming, "Help, goddamnit!" over and over behind him. He trips over a body swathed in bandages.

The power must have gone out, for the corridor is lit only by the faint yellow cones of a couple of flashlights sweeping over huddled shadows and clumps of people moaning a terrible dirge. It smells like a sewer. Shit and urine on the floor. Dubecheck trips and stumbles over another set of limbs protruding into the aisle, eliciting a howl. He gets to his hands and knees and crawls through the tunnel of hallway, sweat pasting his wet fatigues to his back and legs, gasping through his mouth to save his nostrils from the stench of blood, disinfectant and putrefication. He scrambles to his feet and runs toward a door at the end of the corridor, running in perfect synchronization with Mitch Ryder and the Detroit Wheels. "Devil With a Blue Dress On" blares from an unattended radio sitting on the floor by the door.

o   o   o

Outside, in the dark, he wraps his arm around a tree trunk, taking huge lungfuls of the humid, half-ass fresh air that has mercifully drifted inward from the sluggish brown river. He looks about to get his bearings.

With the power blown, the town is black. A few flares drift down in the distance, orange dying embers. Scattered rifle fire cracks and pops nervously over the soft breeze that rustles the leaves above Dubecheck's head. A change of scene would do him good. He figures there is no problem so large you can't run from it. But where to run? He feels like he's in a maze with walls around it.

He starts to run across a grass and gravel enclave and clambers up over an eight-foot wall covered with ivy, having no idea where it will lead. He comes down in an alleyway behind a row of shanties smelling of hot rice. Candlelight flickers through tiny, bead-curtained windows. He comes to a narrow empty street canopied by trees and startles a mess of cats and begins to run, feeling heavy and sluggish. It's been awhile since he has just run, driven himself. His combat boots clump heavily on the tarred road and his trousers snap together, whistling like canvas twill. He starts to hear his labored breathing. In the distance is a broad opening, a clearing that he now recognizes as the soccer pitch. A bombed-out grandstand has collapsed into the cheap seats. He has never seen or heard of a game played there, just seen a mass of yellowed splinters and dirt-colored birds hopping on the scuffed grass field. The field is surrounded by a cinder track; large chuckholes hold deep shadows. He begins to run on the crunchy cinders, hurdling the chuckholes, and finds himself in a race with some leaves scudding before him on a strong gust of wind. He hops a mangled hurdle tipped on its side. There are just no more games to be played here.

He recalls that the tennis court across the street has grass and mosses growing up from the cracks in the pavement where broken glass sparkles like sequins in the sun. The old net sags in tatters, a soggy spiderweb, rotted and torn, a seine for dead leaves and papers. All that's left to do in the local sports world is run. He churns his arms and sprints around the empty track; his chest burns, saliva coagulates in his mouth like glue, his side starts to ache, his bare feet squish sweatily inside his boots. He comes to a ragged halt before the remains of the grandstand, bends over and, with his hands on his knees, spits and gasps. He'd run till he'd drop if he could, but he knows it'd just be in circles, he'd just drop somewhere along this track, having gone nowhere. Pass out and probably die before he wakes with an acute case of slit throat caught from one of the locals.

He cuts across the street and, attempting a shortcut, gets tangled in concertina wire. He gingerly pulls a few tines of barbed wire out of his arms and thighs, then crawls under the prickly slinky like a clumsy sapper. He finds himself near the small charnel house behind his home. He puts his hand on the smooth wall. It still feels warm. Ashes at his feet billow up in a little white cloud. He's probably walking through someone for all he knows. He just can't figure how there can be so many dead people. Maybe there's something in Ripley's "Believe It or Not" he's missed that explained it all. Something along the lines of those Chinese numbers bits. A Sunday comics page picture of four Chinese walking abreast with four more behind and four more ad infinitum behind them in a diminishing perspective of people drawn above a text ending with an exclamation mark, explaining that if you were to stand in one spot on the earth and watch Chinese pass they would never stop coming because they would reproduce enough to keep the line alive before it could ever end. Bummer. That's the human race. Marching four abreast forever into a fucking blender of oblivion, reproducing at a rate to insure constant fodder for the time machine. And there he is, right in near the middle of the march, white guy, second from the right, indistinguishable from most of the others. Just shufflin' off to Buffalo.

Anastasion. He'll have to keep his mouth shut about that. It all adds up to this odd difficulty he's having with women in his life. It never was easy. A guy with no apparent visible means of support, marginally attractive or unattractive, having to rely upon an undeveloped wit or charm is in for a rough go of it. A guy like that can go months without getting laid. But once he gets laid, other women seem to show up like sharks schooling to bloody chum. They must smell when the male of the species is getting laid. You won't see a female for weeks, you mate one and then four more are all over the place being nice to you for a change. Sharks, the closest creature to the human female in the whole animal kingdom. Anastasion. Where does she get off calling him a moral eunuch?

Moral eunuch, am I? So the war is immoral. He remembers hearing that pinch-faced, beady-eyed little woman "correspondent" next to the photographer spitting that same phrase out at someone at the party. Well, good. Dubecheck doesn't want to think that all this they're doing is proper stuff. That would be a hell of a mess. And who are all these people anyway? Anastasion, that correspondent, they come in and out of the war, tune it in and out as if it's a lousy TV program. Fine. This war is immoral and he doesn't want to be doing this stuff and think it's all right. He thinks war is real bad behavior as a matter of fact. But under the circumstances as opposed to what? He's a standing member in the cult of the drone soldier, an able-bodied male in time of war, and there is always war. It is a karma check and he feels quite fortunate to be on the side with the power, a hedge against the actuarial mysteries of survival. If he had been born in Hanoi he'd be with *them*. If he'd been born in Hamburg in 1920 he'd have been in the Wehrmacht. In Orel, the Red Army. If you don't join their armies in times of war they feel quite justified in shooting you, jailing you or ruining you. Dubecheck prefers the moving-target school of survival. If I'm to be shot, let it be by someone I've been trained to dislike. Like these assholes in the NVA. He, meanwhile, personally, will not kill babies, rape women, loot or plunder. He won't frighten old people or shit in the soup. There it is. Dubecheck's Dogma. As for heroics or bravery, he'll try and not let down his friends should he find himself in a position to let them down. No culture rewards or thinks well of those who run from battle. Those cultures are gone. One is fraught with such dilemmas and decisions. Life on the planet is becoming a cruel and unusual punishment. He is not a moral eunuch. If anything, he's an honorable young man or, as Dupree says, "Just a guy. Oh, but what a guy!"

And he has an operation tomorrow and he better start getting serious about it, get serious about the operation and the whole war. Maybe he should get a little more *involved* in it. Maybe he should get his involvement off this *personal* level and try to equate his thankless, fatiguing and dangerous endeavors with the concept behind the whole *event.* Why are he and Recore going out tomorrow to try and kill a tax collector? This is both a multiple choice and an essay question. Actually, Recore and his friends will probably do the actual killing. Dubecheck will just be a knowing accomplice, close at hand, in a routine cemetery ambush. They have done this before, shredding an insurgent tax collector as well as hundreds of thousands of Vietnamese bucks, piasters, with a claymore mine. But the cagey triple agent Phu has indicated there is another guy at it, whipsawing the peasants and figuratively bleeding them white. And though they all realize they won't stop tax collectors, they will make sure this one doesn't collect taxes anymore. And anyway, they're not taxes. They are extortion payments.

Dubecheck always assumes that each ambush may also, with luck, kill the guy who did the Goofy cartoon show. There were forty-four little five-year-old kids watching a Goofy cartoon and one of the opposition threw a satchel charge into the theater. Dubecheck was there too soon afterward, slipping in the ankle-deep blood and falling into chunks of children (hands, spleens, torsos, half heads), trying to help as the sirens wailed and mothers wailed and tiny survivors bleated in horror and Dubecheck found himself looking at, in the bloody, sopping, soggy mess of red meat and torn clothing, a single child's eyeball, lying on the splintered floor all by itself, staring up at him like a confused marble, and the Goofy cartoon still playing because the projector was still running and the screen was half intact and he remembers, before going into a shock he is convinced he has never quite come out of, Dupree screaming over and over: "Shut off the fucking Goofy cartoon!" He hopes every time he goes out he will maybe get to kill the guy who did the Goofy cartoon show.

He'll go find Scoog and bring him back so he'll be shipshape to go in harm's way. Check up on Recore, too. Goddamnit, it's time to become more efficient. Stop being so casually immature about this whole thing. Treat it with the respect it deserves. There's a cause here somewhere and causes deserve the respect of their participants. Cynicism is a cheap and easy way out. Would George Washington act the way you've been acting? he thinks. How about Grant, Lee, Ike, Il Duce or even Uncle Remus? Not that he thinks he's presidential timber, but there are certain qualities anyone wants to emulate. Honor, integrity . . . insanity. Don't people's lives, the jeopardy they're in, beg a sobriety of sorts? This is heady stuff, this for no apparent reason dying and killing business; and one just can't feebly grope one's way through it in some *daze* and feel good about themselves. On the other hand, fuck it. One is being led, guided and directed by absolute imbeciles, fools and pompous asses. There is just no exit.

He sits with his back up against the warm wall of the charnel house smoking a Pall Mall. If he can't be heroic, maybe he can at least get serious. But then again, Dubecheck has come to know a lot of serious and quiet people who are stupid jackals: no-nonsense guys with tight jaws, stars on their collars, distinguished gray at the temples, pudding for brains and just as lonely as the next guy, jacking off, spilling their pearly worth into their dirty socks and handkerchiefs and tossing them into their hampers for some Filipino mess boy to gather up and clean.

Seriously, there's just no way he can pull this gig off well. There's no uplifting sound track, just the buzz of reality: flies, gunfire, white noise and babble. And snoring. He hears snoring from inside the little charnel house. He thinks there might be one way out after all—don't think. Take it as it comes. Easy come, easy go. Relax. A hundred years from now—all new people.

10 The compound is jammed with sailors overflowing from the tiny EM Club, which sits around the corner from the Chiefs' Club, both of those bracketing the O Club, which to Dubecheck's view is packed with about fifteen bodies bumping into each other like drunken robots.

The courtyard has an eerie carnival atmosphere about it; the year-round Christmas tree lights that festoon the low eaves of the buildings surrounding it are the only illumination. The darkroom reds glow off faces twisted in the exertions of drunkenness and laughter. Rock and roll blares from one of the refrigerator-size speakers someone has placed outside the open door of the EM Club. Everyone is shouting and swearing and laughing and singing, like a drunken choir gone stark raving mad. Guys stand in little clusters with their arms around one another's shoulders, everyone talking at the same time. He sees one of his "men," McDowell the intellectual, sitting down with his back against the side of the O Club, next to the black sailor from the pier who wears electric pink socks. McDowell is holding a paperback copy of *Soul on Ice* in one hand. His arm is around the black guy's shoulder and he appears to be crying while talking. The black guy solemnly nods his head and stares, eyes wet, at his electric pink socks and picks his nose with a distracted intensity.

The O Club is a rectangular plywood structure the size of a milk truck, painted green, standing on cinder blocks and shoved up against the wall of an adjoining two-story building. The open door reveals a motley assortment of officers who have come over from the other party, a half dozen or so, and the local contingent of four: the "foreign correspondent," the photographer and Nurse Anastasion's two ugly friends. There is no way they can all stand in that little building and breathe the same smoky air for long without familiarity and the subsequent contempt it breeds raising its ugly head. Dubecheck's been in that volatile little room too many times before not to realize that it can only bring out the worst in people.

Dupree comes staggering out of the building lighting a cigarette. "Hey. Come on in, Diwi. Experience the jocular repartee of inter-service rivalry. The vituperative vilifications of those scarred victims of mental anguish, the tortured angst that seemingly pervades every pore of our peers on the home front."

"Say again all after 'Diwi.' "

"The Army cretins are banging their macho drums along their Mohawks and the weasel-faced little bitch from Yonkers is calling Recore a war criminal."

"I'll pass."

"Remember the Army captain who's supposed to be keepin' Co Lan? He's in there. Name's Tiede."

"Tiede? That pig-eyed, burr-headed guy out at the party?"

"Yeah. Dot's heem."

"Jesus. How do ya figure? What's Co Lan doin' with a guy like that?"

"She's a capitalist. A pragmatist. Maybe she likes him. Who knows why chicks glom some guys? They don't even know themselves. Say, how was the Anastasion?"

"She's a . . . you know, she's sorta weird."

"You expected maybe Catherine Barkley? Alas, but it's a different world, Dubecheck."

"Huh?"

"Never mind."

A high-pitched shriek comes from inside the O Club. Shattering glass thumps a wall. The pinch-faced journalist comes stomping out of the green box; loud laughter follows her. The photographer appears in the doorway, holding a drink in each hand. "Linda! Linda! I've got another for you." He steps down and comes up to Dupree and Dubecheck. "She threw her drink at the lieutenant. Gin tonic. She's quite upset."

Linda the journalist, furiously sulking, leans against a tree trunk by the gate to the compound. Behind her in the shadows, Dubecheck can see a sailor pissing on the other side of the tree.

"What's her problem?"

"She said that the whole war is an example of American arrogance and brutal insensitivity."

"So? What's new?"

"That it's convoluted logic was best evidenced by the Army idiot who said, 'We had to destroy Ben Tre in order to save it.' "

"And Recore said that our logic was no more convoluted than that ideological psychopath Ho Chi Minh's who is destroying a whole goddamn *country* in order to save it."

"She said that was revisionist, right-wing, he-man imperialist horseshit."

"He said she was a really, really dumb person."

"She said, mockingly, that if he couldn't express himself in a more intelligent manner she saw no further reason for discourse."

"He said, 'Forgive me, then, I'll be more precise. You're not a really, really dumb person, you're a stupid fucking cunt!' "

"Then she shrieked and threw her drink at him."

"Both of them, really bad form. But hey, what do you expect? They're both from New York. Hey, take our picture."

"Sure." The photographer hands his drinks to Dubecheck and starts messing with his f-stop.

Dupree gets shoulder to shoulder with Dubecheck and smiles. The heat and recent exertion have made Dubecheck thirsty. The cold little glasses in his hands promise relief and he tosses back the baby gin tonics and eats the limes. A flash goes off in front of his face. He follows a flurry of red dots before his eyes into the cramped little green box, vaguely feeling they might be warning signs of some sort, but walking through them nevertheless, the instant rapport with the gin somehow assuring him that everything will be just fine.

"It tells a lot about a guy's character. But I swear. Everytime. It's one of two things. No shit. I have seen and heard it with my own eyes and ears." An Army first louie is leaning on the coffin-size bar talking to Tiede, another first louie and Snazzy. Dubecheck ducks under the bar to make himself a drink.

"I lost fifty-eight wounded and dead in one month. I never heard nothing like that. Course, I dunno. But I've seen some shit, I kid you not." Tiede pours half a plastic glass full of Johnnie Walker Red for himself and ponders it for a brief instant as if being pensive.

"Fifty-eight guys in a month?" Snazzy makes a sour face and Dubecheck feels he can tell what he's thinking. If the guy's as tough and good as he thinks he is, he wouldn't be using his dead soldiers as a scorecard. Tiede drinks his straight scotch in large swallows as if it was Kool-Aid.

The Army first louie continues, "Well, whatever, I'll bet ya it was one of the two same things every goddamn time. Either 'Oh, God!' or 'Oh, shit!' See, a guy gets nailed, he has two reactions. One of 'em's anger, the other's knicker-shittin' fear. He says, 'Oh, shit' or 'Oh, God.' Even guys that don't believe scream, 'Oh, God!' It must be sorta involuntary. Like there really *is* one whether you believe it or not, and what *you* think don't make any difference."

"I dunno. Don't forget 'Mom.' I was on the bird going back with my first wound." The other louie pipes up. "Those airplanes are shit, man. Pipes and tubes and racks and wounded bunked up inside that goddamn airplane and ever'body so goddamn drugged up you'd thought y'all in the belly of some beast, in bumfuck, Egypt, but even with the drugs there's always these guys screamin' when they wake up again and they still don't have their dicks or feet or their fuckin' face. I mean those dudes can scream 'Momma!' Didn't hear any 'Oh, shits' or 'Oh, Gods' on that plane, but I heard lotsa 'I want my mommys.' Specially in the dark, man. The dark on those airplanes sucks beaucoup.' "

Everybody thinks on that for a quiet moment. Dubecheck wonders what these guys are doing here. He's never seen them before, but from their proximity and bluster they must be Dong Tam 9th. He looks down into the top of Tiede's head with its near Mohawk haircut. The guy is heavy set and perspiring, red-skinned from the sun and booze. He imagines Co Lan's cool, lithe figure smothered by this guy's freckled, hoglike body on a sweltering night. The unthinkable, that she doesn't have her gear together as much as it appears, momentarily crosses his mind.

Tiede quickly looks up and Dubecheck finds himself staring into his narrowly set porcine eyes. They have little pale, seemingly useless lashes.

"What the fuck you lookin' at?"

"I like your hair."

"Huh? What's this? Some Navy fag shit?"

Snazzy chuckles nervously. Dubecheck feels frightened and knows that that is good. If he doesn't feel menace he won't know when to run, hide or hit.

It is quiet in the room. Shouts and laughter from outside seem far away.

"You *look* like a faggot with your fuckin' hair. You a faggot?"

A tiny fringe of hair hangs over Dubecheck's ears and his collar. It hangs a whole inch down his forehead.

"Well? Are you or aren't you?"

"Why don't you suck his dick and find out?" Linda the foreign correspondent has come back in and leans on the bar by the door.

Everyone laughs except for Tiede, who continues to stare at Dubecheck.

Dubecheck figures Tiede has spent so much time pumping himself up to be tough, he believes he really is. He's the type of guy dumb enough to start something and probably vicious enough to finish it. Plus he's very drunk and he's a bully. Dubecheck feels his adrenalin begin to curdle in his gut.

"Hey, lighten up, Earl." Snazzy chucks Tiede on the shoulder and Tiede swats his hand away.

"Goddamn Navy pussy punk."

"This is conduct unbecoming officers and gentlemen. Pour me a drink, Diwi." Snazzy sounds nervous. The two first lieutenants won't say anything because Tiede outranks them, but it's easy to see they are embarrassed. They look down into their drinks as if they've lost something in them.

"Gentlemen, hah! I bet Tiede here's got a field commission they'll take away from him as soon as he hits CONUS. Guy probably hasn't been to knife and fork school yet. You been to knife and fork school, Trunwi Tiede? Or you still eat with a spoon?" Linda the journalist folds her arms across her chest and lifts her chin a bit as if daring Tiede to knock it off her face. The room seems awfully quiet again.

"I'll say one thing." Recore hoists his glass. Everyone swivels toward him for relief. "The chick's got balls." Everyone laughs. Linda smiles and puts an elbow on the bar to prop up the side of her head with her hand. Her dark, furtive face loses its scowl as her lips loosen upward and Dubecheck thinks he likes her and her orange and purple Hawaiian shirt and is about to say so when Tiede hits him in the face with his fat right fist.

A squeaky lightning flashes in his head and Dubecheck feels a slight numbness around his eye. A warm liquid weight hangs on his eyebrow, then slowly slides down his cheek. He blinks at Tiede, who looks at him dully, his face oddly placid as if he really thought this would be the end of it.

Recore swims through the small crowd and yanks Tiede backward and drags him down the length of the tiny room with two large strides and slams him into the television set, knocking it off its mortar box console.

The two ugly nurses dutifully shriek for everyone to stop it—stop it and cover their ears, as male voices sanctimoniously shout for Recore and Tiede to break it up. Snazzy and a lieutenant ineffectually paw at the two grunting drunks, blinking their eyes in protective fear, all of them, combatants and peacekeepers, arms and legs entangled, jostling back and forth in the little room like guys dancing on a storm-tossed deck.

The two lieutenants pull Tiede back onto the seat of his pants while Dupree, Snazzy and some PBR jg hold Recore by the arms. Tiede pulls himself to his feet over the television set, whirls and slams his fist into Recore's unprotected face.

Dubecheck leaps over the bar and jumps Tiede, rolls him over his shoulder and drives him into the wall with a shattering crack that dislocates a corner of ceiling, sending down rotten fishnet bunting, entangling them like big fish. Tiede pounds his fist down on Dubecheck's back, his knees drive up into his stomach. It sounds to Dubecheck like the walls are tumbling down with all the thumping, shouting and screaming. He hears someone shout his name over and over. The voice is twisted in unrecognizable hysteria. Tiede clamps his teeth down on Dubecheck's ear; they fall to the deck in a bear hug and roll across the small floor as if they were going downhill. Dubecheck sees feet and legs hopping over them, nimble folks avoiding the carnage in a wild jig, scrambling to gain enough foothold to flee the room. Tiede and Dubecheck churn about, felling bar stools, while Recore screams, "Kill 'im, John! Kill the sonafabitch!" Dubecheck tries to pry Tiede's jaws apart off his ear, aware of whiskers scratching his cheek, smelling the sweet scotch whiskey sweat on Tiede's thick body. He decides he'd be better off trying to strangle Tiede and starts to do so as he feels people beating him on the back and shouting, "STOP IT! Stop it," and some asshole saying calmly, as if they were playing, to come on and knock it off. He continues to try and tear Tiede's Adam's apple out, contorted strength driven by pain. Tiede gasps for air, releasing Dubecheck's ear. Dubecheck draws back and lays a forearm shiver across Tiede's nasal passage and feels a gratifying crunch of cartilage send a current up his arm. Blood jets from Tiede's nose like a broken hose and his head lolls back and forth as if it were going to roll off his shoulders and onto the floor.

"Dubecheck! Dubecheck! Dubecheck!" The hysterical voice belongs to a livid Lieutenant Kooseman, Lieutenant Commander C. B. "Tuta" Foote's sycophantic aide-de-camp cum executive officer. As OD he wears an armband, schoolboy patrol bandolier and a .45 that he doesn't know what to do with. He stands pointing it up in the air like a track pistol while Recore screams in his ear, "Kill 'im, Kooseman! Kill 'im. Shoot 'im in the head!"

Two sailors with Shore Patrol armbands come running into the wrecked room looking everywhere at once, truncheons high, ready to swing, but stop short, confused over the proper protocol for clubbing officers.

Dubecheck feels himself being hustled out of the plywood box, arms entwined with his, entangled in a noisily shouting octopus, his head a fog, ringing from the smash to the face, hearing his name being shouted and looking over his shoulder to see the two lieutenants rolling Tiede across the floor like some stuffed body bag leaking blood.

The prevailing aura of menace in the air heightens in the courtyard as twisted white faces appear in and out of the humid shadows and Dubecheck is glad that he is drunk. Being drunk obviates any need to really comprehend the situation, christens the chaos with a semblance of normalcy. Lights swirl before his face, his brain whirling in its pan, cutting loose from his skull, his mind, a black nausea rushing up in a gusher of rancid mush from the day's poisonous porridge of warm beer, bourbon, bile, chopped meat and fear. Then falling, like a tall tree in the forest, slowly tipping, then crashing through the saplings and underbrush into a puddle of vomit that feels comfortably warm, a place to lay the head, a pillow of warm pus on which to dream. Voices shout from far away, muffled, confused, angry. But then he hears a choir and assumes they are angels and what he presumes to be his last thought is that, if this is what it is to die, then it is not so bad. He feels himself being pulled along the ground, perhaps to be buried.

o o o

The water is thick, thicker than the air he vaguely remembers sailing through. It feels like a bath that has gone cool. He awakes, treading water in the darkness. Lights from a distance wiggle on the surface like long electric snakes. He looks up to see Recore and Dupree on the floating pier watching him with their hands on their hips. He swims to the pier and clambers up and rolls to his back. He is cold, his fatigues cling to him like a layer of thick dead skin.

"You're in a world of shit." Dupree looks down on him like a basset hound, his face upside down in Dubecheck's vision.

"Kooseman's gone insane. He said you've gone too far this time . . . whatever that is."

The dread feeling that he is not dead seeps back into Dubecheck's thoughts. He is not dead and therefore must continue to deal with other people: peers, superiors and subordinates, Asians, Caucasians and Negroes, males, females and merciless children. Once he saw a caged tiger in a zoo. The tiger paced back and forth behind the bars with powerful, charged energy which suggested the tiger thought his situation temporary. Dubecheck didn't have the heart to tell him he was wrong and locked behind the cage forever, with puddles of piss on the concrete floor and sparrows hopping underfoot. That being back when he talked to animals, something he feels he will have to take up again since he now feels a great deal like the tiger. Not only caged but aware that there are plans for him beyond his knowledge. It's not so much that they're out to get him as that they have plans for him . . . from the President of the United States on down. That he's been sent, directed, commanded and numbered to do whatever it is they wish from the goddamn day he was born. Taught, regimented, fingerprinted, taxed, categorized, pigeonholed, checked, reined, ordered and held with a hammer over his head the size of the United States Government, a large ponderous godlike gray menace hovering overhead like an ugly thunderhead, more likely a fly swatter the size of a Ping-Pong table to thwap down upon any little ant such as he wavering out of line, squiggling single file toward the Armageddon Day picnic.

"Fuck *him.*"

"Hey. That's the spirit. That's my guy." Recore gives Dubecheck an affectionate kick in the back of the head.

"You're in a world of shit." Dupree lowers his voice this time. The phrase comes out of his mouth as if he *likes to say it,* enjoys the pregnancy of grief it portends. "Well, no kidding."

Dubecheck gets up and peels off his wet clothes and combat boots until he stands naked. A baby-breath breeze begins to dry him off.

"If you'll excuse me, I think I'll turn in."

He walks down the float and leaps up into his war boat and descends into the dark hold, grabs a flak jacket for a pillow and lies down on the cold steel deck, listening to the palm fronds ashore rustle like dry paper in the breeze, tapping out the message that the monsoon is on its way. The periodic explosions of concussion grenades the pier sentry tosses into the river to discourage sappers explode beneath the surface of the river. The shock waves ring off the old hull, clank like a hammer off an anvil and resonate through his body.

A calmness overwhelms him, a smug sense of well-being that is the facade of survival. He recalls perusing the log entries of a Nantucket whaling captain in a volume left lying about somewhere in a forgotten library, and how he was taken with the way the old, now long departed salt had ended each harrowing daily catalogue of pain, anguish, terror and bad luck: "So ends this day."

2

PART

11 "Mr. Dubecheck? Mr. Dubecheck, sir? Tuta wants to see you ASAP."

Dubecheck rises to see McDowell peering through the port gun slit of the war boat like a newborn bovine, his wide cow eyes magnified by his glasses.

The soft drowsy half sleep he had been in after a fitful night of slapping mosquitoes and thinking of the day to come and its attendant phantasmagorical aggravations, coalesces into a raging depression. Tuta wants to see him As-Soon-As-Possible. He feels like a child told the principal awaits him, with all the tentative anguish and demoralizing apprehension it entails: What are they going to do to me?

The illusionary highs of the previous day's drinking have crashed into a heap of cold, soggy doubt about everything, at the bottom of which lies the Main Monster . . . someday he's gonna die. The sterile finality of it all makes him wish for sleep, but the day is already hot and oppressively muggy and precludes it. He is sweating as if sleep had been exertion.

McDowell continues to watch him through the slit.

"Thanks for the message, McDowell. You're a good boy."

"You're welcome, sir." McDowell smiles. He strikes Dubecheck as either calmly self-assured or stuporous. He wonders where the kid gets his lobotomized equanimity. There is a familiarity to his benign face he can't quite place.

"Do you really believe in God, McDowell?"

"Yes, sir, I do."

"Why?"

McDowell cants his head like a curious dog. "Why? Why, because."

"For how long?"

"Ever since I can remember, sir."

"What's He look like?"

"Well . . . I'm not sure. . . . He's, you know, just sort of there."

"Looming."

"Yeah, like looming."

"Omnipotent."

"What?"

"All knowing and wise."

"Yes, sir."

"And heaven, too. If you're good you go to heaven?"

"Yes. As a Mormon, I—"

"You're a Mormon?" McDowell nods and bites his nails, suspicious. "Hey, okay. I was in Salt Lake City once. I heard a pin drop in the Tabernacle." He looks around for his clothes and wonders where they went. He slides around some thick belts of .50 cal some fool left out to rust to see if they might be hiding there. "I took this tour of the Tabernacle and we all stood in the back and a guy dropped a pin in the front of the room and we all heard it. Acoustics." Stuck in Salt Lake City by an engine that had thrown a rod out in the desert and killing time with the Mormons while some vulturous mechanic repaired the old clunk of car he drove at the time. Watching a movie about how when you die you go to heaven and all your dead relatives are there, smiling, ready to shake your hand and welcome you, everyone wearing white robes and sitting on what looked like cakes of dry ice that released a misty vapor. Gray-haired Grandpa and Grandma, a whole bunch of white people with suntans, and all the women, looking like Mary Kay cosmetic dealers, wandering around in slow motion with Harriet Nelson grins on their faces. *That's* where he'd seen that lobotomized look on McDowell's face before. In *heaven.* It was a look of the living dead, so to speak. What he got out of the Mormon movie was that, if you were a Mormon and kept your nose clean, heaven was a lock, a lead pipe cinch, a foregone conclusion. When you slid home you were going to be called safe. When you scored that final touchdown and crossed God's goal line there'd be no holding penalties.

He realizes he's still drunk—drunk and naked, and it's getting on in the morning, time for most young men his age to be doing something constructive with their lives.

He walks along the empty dock, naked, McDowell a discreet step or two behind him like some benevolent attendant upon the grounds of a large institution for the stark raving. He spots his clothes on the dock, sopped in the lapping wash from the traffic grinding up and down the wide, flat, mud-puddle-colored river. He looks up to see the morning regatta of sampans loaded beyond capacity with green bananas, caged fowl, tethered piglets, blue-gummed old women and little kids who point, giggle and cover their mouths at the sight of the tall naked American who has decided for the moment he is invisible.

He puts his clothes on, after wringing them out and slapping them against a piling.

"We see the world differently, don't we?"

"Sir?"

"I mean, the same stuff is before our eyes, but we don't see the same thing. It's all broken glass in a tube. I turn it right, you turn it left, we see a different picture. But it's all the same glass."

"Yes, sir."

"Yes, sir, what?"

"Well, everything goes according to God's plan."

"What's the plan?"

"I dunno. It's sorta supposed to unfold according to His will that I guess it's not for us mortals to comprehend." He smiles as if afterthought lets him off some kind of hook.

"You got that right." Dubecheck pulls on his wet combat boots and squishes up toward the Naval Support Activity where the only activity among the drums of diesel stacked on pallets beside several low, tree-shaded Quonset huts is a couple of skinny dogs chattering at fleas on their haunches. The ground is like congealed taffy from spillage, the dead dirt reeking of oil in the heat.

He looks out the barbed-wire gate and hopes there is a God. Recore knows there is a God. McDowell knows there is a God. His mother knows there is a God. Why doesn't *he* know there is a God? He *must* know it. *God* knows he thinks there is a God and you can't hide anything from God, even the nasty thought lurking inside your head that God is an asshole of proportion far beyond the ability of mortals to comprehend.

"Do you pray?" One of the dogs sniffs at Dubecheck, then looks up for a handout, his dripping tongue hanging out the side of his mouth, a Vietnamese dog, Dubecheck thinks. They all look to be the same breed, skinny, plain-brown-wrapper, thirty-two-pound dogs bred to sniff garbage, cower and slink off on their tiptoes with their tails between their legs. Third World dogs. He goes to pet it but it sidles away like a crab and stands ten feet away grinning at him with a look of superior intelligence.

"Yes, sir."

"About what?"

"Well . . ." McDowell strokes his chin like he's probably seen old codgers in movies do when they cogitate. Dubecheck envisions the day when this downy-cheeked pink wonder will be licensed to give advice to humans who are not yet born. He wonders where the unborn are all waiting, perhaps in some cosmic holding pattern a long, long way away from here—drifting in space like the spots that occasionally course back and forth in slow motion across the glazed surface of his tired eyeballs.

"Well . . . you know, like sometimes when we go out at night and it's dark and we're up one of them little canals the boat can barely pass through and there's no way out, you know, like we can't turn around and the trees and brush on the bank are even brushing our faces?"

"Got ya."

"Well, sometimes then I pray."

"Because you're scared?"

McDowell looks at his feet and chews his lips, thinking. "Yes, sir, I am."

"Shitless?"

"Shitless, sir."

"Me too."

"Really?"

"Really."

"I'm not scared to die. I'm just scared of the—the *idea*. Know what I mean, sir?"

"Yeah. The idea."

"I think, though, if some of us die it'll always be someone else. Not me, not you either of course, but even though, I'm scared."

"Yeah. I always think it'll be someone else too. I'm not sure who it'll be. Sometimes I'm so frightened that I'm not afraid. Like I've got too many things to occupy my mind that'll help keep me from dying." A horrible, meaningless death out in the middle of nowhere that not many people would give a fig about, he should add. "What do you pray for?"

"I pray . . . I pray I hope you know what you're doing, Mr. Dubecheck. No offense, sir."

"Go titivate ship and pray for me, McDowell."

"Yes, sir." McDowell salutes and walks off, the dog following, glancing back as if to imply he's after better company.

Dubecheck wiggles the barrel of the snoozing sentry's M-16 to wake him up and let him out of the gate onto the boulevard and into the flow of civilian and military traffic clamoring through the dust and exhaust.

A group of schoolgirls in white ao-dais, conical straw hats looped down their backs and swinging their briefcases, part around him as if he were a pile of buffalo shit in the street. They pass on, quacking like a gaggle of geese.

He flags down a load of ARVNs in a Simonized Jeep and they reluctantly take him aboard. He squats back by the spare tire, hanging on to it like a great ape in a zoo, while the Jeep bounces over chuckholes.

He hops off after several blocks, wearied of the driver continually leaning on his horn as he slowly nosed through the cycles and foot traffic surging in the opposite direction.

Dubecheck finds himself in a moving crowd, a shuffling queue going in a seemingly enormous circle, head and shoulders above them all, the dust stinging his nostrils. Rotting garbage wafts up off a canal.

He seems to be getting more smiles than usual today from the locals: old men squatting next to kiosks and small shops fronting the cracked concrete sidewalk, goatees like wisps of white moss drifting

from their chins; squatting mothers with fat babies whose dark walnut-size eyes watch with wonder the scraps of paper and trash that
wash up in the wind wakes of noisy trucks and Vespas.

They all must know something he doesn't. Of course they know
something he doesn't, for he knows he knows absolutely nothing of
value or substance. He's invisible. He is a scrap of paper blowing in
the wind wakes of trucks. A windblown sailor shipwrecked and ma-
rooned, like flotsam on an interstellar atoll. He should just sit on the
curb and blend, like water I came, like wind I will go, eat rice out of
a beautiful little fragile bowl with his fingers and stare at trash
blown up against the soggy gutter like tumbleweed against a
barbed-wire fence. Listen to the children play. The Homo sapiens as
inanimate object. But pulsing inside the skull, a soft light blinking
in the brain—or is it his *soul* that pulses and blinks like a red light in
the fog? Blinking a code, a complex, ultimately unbreakable code
implying, You are not dead, you are not invisible and this world has
plans for you and you are not privy to them. And you are not a
Mormon either.

He feels a thumping on his back and turns to see his little cigarette girl friend looking at him as if he were injured. He wonders
how she could get so dirty so early in the day. He goes to put his
hand to her cheek, but she backs off like a stray dog, then appears
disappointed when he doesn't follow. He gets up on his cracking
knees, dizzy, despondent and worried, and shuffles off down the
sidewalk, hands in his pockets, loitering in the Orient on a timeless
Asian morning, unable to fathom a thing, oddly at unease because
of the odd Western belief that he should be able to fathom something, feeling out of place upon the planet, locked in the wrong,
enormous room.

He can't imagine Tuta giving him a searing lecture, chewing his
ass to bits and shoving them down his throat. But one never knows
what other men will do, what demons goad them, what they feel
they have to do.

He cannot imagine things to be better if he were in charge. He
cannot imagine them to be worse either, yet down in the boiler
room, with the noise, nuts and bolts, or deep in the bowels of the
body making shit, each entity has its duty and the farther removed
from the bridge or the mind, purity of motive and deed diminish.

Deliberately attempting to kill other humans creates its own
peculiar stress. This is serious business, this war stuff, even though
at times the war seems no more than a holding action against bore-
dom, a void to fill with space and time. He's seen the gray-at-the-

temple colonels and commanders furrow their brows over it all the time. And their younger clones taking it all just as seriously, playing Simon Says with other people's lives, all from the school of "A job worth doing is a job worth doing well." Tight jaws and all, chewing those lips, and he'll be damned if he can comprehend why they don't *see* . . . that nobody cares. That there is nothing to this. That it doesn't mean a thing. He's seen them strut in Saigon where there are more generals than it took to win World War II. He got lost in the hallways of an MACV building and saw little offices full of little men in starched khaki and shiny shoes with maps on the wall, pins stuck in them, red, white and blue-headed pins and grease pencil hieroglyphics, and stacks of newsprint, pink, green and yellow, the color-coded claptrap feeding the insatiable *need to know.* The need to know what?

Most of them have never seen the enemy, the enemy as a *real* guy with hair and eyes and everything, running for his life, zigzagging into the brush, running wildly down a trail, shirttails flying, arms whirling, trying to outrace speedy little bumblebee-size bullets, only to crumple as if blind-sided by some invisible force, the body collapsing like a popped balloon. Dead guys who fall down with their limbs at funny, twisted angles and never move again.

Maybe a little more solemnity about all this is in order. At least out of respect for all the poor sons of bitches getting killed and maimed, the teenagers getting their feet blown off by booby traps while slogging around on their humid hikes, guided by some gray-at-the-temple zealot in a helicopter two thousand feet above the earth, screaming, exhorting his boys to kill those little yellow motherfuckers. The sickening orange flash of explosions, the odd light of fire in sunlight, black greasy smoke, red pins in the maps on the walls of some battalion or regimental HQ, some jerk, "I've got a search and destroy op sweeping five klicks from Cuchi Cuchi, with a company-size op sweeping my left flank right through here. Indian country." And he slaps the map with his pointer and staff nod thoughtfully as the feet and hands fly and land in the mud, looking like bizarre fruit. It all looks good on paper.

He'll start taking this shit a bit more seriously. Fake it if he has to. He'll care that the VC blew up an ammo dump one hundred miles away. That elements of the 25th Infantry in Tay Ninh were hit hard last night up by Cambodia. That twelve Phantom jets, locked in suicidal formation, got shot down over Haiphong yesterday, that his men catch the clap with a frequency that indicates they must be allergic to Asian vaginas. Get involved in the total war effort. The big picture. He can get killed while he's at it, but that's the billet, it's all part of the job and it's just a part-time job while waiting to see what you're *really* going to do with your life. He'll fake it. He'll just try and figure out who means well and who doesn't and avoid them both. Start counting the days—there's not many left—and when he's gone, he won't be missed. And if he won't be missed, why was he here in the first place? But that goes for just about anywhere, doesn't it?

o o o

"You broke his nose." Tuta is perusing a large book on top of his gray U. S. Government desk. An air conditioner rattles in the curtained window. The Hong Kong whorehouse bead curtains to his office click together, swaying from Dubecheck's entrance.

Tuta looks up at Dubecheck, his glasses reflecting the flickering fluorescent tube on the ceiling.

"Sit down, Lieutenant."

Dubecheck looks around for a chair in the cramped six-by-eight room and, seeing none, squats to the floor, his eyes at desk level.

"I've got a problem." Tuta idly leafs the pages before him. He holds up the book and shows Dubecheck a large picture, a painting of what looks like a small-scale riot going on near a big hay wagon with a lot of people dressed up like in the olden days. Somebody on his back is getting his throat slit and a guy looks like he's part fish. There're some nuns. The picture is yellowish with sea greens and strikes the eye with the sort of subtle shading the world must have had before electricity and plastic.

"The *Haywain* triptych, detail, lower portion of the central panel . . . Hieronymus Bosch. The man had vision. Do you have vision?"

Dubecheck wants to tell him that he's probably still just drunk. It's hot and stuffy in the room. He feels like he's sitting in a hot bottle of Mennen Skin Bracer. He could easily vomit if he didn't fall face down asleep first. His eyes keep trying to roll back in his head and take him with them.

"Hieronymus Bosch?" No, he'd never heard of him. Perhaps he was related to the spark plug concern of the same name. "It's a pretty picture, sir."

"Pretty? It's *hell*, Dubecheck. You should see how this guy gets wound up. Talk about some guy who's got the big picture wired, you're talking Hieronymus P. Bosch. Mr. Bosch to you."

"Really?" Dubecheck's head jerks up just in time to keep it from cleaving apart like a nut on the edge of Tuta's desk. He'll have to screw up his vision and concentrate. Concentrate on Tuta's little moon face with its little shiny moon glass eyes.

"Everybody else should just put their work on feed store calendars. This guy was an *artist.* Do you know art, Dubecheck?"

"No. No, I don't know art, sir."

"Well, it's all here. Bosch. Art with vision. You married?"

Dubecheck's mind snaps open and his eyes widen. He's got to get on his toes here.

"No. No, sir, I'm not married."

"Let me tell you something, son." He shuts the book and looks at Dubecheck with his neon glare. "Don't ever, ever . . . ever, ever . . . ever . . . ever, ever, ever, *ever* . . . ever, ever get married."

"Yes, sir."

"You think that might be enough said on the subject but you can't say enough about the subject. The little woman, the better half, whatever you want to call them. I call them Trouble with a capital T. . . ." He pulls out his wallet and lets a foot-long ladder of opaque plastic windows tumble down. "Where is she? Where is that . . . that bitch?"

He thrusts the picture of his wife in front of Dubecheck's face. Through the fog of plastic worn by heat and age stares a Mark I U. S. Navy wife. Dubecheck has seen them at all manner of naval gatherings, tucked away in cocktail party corners like duffel bags, amazingly interchangeable, always slightly dazed-looking, shipped from one duty station to another, trying to be an asset to their husbands' careers, knotted in groups talking about babies. They seemed to be either in foal or calving constantly.

Dubecheck would watch them in conversation, half in and half out of it, their eyes wandering the room as if looking for escape, a frightened "What am I doing here?" look behind the half smiles flash-frozen on their faces. The real pros, the wives of senior officers, were so zoned out they actually handled the hypocrisy, backbiting, social climbing, and political infighting graciously and with ease. An admiral's grande dame would swim about the sharklike power of her husband's aura like a remora sucker, eating the small chunks of offal that drifted down from the rapacious jaws of her benefactor with the efficient diminutive grace of all sea scavengers.

This one, Tuta's, peering through the spotted fog of plastic, wasn't going anywhere near that level with Tuta. Tuta was not bound for high command and knew it.

"You think this shitty little command is to *groom* me for great responsibility? No way." That's how he put it to Dubecheck once. "A slap in the face. That's what this is, a slap in the face. I'm a man who can see the handwriting on the bulkhead, son." Dubecheck wondered why superior officers, although often only in their late thirties, tended to call subordinates "son." Tuta barely had wrinkles. Well, it's simple: their superiors call *them* "son."

Dubecheck considers Mrs. Tuta's face. Nothing remarkable. A nose, two lips, two brown eyes. Each component fine as far as it went, and the whole adding up to nothing that would strike anyone as memorable, a bland homogenized American face with one of those hairdos now in vogue, bangs like an Afghan hound over the forehead separated from a hair bubble on the top with a pink bow that looked like it should be on a toy poodle.

"Hates my guts."

"Sir?"

"She hates my guts. Know what she's doing right now?" He consults his watch as if to confirm it. "She's probably playing tennis and sucking on gin tonics. She can't play tennis. She can't get the ball over the net. She likes to walk up to the net and pick the ball up against her shoe with her racket and flip it up and bounce it off the court and catch it with her hand. She thinks that's pretty neat in her little tennis outfit. Got little hammocks of fat hanging down from her panties and wiggles around in front of all those hard-bellied little fops with Prince Valiant hairdos."

Dubecheck watches Tuta fold up the pictures and wonders how he got together with that woman, for Tuta is one of those men one can't imagine making love to a woman. Like Richard Nixon or Henry Kissinger. Tuta starts leafing the big book of Bosch. Perusing.

"It wasn't easy for me to find a wife. I'm not physically attractive. That's what I love about Madame Phong. She likes me for what I am. Whatever that is. And that's why I'm here too, in this shitty little command with cretins like you to lord over with thanks from no one. Broke his nose. Well, I told Kooseman that war is hell and not to get his feathers ruffled. What's Kooseman got about you? You seem to do your job. You're rather doltish, but if you weren't you wouldn't be here in the first place, would you? We're not fighting this war with the best and brightest now, are we?"

"I don't think so, sir."

"Don't ever think . . . you know. I've been passed over again. Why am I telling you this? That's a point of shame. You think a man likes shaming himself in front of another? Well, guess again. Passed over for full commander. You know why? Do you?"

"No, sir."

"I don't look good in uniform. I'm wide at the hips. Maybe you haven't noticed, but when I have to tuck my shirt in it does not flatter me. It's made me shy. Less assertive. As a teenager at dances I'd stand at the side, you know, usually near the basketball hoop, and when we'd have a Snowball I'd wait for some girl to come and ask me to dance and I'd get so frightened my mouth would get dry. I'd get frightened because I knew no one would probably ask me to dance because I was unattractive and I'd go to the water fountain. You know who made the water fountains, Dubecheck?"

"A . . . a . . . Haws?"

"Haws. Good, Dubecheck. You know your water fountains. Haws does make a good water fountain, but I did most of my slaking from Halsey-Taylors. I drank so much, the name written on that little white ball with the water bubbling up seared into my brain for all time the name Halsey-Taylor."

"What's a Snowball?"

"A Snowball? Two couples would start a dance. Two pretty people, smiling, beaming. Assertive people. After a while they'd separate, and each would pick a member of the opposite sex from the sidelines to dance with and so on and so on, like mitosis. By the end of the song I was always over by the Halsey-Taylor by myself sucking down lukewarm water."

"Really, huh?"

"Yes, really. Did I tell you I've got a problem?"

"Yes, sir. You did. A . . . did Mr. Kooseman say—"

"Kooseman, Kooseman. He's my executive officer. I delegate responsibility to him. Not authority, mind you, but responsibility. Just like they say in the book, or is it the other way around? Feed a cold, starve a fever? But I don't have any responsibility, so that man is just really superfluous. You know what I say about superfluous men? Well, don't bother. Hey, I'm way ahead of you. You don't have a problem. The guy with the broken nose has a problem. You ever have a broken nose before?"

Dubecheck shakes his head, now fully awake, transfixed by a portion of one of Mr. Bosch's paintings. Birds are flying out of someone's ass, another guy is vomiting and a pig with a nun's headdress is kissing a naked man. Dubecheck finds himself twisting his neck a bit to catch what else this guy might throw at him. Tuta is right. The guy seems to have part of the big picture down pat.

"Well, a broken nose, Lieutenant, is a hassle. They've gotta stuff about, well, what feels like a bed sheet up your nostrils to pack it right. Deviated septums and all that. You listening? What you looking at?"

Dubecheck points to the picture lying open in front of Tuta.

"This foot. This foot hanging from this insect's head. The human foot."

"Yeah. Right there! I never saw that before. There's always something you miss."

Dubecheck is on his knees next to the desk. He and Tuta look at the page intently and in silence for a while. Dubecheck can hear Tuta nose-wheeze. Dubecheck's eyes are drawn back to the human foot, severed above the ankle, tied onto not an insect but a thorny branch coming out of the top of a knight's helmet next to the guy being kissed by the sow with the nun's burnoose on its head. The pale foot looks like the one he saw lying bloated in the marshy mud at ebb tide one day fifteen klicks downriver with a bunch of ducks around it. They were pecking at it with their varnish-colored beaks. He hadn't known ducks were carnivorous until then.

"The guy cracks me up, Mr. Dubecheck. Got an eye like a camera. He does not tell a lie."

"Yeah. When'd you break your nose?"

"I was fifteen. I was leading off first." Tuta stands up to demonstrate in the cramped room. He dips his knees and holds his arms out. "I'm not going to steal. Come on. I'm a right fielder. The last guy they pick on the team. A throwing error by the second baseman puts me on. Everybody's still whooping and hollering because I got wood on the ball. Humiliation and shame, Dubecheck. It doesn't build character. Nothing builds character. What builds are dead scabs on top of each other, drying and healing and making scabs. That's what builds."

"How'd you break your nose?"

"Oh. Yeah. My nose." He sniffs through it several times. "The hurler, southpaw, gangly southpaw, goes to pick me off and I turn around and trip and the ball hits me right in the nasal passage. Right in the nasal passage. Blood all over the sack. I remember staring at that dirty canvas base two inches in front of my face and watching my blood look so bright and deep red and then I passed out." Tuta sits down. "That's how I broke my nose. I've got a problem. Get off your knees. Stand up."

Dubecheck does so and wonders if he's come to attention. He's always felt so vulnerable and stupid at "Attention," hands to his side, eyes straight ahead as if he had blinders on, but then he realizes that that's the purpose. He leans against the wall.

"We're going to have visitors." Tuta buries his face in his pudgy white hands and speaks through them. Dubecheck bends to hear the muffled voice.

"A congressman from the United States of America. That's where we're from, America. Discovered by Columbus in 1492." The hands fall from his face and he picks up a piece of paper and looks at it, shaking his head. "Congressman Phillip P. 'Phil' Kealy, R., Missouri. Of course it's 'Phil.' What does he think we'd think it'd be? Congressman Phillip P. 'Ralph' Kealy? . . . Missouri. 'Show Me.' He's on a fact-finding tour for the government of the United States of America. Ever hear of him?"

"No, sir."

"Me neither but, from what I understand, there's hundreds of them. Hmmm. Third term, House panel on appropriations for this —this effort we're undertaking here in Southeast Asia. He'll have an entourage." Tuta leans back in his chair, lets his head fall back and closes his eyes. "He'll have some of his staff. A crony or two. I don't know how much weight he carries, which would determine press coverage. He'll have military aides and sycophants from Saigon and America, maybe from Guatemala for all I know. And a flag-rank liaison. Maybe full captain. Epaulets, three brass bands, four companies of light cavalry . . . Christ. It will be enough to make me vomit, Dubecheck, and why am I telling you this? I need your help and, although I cannot order you to do anything beyond the scope of your minuscule command, you're going to take care of all this for me."

"Take care of what?"

"Congressman Kealy wants to find out the real facts."

"What are the real facts?"

"Don't let me detect notes of sarcasm, irony or . . . did you fart, Dubecheck?"

"No, sir. I just stink."

"Well, stop. And he wants to go out on a 'REAL COMBAT OPERATION.' "

"No. He doesn't."

"Well, obviously not a SEAL operation. He could get killed, which would be a real fact-finding mission. Plus, the overtones of going out on an assassination, or murder if you will, of a local Viet-

namese gentleman of the Communist persuasion might have nega-
tive political ramifications and feedback. Something to do with Nu-
remberg or Geneva Conventions. Proper rules for proper behavior.
Who one can kill, where and how and why. I swear, a man doesn't
need a good gun in this war, he needs a good lawyer. I don't have
one, therefore I'll pass here and there. You'll never hear this man
say, 'I was just following orders.' I just see to it I don't hear them.
So listen up, Mr. Dubecheck.

"The PBR's squadron is on loan-out, I think, but maybe *you*
could take him out, Dubecheck, and blow something up. Yes. That's
it. Go mortar something, call up a helicopter and bomb something.
Do it at night, chat it up on the radio. It could be just the ticket."

"Where? There's usually people out there weeding their gar-
dens."

"Pick a free fire zone. That's simple. Look, it'll help your career.
You could get your name in the paper. You could rub elbows with
the near great. And I want you in charge of the greeting delegation.
They're coming Friday and you're to work in liaison with Lieutenant Dupree and of course my executive officer. I've got to go. Isn't
it real hot in here?"

"Yes, it is, sir."

Tuta rises and pushes Dubecheck out of the way and stumbles
out of his office, slamming the door behind him, leaving Dubecheck
standing in a humid pall of sweat and Mennen Skin Bracer.

As quickly as he departed, Tuta reenters the little room, tangled
in the bead curtain.

"I've got to go but I've got nowhere to go. Sit down."

Dubecheck sits back down on the floor and Tuta goes to his desk
and slams shut the Bosch and sighs.

"I wonder what's on television." He swivels in his chair, slides
some papers off a shelf next to the desk and reveals a small set with
a six-inch screen. He turns it on. Snow. Salt and pepper. Shadows,
then little gray ghostlike creatures begin to coalesce into humans on
the small screen. "A basketball game?" It is the Los Angeles Lakers
and the Boston Celtics tape delay on AFTV (Armed Forces Television). Tuta turns from the screen.

"It's ninety-nine degrees and a hundred and forty humidity and
they're playing basketball."

"I think they're playing in Boston, sir."

"What difference does it make? You take things too literally, but
that's a common error these days. Say . . . do you like me?"

"Sure, sir."

"Really?"

"Really."

"Good. Because I want you to be my friend. I don't have any friends and I never did." Tuta gets up to pace back and forth but since there is nowhere to pace in the tiny room he appears to be doing nothing more than a continuous series of about-faces, at each turn revealing what appears to be a very close basketball game. A shot goes up, but Dubecheck can't see if it went in because Tuta blocks the screen.

"Do you see any problems?"

"With what, sir?"

"The combat operation. You have complete command. After all, you're a CTE and no one else will be CTE. You're captain of your ship when you're under way. Master of your soul. No problems there, right?"

"No. Unless Recore's operation takes some precedence—"

"Cancel it. Recore's little vendetta against the Reds can stand down for this. The war will not end this week."

"Do you think it ever will?"

"Why ask me? You're in it, I just read about it in self-serving batches of military message traffic. It'll end for me in about five months when I muster out with the realization I'm a failure. It's not a comforting thought for a man my age. One day it hits you with a force that you never recover from. Life is good when you think you have a future . . . at least I think it might be. Then one day you look around and realize that there is no future, that this is it and it is."

The air conditioner quits with a cough and a rattle. In the silence the temperature seems to rise suddenly like a sauna. Dubecheck hears a single bird chirp outside. One chirp. He wonders what it meant.

Tuta stares blankly at the Celtics and Lakers running and jumping.

"Between three and five in the morning, if a worrisome man finds himself unfortunate enough to be staring up at the ceiling, doubt and fear come out to dance upon his mind. Like magpies upon a squashed bunny rabbit . . . stuck to a hot two-lane road. Triumphs do not occupy the mind in those mean, lonely and hard hours. It is the humiliations, the failures, failures real and imagined, sorrow and the relentless bullshit that convenes at all sober reflections upon one's life, when it's darkest before the dawn. You can look it up."

Dubecheck has to urinate and wonders if his new friend will let him. And speaking of dawn, it dawns upon him that he has never known any happy people yet and that it's not been, to his knowledge, his fault.

Tuta points to Dubecheck. "Roust a man from his bed in those early hours and he's lower than a hog's jaw on market day. Low tide. He is malleable and the cruelest interrogator is the self." He looks at Dubecheck and sniffs, pausing as if expecting a reply.

"Really?"

"Really. I haven't heard from her in three weeks. Maybe the mail's been misplaced. . . . No . . . no, it hasn't. She's playing gin, drinking gin, flirting with those little preppy tennis fops. But her breasts have dropped, they're sagging. I bet she wants to leave me. Why is *she* my wife? Divorce. Bad for the career. What career? Fourteen years in the Navy and twice passed for the bird. Maybe I wasn't bold enough? And I don't look good in uniform. Did I tell you that? I've wide hips."

Tuta is beginning to sweat profusely. Dark blotches the size of canteloupes appear beneath the armpits of his olive-drab fatigue blouse and his face is shiny under the fluorescent light. He's making Dubecheck pant. Dubecheck feels he could piss in his damp trousers and it would not only go unnoticed but probably cool him down.

"I'd always worn my shirts hanging out for as long as I can remember. Until the Navy. You have to wear them tucked in for the most part. My mother would take me by the hand up the stairs of the local department store to the section for the 'Hefty' sizes. I could hear them all giggling behind my back and she insisted, insisted upon holding my hand. Well, it's all gone wrong and it's too late to change course no matter what they say. You don't start these things over. You get one life and you have less to do with it than you could ever imagine in your worst moments. But it could have been different . . . if only . . . instead of . . . like I should have. Hah! You make one lousy hesitant turn to the left instead of the right and instead of finding the path . . . hah! The path of life."

Tuta resumes his about-faces. Dubecheck notices the game is tied. The Lakers are bringing the ball down court and the Celtics are walking backward in front of them. The game was played last week on another planet and the outcome or score seems as irrelevant as that distant place itself.

"The path of life. Forget the past. Never look back, forge ahead.

That's a hoax. No one forgets those big mistakes they've made. Never. You can fake it, but they're still back there and they come out at night and hang in the air like the smile of that . . . that . . . Cheshire cat!" Tuta is hyperventilating.

"You never learn from your mistakes. You just make the same ones over and over and over. They get bigger, they wear disguises, false glasses and large noses, but they're the same ones and you can't fool me. Oh no. I'm beginning to feel weak and foolish." He taps his temple with his finger. "Shark frenzy. My brain is in a seething shark frenzy of self-destructive doubt and pain. It knows the big picture and it's not going to let me off the hook." He sits back into his swivel chair, breathing heavily from his tirade. "Who's ahead?"

"I think the Lakers, sir."

"Tall sonsabitches, aren't they? Where did all the tall Negroes come from? You don't see them on the street. They just seem to appear, as if by magic, on basketball teams."

"May I go, sir?"

"Of course. I've work to do. You got any medals, Dubecheck?"

"Just the ones for being around."

"Well, maybe I'll give you one. There's a whole pile of paper here about people wanting medals. You want one?"

"No, sir. I just want to take a leak."

"Very well. Don't forget. I'm counting on you." He looks to the TV. "Is there another channel in Asia?"

"Good-bye, sir." Tuta doesn't answer. Dubecheck leaves him turning the channel selector. There isn't another channel.

12 Outside, the ninety-degree heat seems refreshing compared to Tuta's office. He looks around for the bird he heard chirp, half expecting it to be lying dead on the pavement. He goes to the corner of the small alley and relieves himself into a pile of dead leaves as he thinks about the path of life. It's no path, it seems more and more to him that it's like the coyote that's always chasing the

Roadrunner in the cartoons. The coyote runs off the edge of a cliff and stops in midair, looks down and sees nothing but an enormous abyss and starts futilely back-pedaling in the air. He falls down, down, down, turning into a speck, and vanishes in a quiet puff of dust three thousand feet below. That's the path of life.

"What in the hell do you think you're doing, Dubecheck!"

Dubecheck shakes off and turns to see Lieutenant Kooseman glaring at him, hands on his hips—petulant, lower lip protruding.

"You've gone too far this time."

"Really?" Dubecheck buttons up and turns to Kooseman. "What did I do now?"

"What did I do now, *sir.* I still outrank you, mister."

A full lieutenant pulling rank on a lieutenant junior grade takes extraordinary courage or bad manners or both. It's dangerous business, shoving people around, unless you like to do it, as Kooseman does, and then you better be vicious instead of just petty and inept, or something happens to you.

Dubecheck regards the twenty-five-year-old man child glaring at him. Kooseman's been here about two weeks longer than Dubecheck, which makes him act like he helped raise the flag on Mount Suribachi or something. He's not alone in that respect. Give a guy twenty-four hours' more time in-country than another guy and he'll act like John Wayne does in movies when, with a cigar in his mouth, dirty, ill-shaven, tired, beat up, like *battle-hardened,* he has to deal with some helplessly naive shavetail lieutenant fresh off the boat. Guys who act like they were at the Alamo and where the fuck were *you* by the way?

"Mr. Kooseman, sir? What did I ever do to you?" Dubecheck asks, tempted to burst into song and soft-shoe across the concrete as he adds, "to have you treat me the way you do?" Instead he realizes right away Recore was right—Kooseman is shorter than Dubecheck and has to look up to allow for the eight-inch differential in height. Eight lousy inches. Baseball isn't a game of inches, Life is. And some guys take the height business real serious. Much more so than the brain business. Kooseman is a little short in that aspect too. He's an ROTC officer from one of those little dipshit colleges in New England that have about thirty-two students.

But brains don't have much to do with being an officer and never did. There will always be room for the guy who can lower his head and run full speed into a tree trunk for the cause.

Kooseman backs off a step and levels his finger at Dubecheck.

"You were pissing right there! I don't believe it! Right there! Like, like an animal."

Fastidious. He's fastidious too. Best-dressed, neatest guy in Asia. Spiffy and sharp like little guys, for some unfathomable reason, often are. A guy who clips his nose hairs with the same intensity with which Dubecheck's seen some girls apply eyeliner. Leaning forward, peering at the mirror, biting their tongue tip.

He's a sharp-looking guy who looks like he is squared away, and that is probably how he made lieutenant. Guys actually get promoted on that basis. It's called military bearing. Some real Ken dolls, polyurethane to the core, often get the nod just for that reason—which is probably just as good a reason as any.

"Yes, I was," Dubecheck says. "So what are you going to do? Send me to Vietnam?"

"Ha-ha." He says ha-ha like he is sarcastically pretending to laugh. "Real funny. You're really funny. As funny as a rubber crutch."

Kooseman always talks like he's in the sixth grade. Dubecheck's beginning to think that people find an age they're fairly comfortable with in their life and stay there for the rest of it regardless of what happens. Kooseman strikes Dubecheck as a guy who seems to have been comfortable with eleven, probably the last time he was the same size as everyone else his age.

"I've got some plans for you, mister. And I bet you won't like them."

In the officers' mess, a ten-by-six pale green windowless room with a six-foot-long table covered by a red and white checkered oilcloth, Kooseman would always say whatever was served was made much better by his mother.

"You call *these* veal birds? You should see how my mother makes veal birds," he announced one day. And he forked several onto his metal tray and spread ketchup on them.

"No. I don't call them veal birds. The cook calls them veal birds." Recore ate off the platter with his fingers.

"Why would anyone want to cook veal birds? Anyone who cooks veal birds is deranged." Dupree tossed a veal bird toward Dubecheck's semicomatose dog, the one that sometimes follows him around. Its jaws lethargically clicked shut and the veal bird hit him in the forehead. He sniffed around for a moment before he found it and commenced to gum it.

"That's my mother you're talking about, mister."

"No. It's *your* mother *you're* talking about."

"Dubecheck, get your dog out of here. This is an officers' mess." Kooseman daintily cut all his veal birds into bite-size portions.

"I didn't bring him in here. He followed me. It's not my dog."

"Well, tell it not to come in here."

"I can't. It's a Vietnamese dog. It doesn't understand English."

"Didi Mau! Didi Mau!" Kooseman looked at the dog and pointed toward the door. The dog looked straight ahead with glazed eyes as if thinking deeply about what it was chewing.

"There's no place for a dog in an officers' mess. Do I have to order you?"

"Dubecheck doesn't have to leave. He's an officer."

"I meant the dog."

"Why don't *you* go and see if it follows you? Show some leadership." Recore wiggled a veal bird in his fingers in front of Kooseman's face. Kooseman said nothing to Recore, because he was afraid of him and he said nothing back to Dupree because he knew Dupree was rich and someday might be able to get him a job in one of his father's banks. After the war was over and everything was back to normal.

"This is getting too intense for me. Let's change the subject. How does your mother make veal birds, Kooseman?" Dupree arched another toward the dog and hit it on the head.

"Well . . . she stuffs them with a sage dressing. And wraps them with bacon instead of . . ."

"Jesus Christ," Recore sighed. He still had a kind of fired look in his eyes. A sort of glazed intensity left over from an incident two hours before when he and his men murdered two guys they caught wandering into an ambush carrying hand grenades in their pockets. It always takes Recore a few hours to wind down after killing somebody. Dubecheck had picked him up on the riverbank shortly after hearing two short bursts from an M-60, and then they came back and went to dinner. "Fuck your mother and her veal birds."

It was silent in the mess. Just the sound of the dog sloppily chewing a veal bird and a huge fly buzzing around the condiments. Dubecheck momentarily felt sorry for Kooseman. There's nothing wrong with being proud of your mother. He imagined that Kooseman sat down to dinner every night to a tablecloth and a beaming, clean-cut, gingham-plump mother with a frozen warm smile, platter held high, backing out of the swinging kitchen door, saying, "It's your favorite, darling, veal birds." And all the Koosemans, Mom, Dad, and Little Koose—he'd be an only child—would sit down and they'd ask how he did at school and she'd say how she just ironed a fresh batch of clean white T-shirts for him and put them in his drawer and they'd all be very close and they wouldn't know that nobody liked him at school.

And he felt strangely sorry for him because he knew Kooseman, for all his faults, would probably not shoot two teenagers in cold blood on a sunny day with the breeze flapping the palm fronds and the birds chirping until the gun went off, like an air hammer in a pasture.

But somebody had to. There was the vague realization that that's sort of what they must be here for.

Now, in the wretched heat in the courtyard outside of Tuta's office, Dubecheck feels that what he is not here for is to listen to Lieutenant Kooseman scold him.

"We have to set a proper example for these people." Kooseman waves an arm around as if to encompass the whole sweltering nation.

That always got Dubecheck. They were supposed to impress the people of this doomed, forlorn land as if they were timid unwanted guests in it; to behave themselves and have good manners as they plowed the place under and did everything but sow the fields with salt.

In fact, Dubecheck is supposed to be somewhere at this moment. Some psychological community relations types are here today from Saigon to lecture the troops on sensitivity. It all stemmed from an operation a few weeks back when Recore, pinned down with his squad on the riverbank, shouted out on the Radio Net for some air because, "There's a fucking million gooks in that tree line!" He didn't get in trouble for saying "fucking" over the Net, he got in trouble for saying "gooks."

Dubecheck wonders if there'll be giant blackboards set out. They'll all be told to write, "I promise not to call gooks gooks anymore," five hundred times apiece.

"Yes. I have plans for you." Kooseman actually wags his finger toward Dubecheck. That's the trouble with feeling sorry for guys. As soon as you do they'll usually snap back and bite you in the ass.

Dubecheck walks away from Kooseman, vaguely aware that he is being further chastised, not listening fully. What little energy began to build as he left Tuta's office now dissipates as he hits the "wall." It dawns upon him that he is, so to speak, a prisoner of war.

o   o   o

"The trouble with you is you feel sorry for people when you should feel sorry for yourself," Dupree admonishes Dubecheck.

"Really?"

"You don't look out for Number One, Dubecheck. That's what makes America work. Sharp cats looking out for Number One. Sharp *greedy* cats looking out for Number One. You probably think we got great through hard work and sacrifice and a sense of fair play. Wrong, cowboy. Guys like you are always at the back door with your hat in your hand, because you don't know how America works. You probably believe your eleventh-grade U.S. history book." Dupree swivels in his chair and tosses down a copy of *Playboy*, the page open to a naked woman lounging on a huge bed with clean frilly sheets and soft pillows. A room that looks like a display corner in a department store for the wealthy.

"Look at her! You believe that?"

"No, I don't believe that. There's magazine people and people I know." He doesn't recall ever seeing a naked body without moles, freckles, wens, warts or multicolored hues at body sags, curves, ripples and undulations. The girl looks as if she'd been dipped in a light pink lacquer, her body like some unwinged goddess on a tavern softball trophy.

A real human woman sits at a desk across the room from Dupree's desk. She is a short, heavy-set Vietnamese woman with a black thatched-hut hairdo. Co Bihn is Dupree's counterpart in intelligence and is rumored to have connections with the President, like all of the others claim to have.

She is reading a romance comic. She is bulging in her tight ao-dai and smoking a Salem.

Two teenage petty officers sit in the anteroom at the rear of Dupree's Quonset hut facing a bank of communications gear. Smoking. Picking at hangnails. Nobody seems to be doing anything. A row of green filing cabinets lines one wall and maps, tacked onto plywood boards, lean against the other. The room is like being inside a tube of corrugated pipe. It hums with fans that cool all the radios, which hiss and crackle as if anxious to impart news.

"You keep a tight ship here."

Dupree grunts. Dubecheck pokes around in a triple-decked wire basket with In-Out-Hold signs taped to it. Each level holds pastel-colored papers. He pulls out a pink one from Hold and begins to shape a paper airplane with it.

"This congressman, Kealy. You know him?"

"Scumbag." Dupree puts his feet on his desk and looks at the naked girl again.

"You know him, huh?"

"No. They're all scumbags. They hang around my father's house like tongue-dripping puppies. Let 'em know you'll give 'em a few bucks for their reelection campaign and they'll lick goat shit off your shoes. You actually think those guys run for office because they want to help *you?* Once again you strike me as the type of guy who believed his teacher. What was your history teacher, Dubecheck? The basketball coach or the football coach?"

Dubecheck's plane doesn't fly. He opens it up.

"The football coach. Of course I believed my history book. Why would they take the trouble to lie to a guy like me?" Dubecheck scans the crinkled pink paper. "What's this mean? The 205th VC regiment is coming this way. What for? Who says? Are we supposed to know? And if so, why?"

"Maybe they're going to have a unit reunion. How do I know? I'm in intelligence. I figure if they're on their way here they're coming to kill people; that's what they do, isn't it?"

"Better call the cavalry. Hey, give me a free fire zone. The congressman wants to go outside and play guns and Tuta wants me to take him. Tuta wants me to be his friend too."

"Tuta wants you to be his friend?"

"Yes. He says he's never had a friend. I wonder why he wants to start now?"

"Maybe he's having problems with Madame Phong. Maybe he wants you as a sort of a pet. He couldn't, you know, want you as like a human friend. From what little I know, he doesn't think much of you."

"Why? How can you say that?"

"The only thing he's asked me in the last two months is, 'Is that Dubecheck as stupid as he looks?' "

"Really?"

"Really. So maybe he wants you as a pet. Like some lonely people have a dog or something they can talk to and it never answers. It's just there to sort of validate themselves."

"Well, I'm not too crazy about being his friend or the congressman's tour guide either."

"Why not? Maybe you're on the fast track, Dubecheck." Dupree lights a cigarette with a cigarette lighter he took off a VC prisoner who took it off a dead GI.

"Well, to tell the truth, authority figures make me nervous. Hotshots, big wheels, whatever you call them, they kind of upset me and I try and avoid them. Besides, I never know what to say. I don't have much in common with them."

Dubecheck tries to envision what the congressman must look like. He's never seen one alive. A United States senator from Idaho came into a postgame locker room once but he was surrounded by a bunch of men in topcoats and members of the press, so Dubecheck never saw him. He saw John F. Kennedy ride by in a limousine once when he was a senator. He was in the back seat but he was waving out the other side to a larger crowd. He always felt a little uneasy thinking about John F. Kennedy. He was embarrassed by the fact that he seemed to be the only person who didn't know where he was when Kennedy had half his head blown off. It was a Friday. He remembered that.

"But you know, for a lower-middle-class pig like yourself, Dubecheck, you couldn't hurt yourself by fawning before this cat like he's some oriental potentate. They all think they're pretty slick and actually believe it when other people pretend to think so too."

Dubecheck picks up a three-foot-by-five-foot mural of the lower Mekong Delta and puts it on Dupree's desk. "Pick a spot that's good for my op then." He traces his finger over a tributary to the Dong My River. "Hey, how come this is a free fire zone? I've been there. Human beings live there, Dupree."

"Yeah. But what kind of a life is it, Dubecheck? Think about it. Poverty, ignorance, disease, pestilence. That's where the four horsemen work their steeds out, man."

"Who?"

"The Four Horsemen of the Apocalypse, asshole. What do you *know*, Dubecheck? I mean, what do you *really* know?"

"Really?"

"Really."

"I know how to do a Z out, a post, a buttonhook and a basic 'fly.' And to prove I'm a Renaissance man, I can squat on my knees and give one for a fast ball and two for a curve. You know, everybody treats me like I don't know how the world works. Well, I don't, but I'm not sure I want to."

"It's very simple how it works. I've got inside information. The object of life on earth, as we know it, is to make a buck. Anything to the contrary is just lip service from those with chips on their shoulders and sour grapes in their mouths."

Co Bihn chuckles from her desk, intent on her romance comic. Dubecheck wonders what's so funny. Every one of those stupid books he's seen, particularly the ones Co Bihn reads, contains nothing but close-ups of people kissing or girls crying tears the size of dimes. They're certainly not funny. Hieronymus Bosch is funny when you get right down to it.

Dubecheck peruses the map. "This is very interesting. See here where there's an island on this chart? Well, the island moved. It's over here now. This map must be a week old. That's what I like about the Orient. Its changelessness."

"You just said the island changed location. What's changeless about that?"

"Well, things are always changing but it looks the same, if you catch my drift. And then they're not changing and sort of look different. You oughta get out there sometime, Dupree. It'll do things to your head that aren't entirely bad."

"I think you need some R and R."

"I think you should take a hike in a free fire zone. I love that phrase, 'free fire zone.' I like going into . . . *zones*. They sound like unnatural places but you'd be surprised. You know, a free fire zone is so quiet. Like a Japanese tea garden or something. But you can hear insects hum and see little creatures dart here and there. Birds jump from limb to limb on these funny-looking trees that look like they're losing their skin, like they're molting or something."

"Defoliants, Lieutenant."

"Whatever. You move the dead vegetation from your face like cobwebs. It's like walking into an old attic without a roof. If you can see what I mean."

"I didn't know you did pot."

"I don't. Really. I just get drunk. My fingers are too thick to roll joints and it just doesn't appeal to me. Getting drunk appeals to me. Zones appeal to me. People who *create* zones appeal to me. You ever hear that song: 'Who put the Ram in the Ramma lamma ding dong? Who put the bop in the shu-dop du-bop?' Sure you have. Anyway, the gist of it is the guy singing the song wants to shake his hand, whoever did all that, because it made his baby fall in love with him. Gratitude. That's how I feel about guys who create free fire zones and long-range planning contingencies for people who aren't dead yet."

Dupree stares at Dubecheck for a long moment. "You're a strange duck, Dubecheck. You are trying to tell me you're kind. I know better. You're a ruthless thug."

"I'm a running dog of imperialism. You ever hear that song, 'Running Bear Loved Little White Dove'?"

"Of course I have."

Co Bihn has turned to look at the two American officers with a strange look on her face. Bulging at the joints of her tight ao-dai, she reminds Dubecheck of sausages. Food.

"Well, I rewrote the lyrics once when we were out on the river coming back from an op. Except I called it 'Running Dog.' You want to hear it?"

"No."

"I do, Diwi." Co Bihn smiles at Dubecheck, her fat cheeks like yellow dumplings. Dubecheck thinks that after the revolution, when the bad guys win, all those skinny little dudes who've been running barefoot through the jungle on a cup of rice a day are going to eat her.

Dubecheck starts what he considers an Indian dance, popping his palm over his mouth. " 'Uuuga Uuuga, Uuuga, Uuuga Uuuga Uuuga. Running Dog loved little White Dove with a love that wouldn't die. Running Dog loved little White Dove with a love as big as the sky.' "

"Please stop it."

He does and hops up on Dupree's desk. "Look. Find me a nice clean spot where we can't kill anything or where everything's already been killed. I don't suppose the guy wants to see a dead body, does he? Jesus, what if he wants a body count? I bet he'll want to shoot at something, won't he? With a real gun. He probably was in the Big One, right? Why's this happening?"

"According to his PR sheet," says Dupree, flipping through a dossier, "Kealy's among those who believe in the vigorous prosecution of our efforts in Southeast Asia."

"How come they never call it the 'war' in Southeast Asia? Remember that 'incursion' up on the border last week? In the olden days that would have been called a full-scale frontal attack by ARVN suicide squads."

"How about here?" Dupree draws a circle on a patch of map.

"You tell me, you're the intelligence officer. Throwing a dart, is that what you're doing?"

"Why don't you want to kill anything? That's all enemy territory."

"Hey. I like to blow things up as much as the next kid. Geysers of dirt, loud thumps, a whump, a kaboom here and there, hey, sign me up. It's genetic, but as for the killing, I'm not too keen. I don't feel *threatened*, like, until they open up on me and then, when they do, I just want to get outta Dodge. I mean, I'm going home, they gotta live here."

"You got a no-win attitude, mister."

"Just the opposite. It's an all-win attitude. I put it all on a personal level. An equation. X don't hurt me, I don't hurt X. He keeps a low profile, mine's lower. I will advise my relief to do the same and we all go home safe and sound. At the lowest level, I figure it's two less dead guys in the world. Cut the embalmers a little slack for an hour or so. Leave space on the air hearse for someone more or less deserving. One less American flag to sell to drape over my cut-rate coffin. Save everyone a trumpet solo over my dead one at Arlington. Dial everything in the chain down by one. Click. Back one. No Dubecheck in the equation."

"So you won't fight for your country. I get it."

"Right. You and Kooseman can fight for my country. I'll fight for my life. Gotta get back to the motherland and think about makin' a buck, right? And *you* brief this guy. I can't. I don't know what's going on. And I want to know what your horseshit briefing is sorta like so I can pretend to know what you think you know and that guy thinks he thinks he knows."

"No problem. Facts. Nothing but the facts."

"And hurry up. I've spent too much time in this room of yours already. It reminds me of the military. I've got an op this afternoon and I want this congressman crap settled so I can plan that picnic. I want him off my boat as fast as possible and hope he doesn't remember my name."

"What op? Why don't I know about your op today?"

"Why should you? Do you have a need to know? Snazzy wants to go out and try to kill some guys so they can raise the body count and shorten the war."

"I need to know so I can coordinate the activity in this area into a cohesive overall plan. That hurts my feelings. Why don't you guys ever tell me what you're doing? You never, ever tell me."

"Because I, for one, don't know what we're doing. This is intell from Phu. He says an evil tax collector is leaning on some poor peasants in this hamlet just into Kien Hoa."

"My ass. Phu fingers guys who owe him money or he owes money to and we waste them. We're just glorified hit men for Phu's markers."

"Civil war."

"Why doesn't Snazzy ever take a prisoner so I can talk to one and get some *intelligence?*"

"I brought one in yesterday and you gave him to the Gestapo."

"It's the law. The guy broke a federal law. He got caught trying to violently overthrow the government. You know what? You oughta take the congressman on a real hairy dark spooky out in the middle of nowhere that'll make him shit in his knickers."

"Those make me shit *my* knickers and I only do them under strict orders. Besides, what if he died?"

"His wife could fill out the rest of his term. One less U.S. congressman in the world would just make it that more of a safer place to live. You want to hear my briefing?"

"You got it already?"

"Yeah. Just about. See this?" He shows Dubecheck a piece of paper with four columns containing ten words each. "This is invaluable. Take one word from each and match it with a word from the other three columns and it sounds like you're saying something. Read across the top for drill."

"Substantially-relate-viable-input."

"Nice. Give me, ah . . . one, two, three, four."

"Substantially-minimize-overlapping-output."

"Terrific. Even you could give a briefing. Try another. Four-six-seven-ten."

"Exponentially-maximize-primary-analysis."

"See? I just punch in a few heavies like 'VC' or 'National Liberation Front,' 'Chiang Kai-shek,' anything I want, point to a map with a swagger stick, look glum, starch my fatigues and they'll all sit there and nod, solemn as shit, thinking they're privy to grave matters of great import. It works every time." Dupree chuckles and snatches up the paper. "Orally collate optimum alternative . . . fully orient a realistic profile. This stuff is good. Make sure you're at the briefing. I'll start with a few droll jokes—you know, a little jaunty gallows humor to bring home a bit of gallant levity to this portentous event known as limited war—then it'll be stern city from then on out."

"And you'll try and tell them what we try to do?"

"Yeah. I'll try and tell them what they think we're trying to do and then tell them that we're doing it and overcoming all odds while we're at it and couldn't do it if it wasn't for them. You think I'm going to tell them that some jerk like Phu has a hard-on for his brother-in-law, says Nguyen Nguyen is a VC and the whole local garrison of the U. S. Army, Navy and Air Force goes out, wrecks his hooch and half the fucking county while they're at it? You want me to tell them the only way to win this war is to switch sides? It'd be over in a week and everybody could get back to raising rice. These people don't care who's in charge, they just want to grow their rice and live to the ripe old age of forty. So we kill VC. You've seen how these people breed, for Christsakes. There's a never ending supply of them. And I *worry* about my agents. They work too hard. They put in a day shift for me, the swing shift for the enemy and procreate the rest of the time. That guy 'a' yours? Phu? He's worked for the Japanese, the French, the Viet Minh, the NVA, the ARVN, you, them, we, they—and he still does. He must have a stack of W-2s at the end of the year that looks like the Phoenix phone book."

"He wants to go to California."

"They should all go to California. The gangsters in Washington, D.C., claimed, after they cooked the books, to have spent thirty billion here last fiscal year. For each guy they kill, they figure they spent a lot of money. They ought to Chieu Hoi the suckers for what they spend wasting them, get 'em a round-trip first-class air fare to Disneyland and ruin 'em for life. They could probably set each one of them up in business. Buy 'em liquor stores. It's a state law in California that there has to be one every four hundred feet or something."

"He wants to go to California, meet a blonde and buy some Levi's."

"See? Send 'em all. No more war ever in the world as soon as the whole world is America. You ought to take this congressman for a ride and leave him on a small island at low tide. That island that moves. Christ, he'll have some aides with him, though. And some Jimmy Olson-type cub reporter, and they'll all be getting their rocks off walking around in their GI fatigues, just like real soldiers. And I just know it, they'll give Phil a baseball cap with scrambled eggs on the brim like he's top brass. I'm getting ill thinking about it."

"Why don't you come on the show with me? You could frag him. Or come along with me today. You could lie in the sun. Bring your cassette."

"Why would I want to go on a combat operation anyway? I'm not stupid."

Dubecheck gets off the desk and stretches. "Something to tell your grandkids or the boys at the VFW about when you're drunk thirty years from now and the operation is a legend in your own mind."

"Yeah, maybe. I don't know. Lookit all this shit. It's all nothing but drivel." He shuffles a hundred sheets of paper. "We be back by 1900?"

Dubecheck shrugs. "I dunno. Probably. Why?"

"I don't want to miss 'Laugh-In.' "

13 Across an old, ramped footbridge leading to a part of town considered unsafe at night, at least unsafe for people of the American persuasion, lies the chieu hoi camp.

Scoog had told Dubecheck that Recore had gone over there with Phu and Snazzy to see if they could get some "hot intell." That meant finding out where some guys might be whom they could ambush and kill pretty soon and shorten the war.

Dubecheck's vast comprehension of military history has told him that the object of a military force that wishes to win a war is to kill off the enemy until there's not enough of them left to fight anymore on a level that creates big problems. Anybody involved in taking Real War 101 realizes this. To do that, you have to find out where they are. That is accomplished around Dong My by talking to spies, informants, turncoats, prostitutes, tattletales, liars and chieu hois.

The chieu hoi program is another terrific idea probably put forth by a couple of strong-jawed, cleft-chinned squash players in Washington, D.C. The guys whom Dubecheck always sees in his nightmares as the ones coming up with the ideas that keep him involved in Southeast Asia.

It is essentially a half-assed amnesty program for the enemy. If they give up and quit fighting the government, the Americans, the Australians and the Koreans, they can spend the rest of the war in some open-air barbed-wire compound wearing maroon shorts and maroon T-shirts.

Many of the chieu hois don't make up their minds to come over to the other side until they are surrounded by a massive amount of lethal firepower wielded by terribly aggravated American teenagers. The thought of all that awesome destructive machinery in the hands of someone as generally unbalanced as the average American teenager deeply impresses Dubecheck. That most chieu hois shouted "Chieu hoi" as an option to having their brainpans vaporized, as opposed to flat laying down their arms and coming to their senses and capitulating to the good graces and common sense of the other side, leads Dubecheck to distrust them. Walking into a chieu hoi camp is a weird sensation.

Dubecheck enters the chieu hoi compound, leaving his pistol with an ARVN soldier at the huge barbed-wire gate. He is instantly reminded of a swarm of penguins. Hundreds of skinny, knobby-kneed, black-haired Asian men, each one a foot shorter than he, mill about in maroon shorts and maroon T-shirts. They all sulk and glance furtively out of the corners of their dark eyes as Dubecheck passes through them. Everyone in the compound, including Dubecheck, is asking himself the same question: Should I *know* this guy?

The ground is as bare as if pecked clean by a thousand chickens; a few scattered trees cast small circles of shade under which mill some obvious heavies, smoking Salems in their private oasis and trying hard not to scope Dubecheck.

Dubecheck spots Recore, Phu and Snazzy talking to a guy over by the cement cistern, which is the sole source of water for the place. A feed lot. That's what it's like, thinks Dubecheck, except there's no lowing of hungry cattle . . . just a pervasive stench of human manure hanging thickly in the air, the pleasant sound of brackish water trickling into the cistern and bare feet shuffling in hard red dirt. The man Recore, Snazzy and Phu talk to looks nervous. His eyes move quickly so as not to light on anything for long. He constantly sucks at a nubbin of cigarette until Recore shakes out another one for him. He takes it, looks around and lights up with the butt of the other. He doesn't look happy.

He has purplish welts on his face and scabs and scars on his skinny legs and arms. It is hard to tell how old he is. Somewhere between thirty and sixty. Dubecheck can't begin to imagine how many times in this guy's life he's been hit, kicked, shot at and harassed.

Phu says something, sharp and harsh, then slaps the chieu hoi twice, high up on the side of his head. The man cringes and covers his head with his arms and shouts something back. Phu kicks out at him and the man, knock-kneed, backs against the cistern.

"Come on, Phu. I mean, really." Phu, Recore and Snazzy turn to see Dubecheck. "This is embarrassing, isn't it?"

"He's just getting his attention, Diwi." Recore smiles and pats Dubecheck on the shoulder.

The man balances himself with one hand to keep from falling into the cistern and looks warily at Dubecheck and then to the ground where his cigarette has fallen and now sends up tantalizing coils of smoke. He is afraid to reach for it. Everyone looks down at the cigarette, then back to the man. Phu puts his foot out and slowly grinds the cigarette into the red dirt. Snazzy emits a low whistle and looks to Dubecheck.

"These people are stone *cold*. Let's get outta here anyway. The place gives me the creeps and this guy's full o' shit. You really think, Recore, this cat's gonna rat on his friends with four hundred gooks wired to him? Look around, man. If I were this guy I'd sleep on my back tonight."

"Hey, you never know. A man's gotta do what he's gotta do."

"What's that mean?"

Recore looks puzzled by Dubecheck's question, shrugs, then walks off through the idle throng of chieu hois, nodding to his right and left and cheerfully chattering, "Nguyen, Nguyen, morning, Nguyen . . . Nguyen, Nguyen . . . Nguyen, Nguyen."

Dubecheck looks back to see the man at the cistern on his knees intently trying to reshape the mangled cigarette.

"Does this mean the op's off? That would be great because I don't feel too hot. That's why I came here. I don't feel too hot."

"How'd it go with Tuta?"

"Fine. He doesn't feel too hot either. Nobody I know feels too hot unless you're talking about the heat and then everybody I know is too hot."

Snazzy and Recore take their guns from the pimply-faced, four-foot-five ARVN noncom who has kept them in the drawer of a wooden desk that looks awfully strange sitting in the dirt outside the barbed-wire gate.

"What you need then is some fresh air and a little action. So . . . over the top."

"Anchors aweigh." Snazzy smiles and checks the safety on his .38.

Recore rams a clip into the grip of his pistol, smooches the barrel and smiles. "In harm's way. 'Heigh-ho, heigh-ho, it's off to work we go.'"

Recore and Snazzy soft-shoe into the siesta-emptied street, scuffling in the dust, arm in arm, singing, "'Heigh-ho, heigh-ho, it's off to work we go,'" as Phu smiles behind them, skipping to keep up.

Dubecheck again remembers why this war stuff never seems to end. A lot of guys really like it.

o   o   o

More thought would have to be given to the idea that he was among nothing more than an elite tribe of preening chimpanzees. Or more likely the "missing link" between apes and men. Something happened to a guy out in the swamps and jungles. An awareness of one's relationship to something ancient and primordial would surface if you let it. Dinosaurish. That was it. A nagging feeling not too deep inside that hinted of extinction.

He is drawn once again into the concept of the ephemerality of all things past, present and future. Recore, Snazzy and Phu are out of sight. Gone. Memories. All the chieu hois are nothing but phantoms and wraiths in his memory bank, matterless, maybe electrical molecules, maybe nothing. What the hell's a memory made out of anyway? Pictures in the brain. God knows what makes them show. The chieu hois *were* real men in a real cage, now they mean nothing that he could put a finger on.

He would go to the real boys in his command and shake them awake, feel their warm skin, tacky and sweaty, and smell their pungent sour odor. Real boys who will sit up, groan and rub their eyes open and blink in the heat, sitting in their olive-drab shorts with dog tags around their necks that have their name and blood type on them. Information of use to corpsmen, surgeons or Graves Registration. One of those boys he wakes up could be dead in a couple of hours, setting into motion a flurry of official paperwork, telegrams and finally a few Hallmark greeting cards expressing deepest sympathy and regret in the floridly elegant script also found on dollar-fifty valentines.

The sentry in the sandbagged cage at the entrance to the hotel stares ahead with glazed eyes. He sits on a stool in his flak jacket and helmet with an M-16 across his lap, trying to stay awake in the ovenlike heat. He is charged with stopping any suspicious-looking character trying to enter the hotel, but since that covers everyone within five hundred miles, the billet is nothing more than a torture chamber for sleep deprivation.

"The mail get here yet?"

He grunts, which Dubecheck takes to mean either it has or it hasn't and realizes he doesn't care one way or another anyway.

The mail's no longer the big deal it was. The first letters were like transfusions from a happy, clean, sorely missed part of the world. But time made that world an illusion, a bizarre memory, and this world became the only reality. He only got letters from two sources anyway. His pen pals were Mom and his girlfriend, who was really nobody more than some young woman he met at a dance and took to bars and played the ritual courtship game with, a game that has at its conclusion a vaguely assumed marriage. The girlfriend had clung to him with quick desperation, one of acquaintance and desire that confused itself with love and led to a false assumption of possession. And he, like any young man wandering from home, adrift, ambling along in the vast lonely swarm of the military, responded to it, willing to trade loneliness and fear for the comfort inherent in alliance and tagging it love. A couple of suckers at heart.

He never really wrote her, he just responded to her. Soon the letters referred to how "busy" she was getting, a hint that letters might not come with as much frequency as before, which was fine with him because it sometimes became painful to read the tortured, laborious attempts to vary a rather simple and ultimately indefensible theme: how much she loved him and missed him. After a while certain words became meaningless from overuse. At least he couldn't imagine them meaning anything, but one never knows what other people believe. To his amazement he finds that people sometimes do love, trust, honor and obey things he can't imagine people loving, trusting, honoring or obeying.

He should let her off the hook, but selfishly realizes how he needs her letters. They're nothing but a drop in the bucket but the bucket's empty. And how would he go about letting her off the hook anyway?

Dear Honeybunch.
Stop writing to me about the simple, draining inanities of your existence, the weather and the emptiness of your life without me, because these are linking me to a nausea I choose not to feel, for if I am that which can fulfill you, you are in a world of shit so deep it is far beyond my ability to extract you.
Love, Skookums.

Honeybunch and Skookums. Facetious little nicknames they gave each other. Jesus, Dubecheck thinks, what a bunch of hapless comedians.

The letters from Mother, arriving with the bimonthly precision of dunning notes, have a comforting, monotonous similarity to them, as if they were a maternal form letter spit out by the rumbling presses of the U. S. Government. The Mark I American Mother's Letter to Sons at War. He could trade his letter with letters from Scoog's, Recore's or McDowell's mother and get essentially the same news.

The letters consist of the opening weather paragraph. The weather's "beautiful" or "terrible," or the prevailing climatological patterns for centuries have become, of a sudden, unique. It was always curiously comforting, however, to know what the weather had been like when the letter was written. Very curious, for that weather was at least two to three weeks old. Old weather, information either preposterously meaningless or primordially essential.

They could sit around over their letters and talk to each other. "How's the weather in your letter?"

"Hot and muggy. It's never been as hot and muggy for as long as she can remember. How about yours?"

"Rain. She can't remember it raining so much this time of year."

Letters from mothers were no more or less than life carved in stone. After the weather, a roll call of incidents and accidents befalling acquaintances, relatives or friends, how luck is shaking down for a small circle of humans in a small locale, the fact that a distant Cousin Ronald got a trombone, the fact that a bizarre disease attacked an aging neighbor, an old paper route customer, a brief mention of something that has afflicted the writer . . . a pain here or a pain there, a sore back from turning left instead of right, death probing with its indifferent invisible fingers, and over it all a stoic forbearance porous enough to convey a subtle plea for commiseration, condolence, concern or communion.

The final paragraph of the Mark I American Mother's Letter is an admonition to take care of oneself, a "be sure and put your rubbers on" admonition. Mothers didn't have a clue. Dubecheck felt American mothers must see their sons' war as a vague, playground type of affair. Paper hats and wooden swords. Boys whacking each other on flat fields of green grass, stopping to go home for dinner, a warm bath and bed.

The war on the telly, six o'clock national news, was nothing more than clips from an ongoing movie and, since it was nothing more than a movie, could not be entirely believed.

American mothers could never really believe the war was real until some guy walked up to their front door to tell them how sorry the government was that their kid was dead. Dubecheck had seen it, on leave in the States with a friend whose job was to tell mothers their kid was dead and where they could claim the remains. "Remains" was another perfectly apt term for what was left of some of the mothers' sons. Body chunks, a triceps, a shredded pec, tibias, fibias and ulnas, and bone shards, a slab of cooked flesh or teeth like Chiclets in a little transparent Baggy just like the one they use to put his sack lunch sandwich in.

"Please, Dubecheck. Please. Ya gotta come with me today. It's a drag, man. Really." Captain D. D. Scarvie, U. S. Army and childhood chum, pleading with Dubecheck. "You don't have to do anything. Just sit in the car and watch and don't let me drink until I'm done."

So Dubecheck, on leave, in his civvies, rode along in an olive-drab government sedan with white numbers on the side while Captain Scarvie drove to a nice little neighborhood to tell some American mother her son was dead and that he and the whole United States Army and the President of the United States were sorry. Really.

Scarvie went up the walk in a light gray rain, oddly stopping to polish the tip of his right shoe on the back of his left calf before turning to look at Dubecheck with an idiotic, twisted grin on his face. He shook his head, shrugged, then continued up the walk and knocked on the door, a large manila envelope under his arm, a well-dressed door-to-door salesman, erect, his deep forest-green uniform splotched with raindrops.

Dubecheck, listening to a commercial for pimple cream on a rock and roll station, became transfixed by the scene that unfolded at the doorway, as if it was taking place underwater, slowly, soundless, a pantomime of grief as the Mark I American Mother slumped against the doorway, then dragged her hands down her face, distorting it, then gingerly took the manila envelope from Scarvie as if it might explode in her hands, nodding to Scarvie, then wordlessly offering him to come in, but Scarvie backing away a few steps with his arms spread out, looking as if he'd like to turn and run. The mother mouthing, "Thank you," and rubbing her face, staring down onto the doorstep as the pimple cream commercial ended and a commercial for mouthwash started. Scarvie entered the house and the door closed. Dubecheck turned off the radio and could hear the rain tap on the roof of the olive-drab government vehicle in uneven rhythm.

A slow cup of coffee's worth of time passed and presently Scarvie emerged from the little box house and walked back to the vehicle and looked around the empty neighborhood as if to see if there were any witnesses. The door to the house closed behind him and everything looked the same in the neighborhood as it had before Scarvie got there and told the mother her son was dead.

"Now." Scarvie sat behind the wheel and looked out the blurry windshield as Dubecheck reached under the seat and pulled out a pint of Imperial whiskey wrapped in a wrinkled brown bag and handed it to the captain.

"They always want you to come inside for a while. I think they want you to come inside and be their son for a little while. I think. I dunno. You're supposed to go inside and be nice. I mean, what the fuck's ten minutes?" Scarvie slid down in his seat and took a long pull from the bottle, screwed on the top and slid back up. "It's a long fucking time is what it is. Long enough to smell every stinking smell in their house because you can smell better when it's quiet and then they think somehow you were the guy's best friend and can tell them all about it. You know what the hard part is? The hard part for me is . . . to not start laughing. To not burst out laughing in their faces. Know what I mean?"

"Yeah."

"Yeah. Isn't that weird?"

"No." Dubecheck could smell the whiskey on Scarvie's breath sweetly fill the damp air and feel the rain beat into the roof like soft nails. "This is really fun, D.D. We'll have to do this again sometime when I'm on leave."

"Yeah, sure. Sorry. Let's go pick up some chicks. You know how they like cars." Scarvie laughed as he pulled out in the olive-drab government sedan.

o   o   o

Dubecheck gets to the top floor of the old hotel and looks over the railing down toward the little white charnel house and remembers the wailing woman from yesterday and is surprised to see her standing next to "Mama-san," the hooch maid for the third floor. She's apparently applied for a job because Mama-san is demonstrating how to mop a floor while the young woman watches and nods studiously.

"Mawnin', Diwi." Mama-san smiles, showing a mouth full of gold teeth, nodding her head up and down, holding the mop handle, standing barefoot in a puddle of gray water. She had told Dubecheck she walked down from the north to flee Communists twenty years ago. She's had four husbands and sometimes admonishes

Dubecheck for not hanging up his rotten fatigues as if she were a Mark I Asian Mother. He caught her being fucked by Sisler once, her hands against the wall, standing up as if she was to be frisked, except Sisler was thrusting in and out of her with his pants down around his ankles. She made five dollars.

"Mawnin', Mama-san." Dubecheck notices the young woman's eyes are still red-rimmed, her lips pale purple. She stares into the mop bucket and picks at her fingernails, avoiding Dubecheck's gaze. He notices how young she is close up. Time is a funny thing. Things change. He can't imagine what she was doing a week ago, but now she has a dead husband and a new job.

Over the partition separating his room from that of most of his crew, he can hear his men chattering over their mail. On his desk he sees his, a single envelope he recognizes as the same one used by a Chevrolet dealer in San Diego to stuff with flyers about all the great deals he has on Stingrays and Corvairs.

He flops down on his rack, the springs sagging into a hammock, and listens to the crew swap bits of information gleaned from their respective letters. They'd never make it in a Hollywood movie. They're all just plain, ugly Anglo-Saxons. No wiseacre, no lady killer, no coward, no rich kid, no bully, no weakling, nobody from Brooklyn and nobody who plays sad songs on a harmonica. Zeller plays the electric guitar, though. A cheap Fender plugged into an amplifier the size of a case of beer, that he bought from the Japanese. He practices "Louie, Louie" over and over on it until someone rips out the cord and then he quietly stows it behind his bunk until the urge to twang strikes again. Losers. The first indication that they're losers is that they are here. No top-down arm around the floozy with a belly full o' beer bombing down the road for some be-bop-a-lula in one of Weschler-Downing Chevrolet's Nothing Down, Eight Percent GMAC Financing Corvettes.

He should clean his M-16. So it won't jam in case a covey of crazed Vietnamese men come storming out of the bushes like drunken Apaches with their Russian assault rifles, making enough noise to wake the dead. Maybe he'll have Mama-san clean it for him, she cleans everything else. He reaches over and opens the drawer to the desk and pulls out a large manila folder to peruse the Personnel File he keeps on his men. They fascinate him and he has so few in his command, it affords him the luxury of knowing more about them than he needs to.

He is amazed Scoog is only twenty-eight. He looks a lot more worn and haggard than that. He fingers the files, skimming the book on their lives, where they're from, where they get to go, what they did wrong and what he has to do to see that they don't do it again. There's Scoog's sick bay report . . . CLAP at top. And next to it a soiled envelope containing a letter from his irate wife in National City, California, saying she is either going to leave him or start messing around herself like some of the cheap sluts she could name but won't. She had found out he'd gotten a "social disease" from a true rumor that had found its way back across the Pacific like a virulent strain of its own, and eventually Dubecheck became involved in a familial soap opera of less than mythic proportion. Lieutenant (jg) John Paul Dubecheck, Officer of the Line, United States Navy, sucked into a minor maelstrom of marital discord by the tears of his leading petty officer. He wrote Mrs. Scoog—he never did find out her first name, Scoog referring to her only as "that crazy bitch" or worse. And as he wrote he imagined her reading the letter over her ironing board, a cigarette dangling from her mouth, the TV two feet away blaring, "The Price Is Right," standing in black slacks with her shirt hanging out like Tuta, for Scoog did mention she was on the plumpish side, ". . . from all the fuckin' Twinkies she shoves down her throat."

Maybe a tear would roll down her cheek as she read what he wrote and he assumed she would take his letter as gospel because enlisted men's wives believe officers, they believe that officers would never lie because honorable gentlemen don't have to, lying is only for slugs like their husbands, who didn't have the brains or breeding to become commissioned Leaders of Men. In the letter he stated that Rodney was "one of the finest men he'd ever commanded," that his behavior was "beyond reproach," whatever that meant, and that Rodney didn't have gonorrhea but merely a case of, as opposed to a dose of, nonspecific urethritis, NSU, "something altogether different." He didn't tell her that NSU is what clap is called when an officer gets it. The letter worked and Rodney was forgiven via the Fleet Post Office.

He wonders why he helped Scoog by lying to his wife. Maybe it was because it hurt to see Scoog crying real tears before him.

In the confessional atmosphere that can often exist between an enlisted man and his officer, Scoog unloaded. He was one of those people who got to be born so they could be beaten, abandoned and subsequently institutionally abused. He showed Dubecheck the faded, eraser-tip-size pink freckles on his forearms and thighs where Mommy or Daddy put their lighted cigarette butts. Authorities took him into protective custody, a little runt to be shunted from one "Home" to another, terrorized, thrashed, corn-holed and duped until the rising sun was enough to make him flinch.

"Bummer, Scoog."

"Really."

He was touched to see Scoog was really frightened of losing his wife, even though he would refer to her only in the most abusive terms. It always made Dubecheck wonder what all the ugly couples he saw wandering around together back in America saw in each other; other than just another human who would have them. He figured it must be an easier row to hoe, this planet, if maybe two of you could sort of circle the wagons against the daily shit storm of getting by.

Then again, he couldn't have his leading petty officer going around down in the old dumps and not keeping his mind on his job —which was to do most of Dubecheck's work for him.

After that episode, Scoog had followed Dubecheck closely, wanting not only to do good but to be good. He became a model sailor. He cleaned himself and wore relatively clean fatigues into combat for the same perverse reason one wears clean underwear in case they're in a wreck. He didn't drink for a week and seemed to start suffering from nitrogen narcosis or "rapture of the deep" until Dubecheck forced him to have a few beers, to sort of ease up the transition into sobriety. The nicotine stains faded from his fingers and his fingernails lost their black rime. Dubecheck watched the man embarrass himself for the worst of all possible reasons, gratitude. Dubecheck tried to get him to go get drunk with his rotten friends.

"I'd rather not, sir." Scoog stood at attention, his eyes gazing heroically over Dubecheck's shoulder at the wall, a noble Billy Budd jut to his jaw. *"Rather"*—Dubecheck would bet he'd never used the word in his life until then.

"But I'd rather you would. I like you better when you're drunk, hung over and stink." He smiled but Scoog didn't, and for a moment he wondered if he had offended him.

"I'm sorry, Scoog. I—"

"That's okay, sir. I understand."

"Really?"

"Yes, sir. See, when you've been a shithead for so long and all your friends are shitheads and all you're ever going to be is a shithead, your friends don't want you not to be a shithead because they're afraid that if you're not a shithead anymore then what they stand for is just that more worse than they thought their whole shithead life was anyway."

"Really. Huh. Well, in that case, carry on."

And Scoog gave Dubecheck a boot camp salute, beginning somewhere down near his kneecaps and coming to a rigid bow-twanging halt above his brow, snapped it smartly back down, about-faced and walked away with that bouncing optimistic gait reserved for true believers.

Like most great changes in life, Scoog's return to normalcy happened without his knowledge.

Walking around a corner, he was hit on the head by a pallet on the tines of a forklift driven by the black sailor with electric pink socks who carried *Soul on Ice* around in his pocket. Scoog was knocked unconscious and lay in the dirt while a few people looked down on him and wondered if he were alive.

"Who is he?"

"I think he's one a' those guys that goes fucks around on the river."

Strangers in town from a PBR squadron, scratching their heads and their asses and wondering what to do.

"The dude walk around the corner not lookin'." The black sailor with the pink socks lit a cigarette and started covering his ass. Just in case. "And that's the motherfuckin' truth."

"He dead?"

"Sure. Sheeit. That's why his chest still goin' up and down. All the little angels inside pumpin' him up so he can float to heaven. Sheeit—no, he ain't dead. Le's drag his ass in the shade."

They dragged Scoog into the shade and went to get help but then forgot about him and Scoog woke up several hours later with a sunburn because the shade had moved. But he took his reprieve from death seriously. He decided not to spend the gift of life in a somber display of good works and high ideals. He reasoned that, if a man can lose his life by just minding his own business and walking around a corner, then the whole scheme of things was way beyond him and those notions of right living were just useless ballast. If how you live your life doesn't have a damn thing to do with whether or not you get to keep it, then you might as well play it with the hand you're dealt.

"The Lord dealt me a weak hand, sir. Fives and treys. A low-ball hand in a high-ball game, so I gotta go with what He gave me. I'm a fuckin' sailor, sir. Can I borrow ten?"

And he spent it all on Seven Sevens for a day and night down at the EM Club getting back up to speed, vomiting upon himself, and having a good time. Everyone he knew was happy to have him back into the huge fold of shithead existence.

"We're all ready, sir. Is there a briefing?"

Dubecheck looks up to see the star of his reverie standing in the doorway.

"No, Scoog." Dubecheck rolls off his bunk and springs to his feet. "Move 'em out, as they say."

"Yes, sir." And he leaves, cursing his men with that gregarious belligerence which gets lesser people to do things they don't want to.

Dubecheck leans over the railing and watches Scoog walk down the filthy street with his crew. They amble along like scruffy Cub Scouts, chewing gum, smoking, kicking trash before their feet, chattering, laughing and grab-assing until they disappear around the corner. Dubecheck thinks that just a little while ago they probably were Cub Scouts.

14 Traveling by boat is a nice way to see the country. From the air it's just a patchwork plaid of olive drab, but cruising down the river is just right. Beyond the suburbs and out in Indian country the scenery is clean, lush, pleasant enough. Dubecheck sees a water buffalo with horns trying to mount another water buffalo. It keeps slipping off while the cow just chews her cud, oblivious to the bull's frustration.

McDowell has been asking Dubecheck questions, mostly designed to show how intelligent he is rather than to bag some answers. Since his talk with Dubecheck is about God this morning, he has erroneously assumed a line of intelligent communication has been opened up between the two and, like most young enlisted men, McDowell has also erroneously assumed Dubecheck's commission came complete with intellect. He has been using words like "germain" and "destiny" and they have been beading on Dubecheck's brain like rain on a wax job.

"Leave me alone, McDowell. Don't you have something to do?"

"You already asked me that, sir, and when I didn't have anything to do you told me to move mortars and I've already done
that."

"Oh." He sees McDowell standing hopefully beside him. All the
young man wants is to talk to someone a cut above the subhuman
sect he must live with twenty-four hours a day.

"Well, where were we then?" Why not listen to him? As Captain
Scarvie says, "What the fuck's ten minutes?"

Everything seems secure; from down below he can hear the comforting sound of a couple of sailors playing liar's dice with a cup
they stole from some Honolulu bar. The engines grind properly and
the scenery is beginning to suck again. Not that it isn't pretty. The
sun is dipping toward the yardarm, the sky a fuzzy rusty haze, the
palms ragged against the sky, the dry rice paddies turning an unfortunate olive drab as the Delta begins its long afternoon nap. No, it's
pretty but it's just monotonous, and out there in the vegetation and
beneath the clouds and haze is something going on that defies reason, logic and faith and makes it not so pretty.

"Destiny, sir."

"Destiny and whether or not I believe in God. I don't know
from destiny or God. I know I'm twenty-four years old; much more
than that, I haven't a clue and, anyway, I don't have *time* to believe
in God. Maybe later."

The faint sound of a machine gun running off at the mouth can
be heard in the distance. Dubecheck notices everyone reacts to that
as if it were nothing more than a chipmunk in the forest.

Snazzy's bandits sit along the gunwales of the boat with their
legs dangling over the side. Nguyen the Cholon Chick-Killer sits
next to a chubby-faced, perpetually smiling young man Snazzy calls
"Robespierre," always adding, "And you don't want to know why I
call him that, do you?"

There is a thin, high-cheekboned guy who wears glasses, called
"Minh," who sits alone with his M-16 and his rosary. Everyone
steers clear of him, an accolade of respect the basis for which puzzles and tantalizes Dubecheck. On occasion the word "cannibalism"
would be whispered in a reverential, awestruck tone. Snazzy would
only circle his temple with his index finger, regarding the fellow, and
say, "Believe me—he's off the Richter scale."

Nevertheless, out on the river and in front of you where you can
see them, they're good company. They jabber in Vietnamese and
smoke. Their heads are wrapped, Aunt Jemima style, with large

olive-drab bandannas which might come in handy later as tourniquets or sponges to sop up their own blood.

The whole tax collector business had been scrubbed because, according to the cagey triple agent Phu, the tax collector wasn't going to be where Phu thought he was going to be. He was going to be at his brother-in-law's daughter's marriage to a schoolteacher from Bihn Thuy instead and Phu had to go too because his wife's niece was in the wedding. It was going to be a Catholic wedding and they last a long time, so Phu wanted a couple of days off. He even hit Dubecheck up for a little loan, which Dubecheck was only too glad to give. He considered it insurance because one night Dubecheck was awakened in his rack by Phu running his calloused finger across Dubecheck's throat, on his hands and knees, drunk, laughing and saying, "Soc Mau. You dead, Diwi." The guy is as funny as one of Kooseman's rubber crutches.

Consequently, Recore moped off to try and drum up some new business of his own, but Snazzy pretended he had a contingency plan and Dubecheck played along and, to fill a lull and stop Snazzy's whining, agreed to insert him and his men downriver so they could go on a "patrol."

"Snazzy's a fanatic," Dupree once told Dubecheck. "You know what a fanatic is? It's someone who redoubles his efforts after he's forgotten his goal."

Dubecheck and Snazzy sit on M-60 ammo cans next to each other, smoking and taking in the scenery as if it was a dull slide show.

"What's your goal, Snazzy?"

"What the fuck kinda horseshit high school question is that?"

"It's the only kind I know."

"I like the taste of adrenalin." He stands up, unbuttons his fly and takes a leak overboard, a hand on Dubecheck's shoulder to steady himself, as the boat rocks through some river chop.

"I dunno, Dubecheck. I'm stupid. I still think we're the good guys on the block. We don't even know—the other guys really know —how to push the envelope of evil, man. We got the odd psychopath here and there, but the other guys have it down to a science. They're dipshits, Dubecheck. They haven't done a thing for anyone they say they care about except kill 'em." He shakes off and sits back down. "I been wherever they've been . . . armies of national liberation—gimme a break. Assholes. Last month I saw what the NVA did to some folks up on the Plain. Looked like the 328th Veg-O-Matics came through. You know Veg-O-Matics?"

"Now change from slicing to dicing."

"You got it. You know we're making a bad job of it here, but by and large in the scheme of things we still got that 'help the little old lady across the street' mentality, so to speak." He looks over to Dubecheck with a rubbery smile. "Besides, I don't mind killing the right guys. Somebody's gotta do it and, if you don't believe that, you've been watching the wrong channel, sailor."

Snazzy waves and points toward the shoreline. Dubecheck signals Sisler to make the landing.

The stretch of beach appears deserted, a swatch of low-tide scrubland exposing mangrove roots like tangled snakes above the waterline. A flat, green clearing with a few hooches, nearly collapsed from age, sit back off the water.

The PRUs jump off onto the bank. The landing takes place with all the stealth of twenty drunken Shriners entering a bar. According to the chart, there's a little hamlet a few klicks off the river, but by the time these guys get there it will probably be as deserted as the little thatched ghost huts at the shore.

Snazzy is the only one who seems to take the operation seriously. He walks about in a crouch as if he were being shot at, a worried stern look upon his face, then he stands up and motions his men to him with his rifle. Like a coach before the kickoff. A couple of transistors still play "Strawberry Fields Forever." Snazzy gives the PRUs a "Westward ho" with his arm and they start to trudge across the clearing in a head-swiveling ragged formation, looking like a bunch of Japanese tourists. Snazzy turns back to Dubecheck, smiles and gives the thumbs-up sign, some Van Johnson movie-star, bombs-away horseshit silver-screen camaraderie. He seems to stand waiting for Dubecheck to give him the thumbs up back and then, realizing he isn't going to get it, slinks off with a sour look on his face, toward his "destiny," as McDowell might put it. Dubecheck watches the men form up into a file, more dictated by the narrow path they found than any military discipline, and disappear behind a hedgerow and into a tree line.

The boat backs offshore and toward the center of the river. They'll sit in the sun and drift until Snazzy returns from his foray into the bushes with his unit: ex-Saigon pimps, burglars, pushers and gangsters petty enough to have lost in court and been given the choice between the slammer or defending the Motherland. An irreverent lot at best. Young men whose names Snazzy doesn't much bother to learn because they desert at a rate that is officially termed "alarming." He calls them all "Nguyen," which more than suffices since most Vietnamese men are called Nguyen. They desert and end up back in the city, holed up and blending into anthill swarms of refugees on the torpid exhaust-smelling slums on the edges of Saigon or near big American military sprawls. Or they go over to the VC. Or they become chieu hois. They keep moving. The object is survival. It's a right-up-front topic. They have to live here. No matter what. The long noses get to leave. Dead or alive, they do get to leave.

Dubecheck wouldn't walk fifty feet into the woods with those guys, but Snazzy . . . What do you expect? He's in the CIA and they do all sorts of weird things and think it's neat.

Dubecheck sits on the bow, the afternoon sun beating warmly into his face. He holds an AK-47 on his lap, brought up from the potpourri of weapons lying around down below. The AK-47 feels heavy, rich brown and gunmetal blue, a long banana clip curving down from its breech, chock-full of big bullets. In the heat it simmers in a light aromatic coating of oil which it seems to produce from within itself as if it were a live animal.

This is a good gun. Better than the M-16. You could drop this baby in a mud puddle, take it up to the plate, take a few cuts at a hardball with it, forget to clean it for a week and it'd still work like a charm. Not like the M-16, which you have to keep surgically clean or it will jam on you just when some oriental asshole pops up in front of you like a tin duck. Your gas-operated, semiautomatic Colt from Connecticut would "malfunction." That is, the "motherfucking, cocksucking, son of a fucking bitch goddamn" bullets would jam up like a tepee in their rush to the breech and you would be S.O.L.

Dubecheck strokes the AK-47 on his lap as if it were a cat. No problem with this baby. He wonders what loving little hands turned the indestructible parts to such forgiving tolerances. Probably some Slavic chick. He pictures her near the factory, talking with her comrades on a grassy knoll somewhere in Mother Russia or Czechoslovakia, sitting back on her hands after a lunch of cold beets, cucumbers and a cold potato, huge billowing cumulus and nimbo puffo clouds piled on the horizon like colossal cannon balls.

Scoog abruptly brings Dubecheck out of his Russian reverie before he can get to the good part. "Some old gook's trying to get our attention." He speaks through a mouthful of lima beans from a little olive-drab can of C rats, and points several hundred yards downshore with a pink plastic spoon.

An old man, knobby-kneed, waves from the shore. He holds a

long pole and clasps a handkerchief over his face when he isn't waving. He's the only human visible ashore for miles. A huge, dry rice paddy spreads out behind him and several hundred yards be- hind the rice paddy sits a tree line that curves out toward the shore. The old man wears baggy shorts and a dirty, torn T-shirt. He keeps waving Dubecheck in.

The tide has started to flood and the mangrove roots are slowly disappearing at the water's edge. The reeds bend and throb in the current. It is very quiet. No birds chirp as they close the shore.

"Everybody below. McDowell, take that Bible out of your hand and put a loaded gun in it."

Dubecheck enters the wheelhouse with Sisler. As they get closer, Dubecheck takes in the acres of landscape, looking for something different. No bird sounds means no birds or that the birds might be standing on branches, their eyes squeezed shut, plugging their ears.

"Stop."

The boat backs down and drifts in the flood tide. The old man smiles and nods as if the approach pleases him greatly; he waves them in, then covers his face with his handkerchief once more. He points to the reed-clogged, marshy shoreline with his long pole and awkwardly maneuvers it like a skinny lance toward a clump of bushes growing in the scum-covered wrack line of the beach.

A few hooches in the distance appear to be empty. No smoke coils from them, no animals meander about, just Papa-san, out in the middle of nowhere. A tiny breeze blows away the stench of diesel and brings a rotten, sulphurous stink behind it. The old man prods at the bushes, then leans into the pole like a logger and sends out a buoyant black object the size of a small fat log. It bounces against the mangrove roots and bobs free and catches the tide. The fat log seems to pull two more in its train as the old man drops his pole and covers his mouth and nose with both his hands.

The first log is connected to another one by a short line. Then the smell hits Dubecheck like a gust from a stinking furnace. Dead bodies. Three of them, floating belly up, bloated and black, olive-drab fatigues taut across ballooned thighs, chest and stomachs. They look inflated to near bursting and are tied together around the necks, drifting on the tide like stuffed dummies in American uniforms.

"Holy shit."

"Oh . . . yuk, man."

The old man nods and smiles and waves happily and quickly walks off, not bothering to look back.

"We've got to get them." Dubecheck speaks to no one in particular. He can't look at them. He keeps them in the corner of his eye.

"Hey, Scoog, here's your chance to be the tough guy you think you are." Zeller stares down into the brown water and chuckles to keep from retching like McDowell already is. The rest of the crew stuffs their shirts against their faces.

Sisler maneuvers the boat alongside and the bodies bump against the hull like soft buoys. Their eyes have been eaten out and flies dance in the bone-white cavities. Their lips are gone from the quick ravages of tropical rot and their teeth appear in macabre smiles that stand out from their purplish-black faces. Swarms of maggots truck in and out of their half-eaten nostrils like motorized rice.

"I can't reach 'em," Scoog gasps in the suffocating air.

"Get the boat hook, get a line on one."

The boat twists in the current and the bodies start to drift off. Scoog reaches out to grab a hand and the skin sloughs off like an oily glove, exposing a mass of minute insects scurrying for shelter from the light, most falling off into the water like panic-stricken victims of a sinking ship.

"Jesus! Jesus! Jesus! Aaaaaar!" Scoog recoils and wipes his hand over and over again on his pants while staring at the skeletal hand.

The sun burns a languid gold, rippling on the flat brown water. McDowell's vomit, falling six feet from the deck, hits the water in splats.

Dubecheck, Scoog and Zeller cover their faces with their forearms, take deep breaths and lean over the side into the smell. Dubecheck tries not to look at the cadaverous faces so he won't see them again in some bad dream.

"We gotta get them on board." There isn't a handhold of loose clothing; the fabric is stretched over them like tight green skin. Maybe puncture them like black bloated balloons so they'd hiss and deflate and lose their smell. It doesn't look like they can be heaved aboard without tearing loose limbs. They've been tied together around the neck, the nooses invisible beneath the bloated folds of flesh. Two of them have their hands tied behind their backs. A body rolls a bit, revealing a hole in the nape of the neck, and rolls back to reveal a face that looks as if it were made of straggly filament. Gray angel hair, Dubecheck thinks.

Their names are sewn onto patches above their right breasts. Thiel. Thiel's watch band cuts into his wrist and it still ticks and Dubecheck is surprised it wasn't taken.

"Turn this goddamn thing downwind!"

The boat maneuvers around the bodies, which are kept close by the boat hook. The name tag on the guy with no face says Kristofferson. The other name tag is obliterated by a purplish-gray wound that puffs out like an obscene bud.

Dubecheck jumps into the water, surprised by its momentary coolness. The heat of the air and the putrid stench combine to make him dizzy. He looks up to see his crew looking down on him.

"Scoog, have a couple of people look at the shore in case this is some lousy little ambush, for Christ sake."

Zeller and Hatch move to the fifties. McDowell gets up on his hands and knees and gazes down at Dubecheck like a dog.

"Get in the wheelhouse, McDowell." Dubecheck feels strange telling people what to do as he treads water. He wants McDowell to move so he doesn't vomit on him. Little white maggots flail about in the water around him. Dubecheck wonders if maggots can drown.

"Hoist this guy while I take some weight off." Dubecheck cuts the line between Thiel and the kid with no name and loops a bowline around the boat hook.

Scoog and Hatch hoist Thiel's body as Dubecheck places his hands beneath the sopping, stinking mass of the corpse's ass as if he were trying to boost it through a window.

They get it aboard without decapitating it. Dubecheck swims off a few strokes to catch the slowly drifting guy with no name. The body gurgles inside, little squeaks and pops like it's cooking. Dubecheck vomits onto the surface of the water in front of his face. Gagging and gasping for breath, he pulls the corpse and loops the bowline onto the boat hook and boosts it through another imaginary window, wondering why is he doing this. Why are they doing this? He dreads the one with no face. Kristofferson.

Scoog has thoughtfully bent together some line to create a cradle Dubecheck can easily slip over the ponderous body. They haul Kristofferson out, the body farting from each heavy shift of his bloated form.

Dubecheck sits naked on the bow. He's thrown his clothes overboard and tried to wash himself off in the dirty river but he still feels filthy. He's glad they pay him for this. Three hundred and seventy dollars a month, plus room and board. It's the extras that make it such a neat job, he thinks, like food and shelter. He also thinks that he has to do something with the bodies. Give them to someone. Alive, they used to belong to the United States Army. Dead, they belong to him. Three kids put out on a listening post and he bets somebody forgot about them. He closes his eyes but all he sees is the nightmarish vision of what was left of their faces after Mother Nature ate them.

The bodies sit behind him under a tarpaulin and a cloud of insects, a fly frenzy buzzing in a frequency as maddening as the white noise from the radio. They have to sit out in the hot sun with them until Snazzy gets back from his hike and he can't call in a dust-off for Army buddies. He doesn't know the protocol here. If they were gooks they'd just be left to float. If they were Navy they could have gotten a helicopter ride out, first class to wherever. He ought to just transmit in the blind: THREE USA KIA. COME AND GET-TUM. And wait to see who comes. He feels like seeing some new faces anyway, or at least talking to some new voice, because he feels very helpless sitting out mid-river waiting, gently rocking on the wakes of distant sampans chugging silently in the brown distance.

The sky is flat white and the late afternoon heat is searing. His skin broils under a thin sheen of sticky sweat that lies on his body like hot scum. No one is talking for a change. The engines idle, rumbling no louder than heavy heartbeats. The lapping of the almost dead calm brown river against the hull has put a couple of sailors to sleep. He can hear one snore back aft, another whimpering like a puppy having a bad dream, gone under from the heat. Dubecheck himself is incredibly drowsy, gently lulled by the crackling white noise, months without a real sleep that wasn't induced by a big drunk, by flies humming, and an overwhelming sense of uselessness. He drifts back and forth through the membranes of consciousness, aware of all there is . . . the live ones and the dead ones, floating in the smell.

o   o   o

Night comes rapidly at latitude 10 and under the tropic sky a whole new strange kaleidoscope of stars is set above.

"We're so goddamn far from home, even the fuckin' stars is different." Scoog looks up into the night sky as he stands next to Dubecheck, gazing at constellations that fall upon the eyes and ears of a Northern man like those from another galaxy, as alien as Dubecheck feels in his outfit. He wears nothing but a poncho and combat boots.

The slight six-knot breeze caused by the boat beating upriver feels like a chill compared to the humid furnace of dusk that seemed to settle just moments ago.

They had picked up Snazzy and his PRUs over an hour ago. It took Snazzy about thirty seconds to recap his combat patrol.

"It won't go down in history, Dubecheck. It's a walk in the sun until we spot two guys sitting under a tree cooking some rice." He sat next to Dubecheck by the stern holding a rice bowl in one hand and a beat-up WW Deuce vintage .30-caliber carbine in the other. "Spoils of war."

"Way to go, Snazzy. You really showed 'em."

"No, we didn't. Two guys at about four hundred yards having a picnic. Their weapons leaning against a tree. Twenty guys start screaming, pointing and shooting at them. Twenty guys screaming like Apaches, ripping off full auto, and the two guys didi into the woods without a scratch and we end up with a rice bowl and one ancient unloaded carbine."

"Hey, hit 'em where it hurts. The guys got nothing to eat out of now."

Snazzy tossed the rice bowl overboard and Dubecheck watched it rock and bob in the boat's wake, go under, then reappear far astern. "It floats."

"While my guys are screaming like Apaches it occurred to me that the Indians in America are probably nothing but Chinese nomads or somethin'. A long time ago they just walked over that land bridge from Asia into Alaska and trickled down into the lower forty-eight. A long time ago." Snazzy sighed with the heavy weight of the ages. "Asians everywhere. Even the Russians are Asian. Maybe everybody's Chinese except the Africans."

"We're not Chinese."

"I dunno, Dubecheck. Sometimes I look in the mirror real hard . . . you begin to wonder, you look real hard in the mirror."

"Get tough, Snazzy. Mirror time. That's when a guy's gotta get tough. Tough and mean."

"I'll tell you tough and mean, Dubecheck. A guy that can throw out his *National Geographics*." He slapped Dubecheck on the back, then got up and padded toward the bow and the night seemed to become immeasurably darker.

In the distance, high in the air, so far you can't hear it, a Huey gunship hoses down the earth with tracer. It curves down like a stream of red piss from an invisible giant. Two green tracers zip up from earth and vanish into space, like meteors going home.

Dubecheck sees the huddled shapes of his cargo of PRUs glow

and pulse behind the embers of their cupped cigarettes. Most sit on the upper deck murmuring. One is curled up on the deck trying to sleep, his knees drawn up into his chest, his hands clasped prayerfully together around his carbine, which he keeps clamped between his thighs, like a witch riding a broom. Like everyone else, his bandanna is wrapped around his face outlaw style to keep out the smell. The trip back to Dong My is into the wind and the smell from the corpses constantly washes stem to stern. There's nowhere else to put them.

Dubecheck feels like stuffing his nostrils with his fist. Instead he pulls apart two Tareyton cigarettes and stuffs tobacco up his nose like wads of rough snuff. How clever of himself, he thinks. He'll send the hint to Heloise.

Snazzy shouts for Dubecheck to come up to the bow. He has been scoping the bodies with his flashlight, looking like some grave robber against the black clouds on the horizon somewhere up where Dubecheck imagines this river to begin, in some icy clear trickle seeping down out of the Himalayas, a long, long way away.

The breeze over the bow has been a mixed blessing. The smell blankets them, but the flies have gone. Snazzy holds up a corner of the tarp and slashes the bodies with a weak cone of light.

"Murdered. Charlie murdered these guys."

"Really?"

"In cold blood."

Dubecheck's never known what that meant. "Yeah, well, robbery wasn't the motive."

"Huh?"

"The Thiel guy's still got his watch."

"The hell you say? That's not like Charlie. He usually strips pretty good."

So does everybody. Recore claims his men can have a guy's watch from him before he hits the ground. He's seen Recore's guys back from an op chewing gum, transistors to their ears, diddly bopping along like clowns with cheap prizes from a carnie shooting gallery.

"Yeah. It's still on his wrist."

Snazzy plays the beam of light over the body. "Yeah." He bends close. "It's still fucking tickin'."

"Timex."

"Huh?"

"It must be a Timex. You know . . . the Timex is still ticking, but Thiel isn't."

"Ha-ha. Real rich, Dubecheck. You oughta have more respect for the dead. You want it?"

"What?"

"You want the watch?"

"No, I don't want the fucking watch."

Snazzy seems a bit hurt. "Well, excuse me. Somebody might want it. Jesus. I don't believe it. This really makes me sick." He flicks off the flashlight. "Whew. These boys are pretty ripe, aren't they? Mamma Mia."

Dubecheck and Snazzy light up Pall Malls on the bow, two guys out for a boat ride in the cool tropical night. It's actually pleasant, reminding Dubecheck of summer nights on a lake near home, when the heat of day lingered into the night and the water seemed thick, black and inviting, soft puffs of wind sent chills down your sun-burned body and you could hear someone laughing in a boat out on the water, an oar clunk against a gunwale and the sound carry a long way, a warm, rich girl's laughter, wrenching the gut because he was probably lonely and wished he had a girl. It was a night a guy should have a girl to be his pal when the lake was so calm it reflected stars.

"These guys were done in the back of the neck with their hands tied behind their back . . . Jesus, I hate those motherfuckers. Can you imagine kneeling down and being third in line? Son of a bitch, I'd like to get my hands on those sons o' bitches."

Dubecheck doesn't know whether he can imagine kneeling down or not; the cold muzzle pressed against the nape of his sweaty neck, wet pants, crotch full of hot shit, thinking his last thought. What would it be? That this is all some horribly stupid mistake, that this is all so horribly unnecessary? What's new? He can read. People have been shooting people in the back of the head with revolvers and pistols for centuries. Millions and millions of people, and each one with their very own last thought, down on their knees with bowed heads. Bang. Millions. Dubecheck wants to go home.

The closest he'll get for a while is Dong My; it's pale penumbra of night light glows dully beneath dark storm clouds stacked atop the horizon. Pinpricks of descending flares tumble like fireflies in the distance.

The passengers and crew stir and move about in anticipation of arrival. Scoog and McDowell appear in silhouette, uncoiling mooring lines, anxious to do something to break the fatiguing monotony of the long, uneventful cruise upriver. The throttles have been wide open, pushing against the heavy water for hours, and the constant cavitating drone has drained the senses.

They all bunch up on the bow as the pier closes. They carefully watch their step near the large mounds beneath the flapping tarpaulin.

Even in Vietnamese, Dubecheck can tell the PRUs are cracking jokes over the bodies. A couple of them plug their noses and laugh. Some jog in place to keep warm, their bandoliers of ammo clicking like heavy bracelets.

McDowell and Hatch jump onto the float and turn to catch the lines coiling toward them. "That was a long day, Diwi. I feel like I've been in the boonies for a week." Snazzy sighs. "I get tired easier nowadays. I've been getting tired easier ever since the Bay of Pigs. I ought to get out of this racket and do something reasonable."

"Like what?"

"That's the problem. Nothing seems reasonable."

The PRUs jump off the bow, rifles high, their bare feet slapping onto the wet dock. Their elastic shadows dance beneath the weak glow of the naked light bulbs strung between swaying poles as they pad up the gangway to the compound.

The engines shut down. In the ensuing silence soft sounds come to life, the manila mooring lines creaking and twisting under the strain of the boat, the gurgling rush of the ebb tide sluicing between the hull and the dock.

"You got the stiffs squared away?"

"Yeah. I radioed Com Center. These must be the guys now."

Three figures stride single file down the gangway, the metal plates clanking beneath their bouncy, no-nonsense gait.

"You goin' to the club?" Snazzy asks.

"No. I'm a tired sailor. It's been a long one here too." Dubecheck flicks a row of switches off on the console and sweeps the boat with his eyes to put things in order.

"Yeah. No shit. We shoulda stood in bed. Thanks, Diwi, see you later." Snazzy walks off, edging his way between the three figures on the dock, one of whom, to Dubecheck's surprise, is Kooseman. He's never seen the other two before. They look like twins, round faces and crew cuts and horn-rimmed glasses, Americans in civilian clothes, plaid pants and short-sleeved shirts and baseball caps, looking like they just got off the golf course.

"You the guy with the KIAs?" The guy with the Yankee cap snaps his gum and looks to his partner, who wears an Angel hat.

"Yeah. Who are you guys?"

"Just hand them over, Dubecheck. They're in a hurry." Kooseman rocks back and forth on the balls of his feet with his hands in his pockets.

"I wasn't going to keep them, sir. Come aboard. They're up here."

The two men climb aboard and Dubecheck leads them to the tarp. The Yankee snatches off the tarp and kneels down on his crackling knees and sticks his face close. "Floaters. We got floaters, Walt."

"Floaters," says Walt, who removes his glasses and polishes them on his shirttail.

"Floaters. *Uno, dos, tres.* Three floaters."

"Three floaters."

"For sure. We start the day off with Crispy Critters and end it with floaters."

"Start with Crispy Critters."

Dubecheck looks to the Angel, wondering if this is a ventriloquist act.

"Where'd you get 'em, chief?" The Yankee pokes around one of the corpses.

"In this river. Asia."

"Testy. The guy's testy, Walt."

"Testy."

"Don't be testy, Dubecheck." Kooseman stands on the dock, pointing a finger up at Dubecheck. "This isn't easy for anyone."

"We need some help. You got some help?"

"I sent everybody back to barracks. I thought you guys would have it together."

"Have 'em get back down here."

"Take the guys out of the Com Center."

"They're on watch, Dubecheck."

"They're in there jackin' off. They can come down here for five minutes."

"They're on watch. I won't have them leave their post."

"I got a bad back or I'd help get 'em on the dock."

"Slipped disk."

"Slipped disk."

"You got one too, I suppose?"

"That's right, chief."

"Don't call me chief, sport."

"Testy."

"The guy's testy for sure. We don't have all day, Señor Dube-check. You two sailors square this away. We got a vehicle outside the gate and a reefer nine klicks up the road. We ain't too excited about drivin' nine klicks up the road in the dark. We got a convoy meeting us in ten minutes for escort. We go now or the deceased decay right here. Right, Walt?"

"Right. Right here."

Walt has one of those faces that Dubecheck would like to hit with a baseball bat, a perpetual smirk, a bemused look of wry indif-ference which does nothing but agitate.

"Christ sake. Where are the bags?"

"The bags, my man, are here." Walt pulls them from underneath his arm with a flourish and shakes them out.

"Gimme a hand, Warren." It's the first time Dubecheck can recall calling Kooseman by his first name.

"Not me, Dubecheck. I'll be the first to admit it. I just can't handle that action. You'll do fine."

Walt's flashlight holds on Thiel's face, illuminating his clenched white lipless smile and leprous nose. The light plays across the two faces with faces and the face without a face. The faces seem to be laughing at Dubecheck. Dubecheck struggles to fit the rubber shroud over Thiel; the smell's so noxious it does no good to hold his breath.

"Three, four days at least, Walt."

"At least."

"Number ten on the old aromometer, eh, Druveck?"

Ghouls. Stateside morticians. The Army can't get enough people of their own to pump preservatives into dead kids or place scattered chunks in steel boxes under loosely agreed-upon names. Wacky, zany, madcap morticians in on the body boom. Dubecheck figures someday there will be a TV sitcom about them.

Thiel was okay, but Kristofferson's a big thing.

"Lookit the clodhoppers on that dude."

"Clodhoppers."

Dubecheck can't get the body bag over Kristofferson's huge legs and feet. "Gimme a hand here, for Christ's sake." The poncho Dubecheck wears constricts him. He takes it off and is naked except for his combat boots.

"Big sucker. What ya figure this guy went—six-four, two twenty-five maybe?" Walt is down next to Dubecheck.

"You seriously asking me?"

"Yeah."

Dubecheck struggles with a leg, stiff and bloated. It won't bend at the joint. He shoves against it. He never noticed how large the guy was before. He just noticed he didn't have a face and that made him appear smaller than he really was. An optical illusion. He finally gets the limb into the bag and zips it up, leaving only the guy with no name left. He sits on the deck, breathing hard, listening to the light breeze rustle against the palm trees ashore.

"Two down, one to go, Druveck. Where are your clothes?"

The guy with no name goes into his body bag with ease, as if he wanted to get it over with and was being very helpful. Dubecheck drags them to the gunwale and flips them over the side onto the dock.

Kooseman leans against a concrete piling beneath a naked light bulb.

"Help me drag 'em up the gangway, Warren."

"You're doing fine by yourself, Dubecheck. And don't call me Warren."

"Tsk. Tsk. Intraservice rivalry, Walt."

"Counterproductive."

"Get off my boat."

"Happy to, Admiral."

The morticians jump off the side, join up with Kooseman and walk up the gangway, leaving Dubecheck contemplating the body bags.

It's a pretty night, he thinks as he looks up into the sky. Stars flick on and off among soft, high, gibbous moon clouds that scud along on the breeze. The monsoon is sniffing about, stirring the air with cool currents of wind, scattering soft pads of silver and gray across the darkness. It's nice not to be around people for a moment. He lights a Pall Mall and enjoys the tropical wind against his naked body. Something about wearing nothing but shoes to really make you feel really naked. The tobacco tastes good, as it always does after cheeseburgers, sex and hard work. He flicks the butt into the river where it hisses, puts on his poncho and leaps to the dock. He throws one of the body bags over his shoulder. Damned if he's going to drag these guys up the gangway and across the oily dirt like sacks of cement. No way. Lieutenant (jg) John Paul Dubecheck is going to carry these guys. He gets to the top of the gangway and flips the first body down onto the ground. Out of the corner of his eye he sees a cigarette ember glow and fade in the dark shadow near a Quonset hut. Kooseman and the ghouls are across the compound by the gate. Good name for a rock 'n' roll band, he thinks. Warren and the Morticians. He clumps down the gangway and picks up another body.

The last one, the big guy, is a bitch; he staggers under the load, zigzagging up the gangway, pausing halfway to hyperventilate. Two twenty-five easy. The thought that this dead guy used to be a baby enters Dubecheck's mind. And that his parents were proud of him and his size. And all his relatives too. They'd look at him and say, "My, how you've grown," every time they saw him on his birthday or Thanksgiving or Christmas. And he had big feet. He wondered if people looked at his big feet when he was a baby, like they look at a puppy's feet, and if they're large everybody would say, "Oh, he's gonna be a big one."

He leans against the railing with the heavy body over his shoulders, exhausted, and feels like crying. He'll have to get ahold of himself. So the morticians won't come back and see him being some fag ass pussy. He rolls the body over off his shoulder and it hits the ground like it's full of broken watermelons.

The cigarette ember he saw in the shadow flies through the air and hits the ground in a shower of sparks. Out of the darkness comes the black sailor with the pink socks. He stops, steps on the butt, then comes toward Dubecheck.

"Need some help, man?" He walks past Dubecheck toward his forklift. He climbs aboard, starts it up and wheels over to the clump of bodies, lowering the long tines on the way. He helps Dubecheck load the bodies onto the steel arms. "Hop on, bubba."

They drive the bodies on the forklift through the dark, deserted compound over to the gate. Dubecheck hops off. The black sailor with the pink socks lowers the tines, backs off and drives away.

Dubecheck sits down in the dirt next to the body bags. Warren and the morticians are nowhere to be seen. They must be in the Com hut drinking coffee and looking at *Playboy* Playmates. The mangy compound dog comes over to sniff at the bags and look to Dubecheck for an explanation. The dog whines and roots at a bag with its nose.

"Beat it."

The dog skitters away a few steps into the dappled amber shade of a tree swaying beneath an electric light and regards Dubecheck with sad eyes.

The street outside the compound is deserted and Dubecheck seems all alone. The black sailor with pink socks has gone to wherever he goes. Dubecheck looks back to see if he can see a burning ember in the night. He wonders how he ended up alone, sitting naked under a poncho with the mangy dog, who sidles up to him looking for a scratch behind the ears. Dubecheck figures there ought to be something a guy should get out of this, that it must mean something, that everything connects, that perhaps underlying it all there is something *good* here, that something should come of this, that he should be able to bring away from all this something of *value.*

He unzips one body bag, but it is the wrong one. The second one is the one. He jogs over to the sentry drowsing in his sandbagged bunker and borrows his knife. Something of value.

He gropes in the body bag and finds the arm and, if he can listen hard enough, imagine enough, he can already hear it. He takes the knife and works it about, his hand ready to catch, and he gets it quickly and cleanly. He zips up the bag and under the candlelike light cups in his hand something of value—Thiel's watch, ticking wildly in his palm.

15 There really is no problem large enough that you can't run away from it. Any horseshit to the contrary is lip service from people who really don't understand the magnitude of the Big Picture and one's irrelevant and ephemeral place in it. And through the foreseeing care and guidance of blind luck, on the way back from Snazzy's operation the huge bump in the night the boat experienced, like a full-on collision with a whale, turned out to be a damaging incident. Sisler had apparently run the port shaft of the big boat through an unseen sand bar, twisting it and rendering it inoperable; out of commish, and the nearest repair facility was the U. S. Army's, klicks upriver. Their haul-out facility was backlogged with a half dozen of their own problems. With a semilegitimate straight face, some Spec 4 with a clipboard told Dubecheck he was sorry he couldn't fix his boat for at least a week.

"Bummer."

"*Quel* bummer, Lieutenant," said the Spec 4 with a heartfelt smirk.

"Well, I'll just have to take a number and wait my turn then, won't I?"

"I can see you are a team player, sir. How long would you like to wait? Ballpark?"

"Ah . . . how about a little *while?* I wouldn't want to impose. I can see you have your proverbial work cut out for you."

"Très bien, mon capitain," said the Spec 4, jotting upon the clipboard. "A fortnight."

Two weeks the boat will be down. It's not that Dubecheck doesn't want to vigorously prosecute the war, it's just that it doesn't seem to make any difference whether he does so or not. One can only shovel sand against the tide for so long before one decides it's time for a smoke break, so to speak. So after filing his CASREP, notifying the Chief of Naval Operations (CNO), the Commanders-in-chief of the Atlantic and Pacific Fleets (CINCLANT and CINCPAC), the Commander of Naval Forces Vietnam (COM-NAVFORV), his Task Force Commander (CTF), his Task Unit Commander (CTU), the Commander of the Pacific Amphibious Fleet (COMPHIBPAC), Dubecheck's nominal superiors in San Diego and Saigon, the Bolivian delegation to the United Nations and the Student Council president of Edgar Allan Poe Junior High School, he had a good idea.

The yeoman petty officer at the Com Center was only momentarily thrown by the Bolivian delegation and the Student Council president and would only send out Dubecheck's Casualty Report if he could change those two info addresses to BODEGU and STUPRESPOE. Dubecheck thought that was fine and on his walk back to the hotel he saw Madame Phong buying tomatoes in the open-air market and told her to tell Tuta "Dark Singer's" big boat was broken and said "Singer" was going on a trip.

One of the perks of having one's own command, other than being able to make off with everything that isn't nailed down, is that you can write your own orders to a certain extent. Dubecheck realized he could write himself orders to leave for a bit, seven days to be exact, to go on R and R. To rest, relax and/or recuperate. The only hitch might be the dingo up in Saigon who ostensibly oversees what Dubecheck and his ilk are doing but hasn't the faintest.

His orders for R and R, endorsed by himself, went through the small chain of command like a whisper and in less than four days Dubecheck found himself in possession of the proper papers to leave the country. The urgency and suddenness of his request narrowed down his options as to where he could go, but since his main priority was to get out of the country, anywhere that a plane could land would be fine. There was space available to Hong Kong, Tokyo, or Honolulu, the other ports of call having been booked solid for months.

Hong Kong is a first-rate joint. Fish and chips wrapped in newspaper, a crowded ferry ride over to old Kowloon to play the ponies of Happy Valley race track, the overwhelming smell of the Orient hanging in the air, the commingled scent of a thousand generations of people swarming up against the steep, lushly foliated hills and upon the crowded harbor thick with rafted boats and ships, from sampans the size of kayaks to aircraft carriers the size of small cities and just as populous, thousands of vessels scattered across the foul-smelling, oily expanse of harbor like sea wrack washed up high beyond the tide line after a storm. The air seems to buzz with the whispers of eight million people. And more importantly, the girls have big firm breasts and fat cheeks when they laugh and take your money. Down in Wan Chai the bars are packed with them, and the bars and the soft round girls who laugh with crinkly eyes, who lightly touch your thigh and smoke your cigarettes, are far more fascinating than the statues and museums or the cricket games the insane-asylum-white-clad British play on the green expanse in front of the huge hotels for Europeans.

But Dubecheck didn't really feel very Hong Kongish at the time. The fact of the matter was that Dubecheck was getting a little down on Southeast Asia, the Orient in general.

Japan was out of the question. It seemed the acme of the Orient. Yokosuka and Tokyo, to him, were like industrial New Jersey with raw fish and rice. No more Orient. However, had Bangkok been available, he might have gone there. Returnees from Bangkok can hardly talk, their tongues snarl and loll as they try to describe the beautiful young women with blue-black hair down to there and waists you can encircle with thumb and forefinger and high butts as smooth as warm marble, gliding through the streets like swans. So it was space available Hawaii, take or leave it, and he took it.

But Dubecheck had forgotten how weird and bizarre Honolulu is, and as he stands in the doorway of a Flying Tiger Airlines R and R charter, elbow to asshole with two hundred noncoms and E-4s in an aroma akin to a three-hundred-pound sweating drunk, waiting to descend the steps to the tarmac of Oahu, he fears he may have made what is often referred to as "a terrible mistake."

O   O   O

"Aloha," says the flight attendant. Across the tarmac, waving wildly through the terminal windows, looking like some exotic jungle tribe of whites, are the wives and loved ones of the brush-cut, khaki-clothed men and boys Dubecheck has spent the last hot and stuffy eight hours with.

As Dubecheck, wifeless and unencumbered with a "loved one," stands back, the two groups rush toward each other in a colorful frontal assault. "Hefty" is the word Dubecheck would use to convey the general overall appearance of the women. Breasts bouncing, double chins jiggling, bedecked in leis and parrot-colored muumuus, and sporting crunchy beehive hairdos lathered with yellow or chocolate frostings, they storm the half-drunk, half-hung-over soldiers in a shrieking wave.

The collision is noisy and weepy. Carefully applied mascara runs down faces like rivulets of mud. Pink lipstick, freshly shaved and powdered armpits, two hundred flowers of American hygiene sobbing and hugging deeply tanned, confused-looking GIs stunned in the first bloom of their disappointment. R and R can be a bitch.

The couples rush customs in a frenzy of rutting lust and are herded onto waiting buses, the diesel fumes mingling with the scent of orchids, Ban roll-on, douche and cologne.

First things first. A crowded bus ride and then a large room where everybody sits down and holds hands while a wisecracking Top gives everyone an "orientation" with the demeanor of a cheap, stand-up comic, heavy on the double entendre and sexual innuendo. Everyone sits squirming in their seats, occasionally exchanging glazed smiles and wondering if they are having fun yet. Dubecheck surveys the sea of expectant faces sitting under the skylit ceiling, the mist of hormones hanging as thickly in the air as pollen and dog dander. There will be furious, groping, battering sexual collisions in a couple of hundred hotel rooms within the hour, the TV on in the background. They won't start fighting with each other for the first few days. Then the wife, at first curiously, then angrily, will ask her soldier why he has to drink so much. There will be one fucking hassle after another. Drinks like cans of Libby's fruit cocktail with half a jigger of rum in them at five bucks a pop. Hula dances and the "little woman" will want to go see that jerk who pretends he's drunk on champagne all the time, really cute when he pretends to hiccup and the audience laughs like chimpanzees. Ukuleles and slide guitars playing music that, if you were stuck in an elevator with it, would drive you mad within an hour. Dubecheck had forgotten how much Honolulu sucks. Like a terrible television program you can't turn off.

Choosing Hawaii may have been a terrible mistake. A claustrophobic feeling washes over him as he realizes he is on an island surrounded by the whole Pacific Ocean. He doesn't know anyone on the whole volcanic chain. But he can solve that easily enough. Just go to a bar. There are some real depressing ones in this town as he recalls. Just off the back streets of Waikiki, sailor bars with lousy overpriced drinks and surly-looking strippers who look like someone is putting a gun to their heads and making them take off their shiny, sweat-stained satins, sequins and fringes. More than once Dubecheck has pulled his men out of such joints. The strippers always seem to have a dime-size hole in their black mesh stockings, and the smoke hangs in the air as if the place was just about to burst into flame. And he'd wonder who makes pasties and, blinking in bright daylight, view the bleached-out world in pale noon wash.

He could go to a bar in one of the big hotels but there would be that fucking music again. He wishes the fat comedian of a top sergeant would get to the point of this orientation: when does he have to catch the airplane back to Asia? Miss that baby and, if they don't tie him to a post and plug him, it's pounding rocks in Portsmouth brig until the apocalypse.

After a good, tortuous military hour, the orientation mercifully ends and Dubecheck finds himself leaning against a palm tree watching all the agitated couples wildly flag down the cabs which have noisily descended upon the intersection like sea gulls over a garbage scow.

The war ceases to exist when you are not in it. The only similarity to where they're holding the war and where Dubecheck now finds himself loitering is the temperature. It's starting to get hot. He wears a Hawaiian shirt he bought at the PX and a pair of baggy yellowish slacks crisscrossed with green, red and black stripes creating a sort of Polynesian plaid. In his right pocket is the pistol he glommed from the guy he fished out of the river. Another perk. For some reason it's in his orders to carry around a weapon when he travels from A to B. A pair of forty-nine-cent shower shoes flap on his feet. He's traveling light. If he needs something, like a tuxedo, he'll buy it. In his other pocket is a roll of cash the size of his fist that he intends to blow "as if there were no tomorrow," which is always a distinct possibility. He can see getting through this day is going to take some work, but with a clear conscience he feels up to it and heads toward the familiar dives hard by Waikiki.

Dubecheck comes out of the "world-famous" Seven Seas Bar and Grill blinking in the bright afternoon sun, his head feeling packed with wet sand, sluggish. The five Manhattans, fifteen maraschino cherries and a half pack of Pall Malls on an empty stomach haven't done much for his disposition. Jet lag. He figures it has to be jet lag that has caused his crankiness. His body clock has unwound but the alarm seems to be stuck and he can't shut it off.

The day is always much brighter when you come out of a bar. In fact, the whole Honolulu scene is a little too bright for him. Old guys with white, wormy-veined legs walking by in baggy shorts and Hawaiian shirts looking like Easter eggs on stilts. Their wives in muumuus looking like Easter eggs on tiny feet. His eyes blink at the assault. He heads down to Waikiki, driven by some foolish notion of tourism, as if fulfilling some obligation to see what all the local fuss is about.

Time to go scope out civilians for a while, like going on a trip to the zoo to see exotica. He'd spent the last several hours decompressing into the civilian world by sitting in a sailors' dive listening to some jarhead who'd been in a running argument with his wife ever since he arrived on R and R four days ago.

"How the fuck you talk to your wife about the war, man?"

Dubecheck didn't know. The young Marine and Dubecheck were the only guys in the bar outside of the bartender, an ex-non-com with faded blue tattoos pasted on his freckled arms like dead leaves. He absently polished glasses and commiserated with the kid.

"They don't like to talk about war."

"Yeah. And what else am I supposed to talk about? Like I been in it deep, man, for a long, long time and I'm supposed to want to talk about *shopping?* I mean, gimme some fuckin' slack. She says I drink too much. Shit, I can't drink enough." He chuckled and drained his rum and Coke.

"There you go. Civilians. They're born on third base and go through life thinkin' they hit a fuckin' triple." The bartender felt good and comfortable with Dubecheck and the Marine. He made a couple of refills without being asked and slid them across the bar and gave a little flick of the wrist to show they were on the house. "Dog breath. Fuckin' dog-breath civilians."

There was a long, quiet pause as they all contemplated dog-breath civilians. Dubecheck could hear traffic going by outside in the street through the open door.

"There was this fuckin' new guy. We get jumped, night ambush, I'm talkin' world o' shit and he freezes. Right next to me, he freezes until Gunny comes along and slaps him upside the head with his butt and his helmet goes flyin', then he picks it up and starts firin', puts the sucker on rock 'n' roll for about three clips, then turns to me and says, 'Can I borrow some bullets?' *Borrow* some bullets. Jesus Christ. Just what I need, instant brother-in-law. I mean, can you believe that? *Borrow* some bullets."

Dubecheck left the guy pissing and moaning and wondered where the guy's wife was. Shopping, probably. Maybe watching "The Price Is Right" back in the hotel room, sitting on the bed clipping her toenails and wondering if she did something wrong.

Dubecheck sits in the sand and watches Japanese tourists trudge through it in packs, looking like they're lost in the desert and photographing every square inch of it. The men all wear black suits and white shirts and black ties and the women wear black dresses and hold their purses in one hand and their shoes in the other, negotiating their way through a few pink newlyweds lying on beach towels, turning lobster red and listening to transistor radios advertise new cars and Clearasil.

Burly Hawaiian guys, thick and bronzed, almost fat but hard and powerful, walk by carrying a huge outrigger, sons of the sons of sons of proud Polynesian gods and warriors now paddling shrieking American tourists around on the turquoise bay, tourists who look like county seat clerks, Anastasion's polyester parents, and, like the Japanese, every one of them wearing glasses.

The eyes go, the teeth go. The Homo sapiens creation seems to be ill designed and Dubecheck thinks Tuta was right: every damn component not only capable of crapping out but designed to. He notices how all the white people seem to be uncomfortable inside their bodies. Whereas the Japanese, Hawaiians and the rest of the Asians seem to have some consistent proportion to their appearance, white people seem to be falling out of their initial shape in any number of variations. The odd bulge, ballooning shifts, elongations, foreshortenings. As if the body's boundaries are too easily willing to give at any plane or surface, gravity wreaking havoc as chests cave, breasts sag, hips balloon, thighs bulge, wattles and jowls droop, noses grow.

The Japanese tourists are all smiling and Dubecheck wonders what they're all smiling about. Even when they chatter to each other they are smiling and they're always ready to laugh. They laugh at the same silly things kids do. Someone stumbles in the sand. They all laugh. Big deal to them. A woman hops in the sand like it's a hot griddle and they all laugh. They take a group portrait and they all smile like someone's pulling hard on their bridles, and the guy taking the picture smiles and takes the picture and they all laugh. Strange people. He hears they are a smart race. These are at least smart enough that they aren't out at the sunken graveyard in Pearl Harbor where the skeletons of long-dead American sailors rattle silently down in the submerged bowels of the battleship *Arizona*. And Dubecheck knows why. He's heard they are very polite people.

He's starting to get sick. The maraschino cherries are in his stomach, up near the top, planning a break. He could get on his hands and knees and let them go, but he'd be embarrassed. And he might ruin the honeymoon of the couple lying on their backs in the sand ten feet from him, their eyes closed, holding hands.

"You won't *believe* what happened to us on our honeymoon. I mean, this, this *guy* . . ."

He gets up and makes it to the sidewalk and rushes along looking for a place where he can relieve himself with a modicum of grace. He breaks into a run and turns into a little alleyway and shoves open a wooden gate and vomits into a flower bed. A nice brown stream of bourbon and sweet vermouth and every maraschino he had. Cherries jubilee, each one still the shape in which it came off the tree. He starts to count them and hears a hoarse whisper.

"Oh, my God!"

He looks up through his watery eyes to see the blur of four white-haired women playing cards at a round table beneath a brilliant umbrella. He blinks as the scene comes into focus; they're all staring at him, fifteen feet away across the grass, their cards close to the vest. He scans the riotous growth of tropical vegetation and neatly trellised patio and feels he should give some explanation.

"Your yard makes me sick," he says.

He shuts the gate behind him and walks off. Maybe he ought to get a hotel room and go to sleep for a week.

o　　　　o　　　　o

Fitful sleep. He wakes in a dark hotel room without a clue to the time. Thiel's watch is in his pocket but it ceased ticking soon after he took it. He hasn't bothered to wind it since. He wonders why he keeps it. It must be his *war* souvenir, just like a samurai sword or a pair of Nazi binoculars. Maybe he kept it because he is mentally ill. He gets up and parts the curtain and it is dark outside. If he is mentally ill he's in the right place; Honolulu seems to him an enormous padded room with flowers on the wall. He's got to get out of the room at all cost. Really.

The hotel was picked on the basis that it looked like no one else would stay in it. A pale yellow job about seven stories high, wedged between two big ones, fire escapes down the front. A small lobby with two brown leather chairs and a couple of palm trees in big brown pots. There was supposedly a restaurant and a small bar down the stairs to the left, "Featuring the Piano Stylings of Recording Artist Lamont Shay." There was an easel with a picture of Lamont on it. An eight-by-ten black and white of him with his head tilted at an angle, wavy hair, his cleft chin resting on his fist as he looked out with a blissful expression that conveyed the impression his heaviest number might be "Mairzy Doats."

As Dubecheck descends the stairs, he can hear the opening bars of "I Left My Heart in San Francisco," a song that would normally send him racing for the exit, but a raging hunger drags him down into the dark room. The room smells like chicken à la king in one whiff and pomade in another. He makes his way through the darkness, focusing on a tropical fish the size of a hand fanning back and forth in a brightly lit aquarium behind the small bar. He bumps into a bar stool and climbs up on it to get his bearings. Unfortunately, it's right next to the service station, where he finds himself staring down into a tray of maraschino cherries, limes, olives, onions and lemon twists. He looks up to focus on his face as it slowly emerges in the darkness of a little mirror behind the bar next to the aquarium. The pianist is only at the part where little cable cars climb halfway to the stars and Dubecheck is about to leave when the bartender flips a coaster in front of him and gives him the "What'll it be?"

"A beer. A cold beer. In a bottle with little droplets on the side to prove it."

The bartender gives him a look, then shrugs.

"What kind?"

"Not Hamm's."

"A cold bottle of not Hamm's. Oh boy. A game. How about Budweiser?"

"That's not Hamm's." He smells vanilla in the dark air and turns to see he's seated next to a Negro woman. That in itself isn't very startling, but he never really correlated Hawaii and Negroes. What he did correlate was that his father once said poor Negro women used to use vanilla extract as perfume. He always thought his father was nuts on that one and wondered how he knew anyway. His father didn't like Negroes. Colored people. Dubecheck knew and still knows a lot of people who didn't and don't like Negroes and colored people. White Americans mainly. His father, to his knowledge, didn't know any Negroes, but that didn't seem to make any difference. There was always the tacit assumption that he knew enough about them through some sort of social osmosis that their reputations preceded them and if one ever showed up he would be well prepared to dislike the black colored person.

Dubecheck knows some people who are colored black and likes some and doesn't like others and, like most of the world, he can take some people or leave them. He is having a difficult time mainly with white people in his life now and yellow people whom he wouldn't know if they stood next to him in a crowded elevator. Pale caramel Communists.

"Nice perfume."

The woman looks over at Dubecheck blankly. She has a dark mole on her cheek, a chocolate chip, and in the aquarium's glow he can see she wears thick shiny red lipstick and has baby blue eyelids freckled with silver sand. A "colored" woman, he thinks. Her hair is like a blue-black Dynel helmet with the sheen of glare ice.

"The King of Beers." The bartender slides a bottle of Budweiser across the bar toward Dubecheck.

"The King of Beers. Hey, that's real good."

"Maybe next time you can have a Miller. 'The Champagne of Bottled Beer.' "

"A Tall Blond."

"Right on. Will Monsieur be having dinner or do you want to cough up for the brewski at this time?"

"Would you eat here?"

"The Bud's one-fifty."

Dubecheck pulls out his wad and sets it on the bar. "You got a flashlight so I can see what I'm doing?"

He feels the leg of the lady next to him brush up against his thigh and looks to her. A demure smile, he thinks it's called, softens her face.

"It's Fabergé."

"What is?"

"My perfume."

"Really? I'll remember that." He smells the pomade now. Next to him at the service stand is Lamont Shay himself. Dubecheck vaguely remembers the song ending and what sounded like six hands clapping together for a few beats.

Lamont Shay wears tight maroon bell-bottom pants with a bib and shoulder straps over a frilly-fronted white shirt with balloon sleeves. His shoes are white and he has rings on six fingers.

It's been a long day for Dubecheck. The few and short conversations with humans he's had have been difficult, as if he had been talking in a foreign language that he has not mastered, making him feel alien. The unaccustomed daytime nap and his skewed body clock have conspired to make him *cranky* and he knows it.

"Do they make you wear that?" Dubecheck says.

"I beg your pardon?"

"Do they make you wear that outfit you've got on?"

Lamont looks down at his crotch, then back up to Dubecheck.

"I'm afraid I don't understand."

The bartender starts to chuckle. He is squirting soda from the bar gun into a couple of cocktails.

"He's just wondering if you look like a screaming faggot by choice, Lamont."

"Bite mine, Jerry. I'll have a daiquiri. Christ, what a crowd. I've had more action in a funeral parlor."

"Maybe it's the tunes?"

"I beg your pardon?" Lamont raises an eyebrow at Dubecheck.

"You heard him, Lamont. Cut the 'I beg your pardon' shit. What was he playing when you came in, sir? I sort of pretend I work in an elevator. I shut it all out. Forgive me, Lamont, but it's for my mental health."

"He was playing 'I Left My Heart in San Francisco.'"

"You *weren't*. Tsk, tsk, tsk. Lamont, whatever are we going to do with you?"

"Allow me to buy Lamont's daiquiri. And this lady next to me, whatever she's drinking, and that guy at the end of the bar." Dubecheck jerks his thumb over his shoulder.

"That's a plant at the end of the bar."

"So, buy the plant a drink. I'm on vacation."

"Sure, sport. I'll get it a Hamm's."

Dubecheck peels off a couple of fives and tosses them across the bar.

"What business are you in?" The lady lights up a cigarette and squints at Dubecheck through the smoke.

"Boating. I'm in the boating business."

"Do they make you wear this?" Lamont tugs at Dubecheck's shirt.

"Don't be catty, Lamont. Here's your daiquiri and don't forget to thank the gentleman."

"Thank you. Any requests, just send them over. One of your favorites and I hope it's not one of mine. Excuse me if you will."

"The least you could do is give him your autograph. You want Lamont's 'John Henry'?" the bartender asks.

"Of course I do, don't we?"

The black lady shrugs, nods. "Sure."

Lamont sighs, puts down his drink and takes a pen from the bartender's pocket and writes on the back of a round coaster. He tosses the coaster in front of Dubecheck and walks off. The coaster says, "John Henry."

Dubecheck absently puts it in his pocket. "This might be worth something someday."

"Yeah. This may be your lucky night."

"Let me see that menu."

"Sure. You can keep it for a souvenir if you want."

"As long as I'm here, maybe I should have something Hawaiian." Dubecheck peruses the menu in the near dark. "Pineapple. I don't see pineapple on the menu. Actually, I don't see anything on the menu, it's a bit dark in here. You have any pineapple?"

"I got pineapple juice and crushed in simple syrup. But not your real pineapple."

"That looks like a big hand grenade."

"Right. *Au naturel,* no can do. Sorry."

"That's all right. I can take a hint about this place. Anyway, pineapple I can also take or leave." For some reason Dubecheck seems enthralled by the sound of his own voice. A need to use it. To babble. Two sips of Bud have put him right back where he was before bed.

The woman next to him raises her glass to him and takes a little sip.

"Don't mention it," Dubecheck says. "What is it?"

"She drinks scotch and Coca-Cola, which is a shitty thing to do to both of them, if you ask me, which you didn't."

"Huh. Scotch and Coke."

They all seem to ponder that while Lamont tinkles and trippingly runs his fingers over the keyboard as he makes his run into a song called "People."

"All-time horseshit song of the century. You've got me listening to that clown now, pal. You owe me one."

"I kinda like it. It's, you know, friendly. I mean, the words and all, you know?" The woman looks to Dubecheck for support.

"It's okay, I guess." He was going to add, "if you like people," but decided that might hurt her feelings. What he'd really like to do is lob a grenade over by Lamont and watch swatches of his maroon jump suit float down upon the diners while they shrieked and knocked over their tables, clothes in smoky tatters, on their hands and knees scrambling for the exit over broken plates, chunks of mahi-mahi and bent silver while the piano strings twanged and parted from the fire consuming it in a greasy black pall.

But not really. Just a fun grenade. A Roadrunner cartoon grenade, which when it's done blowing up in the coyote's face and singeing his fur and scorching his eyeballs still allows him to receive more brutal yet harmless carnage upon his body. An ACME grenade, from the ACME Munitions Company, the same company that makes ACME Rocket Roller Skates and ACME Bird Traps with ACME Bird Bait. He thinks it would be very neat if the ACME Company made everybody's weapons and explosives and all anyone would die from then would be laughter. Whole battalions rolling on the ground holding their sides in hysterical laughter and pointing to the enemy troops standing with their hands on their hips, petulant looks on their singed faces black with the explosive soot of ACME artillery shells and ACME airplane bombs, and ACME anti-personnel mines, enemy soldiers standing perforated with holes, sievelike, through and through to daylight made by the ACME Bullet Company, guys standing like Swiss cheese and the air running out of them through the holes, their bodies deflating like punctured balloons while quizzical looks freeze upon their faces and the other soldiers point and laugh and go "Beep-beep." Sort of just like it is now in a way.

He looks over his shoulder to see if Lamont is still intact. He smells a gust of Fabergé and thinks maybe he's being rude to the woman next to him. She seems to be pleasant enough since she saw all his money. But maybe that's just a coincidence. But she does like the song "People," so conceivably she doesn't have a mean bone in her body. Right. It's these truly stupid turns of mind that are starting to bother Dubecheck. He feels like he's spinning in the proverbial whirlpool and needs a bit of flotsam to cling to as he sinks. Not only can't he hold thoughts, he figures he's better off losing them.

"What's your name?"

"Mine?" She opens her mouth in a yawn and pretends she just meant to wipe the corners with her thumb and forefinger. The dim light from the aquarium makes the inside of her large mouth loom up into Dubecheck's vision like a glistening wet purple cave. The thought that she could put a baseball in there crosses his mind.

"Rewbella."

"Rewbella . . . Huh. I don't think I've ever met anyone named Rewbella before."

"And you probably never will. These people name their kids with *imagination* and *soul*. Don't ya, sugar tits?"

Dubecheck turns to see a stocky white man in a light suit and dark tie. He wears horn-rimmed glasses that sit on a puffy little pig nose. Even in the dim light he appears flushed. Short, sandy, curly hair, like a Chesapeake Bay retriever, caps the top of his large head.

"Duwayne Follette. Not Dwayne, but Du-wayne. Duwayne from Wayne." He holds up his pudgy little hand for Dubecheck to shake and Dubecheck takes it. It feels like a bunch of little peeled bananas.

"John Paul Dubecheck."

"I see you've met." He puts his arm around Rewbella and gives her a squeeze. "C'mon. Great big greasy one." They kiss with a great amount of noise. Duwayne comes up for air, lipstick smeared over his plump lips, and takes off his glasses and begins to clean them with his tie. His eyes suddenly look half their previous size.

"Rewbella. You know how she got a name like that?"

"No, I don't."

"Her mother's in the hospital, right? She's all drugged up. Twilight sleepytime. She hears the nurses talking about childhood diseases. Measles, mumps and *voilà!* Rubella. The lady here is named after a disease. Of course it's spelled wrong. Niggers can't spell. Just check out birth certificates, wills and what not. I oughta know. I'm a banker. But I dunno, you know? I think they do it on purpose. You do that on purpose, sweet meat?"

"I do believe we do." She laughs and snuggles into the crook of Duwayne's arm.

Dubecheck looks out of the corner of his eye to see if the bartender might help him out of this but the guy is all of a sudden busy pretending he has to replenish the swizzle sticks and it's going to take his undivided attention. Duwayne puts his arm around Dubecheck's shoulder and the other one around Rewbella's. "Hey, what are friends for? Whaddya say we all go get some mahi-mahi? Whaddya say?"

"I'm sorry. I have to go bowling."

Duwayne backs off from Dubecheck and his mouth drops open, just like the mouth of the tropical fish staring out of the aquarium at the jerks at the bar.

"You're kidding?"

"No. I guess I'm not. I . . . I've got to go bowling."

"I *love* bowling. I love it!" He slaps Dubecheck on the shoulder twice and looks to Rewbella with beaming disbelief. "Tell him. Tell him, baby, how your daddy loves to bowl."

"That's right. The man do like his bowling." Rewbella smiles at Dubecheck, nodding vigorously. "It's the truth. The man loves his bowling."

"But where do you go? I mean, Jesus, I never thought of bowling in Hawaii. John, you know a good place to bowl in Paradise, you just come clean with Duwayne from Wayne and all the lines are on me!"

"I think I'd have to look it up."

"You mean let your fingers do the walking?"

"Right. Walk through those yellow pages."

"Nah. Just start with the B's, save some time. Be honest with me, all of you, and think about it. Is there anything on earth more comfortable than a pair of rented bowling shoes? Now come on, think about it."

"Come to think of it, when I think about it, you're right." Jerry looks at Duwayne, then quickly looks off into the dark toward Lamont. " 'Feelings,' the guy is actually playing 'Feelings,' and I'm listening to it."

"Pussycat, go powder your nose. Prepare to spread your wings and fly. Bowling. A time whose idea has come."

Rewbella slides off her bar stool and, taking her purse, moves into the darkness of the lounge.

"That your wife?"

"Me? Duwayne from Wayne? I'm a banker. Would you put money in my bank if you knew I was married to a woman of the colored persuasion? No. You wouldn't. Not in Indiana. Rewbella is my pal. Every year. Right here. A dusky princess. My Haitian honey."

"She's a whore from Compton."

"*Jerry!*"

"She comes here for two weeks every year for the last ten to nail guys like Duwayne 'cause she's got ambition."

"I like a woman with ambition. And big tits. She's got big tits.

Like . . . like *bowling* balls!" He slaps Dubecheck on the back, happy with his clever analogy. "You hear that one, Jerry?"

"Yeah. Good, Duwayne. Be sure and tell her when she comes back."

"What's she do with all her ambition?"

"She wants to open her own beauty parlor."

"And call it Black Is Beautiful. Sharp, huh?"

"That's—that's very clever. Black is beautiful."

"Hey, John. You'll like this one. What's the difference between a Negro and a nigger?"

"I don't know, Duwayne."

"One is a 'Negro'; more than one, then they're 'niggers.' Black is beautiful. See her hands. She's damn near burned the suckers off straightening hair. 'Conk.' I've tried it myself. Burns the hell out of your head. Say, I can't tell you how excited I am about going bowling. You in a league?"

"No."

"Rolled a six-seventy once. Though I've never kegled a three hundred. Close, but no cigar. Left a seven-ten split and almost had a heart attack. As a matter of fact, I've had a couple of heart attacks but that's not your problem. Jerry, call us a cab."

Dubecheck wonders why he is finding it impossible to say, "I don't want to go bowling." But why, why not?

16

No doubt about it, the shoes are comfortable. Red, green and yellow with the number 12 written on the heels. And he hasn't done bad. Duwayne has been very helpful and after a first game of one-twenty, Dubecheck rolled a one-sixty then a one-eighty, and Duwayne is excited because he says Dubecheck is a "natural." He gave him his business card and said if Dubecheck ever gets to Fort Wayne, Indiana, they'll go bowling together and have a good time.

Rewbella can barely bowl her weight, but it's been fun watching her bend over and drop the ball on the lane and wiggle her ass during the ball's three-minute roll down the boards where it usually just went "clock" and sort of shoved over a pin or two. But Duwayne has been pretty thoughtful about the whole thing.

"When you really think about it, your black person hasn't really entered bowling's mainstream," he confided to Dubecheck as they watched Rewbella put one in the gutter about ten feet down the lane. "Which is odd when you consider how good they are with balls as a rule. You ever had sex with a colored woman, John?"

"What color?"

"Black. Purple pudenda. Africa. The dark continent."

"No."

"Well, believe you me, do. And you can take that advice to the bank." He elbows Dubecheck in the side and tips up a bottle of Bud, empties and places it on the bench next to the score table with a dozen of its friends. He belches. "It's nice to get out of Indiana now and then. Don't get me wrong. I'm a Hoosier to the core."

Rewbella comes to sit on Duwayne's lap and writes on the score sheet. Her doodles appear on the overhead projector. She doodles the head of someone with an Afro hairdo while Duwayne pulls her dress up her thighs.

Dubecheck looks away for modesty's sake, he guesses. The bowling alley is half empty. The thwocking, clumping sounds echo about. He is very bummed and is seriously thinking of begging off for the evening. There really doesn't seem to be a human being he wants to be with at the moment, which is a very lonely feeling. He could go to his hotel room, but it has a phone, and a room where the phone will never ring is also a very lonely place. Duwayne is one of those very difficult people whom you don't like but don't really mind altogether, and Rewbella seems to like him and the pleasure they seem to take in each other provides a small thermal ball of energy that Dubecheck can warm his chill feelings with. Nevertheless, it's a shitty way to live or at least spend your vacation, so he gets up to say good night and that's when Duwayne has his heart attack. At least that's what Dubecheck thinks it is as he gasps and gets to his feet, spilling Rewbella onto the foul line, and clutches his chest while his eyeballs try to leave their sockets.

"Oh, Jesus!" Duwayne gasps. "Get me outta here." And then he falls over and Dubecheck can only think of what a stupid place a bowling alley is to die in. People in bowling shirts come running over, asking what the matter is, and stand watching as Duwayne lies on his back inhaling and exhaling like a giant bellows. Dubecheck looks up and sees a guy watching Duwayne die while he absently eats potato chips from a tiny cellophane sack.

"Does anybody know what to do?"

Rewbella is shrieking and being of no help and between her shrieks Dubecheck can hear a bowling ball crash into some pins at the far end of the alley. He turns to see two guys whooping it up because one of them got a strike.

Duwayne's mouth is gaping like the tropical fish in the hotel bar, his eyes beseechingly roll to Dubecheck. "Not here," he croaks. "Not here, John."

Dubecheck picks Duwayne up and throws him over his back and staggers toward the exit. He vaguely senses the puffy, pale-skinned manager shouting in his ear that you can't leave the premises with rented shoes and someone else yelling, "Call an ambulance." And Rewbella shrieking and pulling at the sides of her face as she trots backward in front of Dubecheck, who is starting to see black spots in front of his eyes because Duwayne must weigh two hundred at least.

Outside on the sidewalk he flips Duwayne down on his back and a crowd of people seem to emerge out of nowhere and stand looking down at Dubecheck, who kneels next to Duwayne, who is trying to say something.

Dubecheck puts his ear to Duwayne's mouth and barely hears him say, "Pound-on-my-chest."

Dubecheck starts to pound on Duwayne's chest with the heels of his fists.

"What you doin', man?"

"Give him air."

Dubecheck is surrounded by a picket fence of legs.

"Press on it, man. Don't beat his ass."

"How about mouth-to-mouth? Somebody know how to do mouth-to-mouth?"

"Go mouth-to-mouth, man. He needs air."

"Yeah, give him some air."

"He needs air."

"What's the matter with the cat?"

"He's shitfaced."

"Somebody call an ambulance. Did somebody call an ambulance? Somebody should maybe call an ambulance."

"Is he drunk?"

"He needs air. Give him some air."

"How come the colored chick's screaming?"

"The guy's on his lips."

"Somebody should calm down the colored chick maybe."

"Why's the black chick cryin' for the honky dude?"

A siren mercifully approaches in the distance. Dubecheck has a feeling he should be doing something, but since Duwayne isn't bleeding from anywhere he doesn't have a clue. Massive hemorrhage is Dubecheck's bailiwick, but Duwayne is just lying there looking like he's doing a slow broil, staring out of blank eyes and breathing in shallow little sips.

The ambulance siren drones to a moan and two attendants leap out, the red flashing light painting their white shirts and pants pink. One carries a little suitcase. A stethoscope hangs around the chest of the other. They push Dubecheck out of the way and start to poke around and look at his face with a flashlight and stick the stethoscope to his chest and take his pulse and finally one attendant looks up and asks, "What's the matter with him?"

"He's shitfaced."

"He needs air."

"I think it's his heart."

"Take his shoes off."

Dubecheck turns to see the bowling alley manager behind him, an embarrassed little twist to his lips. "For circulation, I mean."

They defibrillate Duwayne and he flops under the current like a beached fish. And then they put him on a gurney and wheel him into the back of an ambulance. Dubecheck and Rewbella climb in with him, Dubecheck holding onto a large CO_2 canister, thigh to thigh with Rewbella as the ambulance moves out, slowly, in curious relation to the wailing siren, which gives the impression of much more speed.

"Mothafuck, you know?"

Dubecheck looks into Rewbella's wet face. She looks more confused than upset.

"Yeah. I guess."

"I mean I was set, you know what I mean? The mothafucker die on me and it's shit city, you know?"

Dubecheck feels curious. People you bowl with don't die. Neither do people you've only known for an hour.

"Any of you related to this guy?" The ambulance attendant in the back looks straight at Dubecheck.

"Yeah. We're triplets," Rewbella shouts, startling Dubecheck.

"I just met the guy and his . . . his friend here when we decided to go bowling."

The guy looks down at the shoes on Dubecheck's feet and nods solemnly. "He like bowling?"

"The man likes his bowling."

"That's nice. He dies with his boots on."

"What you say?" Rewbella's voice trails off to a high angry whine. "What you say, he *die* with his boots on?"

"The dude's dead, sis."

"Mothafuck." Rewbella sounds astonished. She leans over to look into Duwayne's face as if he could verify it.

Dubecheck wonders if that means they can shut off the siren now. It is a sound he hates worse than helicopters.

Rewbella, a puzzled look on her dark face, frowns, leans across and shakes Duwayne as if she were trying to get him to stop snoring or something.

"That won't do any good, lady."

"Who-*wee.*" Rewbella leans back against the side of the ambulance and stares out the window. Nifty little venetian blinds come halfway down the windows. Dubecheck sees storefronts and the silhouettes of people parading darkly, like zombies, in front of them. Brightly lit mannequins behind plate-glass windows wear Hawaiian shirts and swimsuits. He looks at Duwayne, whom he could take or leave a while ago, and now feels a surge of real remorse and realizes he misses him. He wasn't without a mean bone in his body, but he was full of life, so to speak, and Dubecheck feels a mild resentment that he doesn't have it anymore, that it was suddenly snatched away from him as if it were cheap and ethereal and insultingly meaningless.

But maybe he isn't *really* dead. Maybe he's just having one of those "out of body" experiences where the "person" hovers below the ceiling and watches and hears what everybody is doing and saying. Good old Duwayne from Wayne's spirit riding along in the ambulance, deciding whether or not it should split and take Duwayne into heaven, traipsing on his size 9s. Dubecheck looks at the two 9s on Duwayne's heels; his feet look really useless now that he's dead.

"Can you turn off the siren?"

"Sure. I'm going up front. You two maybe like to talk it up a bit and let us know where the guy goes, okay?" He moves up through the narrow passageway and sits in the passenger's seat next to the driver.

Rewbella leans forward. She starts to stroke Duwayne's body, then pat it, then awkwardly massage it until Dubecheck realizes she's sort of frisking him. She leans back with his wallet in her hand and opens it up.

"Whatcha doin', Rewbella?"

"Whatchew mean, 'Whatchew doin', Rewbella?' Rewbella takin' care o' business, Dipshit."

She pulls out some currency and tosses the wallet on the floor of the ambulance. Duwayne smiling on his driver's license. "He ain't gonna be needin' this where he gonna go anyway."

"Where's he goin', Rewbella?"

She whispers and shakes the money in Dubecheck's face. "Up yours, mothafuckah. I got this comin' and more. An' where he goin' ain't no bizness mine. You can take care the 'rangements. For your *bowlin'* buddy." She chuckles. "Sheeit. *Bowlin'.*"

"Hey, Rewbella?"

"Hey, Johnny?" She mimics his quiet question.

"Fuck you."

"Maybe for that wad in your pocket, but then I'm particular and maybe don't want your little chuck pecker. Hey! Hey, you up there! Stop this 'bulance!"

The ambulance stops and Rewbella gets out the back, gives Dubecheck the finger and slams the door. It bounces back open and he sees her trot off into the night, looking awkward in her size 7s. She looks back once.

"Could you tell us what's going on, mister?"

"Me?"

"No. We're talkin' to the dead guy. *Yeah,* you. What's goin' on?"

"I don't know."

It probably isn't good manners to just leave Duwayne lying dead, alone in an ambulance five thousand miles from Fort Wayne, Indiana, but the option is truly tempting to Dubecheck. The back door of the ambulance is wide open.

"I've known this guy for an hour." He reaches over and picks up his wallet. Credit cards gone too. This incident has the potential to get way out of hand. There's two ambulance drivers looking at him holding the nearly empty wallet, and meanwhile he has a large roll of cash in his left pocket and, as he recalls, a Chicom Tokarev pistol back in his hotel room. The ambulance drivers look at each other and Dubecheck looks down into the small photograph on the Indiana driver's license of Duwayne smiling at him as if he was pleased about how much trouble he might have Dubecheck in.

He pulls the driver's license out of its plastic case and lays it on top of Duwayne from Wayne, and slips the wallet in his back pocket while the ambulance drivers are huddled together, whispering, which Dubecheck has always been smart enough to realize is not only bad manners but a bad sign if you're not involved in the conversation.

"Well, pal. What's it going to be?"

"Aloha." And Dubecheck leaps out of the back of the ambulance and didis down the street, hearing the guys shout and wishing he were drunk so the gravity of the situation would be lost on him. The only up side is that, although he looks like a clown in his eye-searing outfit, he's in Honolulu and everybody sort of looks like him. And he'll be damned if he'll chuck the bowling shoes. Duwayne was right. They're the most comfortable damn things in the world and he feels like he's running with the wind, his legs feel full of spring as the pavement glides beneath his feet. He's lost but that doesn't make much difference, he'll just follow his nose toward the sea. He does a quick celestial fix, looking up through the glow of Honolulu night light to see a few set pieces of familiar constellations stuck in the sky, forever trapped in an eternal merry-go-round, and smartly places east and west and veers to the east, heading toward the sea, Waikiki to be exact, to find the hotel and check out.

o   o   o

He can't pinpoint the exact moment the brilliant idea hit him, but it must have been moments after he checked out.

Now he feels the nervous adrenalin rush of doing something so preposterous it probably has the potential to alter one's life. For he has also decided to check out of Hawaii. That makes him feel better in itself. That it violates every law and statute he is supposed to abide by is the only unsettling part.

17

CONUS. Continental United States. For months he'd been OUTUS, as the military cleverly called being Out of the United States. Well then, CONUS it is, because Honolulu is definitely bad for his morale and what's R and R about if not for morale? If he wanted to stay as flaked as a rat undergoing a battery of tests to induce insanity, he wouldn't have left Dong My in the first place.

And to avoid further complications, he is cleverly disguised. He took off his bowling shoes and put them in a little flight bag he bought to put his Hawaiian shirt and pistol in. Now he wears a blue T-shirt with a picture of the sun setting on a lagoon, his plaid slacks, new shower shoes and a straw hat. So he relaxes, leans back and looks out of the window of United Airlines Flight Blah-blah-blah at the sparkling little lights of Honolulu receding at a joyous rate to the rear and out toward the vast blackness of the great ocean below; bound for CONUS. And the first and immediately departing flight for CONUS was good old Flight Blah-blah-blah bound for where Lamont had left his heart. San Francisco. What the hell? Dubecheck would gladly have caught the plane to Trenton if that was the first. He is feeling good. He'd forgotten how it felt to feel good. He grins. First class to himself, the smoking lamp is lit and he bought a fresh pack of Camels at the airport, along with *Sports Illustrated, Time,* so he could find out who was winning the war he was in, and an Almond Joy. By God, he might even have a complimentary drink as he wings his way toward the sunrise. And here she comes now, his gracious hostess in her tasteful powder-blue flower print muumuu, reeking from the glorious floral lei around her neck.

"Good evening." She looks at her manifest. "Would you care for a cocktail, Mr. Kooseman?"

"Why not?"

o   o   o

The inanimate world, far from being a passive, looming realm of indifference, chance and coincidence, is an active determinant in the lives of the animate.

Somewhere over the Pacific Ocean, just before dawn, thirty-three thousand feet above the undulating mass of dark water, a crack decides to give birth to itself in the plastic window in front of the sleeping pilot's face.

The copilot, leafing through a stock issue prospectus, does not notice it until the flight engineer, stretching and yawning, leans back in his chair and decides to look out the window with his head upside down for a novel look at the stars.

After a rapid descent, which Dubecheck mercifully sleeps through, a flurry of radio communications to the United Airlines repair facility in San Francisco indicates the window had no relatives in the stock inventory. The crack that gave birth to itself has plans other than going to San Francisco and will have none of this redirection to Portland, Oregon, where the low-flying plane could find surcease from having its pressurization system blown all to hell. No, Portland International is fogged in.

To fix the airplane and save human lives, the United Airlines company tells the people flying the jet to land at Sea-Tac International and Dubecheck subsequently finds himself at eight in the morning standing in a chilly gray rain with a lei around his neck in Seattle, Washington. Since the plane wasn't expected, it doesn't go to a jetway but parks on the tarmac and a staircase is wheeled up to it. Dubecheck stands in the wind and rain at the top of the stairs and looks out to the terminal, feeling somewhat like a low-grade visiting dignitary from a foreign land. But it is America that feels foreign and he doesn't figure it until he realizes it is the first time in nearly a year that he has stood in fifty-degree weather. Springtime in the Pacific Northwest, a territory he is not totally unfamiliar with. A place where he's spent his formative years, that formed him like spilled mercury. He takes off his straw hat to savor the cold rain pelting his face and descends the steps and walks to the terminal.

Spitting. They're spitting at the troops in airports, so the rumor goes. You hear it all the time. "Man, some chick came up and spit at me." Dubecheck figures it for horseshit. A lot of guys are weird that way. They hear something happened to one guy and then they'll say it happened to them even though it never did. The strange part is that they even start believing it themselves. There's not enough spit in the world to hit all the guys he's heard say they got spit on in the airport by a hippie chick. It's always a "hippie chick." Dubecheck wonders if it's the same one. She's flown from airport to airport by angry people, a beleaguered auxiliary of the Hare Krishnas or something. Maybe there's more than one of them, but it'd be hard to tell, because all the hippie chicks look the same to guys in uniform. And vice versa. Old vice versa raising its two-faced head again.

Well, it will be a cold day in Asia before he'll let some hippie chick spit at him without him wiping it off his face with a ball of hair he'd rip out of her armpit. Chicks spitting at guys in airports. What next?

But nobody's likely to figure him for a baby-killing, drug-hooked, bloodthirsty pawn of the military/industrial complex today. He looks more like a clown and he's a little cold, so he puts on his Hawaiian shirt so he'll look like a tropical clown and his bowling shoes so he won't get his feet wet. He sticks the Tokarev pistol in his pocket, tosses the flight bag into the garbage and wonders what the hell he's going to do in Seattle, Washington.

But better Seattle than Honolulu any day. Besides, there is probably an all-points bulletin out on him for either the murder of Duwayne from Wayne or the theft of bowling shoes. But checking out of Hawaii as Mr. Kooseman was a clever ploy, he thinks. Rerouting the plane from San Francisco to Seattle will throw off even the best bloodhounds, and he also cleverly kept Duwayne's wallet, which would have been left at the scene with all ten of his fingerprints on it like filigrees of guilt. Poor Duwayne. Lying on his back in a coffin-size refrigerator somewhere in downtown Honolulu and his wife back in Indiana probably wondering why he hasn't called in from the savings and loan convention to tell her how much he misses her and the kids and what flight he'll be on when he returns. He looks at the picture of Duwayne's wife in the nearly empty wallet and feels a little sorry for her, so he can't bring himself to throw the wallet into the garbage with the flight bag. He considers her narrow, sharp-nosed face, her posed, somewhat distracted gaze set off by the glasses which supersonically wing out to the sides. She looks like a bird listening to worms crawling underground. She reminds him of Tuta's wife and all the other marital mug shots guys seemed obliged to carry around in their wallets like identification. He sticks the wallet into his pocket next to Thiel's watch, feeling like some sort of psychopathic pack rat, and wonders if the Black Is Beautiful Beauty Shop will be opening soon in Compton, California. He imagines showing up someday for a little off the top, leafing through a worn copy of *Ebony*, Rewbella chuckling as she reminisces about her gutter balls. "Oh, the man did like his bowling." Bygones becoming bygones. Whatever that means.

Outside a refreshing grayness colors everything. The sky is a mass of low, fast-moving, dirty-bottomed clouds dropping cold rain, and it is invigorating.

Out of all the taxis parked out front, from golden-orange Yellows to chartreuse green Farwests he happily chooses a dirty gray and white Greytop at the back of the line. This causes some petty bickering to break out between the curbside dispatcher and the guys first in line, a half dozen or so pissing and moaning drivers who had been snoozing or drinking coffee and reading the Seattle *Post-Intelligencer* inside their vehicles, waiting for fares to haul into the city. He shuts the door to the sound of the dispatcher shouting, "It's a free country! He can take any fucking cab he wants!"

It is sort of a toy airport, clean and small, and the city too, as it appears over the horizon of the single freeway leading into it, is like a little toy city. All of a sudden a small thicket of buildings, sky-scrapers because the sky is very low, pop up from the edge of a large gray salt-water bay surrounded by dark, mud-colored hills misted in the rain. He likes Seattle. It's sort of a half city, not altogether a noisy, dirty concentration of people and not altogether a lushly foliated clearing hacked out of the surrounding huge green-black forests that sit on the shoulders of the mountains that look down into the narrow valley where the city camps alongside a wide cold arm of the North Pacific.

He figures his cabby isn't too bright, but then again it's early in the morning. The guy took a long, lingering look at Dubecheck before he put down the meter and asked for Dubecheck's destination. Dubecheck told him to just start going and he'd think about it on the road and they traveled in silence for a while until the cabby decided to break the ice by asking Dubecheck if he's just come from Hawaii. That's when he figured the cabby wasn't too bright. But then maybe he was trying to be friendly. People often confuse people trying to be friendly with not being too bright. At times it's a really thin line.

"Yeah. Hawaii in the Pacific. I want to go to a hotel."

"Cheap or expensive?"

"In between. Just right."

"Like Baby Bear's porridge, huh?"

"Exactly."

A lull in the conversation gives Dubecheck a chance to scan the scenery. Little boxy houses stacked on hills. A lot of bare brown trees dusted in a soft baby green look ready to explode into leaf. Early April alders.

"You ever been to Seattle before?"

"No," he lies. Lying always sets up so many more interesting possibilities when you're on the road.

"On your left there's Boeing."

"Where they make Boeing airplanes?" Let the guy think he's

stupid for a while. He sees the cabby give him a worried look in his rear-view mirrow.

"Yeah. Right there. You probably flew in on one of those babies."

"I flew in on a Douglas DC-8."

"Oh."

Dubecheck scans a large two-mile runway in the middle of a vast industrial garden sunk in the valley to the left of the freeway. Partially painted airplanes sit parked on the runway, color schemes and logos like half-completed puzzles on their fuselages and two-story tail fins.

"I don't think they're as good a plane as your Boeings, though."

The guy gives a sheepish smile and nod back to Dubecheck in the mirror. That's the way it is around here, he recalls. People actually think because they live here they sort of have something to do with how good the airplanes are, just like they all think they are personally responsible for Mount Rainier being so beautiful.

"Too bad you can't see Mount Rainier today."

"Mount what?"

"Mount Rainier. It's over fourteen thousand feet in elevation. Beautiful mountain."

"Where?"

"Back there. Over your shoulder. You can't see it, though, because o' the clouds and shit."

"The hell you say. Fourteen thousand fcct, huh?" Dubecheck turns in his seat to pretend he's trying to see. This has got to be killing the guy. That Dubecheck can't see the mountain has put a pall of pain over the guy's face. He actually hits the steering wheel with his fist in frustration.

"Rats. That sounds like a swell sight."

"It is."

"When can I see it?"

"Aw, shit, when it clears up or somethin'."

"Gee. I almost wish you hadn't-a told me about it now." Dubecheck looks out the back window again. "Fourteen thousand feet. Whew!"

"What do you do for a livin'?" The guy wants to change the subject.

"I own a beauty parlor."

"No shit?"

"No shit."

The conversation stops until Dubecheck finds himself on the

sidewalk outside the Vance Hotel and the cabby thanks him for the fare and a twenty percent tip.

o   o   o

Dubecheck finds it perversely rewarding to be back home while everybody he knows thinks he is someplace else. To be totally anonymous. He has a few acquaintances in Seattle he won't bother to look up, since they are a little embarrassed by him being in the Navy, what with war now out of fashion among the young and intelligent. They sort of treat him like a mentally retarded cousin at a family reunion, smiling nervously as they edge away to talk to someone with more hair on his head and face.

Hair. How does a guy explain away his military haircut? Without bald spots and ugly tufts, it's hard to say it has just grown back after chemotherapy. Maybe he'll get a wig. He recalls a novelty store down by the waterfront. A wig and a coat for the nip in the air. Definitely a wig, because people really are preoccupied by hair. His civilian friends have let theirs grow, along with a few silly-looking Fu Manchu mustaches drooping down the sides of serious against-the-war mouths. As if every kid with a Mark I military haircut is for it.

In CONUS, if you are against the war your hair should be worn long, and if you are for the war your hair should be shorn. Only in a country where the war isn't being fought does one have the luxury of being for a war or against it.

A rheumy-looking grown-up in an overcoat walks past Dubecheck as he stands in front of the Vance Hotel. He smiles at Dubecheck with a conspiratorial wink. The man has a gray crew cut, and between him and Dubecheck flows a flood of political camaraderie distinguished by their hair.

Dubecheck is elated. He feels absolutely invisible, invincible, unaccountable, omniscient, like he's having Duwayne from Wayne's near-death experience for him. He is hovering over all the Americans in Seattle and they don't know he's there. He's a mere apparition in mufti. He feels the terrifying excitement of being behind enemy lines.

He isn't going to check into the Vance. He's just going to float invisibly through the city, among all the hamster-like humans preoccupied with the furtive little stories churning away inside their heads as they trudge up and down the steep hills leading from the waterfront, holding umbrellas over their heads, staring down into the wet sidewalks beneath their feet like dogs staring into a whirl-pool. His name is Mr. Kooseman and he has a picture of his ugly wife in one pocket and an unwound watch in the other, right next to a pistol as hefty and comforting as gold bullion. Ace Novelty hoves into view at the bottom of the hill as a huge green and white ferryboat looms up and makes way from the terminal with a long horn blast that echoes against the brick walls and alleyways off the Alaskan Way Viaduct, sending an explosion of pigeons and sea gulls flapping in ever widening concentric circles, awash in the soft gray rain-splattered air.

O   O   O

Well now, this is better. He's got a black fright wig on his head and has picked up a tight-fitting but serviceable military coat from an Army and Navy Store on Second Avenue. Was irony the word? He couldn't quite recall, but somehow the olive-green Army coat, com-plete with a yellow chevron on the left shoulder indicating the bearer or wearer as a private first class in that vast, seething, som-nambulant organization, seemed appropriate.

The Army and Navy Store had been guarded in front by a small paramilitary force of winos and scraggly-looking youths with filthy hair, bare feet and private first class coats all panhandling in the drizzle. Obviously assuming he was one of them, they left Dube-check alone, and he realized the wonder and joy of being armed with the best pistol the Communist world could buy, flush with a bulging erection of American dollars in his pocket, and if not willing yet still being able to die for his country, but knowing, with the certitude of youth, that that will never happen.

He sits on a bench beneath a totem pole, brooding, purplish pigeons clucking and waddling around his feet. Tattered pale blue flags of sky softly tear away at the overcast. It will be a glorious spring day. Dubecheck is tense with the realization that such joy is short-lived, and a nervous energy trembles through him. This joy must be seized and milked for what it's worth before it turns to the usual shit. The last thing he wants to do on R and R is rest and relax.

The rising wind knocks some bare tree limbs together over his head, bare limbs barely budded, pregnant with leaf ready to ex-plode. The sheer idiocy of being able to do what he wants with a spring day in the land of the brave and home of the free is almost too much.

Dubecheck gets up, afraid the day is going to end, afraid the moment is going to end, knowing it's going to end.

He bolts off through the bums and winos scattered on an island of bricks and pavement like human wrack. They suck on Nawico wine from pint bottles wrapped in paper sacks as if the stinking sots had manners. The clear bottles have bas-relief clusters of grapes on them, the only thing remotely close to grapes in the product at all. A couple of Indians, cross-eyed drunk, sit on the curb, looking like a couple of little kids who've been playing in the dirt all day. The smell of the waterfront hangs in the air like thick brine. Dubecheck follows his nose up a brick alleyway, two rats scurrying before him to hide beneath a row of dumpsters being picked over by a couple of old, dirty, bearded men, moving in slow motion, intently poking with long sticks that look custom made for the job. The last time he felt like this was when he stumbled out of Anastasion's boudoir in the provincial hospital. That seems like a different life, yet was not much more than a week ago. Maybe a hundred and fifty hours. And maybe there's sixty thousand hours in a life, if it lasts as long as the Biblical Bookies Actuarial Tables say. Well, boy, then get moving.

Briskly walking up First Avenue, he spies the Space Needle sticking up into the air like an orange Frisbee atop a tripod. The wind is coming from the north, sweeping the dirty-bottomed cumulus clouds from the sky.

He walks past cheap arcades full of magazines of women with bare tits and wide-open beavers, and pawnshops like iron-grilled armories, and heads toward Pike Place Market, a colorful outdoor bazaar full of fresh, shiny, bright-eyed dead fish, clams, black mussels, pinkish-orange crabs and crusty gray-barnacled oysters stacked in piles on beds of crushed ice. Real mongers are out there hawking the stuff with raucous, pushy voices. Pyramids of vegetables and fruit are dewed with a lacy mist, lush and glistening under naked light bulbs, price signs scrawled on paper bags in infant script and stuck in the piles on sticks. As he remembers, there's a joint that sells peanut butter from a twenty-gallon crock, the oil floating an inch thick on top of the salty muck, and next to it is a bakery with golden, ambrosial-smelling loaves stacked cattywampus behind glass windows and next to pastries that look like flowers.

And that's it. Seattle. He'd done it all. The Space Needle, winos on Skid Road, Mount Rainier and now the Pike Place Market.

Some trucks are backed up on the narrow brick street unloading produce into the stalls. Guys unloading their wares to swarthy, Levantine-looking salesmen in dirty aprons sucking on steaming, dirt-colored cigar butts. Dubecheck likes this place. Out of a dirty window he can see Elliott Bay, four or five stories below, loop in off Puget Sound, the market being built on what appears to be a huge railroad-trestle-like foundation. And beyond the blue, white-capped bay, where several anchored freighters nose into the wind, the jagged Olympic Mountains, late winter snow glowing on their crest in the morning sun, guard the fir-choked slopes to the Pacific. And somewhere over there his father lies buried, his bones probably now as clean and white as the driftwood littering the stormy ocean coastline to the west.

Fried oysters at the Athenian Café. Two orders from the whiskey-voiced waitress with a white prune face highlighted by ketchup-colored lipstick and plucked eyebrows, a rust-colored hairdo someone told her she looked good in back in 1942 and she hasn't bothered to change since. French fries and coleslaw and toast and a couple of cold Rainier Beers and Dubecheck is talking serious breakfast, full and buzzed, picking his teeth, looking out a window down onto the sound and feeling better than he seems to have a right to. He's the only person in the restaurant during its midmorning lull. He might just sit at the table and watch ferryboats and sea gulls until lunch. Curious how few people seem to be about and out on the streets, a large city with small-town pedestrian traffic, people sort of ambling.

As he leaves the Athenian, the waitress gives him a surly look he enjoys all the more for having overtipped her. She passes Dubecheck on his way out, her white nylon dress whishing, eyes straight ahead as she swooshes down on his table like a magpie on a road kill. Salt of the earth, the kind that has a bug-eyed Pekingese at home that yaps constantly, banging off the front window like a noisy moth off a light bulb, barking at the postman. Or maybe a chihuahua named Pepe. The sort of dog that belongs in a blender.

Down the corridor, under muddy skylights, are a line of tables with a scraggly gaggle of young people standing behind them selling beads and trinkets like white Indians along the roadside of a wretched reservation.

Behind one open table a young woman and two morose-looking guys are trying to sell some hand-thrown pottery, macramé and some turquoise baubles set in silver. Crafts. A whole tray of crafts. A sign above them says, NATURAL ARTS AND CRAFTS. Dubecheck wonders what "Natural Art" is.

The girl unfolds a "natural handmade quilt" on the counter. She wears a long dress, tie-dyed, and a pair of wire-rimmed glasses. Her long brown hair is parted in the middle. She has a thin yellowish face with a jaw like a shovel. She looks up at Dubecheck and smiles without showing her teeth, with a smarmy-looking "I love trees" smugness he finds grating. He wonders if she spits on soldiers at airports.

The guys both smoke tiny corncob pipes and wear Air Force greatcoats, their hands shoved in their pockets, hunched over like they're taking a break from the retreat from Moscow.

"Hi."

The voice is soft and gives the word "Hi" two syllables. Dubecheck looks up from the egg-size bauble of turquoise he was staring into.

"I said 'Hi.' " She has a smile with a lot of teeth, but to Dubecheck they appear to be just the right amount and they are white and it is the type of smile he imagines is called "dazzling" in books and magazines. The smile is on a pretty face about eighteen inches from his. The girl's blond hair is a flowing cape that hangs over her shoulders to the top of her thighs. She has sky-colored eyes as big as Ping-Pong balls, and when she turns to look over her shoulder for an instant at something that might have followed her, the large, loose breasts beneath her peasant blouse shift and roll like sacked kittens. When her face snaps back around, her hair following a second later like a golden curtain, Dubecheck still cannot speak because he finds himself in the presence of one of those women who not only make guys moan but render them essentially mute.

She winks at Dubecheck and turns away. Her long denim skirt, as flowing as an ao-dai, whips about her leather-sandaled feet but hugs her hips where her blouse is tucked in. She slings a huge leather purse off her shoulder and slams it down on top of the handmade quilt while the other people behind the Natural Arts and Crafts display irritation at her arrival.

"Shit, *man*. I mean real punctual."

"Yeah, really." The two guys come down pretty hard on her.

"Hey, sorry. I mean, like I got caught in traffic, okay?"

Dubecheck walks off in a fog. Beautiful women do that to him. Like Co Lan. They make you mute and they usually belong to some guy already anyway. Guys can't believe beautiful women drift around like something loosed from a mooring, although a cheer-leader told him once, when she was sad and decided to confide in Dubecheck on the team flight right after USC had just finished kicking the shit out of them, as they always did, that beautiful women are often very lonely.

"Really? Why?"

"Because guys are afraid of us." She was slightly maudlin because she had been drinking vodka from little airplane bottles, and
her breath smelled like she had just thrown up. She was one of those
cheerleaders Dubecheck found annoying, because she would actually cry when the team got beat and they got beat a lot that year.
He remembers standing on the sideline and catching himself watching her and her cronies stand forlorn, with tears in their eyes and
muddy mascara stains on their faces, as they held fistfuls of crepe
motionless beneath their beautifully sweatered breasts and the band
sounded flat and far away, burning forever into his mind a hate for
bleating trumpets and trombones and restless, persistent drumming.
A couple of the cheerleaders were criers and he often wondered
what they'd do if something really terrible happened in their lives.

The one on the plane confided to him that a lot of beautiful
women like her felt the same way, that guys would never come up
to them and talk to them like they were real ordinary people too,
that they had feelings, hopes, dreams and aspirations just like normal people and that beauty was, in its own way, a burden.

So during the next week Dubecheck asked her out for a Coke
date, but she said she had to study. Then he asked her out to a keg
party and she said her sister was sick, and then he asked her out for
a walk or something and she said she'd just washed her hair, which
they both took to mean she obviously had to remain in traction
until it dried sometime in the vague distant future. And that same
night he saw her out with a real beautiful guy who was driving a real
beautiful Corvette and that sort of ended Dubecheck's plan to start
treating beautiful women as if they were normal people, because
they obviously weren't and they are always somebody's baby. Even
if they think they're not.

But they are always more exciting than women like the whiskey-
voiced waitress, whom Dubecheck could talk to all day and feel
comfortable with. But the fear of them was part of the fun of it
when you got right down to it. So when he turns around to go back
and stare at her, his heart gains five quick pounds and sinks in his
chest as he sees her walking toward him, head down, a purple pais-
ley scarf wrapped around her head like an Indian and flowing off
behind her in the wake of turned heads that spin to gawk after her
in awe.

"Hi." The sound fights itself up over a large lump in his throat.
He coughs.

She looks up briefly and he sees that her eyes are watery, as if her team just lost the big one, and she walks right past him. He turns and follows her, impressed with how fast she can walk, her hips moving beneath their denim sheath, soft rippling muscles like watery current.

"Hey . . ." He catches up to her without the faintest idea of what he might do if she stops and turns. She stops and turns.

"Hey what?"

"A . . . a . . . you're beautiful." Smooth. Brilliant.

She turns away and continues walking through the market, her purse bouncing off her hip, and he follows, in too deep to stop, somehow assuming that if she didn't say, "Get out of my life and drop dead," walking away from him at ten miles an hour was an invitation to share the rest of their lives together in a swoon, in that vague timelessness that exists in a mysterious future of enchanted bliss.

She stops and leans against a No Parking sign, breathing heavily from her sprint through the market. Nearby a straggly, dirty, blond-haired guy dressed in patched Levi's and swathed in dark scarfs is playing an intense folk song. His guitar case is open and small change lies in it like coins in an empty wishing well. A small semicircle of people who were watching him now watch the girl, thinking she has to be somebody's baby.

Dubecheck, for some baseless reason, assumes she's his baby, a feeling that seems so natural he's lost all trepidation, a rare, effusive feeling of rightness which renders apprehension absurd.

"What's the matter with you?"

She looks up, a tiny opalescent bubble pops at her nostril. Her dark lashes are wet and tears pool at the corners of her eyes. Her face is extremely young, smooth and tight, a face caught in the quick flight between late adolescence and whatever's next. Her skin has a pink Pacific morning glow to it and her wide lips, the lower one pouting either naturally or due to her present sadness, are plump. She heaves a sigh, as if contemplating whether to answer or not; her breasts rise, inflating her blouse. Dubecheck is about to moan when she starts to shake her head in disbelief.

"I mean, shit. I just can't buy those vibes, man." She wipes her nose with the back of her hand, then wipes the back of her hand down her thigh. "Like, I'm the one who *rents* the stall. Really."

Dubecheck doesn't know what to say. Although there is something in him that makes him want to help, he can only think of sliding the blouse over her smooth shoulders and watching her bullet-tipped Texas pinks spill out like fruit.

"I'd like to throw a pie in his *face,* man." The belligerence in her voice, together with the innocuous weapon, strikes an odd note.

"A pie?"

"Yeah. A pie. A cream pie."

"I'll buy you one."

"Yeah?" She thinks a moment, running her pussy-pink tongue around her lips, and gives a little grunt. "Huh. You would, huh?"

"Right over there." He points to the bakery across from the vat of peanut butter, his mind clouded with visions of slathering peanut butter, whipping cream, unguents, oils and balms all over her body.

He sees the guitar player's audience watching him. Even the guitar player is watching, strumming some song that's supposed to stop wars or something; the drift Dubecheck can't quite follow as he watches the girl shift her pony-express-bag-size purse from one shoulder to another.

"Well . . . I'd like to do that, but it'd be a waste of good pie." She looks over her shoulder at the bakery as if she might change her mind. "Thanks for the offer. Haven't I seen you, you know, like somewhere before?"

"Yeah, back there."

"Over there?"

"No, down back there."

"Is that you? The same guy. Is that you there?" She points down the arcade toward where her crafts stall is.

"No. I'm right here."

"Yeah. I can see that."

She starts to walk across the narrow brick street and he follows a step late. He's got the feeling they're supposed to be together or the airplane window wouldn't have cracked thirty-three thousand feet over the Pacific Ocean.

"Where are we going?"

"I'm going to my car. I told them if they wanta step in my shit they can kiss my orka dilly dally dariolious." She walks with her head down but somehow seems to know where she is going.

"Say that again."

"What?"

"What they can kiss."

She looks up with a bright smile and shifts her huge purse to the other shoulder and singsongs like a kindergarten kid, "Orka dilly dally dariolious." She laughs, throwing back her head, exposing the curve of her neck, her wide-open mouth full of tightly packed molars, a wonder tongue, a glistening cave of mauve and puce textures

that Dubecheck imagines himself parachuting into like a tiny para-
trooper.

She stops. A frown tries to mark her forehead but has to settle
for only making her look petulant. "I forgot where I parked my
car!" She says it like it doesn't happen very often.

"I'll buy you one."

She regards Dubecheck for a moment, looking up at him with a
quizzical squint. "Okay. How about a banana-cream Cadillac?"

Dubecheck laughs and when he finishes realizes he hasn't got to
laugh much lately.

"What's your name, dude?"

"Raoul." He wonders why he said that the moment it came out
of his mouth and decides to be honest. "Actually, it's John."

"I like Raoul better."

"I'll help you find your car."

"How could you? You don't know what it looks like."

"What kind is it?"

"It's a green car."

"They're good cars."

Her car is three blocks away with a parking ticket under the
windshield wiper. A seven-ton 1948 Dodge coupe, faded British
racing green with a little cancer on the lower wheel wells, a roof as
oxidized as a penny left in the rain.

"This is a nice car."

She takes the parking ticket and rips it into little pieces and
sprinkles it down a storm drain. "Tickets are biodegradable."

She lifts her purse up on the hood and, after fishing in it for a
moment, pulls out a tissue. She hands Dubecheck her purse and
pops the hood. The purse feels like it holds a bowling ball. A slit in
the top reveals a pharmaceutical explosion.

She wipes the dipstick with the tissue, inserts it, withdraws it
and squints. "Ding dong, this dog's hungry."

She opens the driver's door and lugs out a two-gallon white
polyurethane jug of Raylube thirty-weight and proceeds to pour
several quarts into the crankcase. She replaces the dipstick, slams
down the hood and says, "Get in."

"Really?"

"Yeah, really."

He gets in the passenger door, sliding a huge potted fern over
toward the center. She slams her door shut; her breasts quiver like
pudding in the aftershock. He holds her open purse on his lap.
Mixed fragrances waft upward from it: marijuana, chewing gum,

incense, Bag Balm. She reaches in her purse and, eyes closed, gropes around for a moment before pulling out the ignition key. It's tied to the end of a rawhide braid with white feathers.

The girl drives fast. They are speeding along the Alaskan Way Viaduct, an elevated one-way with Elliott Bay and the piers a hundred yards to the west. The lumbering Dodge hunkers down on the road like a tank on tracks. Dubecheck turns on the radio next to an open ashtray full of roaches. "KJR, Seattle, Channel 95." A jingle as happy as a Christmas carol and that's how Dubecheck feels now. Like just before Christmas as a child. She drives with intensity, hands at ten and two, west on Spokane Street, through a gray industrial flat of mud-colored waterways, ramshackle piers and a steel factory with mountains of rusty scrap metal sitting on poison dirt. Steam billows from stacks and boils south in a snappy breeze that scallops the big blue bay northward with whitecaps.

The car charges up a long curving hill that rises from the bay and leaves the city skyline behind to the east. He is not about to ask where she might be taking him since he doesn't care and he leans back to relax. They haven't spoken since he got in. Maybe she's going to kill him. He's heard all those sordid hitchhiking stories. It's not safe. Strangers. You gotta watch 'em. What could she do to him? A slight growing erection pushes up against the fifteen-pound purse on his lap. Isometrics.

She runs an amber and a block later a baby red and turns hard left.

"I'm trying to catch a ferry."

"Oh."

"Do I scare you?"

"Yes."

"I don't always drive this way."

"That's not it. You're a good driver."

She looks over to Dubecheck and smiles. "I like your aura. I think we're going to get along fine."

"Really?"

"You're very gentle."

"Yes, I am." He wonders where all this happy horseshit is going to lead. He's found you can't sustain these tippy-toe-type fabrications for too long without them coming back and stepping on your dick. His career as a junior officer in the military at least taught him that.

18

The ferryboat pitches and yaws gently through the four-foot waves that roll southward under the north wind, spindrift whitely lacing their deep green faces. Sea gulls veer and dive in the air like tossed leaves.

Vashon Island sits several nautical miles off the West Seattle coastline, rising out of Puget Sound in that dark muddy Northwest green of fir and madrona trees, huckleberry, Scotch broom and salal growing in junglelike profusion from clifftops down to the rock and gravel tidelands.

The noon sun, still low along the southern meridian, blasts the surface of the sound into an undulating shattered mirror.

Dubecheck can see a few cabins scattered along what looks like a twelve-mile coastline; otherwise the place appears nearly uninhabited, a huge bushy hedge surrounded by lapping cold waves.

The crossing takes about fifteen minutes. Dubecheck spends most of it on the bow of the boat, feeling the cold salt spray mist his face, listening to the rattling, rumbling percussive beat of the drive shaft and screws spin and bite into the water as they send out a frothy rapids astern of the long steel hull. The girl stays in her green car in the front row of the auto deck next to a bread truck, a UPS van, a Volkswagen bus, sucking at a roach and flipping through her new pack of tarot cards. The vanguard of sea gulls screeches and cries into the wind and he wishes the ride would never end.

o   o   o

"Should I know your name or something?"

They are rolling down an empty two-lane blacktop road with old orchards, the trees gnarly and bare, off to the side, orchards in clearings hacked out of the evergreen stands and overgrown with tall yellow grasses and tangles of blackberry vines.

"Lulu. Lulu Turrentine."

"That's a neat name. Is it real?"

"It's what I call myself."

A few old wooden farmhouses appear and disappear in small clearings among the thick groves of alder and madrona that come up to the sides of the road. Rutted dirt driveways poke into the filtered light of the groves and vanish into dark shadow. After they had driven through the little town in what she said was the center of the island, they hadn't seen another car or person. Just a horse standing motionless in a pasture, staring off as if it were thinking about something, a flock of birds swarming in the distance looking like little flies. Everywhere the trees bend and sway in the wind.

"Stop."

She pulls over to the side of the road and Dubecheck reaches over and turns off the engine and gets out and stands on the gravelly shoulder of the road beneath a medium-size fir tree rising six stories into the blue sky; its drooping, needled limbs, high up, swimming in the air, make a soft seashell-to-the-ear roar. A cone dislodges from above and falls near his feet and rolls into the ditch at the side of the road to join dozens more. He sees the thickly barked trunk sway and give before the wind, the huge plant creaking like a mast under strain. He hears a crow cawing nearby and the constant sigh of woodwind and wonders if he could think the same thoughts as the horse in the pasture. Horse sense. The crow persists, cawing from the top of a snag looming up from the center of a madrona grove across the road.

"What's that crow saying?"

"What crow?"

"The black one. On top of that tree across the road."

She gets out of the car to look, the wind snatching her hair and whipping it wildly about her head. She grabs it with her hand as if it might fly away and squints up at the snag with her hand bridged over her eyes.

"I don't speak crow," she says. She turns to Dubecheck, holding her hair, looking like she's saluting him, the start of a smile on her face. "You're shivering. Get in."

"I like it." He gets in anyway and she drives off, the semiautomatic transmission clunking its way up to speed. The sunlight strobes through the trees as he looks out his window and, even though he doesn't know her, it reminds him of her smile.

o   o   o

"I'm taking care of this guy's ocelot." The car lumbers and lurches down a heavily rutted switchback road. Dubecheck can catch glimpses of the sound sparkling through the thick trees and fern-choked gullies that cleave to the unseen shoreline far below. "Like I haven't been here for about a week. This could be a bummer. This ocelot and I, we don't hit it off. I mean, it's a beautiful animal, but it's got a rotten disposition. Like it should be back on the Amazon or something. The cat's in Mexico. I mean the cat who owns the cat."

They break out into a narrow, marshy gully and the road dead-ends at the edge of the sound. Old pilings sit a hundred feet offshore and a collapsed deck hangs ten feet above the water, rotting from decayed joists. Water roils around the barnacled pilings, blackened from creosote and nearly a century of damp weather. Dubecheck likes the old wreck, whitewashed with sea-gull shit, standing against the current.

Across the passage of the sound, now like a wide wind-whipped river, lies the western mainland, a mile or so away. A few cabins, hunkered down beneath a jagged fir ridge, line the beach, now already in afternoon shadow.

An old two-story house with a broken shake roof, bleached from years of neglect, stands sagging under a blanket of ivy that has snarled out from its base; a crooked brick chimney seems to hold up one side of the house. A veranda with a rickety railing around it holds a tattered lawn swing. Flower boxes line the porch and weeds as beautiful as flowers erupt and grow in profusion from them as if they belonged there.

The key is cleverly hidden under a tattered rattan welcome mat at the front door. She opens the door and a gusty whiff of cat shit floods out the door.

"Quick!"

They step inside the door and see vandalism. The ocelot snarls in a corner on top of a couch it has shredded. Piss, little Tootsie Rolls of feces and cat food are scattered over the floor.

"Bummer."

"Really."

"Get him for me while I clean this shit up. Man, Rudy is going to be all bent out of shape when he sees his joint."

"What do you mean, 'Get him'? That animal is pissed. Lethal."

"There's his cage. He *opened* it. Oh, man! I don't believe it."

A yard-square wire mesh cage lies on its side, shredded newspaper scattered all about it. Dubecheck eyes the cat and it eyes Dubecheck. It blinks.

"Does it have a name?"

"Ceylon. Its name is Ceylon."

"Cute. The sucker weighs about fifty pounds."

Ceylon meows and snarls like a cat that weighs fifty pounds. It whines, its back muscles rippling, coiled, a four-legged barrel of gristle with a black-spotted orange crew-cut coat and claws that rip at the couch like a quiet chain saw.

"Is this why I'm here? Did you know . . . ?"

"No. I didn't *know.* You're here because you're here. You want to be here. You've chosen to be here."

Dubecheck regards her face, which suddenly appears more childish than he can recall. She's serious. He thought she was kidding.

"You're serious."

"Really."

"Is that how it is? All the time?"

"I don't understand you, man. I gotta get a broom."

Dubecheck looks over to the ocelot, then sees a salmon net leaning against the wall. The net wants to be there and the ocelot has chosen to be caught.

Dubecheck has found that women sometimes don't get it. They don't seem to know that, between wanting to get something done and getting it finished, something has to happen. Like actually doing it. Lulu has left the room and, if he gets the ocelot back into the cage before she gets back, she'll say, "Oh, good. You got the ocelot back in its cage," and all will be well because that's what was supposed to happen.

What really happens is that Dubecheck gets into a slight palms-down crouch like some TV wrestler circling the "Cat Man."

Ceylon leaps up on the back of the couch and gives Dubecheck a "You gotta be joking" look as Dubecheck reaches blindly for the salmon net. The ocelot coils down into a crouch of its own while emitting some guttural sound. The hackles rise on its back and it slowly rips at the couch back with claws the size of pocket-knife blades.

"Is Ceylon a guy or a chick?" Dubecheck shouts out.

"He's neutered," Lulu shouts from back in the house.

Great. The ocelot regards Dubecheck as if he was the guy who cut his nuts out, then springs for the door, and Dubecheck tries to trip him but gets his leg knocked out from under him and falls, hands down, into a pile of cat shit.

The ocelot bounces around the room like a pinball while Dubecheck chases him with a salmon net. All things that can be broken are being broken and knocked over as the cat runs into walls and in frenzied circles, trying to get back to the Amazon *right now.* The only thing that crosses Dubecheck's mind is what this cat would be like with his balls on. Dubecheck swoops him up into the salmon net, where he thrashes wildly, like a huge noisy butterfly from hell. Dubecheck rams the net into the cage and snaps the long handle off at the door and slams it shut and sits on the floor as Lulu comes in and says, "Oh, good. You got the ocelot back in its cage."

"You asked me to." Then he becomes aware of his hands on fire.

"Oh, poor *babeeeee.*" Lulu grabs his hands in hers and looks up at him as if he didn't know he was in pain. Only young women who are very pretty get away with things that other people would pay dearly for. He doesn't know how long they get away with it but suspects only as long as they are pretty.

Lulu pours hydrogen peroxide on the gashes across Dubecheck's hands, the foam turns pink in the deep gouges and his hands feel like he's been playing tug-of-war with barbed wire.

The ocelot, entangled in the fish net, angrily rolls around the cage, snarling and spitting. Lulu frowns, then brightens. "Oh, wow, the salmon net . . . that was really clever of you. I'm sorry you got so cut up." Dubecheck watches her bite her tongue as if she was in pain while she pours another dollop of hydrogen peroxide on his shaking hands. His war wounds. He'd almost forgotten that this little interlude is only a time out from the more important matters at hand, like the war he has chosen to be in, the war which is now, to him, like a poorly remembered dream.

"I'll put some Bag Balm on them."

She dumps her purse out on the seat of a rocking chair. The can of Bag Balm tumbles out among a small avalanche of envelopes, tissues, tampons, lip gloss, an amber vial, a Baggie of vegetable matter, a bottle of aspirin, a loofa sponge, cocktail napkins and paper coasters covered with phone numbers, a rolled joint, Pepto-Bismol, a ring of keys, a fat purple wallet bulging with papers and photos, a half a roll of Life Savers, a few sticks of Black Jack chewing gum, a dozen or so matchbooks, and a half dozen sticks of incense.

"I think I'll fire one of these dogs up. Get the stink out." She lights a punk of incense and sticks it in the dirt of a flowerpot on a windowsill, then goes to the pile on the rocking chair and holds up a small plastic vial. She unscrews the top and shakes what looks like a narrow slip of paper into her palm and walks toward Dubecheck.

"Here. Take one." She rips off a quarter-inch tag of paper. He sees there is a picture of a little bald man with a long flowing beard and he wears a toga.

"Who's the funny little guy?"

"Mr. Natural. Say ahhhh."

He opens his mouth and she places the tab of paper on his tongue. She does the same and smiles. She sticks the vial into her skirt pocket and combs her long hair with her fingers. Her breasts loll about like lazy golden swells.

She fingers out a golf-ball-size scoop of Bag Balm and smooths the sticky amber-colored salve into his hands. The warm sting soothes them. He swallows the paper tab with a dry gulp.

Lulu takes Dubecheck by the hand down the cracked porch steps and leads him over a rotting wooden bulkhead made of pilings sunk into the sand and gravel beach. The beach slopes gradually down to the shore a hundred feet or so away. The tide is low. Near the waterline the damp rocks are strewn in gray-black profusion, encrusted with barnacles. A couple of tide-stranded starfish, fading orange, cling to the lumpy bed of stones. A boulder is mantled with a black woolly coat of mussels and shaggy doilies of rubbery olive seaweed. Lulu lifts a small rock with the toe of her sandal and two dime-size crabs scurry from the sunlight as water seeps up and muddily fills the indentation left in the land by the upturned rock. The little purple crabs disappear among the stones. Dubecheck wonders if their hearts are racing. If they wonder.

Through the clear shallows Dubecheck sees the rippled sand floor of the sound, scalloped by the steady wave action. He turns to see the cliff behind him, eighty feet high, yellow clay and sand, with the tangled snare of exposed roots of the huge madronas that reach out over the edge at the top, looking ready to fall and bring down with them the bluff, calving the land into the sea as they must have been doing for a long, long time. Some large firs are swaying up there also and some crows spinning and falling and cawing in the clear blue maelstrom above the trees.

"I just got my mantra." She puts her hands on her hips and squints out into the glaring expanse of water.

"Really?"

"Really."

He doesn't know what she's talking about. A mantra. Perhaps it's something like an ocelot. His jaw is beginning to ache, not unpleasantly, but enough to let him know something is going on with his central nervous system. He knows she gave him a drug he suspects to be acid but, being shy and naive and a little embarrassed about both, he had recalled Dupree's dictum about drugs: if someone is kind enough to offer you one, don't refuse it or be so rude as to ask what it is.

A ripple, somewhat like a pleasant chill, goes down his back. The back of his head is numbing, like a novocained orgasm, and his throat seems to be constricting, which doesn't bother him at all, because he realizes he doesn't need his throat. For anything. Ever. Again. Except to forever tell the truth.

"I don't know what a mantra is."

She looks at him with eyes that seem more *burrowing* than they seemed before. Frightening for a brief moment, which is fair: after all, she is another human. He blinks and works his aching jaws a bit, as if that might stop his cheekbones from constricting his face like a soft vise.

"It's a word, a sound you use in meditation."

"Really?" Who cares? Or wait . . . is he interested?

"You repeat it over and over again as you relax and meditate as you transcend the material world."

"Huh . . . What is your mantra?"

"I can't tell you. It's a secret."

"Why? What difference does if make if anybody else knows?"

She works her own jaws a little and nervously scratches at her head as if it has just been infested by bad bugs. "Well . . . well, I dunno. Maybe somebody, like I mean if somebody knew your mantra, they'd like, I dunno, *use* it themselves."

"So what?"

"So, it like maybe *dilutes* your mantra, man. I dunno."

"I've got a mantra."

"I thought you didn't know what a mantra was."

"I didn't. That doesn't mean I don't have one."

"Yeah. That's cool."

They wander up the beach. Dubecheck can't see another dwelling or human being anywhere in either direction along their coast. All he can see is just trees, waves, rocks, the sun and sky. Quite a lot actually, when he starts to think about it, which he is starting to do. It is like his mind has a tremendous agenda that has to be addressed, coupled with the calm realization that it will be. In his own sweet time.

"I'll tell you my mantra."

"You really shouldn't. I appreciate it, but . . . maybe you could get in trouble or something. Don't you think?" She stops and screws up her face in curious consternation at the thought. For an instant she reminds him of . . . McDowell and then, in a flash as sudden as the last, she reminds him of everyone.

"It's Dark Singer."

"Oh." She whispers. "Oh, that's beautiful. That's a beautiful mantra. I . . . I always thought they were one syllable, though."

"I've had it for a long time, it's . . . maybe sort of grown." He thought he was always going to tell the truth forever moments ago. Then he realizes that it *is* the truth. *Everything* he says is. *Anything* he says is the truth. Or he wouldn't be saying it. Right?

"Oh, look at that!"

Lulu runs across the rocks toward a sand oasis beneath a foot-thick arch of a madrona limb curving twenty feet out over the high bluff falling to the beach. Driftwood is rammed hard up against the bank like long thick shards of damp marble, rippled and veined by water and wind. Old stumps with root systems jeweled with barna-cles and sprat tilt like phantasmagorical wagon wheels. Lulu sits down, wiggling her toes in the light brown sand, her skirt above her knees, which she holds to her chest, sand on her thighs like a sugar cookie, and where the slow curves of her thighs sweep into the beach, Dubecheck can see, between those pale golden lobes, what appears to be a little baby hamster curled up, sleeping, out of the wind, nestled in her bare crotch.

"Raw-ouuuuulll!" Lulu howls into the wind like a coyote and laughs, rocking on her butt, tightly holding herself as if she might explode should she let go.

Her face moves like it's under water, like lichens pulsing on a rock. Something is happening in Dubecheck's soufflé brain he can't put his finger on. His legs feel like strands of thread and that is good. He falls to the sand and digs his fingers into the cool, grainy earth, kneads it and feels his fingers become the sand. His hands and the beach have become the same thing and that is okay with him. In fact, he figures, it's about time. He wants to flip the shower shoes off his feet and grind his toes into the sand and root himself into the beach like a thousand-year-old piece of driftwood, but discovers he doesn't have the energy for all that. He looks up to the blue sky and finds the color worthy of laughter and laughter worthy of more laughter. What seems like hours pass as he marvels at the stones lying at the edge of the sand. The wind blows through his head as if he had left the door to it open. He turns to Lulu and sees her eyes and teeth and a little fear and snatches his glance back toward the seething sound, which rolls before his eyes like a river on a roller coaster. A sea gull slices through the air and tilts, exposing its white belly to a golden blast from the soft early spring sun, and in that instant everything in the world seems right. His body sways like the limbs of a tree he sees high above as he falls on his back. But he has no back and no body, and high in the sky is nothing but molecules, nearly invisible bubbles gliding across his vision so slowly, so slowly, back and forth like a weather vane in an aimless breeze. And then the voices come, sweet crows crying, "Cawwwwww!" like the sigh of a long-drawn bow on some instrument from another world. Soon it is Lulu on her feet, walking down to the shore on tiptoes with her arms flung out and her blouse snapping in the wind like a loose sail, and then it's off and she stands arched against the wind with her head back and her arms dissolving into the sky. He gets to his feet, smiling, and goes to the shore and stands with the water lapping about his ankles, his feet dissolving into it, shimmering and wiggling until they appear as pebbles and sand, and fearing monsters possibly reaching out from the depths to drag him into the dark cold. He backs away and finds a boulder to climb upon and clutch like a large ball, the mussels and barnacles like a soft blanket, yet his cheek feeling the rough, knifelike pressure of the encrustation, his head sideways looking out to the water surging, and then the rock begins to breathe, just like he knew it could, and he becomes the rock and he is no more, just the breathing, inhaling, exhaling, bellows of the living earth, and he is nothing but vision, a rock that can see, and he sees only the pale blue of space and forever.

"Hey!"

"Yes?"

"The tide's coming in."

Dubecheck knows he must leave the rock and slides down, his feet entering the now cold water. Prickles of brine enter his cuts and he realizes he is coming back from somewhere else. Still he floats. Lulu takes his hand and they walk up from the beach, stumbling over the rocky footing. He is full of energy; spasms rush down from the nape of his neck and disappear into his heart. His scalp tingles pleasantly, but his legs feel heavy.

The wind has sat down. The water seems to be resting after running a long way and the waves are smaller and Dubecheck turns to look back with the surge of sadness that you feel when you know something is going to go away forever.

"How long have we been here?"

"Where?"

"Here." He stops and points down to the beach.

"The past does not exist. It has passed and the future doesn't exist yet, it isn't here. A short moment is fiction. Think about it. The world does not exist."

"Really?"

"Everything passes away and nothing returns. I mean, like events. The present is an instant. The past is gone and the future isn't here. Nothing exists, Raoul."

Dubecheck ponders, but all he can think of is the international date line and what that might do to things. The international date line *must* mean something in the scheme of things. Maybe that's why the war means nothing here. It's always really held on a different day.

"What exists is an eternal present. An eternal now. Time is an abstraction, the fourth dimension of space, a line of eternity, a spatial conception in relation to the world and our consciousness." She pauses to scratch her back with her balled-up blouse.

"Is that really so?"

"Think about it. Time, somehow, translates itself into space. The atom is the entrance of the fourth dimension into three-dimensional space. Look! Look closely." She holds her cheek up to the slanting sun. "Try and see where my flesh ends and the air begins."

Dubecheck leans closely and, by God, she's right. Her cheek looks like the surface of the sun as he's seen it in textbooks, spumes of light and fire and molten gas leaping from the globular surface in an incandescent fountain of chemistry and physics. And he can't tell where her cheek ends and the world begins. Wait a minute! She doesn't have her blouse on and her bare breasts sit upon her torso like the golden lobes of a tavern softball trophy goddess covered with a million little goose bumps from the chill spring air and her thimble-sized nipples on a silver-dollar-size field of pink stare at him like some benevolent sad-eyed animal.

"Oh, Lulu."

"Raouuuuuuuuuuuuuullll!" She throws her arms back and howls. Her ribs make flesh-colored bars beneath her breasts, her belly sinks into shadow and the sun makes golden the down that curls from her bare hip like geysers from the sun.

Dubecheck wraps his arms around her waist, feeling the soft lobes of her chest press into his Hawaiian shirt, and he buries his nose in the cold corn silk of her hair. As he lifts her up and swings her around he sees over her shoulder, sixty feet away, a deer stumbling awkwardly down the bank, staggering onto the beach to stand, head down, panting, on wobbly legs. A doe. A deer. A female deer. Rey. A Golden Drop of Sun. Me, a name, I call myself, and then he hears the barking and yelping of dogs and a landslide of gravel and dirt. He sees the deer walk toward the water on spindly legs, its tongue hanging out of its mouth like a dog's. It enters the cold water and starts to swim. The waves almost engulf it, but it plunges into the sound and as the barking gets louder, the deer starts going in circles in the water as if it had lost its bearings.

Lulu turns around as the pack of dogs tumble down the cliff, somersaulting and yelping, six of them, salivating and panting from the chase, sprinting across the rocks and gravel into the water toward the deer, which circles in confusion forty feet offshore.

The dogs churn out toward the deer, their barks turning to gurgles as the waves wash their muzzles.

"Can't you do something?"

Well. Isn't that the way it always is? *Do* something. A thrashing fountain of white water surrounds the deer. Dubecheck can see a brown dog with its jaws clamped on the doe's ear. It snaps its head back and forth like a shark. A tiny puff of brilliant red tells Dubecheck that part of the ear has come off, and the brown dog, gasping for air, paddles toward the beach, coughing salt water, spitting out the ear. It reaches shore and shakes off the water, sending diamonds of spray into the air, then turns to bark at the frenzy offshore. It wears a collar and a shiny little license. The dog must be drunk. Other than that, he's a good dog. Dubecheck throws a rock the size of a baseball and it yelps and backs away. Dubecheck runs into Puget Sound screaming, and stumbles, pitching forward into the water, losing his fright wig, going in harm's way, invincible. He swirls in the near freezing water, slapping at snarling muzzles, trying to break forelimbs. He hears Lulu scream from the beach. He looks up to see a hovering gull peer down with mild interest, then realizes he's doing the dog paddle toward shore with the rest of the animals and they all hit the beach at the same time. The dogs shake off the water and Dubecheck drips, nearly blind from salt water, and feeling about thirty pounds heavier than when he entered the water. His wig is washed up against the beach like a black jellyfish and the dogs, grouping on the beach, look angry. The deer churns out into the sound, blown off course like a rudderless wreck.

"Where's your hair!" Lulu reaches down to pick up his wig. She holds it in her hands and looks up to Dubecheck. He realizes that his money and his gun are probably wet too. The German shepherd growls at the humans. The other dogs start to growl also and they all V-up into a pack with the big one at the front showing his teeth. The dogs creep forward in slow motion with one brain.

"Hey, Raoul . . ."

"Yeah. I know."

A German shepherd, a springer spaniel and four middleweight, caramel-colored mongrels. Invincible, Dubecheck imagines he sees their hearts and lungs, platelets and leucocytes slithering at speed through their arteries, their eyes incandescent brown. They growl like ocelots. He gets on his hands and knees and creeps toward them, growling low in his throat. He stops three feet from Rin Tin Tin. Rin Tin Tin quiets and licks his worm-colored lips, blinking. Dubecheck looks into its eyes and sees dog brain, like a wet road map of Indiana.

He sits down in the wet sand and crosses his legs. The shepherd comes forward to lick his face and Dubecheck scratches it behind the ears. The other dogs swarm upon him, wiggling their asses, wagging their tails as they climb over him, jealous for affection.

Walking back to the beach house, the dogs strung out behind, tongues lolling from their smiles, Dubecheck is aware that only moments have passed, yet the sky has darkened some; it's a rich blue and the sun is low enough in the sky that he can look at it. The greens of the trees and bush have deepened, minute flashes of lightning course through them. The world seems an incredibly busy place; more is happening than a person could imagine yet he senses it all. Everything is in motion and, shirtless and wigless, he feels bathed with the most perfect temperature on earth.

"Why do you wear a wig?"

"I don't know."

"That's okay you don't know."

"That's good that that's okay."

"That was a beautiful thing you did for the deer. That was the most beautiful thing I've ever seen. That deer spirit is with you."

"I want to take my pants off." The rest of his naked body wants to swim in the air.

"That's okay to want to do that. That's beautiful."

He takes off his pants and carries his wet clothes in a bundle under his arm. His waterlogged shower shoes squish over the barnacled rocks beneath his feet.

She has the black wig clutched to her milk glands; she hands it to Dubecheck and zips down her skirt at the hip. She wiggles out of the denim, sliding the skirt down over her hips and, bending forward, her tits balloon as they hang and sway. She steps out of her skirt and picks it up and walks ahead. She turns to see him watching her, the sun spreading over her shoulder and illuminating round edges like a cloud with silver lining.

He moves up to her and, when they kiss, her mouth feels much hotter than her skin. He digs fingers into her back and they seem to enter her body. She pulls back and takes his hand and leads him toward the house, backing up the steps, staring into his eyes. He is suffused with the same joyous warmth of one who has hit a home run.

Inside, she chops kindling with a hatchet by the hearth and builds a tepee with it over a bed of balled-up newspaper. "You must be cold."

"No. I'm just right." The house is dark with the shadows of plants. Outside the open door, the horizon turns pink and he sees a large ragged V of sea gulls heading southeast. Moments afterward, a flock of crows spill from the sky in no formation; they flap erratically in the same direction, bringing up the rear in noisy anarchy, ne'er-do-well drunks.

Lulu has returned from a dark hallway with a blanket and sets it down before the hearth on the floor. The fire of salty-smelling driftwood pops and cracks.

She kicks off her sandals and sits Indian style upon the blanket. "Come here. Do as I do."

She sits naked, her thumbs and forefingers touching, her back straight, one of her feet on her hipbone. "This is the half lotus."

Dubecheck sits naked across from her and does the same.

"I'm going to do my mantra."

"Okay."

"So . . . like don't be alarmed or anything, like I might zone out a little."

"Have at it." Transcendental meditation. That's it. He's heard of it. You bury yourself inward and, irony of ironies, it gets you out of this place. You can didi to the cosmos or wherever with a word for a ticket. It would take a brain stronger than his to pull it off for himself. He can hear the noisy crows, their loud caws fading, but they sound like jungle birds in this cramped, atrium-like house, and with that tropical cat staring at him from its cage, the room's too much like Asia for the moment, especially with this naked chick on cruise control with her Eastern religious trip she got from Sears Roebuck or someplace nearby like it. The sweetly putrid scent of incense fills his nose like the stink from gook funerals and he's like sorta gotta get outta here. For some fresh air. Maybe climb naked up the clay bank behind the place and crawl out on a big madrona branch that hangs over the cliff and look down into the sound and hope the wind is strong enough that the branch will sway as he clings to it, afraid to fall and then again not really giving a shit if he does.

Hell with it. Maybe it's a gut check. He stays and watches her lips move soundlessly. Her eyes are closed. He looks at her right nipple; the left is covered by a cascade of thick blond hair. Maybe he'll stare into it and hypnotize himself and find enlightenment. It has goose bumps around it from the slight breeze coming in the front door, goose bumps where the hairs of thousands or millions of years ago would have grown. He can hear the dogs outside on the porch, as restless as ducks on a pond smelling Mr. Fox, their toenails clicking on the wood, and they whine, bored and confused, maybe thinking about tearing into him and gnawing on his spine. The hackles go up on his neck and a chill shudders his body, and then her body too, ripples, like a thoroughbred's flank. She smiles, lids closed, and he wonders what cerebral cotton is inside her head that can give her face, her whole *being,* whatever that is, such mindless, obvious ecstasy. Doesn't she know what's really going on?

He wonders if he is supposed to sit here in this excruciating position until she finishes whatever it is she is doing, whether it is a test or something he has to pass before she decides she wants to fuck him. He thinks chicks might be nuts. He looks into her face with its smarmy smile, a brief subliminal Jolly Roger shot of her skull gives him the yips for an instant, but he toughs it out. Her face undulates and then he seems to see each feature separately, an eye, a nostril, a lip, a cheekbone, a brow, and so on, and scattered separately, like a quick slide show, it's not a pretty picture and he doesn't like her a bit for it. He's afraid for a moment what she might turn into and the idea of coupling with this thing seems dangerous and preposterous and out of the question.

And before his eyes she has curlers in her sparse colorless hair, and her breasts sag like they're being tugged, and the lines come out on her face like time-lapse photography and the flesh behind her arms droops and desiccates and her legs mottle and the veins bulge purple, her belly becomes a gut and sags, a wrinkled hammock of flesh. She grows jowls and her face is dusted with a white mortuary powder that smells like incense and her lips are red and leer and she's blind, eyelids crusted shut. Bummer. He tears his eyes away and locks his mind on the fire, which turns out to be a poor choice

since his head explodes like a flashbulb popped off inside his cerebel-
lum. He leaps to his feet, dogs on his left and the ocelot on his right,
and sees Lulu wide-eyed, out of her transcendental meditation with
a start.

"Hey, Raoul. Good to seeya. You okay?"

"Yeah. Yeah, sure." He is surprised to see it is dark outside and
the only light in the room comes from the orange flames in the
fireplace. Camping in the jungle with Jane.

"I'd like to do a tarot reading for you."

"A what? Why?" Dubecheck is coming back from wherever he's
been all day and is not sure that it's where he wants to be.

"Come, sit by me."

He sits by her, feeling the sandy rug beneath his butt, staring
down into the soft bird's nest between her legs, mesmerized by the
airy coils of dark filament spreading like a little fan halfway up her
belly. She is leaning back on her palms, her knees up, her thighs fall
open. Dubecheck looks up and she opens her mouth in mock surprise and his penis suddenly feels like lead as it fills rapidly with
expectation. She puts a fingertip over the little hole in the top, as if
shushing it, while staring into his eyes. This is all new territory to
him. He figures she knows what she is doing, because he hasn't a
clue. She wraps her hand around his hard-on and closes her eyes and
looks like she might go into transcendental med again, which might
be a bummer.

She whispers, "I've already had an orgasm."

Jesus. Chicks are nuts. "I haven't."

"Oh, baby. Oh, baby, baby, baby. You will." She gets up and
walks to her purse. "I gotta like put in my diaphragm." She digs
into the purse and after a moment turns and walks, in that flat-
footed manner naked women seem to have, down the dark hallway.
And that's when the dogs start barking and a noisy engine comes
backfiring down the road into earshot.

"Bummer." Lulu runs back to the living room, her nakedness
making her look suddenly vulnerable, and starts to put her clothes
on. "You better get dressed, man."

His clothes are wet and clammy and go on hard. Two car doors
slam and the ocelot starts to growl and bang against its cage.

Two guys appear in the doorway. A tall thin one whom Dubecheck remembers from the market, standing in his Air Force great-
coat, wild straggly hair, his eyes on fire like a revolutionary. He's
standing next to a guy who looks like he thinks he's Cochise or
something. He has a band across his forehead and a big white

feather sticking up in a no-frills, no-nonsense, low-key Tonto head-dress. He wears a fatigue jacket and Levi's and looks sullen.

"Hey, what the fuck, man?"

It beats Dubecheck what the fuck is. He's cold and his muscles feel like they've all taken a vacation and he doesn't know what's keeping his body upright.

"I mean, what the fuck you doin' with my ol' lady?"

Dubecheck looks to Lulu and wonders if she has the answer.

"Lighten up, Chad. Look at him. He just washed up on the beach, all right?"

"Yeah, sure. Whose fuckin' dogs, man?"

"They're his."

"Can't he talk? Where's your fuckin' *hair*, man?"

No, he can't talk. The idea of talking seems completely out of the question. Besides, what could he possibly have to say to Chad and the shady-looking creep who's being the silent type himself? They come in the room, keeping Dubecheck in the corner of their eyes as they pretend to scope the joint out. Chad's a little angry Dubecheck's so large or he'd probably *really* be a little more pissed about his chick.

"Man, the traffic was a bummer. You got any weed, Lulu? Like I'm strung out, the stoplights and all."

They all sit down in chairs and do a number and the Indian says, "This is good shit, man," and everyone nods sagely that this is so.

Then Lulu pulls out a little hash, "Afghani Red."

"Outta sight," says Chad. Lulu makes a little pipe with alumi-num foil and drops a pea-size chunk of hash into the bowl and fires it up. Dubecheck takes a hit of that. All of a sudden he feels like having a highball, but instead zones out while the Indian goes into a rap about how the white man has ripped off the black man's music. That black music comes from their pain and only out of pain can soul come.

If that's all it takes, every gook Dubecheck's ever met should be on the Lucky Strike Hit Parade. He watches the Indian and sees he is no more an Indian than he is; he's seen Indians before and their eyes are empty and beaten and forlorn and this guy's eyes are beady bright from more than just the hash. His eyes aren't sad enough for an Indian's; they're like a lizard's and Dubecheck makes him for a Mexican trying to cash in on the Noble Red Man scam. Real Indi-ans are like gooks, lost at sea, adrift and hopeless. He's seen them in between their drunks in logging towns and on the bleak, rainy reser-vations and they all look like they've been captured and are just going through the motions, and none of them seemed noble, they just seemed pathetic, like they'd had the shit kicked out of them.

"What tribe are you from?"

The guy looks up at Dubecheck and pauses a moment. "Sioux, man. My grandfather was a chief."

"That's beautiful." Lulu sucks on the hash pipe and holds her breath. "Beautiful." She exhales and coughs.

Dubecheck looks at the "Indian" and smiles. "How."

"That's not funny, man." It's Chad again. "The white man raped the Indian. He's raped the land."

"And stolen black music," adds Dubecheck.

"Right."

"Yeah, really."

Dubecheck would like to take them all on a field trip of an Indian logging operation. They leave the forest looking like they harvested it with seven-hundred-and-fifty-pound bombs. Show them selling a pickup load of ungutted doe for a couple of fifths of Town Club whiskey. The ones he's seen weren't particularly noble, they were just plain folks, no more, no less.

"Hey, Lulu. Drifting Cloud's gonna take me to his power spot, man. You wanna like trip along?"

"That sounds really heavy."

"Really."

"Your name's Drifting Cloud?"

"Yeah. Yeah, it is. What's yours, 'Water Faucet'?" Even Dubecheck laughs. They all giggle for a while and when they show signs of stopping, someone says "Water Faucet" again and they all laugh. The dogs on the porch smile and the ocelot seems to chuckle, blinking its eyes like a wise old owl, and Dubecheck is caught up in the wonderful warmth of the family of man and all living beings in harmony and wonders how he can get out of here, ideally alone with Lulu.

"Drifting Cloud had a bitchin' vision the last time he was up there."

"Where?"

"It's a special spot near a waterfall, right?"

Drifting Cloud closes his eyes and nods.

"I mean the vibes are so heavy, so positive, it's gotta be like just magic."

"Yeah, really."

After the field trip to the Indian logging site he'd like to take them down a ten-foot-wide slough in a pitch-black Asian mangrove swamp to check out that power spot, with the cheeks of their asses pinched so tight together you couldn't pry them apart with a crowbar.

Momentarily, he wonders if the drunken Marine in Honolulu is still hiding from his wife and who the lady in the backyard playing cards had clean up his vomit. Maybe she did it herself, her nose pinched up, holding her breath, hosing it away with a garden hose as she too wonders who people are and why they come into your life and if it all isn't nothing but aimless molecules colliding in a vast chemical stew. He's had his own vision, the Armageddon Day picnic, the culmination of human history, or what he knows of it: cave men, flint and fire, clubs to beat animals and each other with, and kindergarten drawings on the walls and, after swarms of humans built the pyramids, Greeks in togas, marble statues and columns, wise guys with bright ideas like truth and beauty, the rise of Rome, followed by the fall of Rome, the little baby Jesus, the Dark Ages, the plague, rat fleas, cathedrals, wars with swords and crossbows, people burning at the stake, hungry people splitting for America, Pilgrims, Thanksgiving, the Boston Tea Party, wars with cannons, the French Revolution, guillotines, wagon trains, Civil War, cars, war with tanks, Babe Ruth's sixty homers, the Japs and Nazis eat it, the atomic bomb, television: the whole history of the world, not counting the Chinese, right up there in his head, a Rolodex of information leading right up to his vision, the final day when, among lakes of blood and rivers of pus, the sack races will be held, the three-legged races, and people laughing as Frisbees fill the air and people stuff themselves with potato salad and watermelon and run with egg-laden spoons in their mouths. Oh, what a panorama of joy will prevail at the Armageddon Day picnic! Balloons in the air when the stars begin to fall and then *fini*. No more. Just like the dinosaurs, poof! Cenozoic, mesozoic, paleolithic or whatever all those chunks of time mean, all folks gone, nobody more to keep score, no more diet dog food, just space and eternity.

"Time is an illusion anyway."

"Really."

Lulu, Chad and Drifting Cloud have been talking about time.

"If time isn't real, then what's eternity mean?"

They all look at Dubecheck.

"Yeah, really," says Lulu.

Dubecheck says, "I think time is real and is what keeps the light from reaching us, and there is no greater obstacle to God than time."

"It depends what you mean by God, man." Chad pinches out the tip of a roach and then puts it in his mouth and swallows it.

"I have no idea what I mean by God," says Dubecheck.

"You Wasichus are blind in the world. The forces of being, the Great Spirit, is something that is lost to your dead eyes and souls." Drifting Cloud returns from the kitchen with a half gallon of Cribari wine.

"Really," says Lulu.

"Horseshit," says Dubecheck.

"Hey, man, cool it." Chad starts his "I bet you'll blink before I do" thing with Dubecheck. "His people have suffered and nearly vanished because of us white people, man."

"Bummer."

"Really."

"Like Wounded Knee. I had ancestors there." Drifting Cloud hits the Cribari pretty hard.

Ancestors at Wounded Knee. This guy had ancestors maybe doing pleats and rolls in a Tia Juana auto shop or chasing the fruit crop in the Yakima Valley, but Wounded Knee, no way, the guy is too street smart for a brave, the guy is much too far into the real world.

"What's Wounded Knee?" Lulu gets up and stokes the fire with a couple of snowshoe-size slabs of fir bark. The firelight glows through her blouse and reveals the shadowy lobes lolling wasted on her chest, and Dubecheck is reminded how much Drifting Cloud and Chad have cost him in the larger scheme of things.

"Jesus, Lulu, Wounded Knee, like the white man slaughtered women and children in the snow one winter morning. The fucking macho cavalry stormed in at dawn and hacked up a sleepy village of starving, freezing, defenseless Indians." Chad seems pretty angry, like maybe he was there.

"There were a lot of Negroes in the cavalry too."

"What's that supposed to mean?"

"*Negroes*. Listen to the guy. They're *blacks*, man."

"What it means is the whole cavalry wasn't white. It was black and white and even had red Indians in it."

"So it wasn't *their* idea. They were just pawns of the white man, man. What the fuck you know about it anyway?"

"I don't know anything about it, really. I don't know anything about anything." Dubecheck feels very cold in his wet clothes and remembers he's supposed to be resting and relaxing and that that is very hard to do around people you don't want to be with. He gets up and goes out onto the porch where the snoozing dogs get to their feet and look at him expectantly. He walks down the steps and takes a piss into a mud puddle in the driveway just above the beach. The tide is coming in and the short, choppy, noisy waves lap rapidly upon the diminishing beach. It is deep dark and he can't see beyond twenty feet and the light rain feels like the mist beneath a waterfall. The dogs wait with polite restraint until he finishes before they go to sniff, then drink from the puddle.

He feels very tired all of a sudden and sort of feels bad about Wounded Knee, but he knows Wounded Knee was just another place where shit like that happens all the time, just like the weather, like it was part of the yearly unfolding of seasons, like night following day, like breathing, like life on the planet, like the sour, bad breath of an uncle, drunk and weepy, whispering in the dark one Christmas Eve when ten-year-old Dubecheck got up in the middle of the night to take a piss and got waylaid by Uncle George, who sat in the dark drinking a fifth of Four Roses out of a jelly jar, smoking Philip Morris cigarettes, a small one-candlepower night light on in the breakfast nook and the rain coming down in heavy torrents upon the composition shingle roof like BBs pelting a pillow.

His father's brother, with his heavy, clumsy, menacing accent, one his father had fought to lose and did, a guy who came around every couple of years, not enough to grow close to or fond of, who never had a clean shave and always smelled, sweetly reeking of the flowery musk of a drinking man's sweat; who always wore a wrinkled dark suit that seemed several sizes too large, and the tie and shirt never matched. He remembers they picked him up where the Greyhound or the trunk line let him off, holding a small hard suitcase in one hand, the tips of his shirt collar curling up out of his lapels, not quite a fat man—"dumpy" would be the word—waving with a pained smile as he stood on the sidewalk. Dubecheck would see him through the blurry sweeps of the windshield wipers of his father's pale green De Soto. Of course, the man embarrassed young Dubecheck, but he was surprised to see that the man could somehow move his father like nothing or no one else. His father would stop the car and get out into the rain and George would put down his suitcase and they would hug each other, standing stock-still in their shabby clothes for a long moment, his father's tan gabardine topcoat getting freckled by the rain, an occasional pat on the back, a "There, there, everything's all right" pat, and after a long time with their arms around each other, like two tired dancers, they would disengage, then squabble quietly over who would carry the ridiculous little suitcase all the way to the car, which was parked about eight feet away.

"I won't hear of it, George." His father would smartly end the discussion and pick up the suitcase and carry it to the rear of the car as if it were a steamer trunk going first cabin.

Then George would get in the car next to Dubecheck, and with that clumsy gregariousness of a man who'd never had children of his own and thought you always had to be nice to them, he'd hug little John Paul, scratching a forty-grit sandpaper beard across his cheek, and call him all kinds of unfathomable foreign names of endearment and love that needed no translation. Both George's and his father's eyes were brimming with tears when they got into the car. George slapped the top of the dashboard.

"Cheezus. Vat a car you! You gotdam millionaire!" He'd laugh and give Dubecheck a hard squeeze. Dubecheck felt small between the two men. And safe.

His mother didn't like Uncle George. But what *did* his mother like? Uncle George would only stay a couple of days and then he'd leave for somewhere, off into that vague world where people who don't much concern you seem to spend their lives and get by. A guy you remember only when he shows up, or you hear he dies.

That dark Christmas night, Uncle George beckoned him to the nook, waving his smoke-wreathed hand. He smoked his cigarettes until they were the size of roaches and his fingers were dirty orange from the nicotine. He wore an undershirt with straps over his hairy shoulders. "Seed down, little pony."

He ground his cigarette out and lighted another one and pointed to the bench across from him. He poured straight Four Roses into a glass Dubecheck remembered holding Concord grape jelly.

"Your father is a brave man."

Ten years old, his feet don't even touch the floor and he's wearing pajamas whose cuffs reach the middle of his calves as he swings his legs nervously and sits while his uncle recounts how he and Dubecheck's father, when they were nearly half Dubecheck's age, watched, with their own mother, while the Bulgarians, the *Comitadji,* spurred on by the Germans, hanged their father by the neck with a pillowcase over his head from a gibbet that left his feet a foot from the ground, his calves tied together and his hands tied behind his back so he wouldn't flail and kick as he strangled, and the German colonel, way back in 1916, laughed with his junior officers afterward, dressed in their baggy jodhpurs and knee-length leather boots, swords at their hips, smoking cigarettes between their thumbs and little fingers, the stink of shit and piss in the stained and soiled pants of the eight men and two women hanging from gibbets dug into the ground by sweaty peasants, friends and neighbors scared shitless. When they hanged his father he was six and they made him watch it with his brother and mother and friends and neighbors in a dusty lot overlooking the plain and he said his father's knees buckled and they had to pick him up and drag him to the gibbet while his wife screamed and had to be held back from the Bulgarian executioners. The priest just stood there making the sign of the cross and wiping his sweaty brow. It was a beautiful day! Hot and sunny, and you could hear chickens clucking in the silence before they hoisted the men up on pulleys that squeaked as the nooses tightened.

One of the men had had his arm shot off in the war, his coat sleeve was limp, and nothing to tie it to, so the lone one flailed wildly as he strangled. And it was a beautiful day! Jagodina. "The kingdom of Serbia, my little Johnny Johnny! Monastir-Bitolj. Every day the scum would bombard us and over a time they killed five hundred, and they were women and babies and old men. But who knows how many dead? The children lay piled in the street, laid out on their backs, angelic, sleeping with sweet dreams, but dead from the gas.

They drove us out of town on foot after they killed all the men, our father. They took our mother, who knows? and we walked four days with no food or water and people fell down and they clubbed them to death or slashed them with their sabers as they lay coughing from exhaustion."

Uncle George's eyes filmed over with the scum of memory, and he drank deeply from the jelly jar. He put his palm to Dubecheck's face and slapped it roughly with affection.

"If you see any time they coming, yust focking run, keed."

Uncle George wiped his nose and then blew it with a huge snort into his hands and wiped his hands on his pants.

Uncle George and his father had run away when some guards ran off to put a bayonet through the side of Lazar Nusi's head, a sixty-five-year-old man. They never saw their mother again.

Merry Fucking Christmas. It wasn't "White" like Bing Crosby dreamed of on the record player. It was gray and muddy. Dubecheck went back to bed after his Uncle George passed out on the breakfast nook table, too petrified to leave before. He lay awake on his bed until first light, his eyes wide and his throat thick. Only with dawn did his eyes close, and he awoke to his mother shaking him, surprised he would stay asleep so long on Christmas Day, puzzled as he staggered lethargically to the living room to see what Santa had brought him for being a fairly good boy.

Monastir, Wounded Knee, what's the diff? He remembers lying in his rack in Dong My watching Mamma-san, the hooch maid, mop the floor as she matter-of-factly told him of how she was on Saipan during the Japanese occupation and the American invasion, how all the Japanese women ran up to the highest cliffs to throw their babies to the sea, then follow them in suicidal leaps into the foamy swells upon the rocks far below, just so as not to fall into the clutches of the red-bearded devils from America. She said she didn't do it. She hid in a cave with her son and came out days after the battle, scorched, hairless, dying of thirst. The first American devil she saw gave her a Hershey bar. She had saved her son's life so the French could kill him ten years later just outside Hanoi up Red River way on the Chinese border.

"What was a Vietnamese like you doing on Saipan anyway, Mamma-san?"

"Just lucky, Diwi." And she laughed and slathered the mop over the floor and began to hum.

He sees Uncle George and his father hugging in the rain on some vaguely remembered street corner, a "There, there, it's all right" double pat against his father's back. It is all right. Both those guys are dead now. The corner's probably gone too, paved over in asphalt for a 7-Eleven. The rain is still here, though, and it slides down his face with his tears.

He feels someone at his side and starts quickly. Lulu has come up as quietly as his memories.

"You're shivering."

"Yeah, I'm all right."

"Hey, Lulu. Get your ass back in here and tell that dude to hit the road!" Chad appears on the porch with Drifting Cloud, who is whistling into the bottle of Cribari, making tugboat sounds.

"Don't pay any attention to them. They're just being assholes," loud enough for them to hear.

"Man, I really don't dig you hangin' round my ol' lady, I don't care where you come from, the beach, Mars or from under a rock. If you don't split we're gonna kick your fuckin' ass, okay?"

Dubecheck walks toward the porch and stops at the bottom of the steps. The two are silhouetted against the firelight that shimmers on the ceiling of the living room.

"Sure, guys. I wanna just go get the ocelot."

"Whadda you mean, 'get the ocelot'? It's Rudy's ocelot, man."

"I don't care. I don't even care if it's *your* ocelot, Chad."

"Like you want trouble, Water Faucet?"

"No, Drifty Cloud. Nobody wants trouble. I find, when it comes, you never had a choice. Right, Chad? So me and my wonder dogs are going in there and take that ocelot to fucking Zanzibar just for the hell of it and just because I don't like your whiny face, and you aren't going to kick anybody's fucking ass, because you haven't kicked anybody's ass in your life."

Dubecheck shoulders his way through the two and enters the house.

"Rudy'll blow your ass away, you take his ocelot."

"Rudy can suck my Uncle George's dick."

Dubecheck grabs the cage by the handle on the top. The ocelot scrambles, his weight rolling in the cage like a giant bowling ball. Chad and Drifting Cloud block the doorway and look nervously at each other.

"Hey, man. Cool it, okay? You take the ocelot, Rudy'll kill us, man. Take it easy."

"Yeah, shit, man. It's cool. Have some Cribari. Let's do a number."

The dogs peek in from the porch, their snouts between the legs of the guys blocking the doorway, accurately smelling trouble.

"Hey, c'mon, guys. Stay cool." Lulu is whining from below the porch. "Jesus, I mean, really."

Dubecheck feels cornered. Like once in junior high school, two guys cornered him. Ninth graders, big guys, two years older, in the boys' locker room after everyone else had gone home for the day. The smaller one slammed Dubecheck's head against the wall with his open palm while the taller one just grinned that sick grin assholes have and then ripped Dubecheck's Pee-Chee out of his hands, scattering his schoolwork. Then the little guy hit him in the stomach with his fist and they did it just because they felt like it and left him on the floor, crying and ashamed, frightened and humiliated, twelve years old, not having known yet that people really do those things to you. And later, rather than single them out and fight them back, he became a coward and tried to become their friend. And he was cowardly, because if something isn't right and you know it, and you do it anyway, you are cowardly and it wasn't right to try and befriend the cruel.

"If you see any time they coming, yust focking run, keed." But they're always coming, there's no place to hide. You just need sheer luck to survive, sheer luck to live from one goddamn day to the next. Luck and a little rage, and he isn't going to befriend these guys because they are finally having second thoughts.

"Get outta my way."

"Please. C'mon, man. Don't be ridiculous."

The ocelot is snarling. It is an ugly sound, and fits Dubecheck's mood, for he is feeling ugly and full of rage, and cold and wet and a long way away from everywhere, because he has no place to go, no place anywhere to go and no place he can think of that he wants to be. This dingy dark living room, where he holds a smelly, fifty pound ocelot in his hands, is not where he wants to be either. He whirls, swinging the cage by the handle, and lets it slam against a wall, springing the cage open as the dogs burst in snarling and yelping.

Outside, with Lulu clinging to him, the inside of the house sounds like it's undergoing reconstruction. Drunks tipping over closets of crystal and china. The ocelot seems to be holding its own; its piercing cry slices through the barking, cutting it into agonized canine howls. Chad and Drifting Cloud stand next to Dubecheck and Lulu.

"Jesus, that's impressive. Outta sight." Drifting Cloud starts laughing and slaps Dubecheck on the back.

"It is far out, man. I mean, like it's . . . animalistic in there." Chad ponders the hidden cacophony.

"Yeah, really," Lulu says.

It becomes quiet in the house as Dubecheck, Lulu, Chad and Drifting Cloud stand huddled, shivering in the cold spring rain.

While all the dogs and the ocelot went to sleep inside the house, the people sat in the back of Chad's VW van and drank a half case of Rainier beer and listened to tunes from the eight-track cassette at the little table that folded out, and to Dubecheck's complacent acquiescence, they all became friends and smoked hash.

Later Lulu and her old man, Chad, make up and tiptoe into the house while Dubecheck gets to spend the night listening to Drifting Cloud snore and fart in the front seat of the van as Dubecheck shifts and squirms and nearly freezes to death balled up on the floor beneath the table.

He can't sleep, and as often when you're the only one awake you get a sense of standing watch for everyone, so Dubecheck shudders in the cold, standing watch over the dogs and people and even the ocelot and maybe the crows and sea gulls wherever they snooze. It is just Dubecheck and the nocturnals, an occasional mouse scurrying through some dead leaves, the cry of a house cat on the prowl in the distance, the wind through the madronas and the water lapping the shore and Puget Sound hissing in the blackness.

Drifting Cloud had admitted to him in the confessional of fatigue and darkness that he was a "beaner from St. Pete," a Mexican from San Pedro south of L.A., a fruit bum following the crop, picking apricots and peaches and pears and apples in eastern Washington and playing Indian and Dubecheck once again wondered why people always told him things he really didn't want to know and then he realized it was because he was usually the only other one awake deep into the night and that everybody wants to tell someone everything. And when they do they don't want to know a thing about you.

Dubecheck looks at Drifting Cloud squirming in the front seat, whimpering like a dog having a nightmare, maybe having one of his own, about Wounded Knee, for all Dubecheck can imagine or figure. Or more likely dreaming of nights spent sleeping in boxcars with a hand on his knife and a tight asshole, living on Wonder Bread and bologna sandwiches, sleeping with his body awake, riding a noisy, rumbling freight toward the rich orchards of fruit for America, twelve hours up a ladder filling bins the size of Cadillacs with apples the size of baseballs for the chance to get to do it tomorrow.

Dubecheck gets out of the VW and stands in the drizzle and looks out to the sound; a few specks of watery light shimmer across from the black mainland. If he's standing watch over these people, what is he watching for? From what is he protecting them? The man bringing them their invitations to the Armageddon Day picnic? He likes all these people within fifty feet of him. The only people within five miles as far as he knows. You stay with anyone long enough, you seem to warm to them. Hostages and captors. Happens all the time. Read about it in the papers. Some guy could stop torturing some guy for a minute, shoot the breeze, smoke a J, they'd be friends. Might not stop the guy from torturing the guy some more, but what the hey? What are friends for? Fucking people. Hostage to each other is what they are.

Dubecheck climbs back into the VW van and curls up to get some warmth on the floor. He resigns himself to staying awake all night, which is always good for a buzz around dawn and early morning before the body hits a wall near noon and you could lie down and die.

 In the morning, when everyone assembles, there is not much to say. They are not close, dear friends after all. The house is a wreck, everyone is hung over and only the fact that they're basically strangers keeps them from becoming rude to one another. Chad has an economics class he's going to be late for at the University of Washington. Drifting Cloud's face twists up in the consternation of one facing the day and wondering what he's going to do in it. Lulu's car needs a jump start and Dubecheck feels, as far as the day is concerned, he may need one himself, or at least advice from Drifting Cloud on how he's going to deal with it. It's cold and drizzly. What the day before was beautiful and glorious now lies wrapped in damp hues of gray and lighter shades of pale. Only Lulu seems to work as a visual force. She appears to Dubecheck as something in Technicolor, a bit out of place, strawberries and whipped cream on the dirt, but his feelings for her have diminished somewhat, like they do when you've found out you don't like the company someone you like has chosen to keep. Any chick that could like Chad can't be as squared away as Dubecheck had hoped. And with that realization, she doesn't look as good as she used to and he thinks of the Girl Who Thinks She's His Girlfriend, and because she is not around, she seems a paragon of virtue and nobility, as he envisions her standing stoically in her little paramilitary stewardess uniform, patiently waiting for him to see the light, to realize there are deeper feelings, emotions and tuggings upon the groveling, grappling human soul than self-serving gratification. But he's not sure she's right. Anyway, what does she know? At least Lulu knows how to jump-start her car, which Dubecheck finds alluring. She clamps the ends of the cables onto her battery and shouts to Chad.

"Crank that dog over!" She starts up her car and leaps out to disengage the cables and coil them up before tossing them into the jumble of flora in the back seat.

There is a moment of awkwardness as people wonder who's going with who. Dubecheck climbs into Lulu's car and stares straight ahead at the milk-colored sound.

"You comin' tonight?" Chad asks Lulu. She nods and runs to give him a peck on the cheek which he receives morosely, giving Dubecheck a look he might think menacing. He motions to Drifting Cloud to go along with Lulu and the guy gets in the front seat next to Dubecheck. He smells like flat beer.

Lulu drives for a long time before she gets to the ferry and after the crossing, when the ferry arrives in Seattle, she drives for a longer time and no one talks because they said all that could ever be said last night while they babbled away the hours in the back of the VW van. They drive across the Lake Washington Floating Bridge in the flat, milk-of-magnesia light. Lulu is going to take them to her parents' house.

For sheer aggravation, Dubecheck imagines. Her parents' house is a low-slung earth-toned monstrosity on the edge of the lake on Mercer Island, looking across to Seattle. The four-car garage houses a huge station wagon and a little black Porsche that looks like the station wagon's pet. Two large clumsily happy golden retrievers come running out, slathering like they're in a dog food commercial, padding around in circles and whining as Lulu leads the way to the front door, which is nearly canopied by bonsai trees which look to have been tortured into twisted convolutions by some mad oriental gardener. A set of wind chimes hangs silently by the front door. Drifting Cloud is rubbernecking around as if he just got off the bus at the Taj Mahal.

As she baby-talks the dogs into a slobbering frenzy, Lulu rings the doorbell and looks in her purse for a key.

Dubecheck is familiar enough with the English language that he would characterize the look upon the face of the woman answering the door as "pained."

She says, "Ohhh," very quietly, as if just learning of the death of a nodding acquaintance's cat and hoping to sound sufficiently concerned. Lulu's mother is a white lady and already, before nine in the morning, is put together for the day with a beige cashmere sweater, pearls, nails as pink and shiny as Ford bubble gum balls, tweedy slacks and tan loafers.

The dogs nearly knock her aside as they skid and click on the terrazzo tile of the foyer. Lulu barges in after them. Dubecheck and Drifting Cloud, who only Dubecheck knows is really Jesus Camarillo from San Pedro, California, stand at the door.

"Aren't you going to invite your friends in, Jane?"

"Yeah. Like come in, guys. Jesus, Mother. I mean really. Don't make such a big deal out of it. They're friends of mine."

"Oh." She tries to smile. Her hair is short and Dubecheck is sure he can see every strand neatly swept back into what the Girl Who Thinks She's His Girlfriend calls a pageboy. She might be fortyish. Her pleasant face puckers and puffs neatly around the eyes, lips and nose. She's squared away in a world where neatness counts. She smells a bit of the shower as Dubecheck slides in past her, buzzed from fatigue, feeling a bit whacked out.

"Aren't you going to introduce me to your friends, Jane?" The woman is trying very hard to be civil and mannered and Dubecheck feels a little sorry for her because her daughter seems rather *unkind.* Lulu-Jane is looking in the refrigerator that stands in the kitchen several rooms away across a vast expanse of beige carpet broken up by islands of white sectionals and leather-topped tables with lamps the size of jockeys.

Dubecheck looks out a living-room picture window as big as a billboard at a dock protruding into the gray rain-pocked lake. A Chris-Craft runabout hangs out of the water on slings, and a large cabin cruiser sits in a slip as motionless as a painting. It reminds Dubecheck of something. He extends his hand toward the woman. "I'm Lieutenant (junior grade) John Paul Dubecheck, United States Navy."

She tentatively takes his hand and shakes it with a slightly crazed smile, looking up at Dubecheck, who, bewigged, looks like a deserter from the Hawaiian Army.

"And this is Drifting Cloud of the Hunkpapa Sioux."

The woman nods and says, *"Hunkpapa* Sioux. Well . . . that's very nice. Would . . . would you like something to . . . ?"

"Make us something to eat, huh, Mother? You guys hungry? I'm hungry."

"Of course, darling. What would you young men like?"

Dubecheck would like to eat Lulu. He doesn't like Lulu anymore, which somehow would make it easier to eat her. Right on the inch-thick beige rug, with her mother quietly going "Oh dear" as Dubecheck rips her blouse off and throws her down onto the carpet and tears her skirt off with his teeth, spitting out chunks of denim while the dogs prance around and bark in confusion, glancing occasionally at Drifting Cloud for guidance.

The house seems like a museum. There are pictures hung on the wall that you wouldn't want to look at more than once, paintings in frames more imposing than what they enclose. Magazines fan out on a table in perfect symmetry. *Sunset, Madamoiselle, Fortune* and *Life.* The three rooms Dubecheck can survey have the antiseptic quality of a department store. A sootless fireplace, in a wall of heavy stone masonry, is coldly empty.

"I'm going to take a shower." Lulu-Jane treads down a long, beige-carpeted hallway and goes in a doorway. In the human silence that follows, Dubecheck can hear the sound of helicopters in the distance. It's coming from a little black and white TV sitting on a tile counter in the kitchen. He watches and leans close. A heavily breathing "correspondent" is saying something about being with an element of some regiment or battalion in Quang Blah Province. Sure enough, the heavily breathing correspondent appears upon the toast-size TV screen, and behind him a Huey gunship is descending, bending the grasses behind him like wind through a wheatfield, and the pop of automatic weapons can be heard going off as erratically as wet lady fingers in the background. Dubecheck is watching the morning news. He can hear the water from Lulu-Jane's shower coursing through the piping of the house and dog toenails tapping on the kitchen floor and Mother Lulu-Jane saying, "So . . . the Hunkpapa Sioux. Now are they, I mean, different from, say, the . . . the . . . other Sioux?"

"My grandfather was a great chief."

"Oh, that's nice."

"Got a light?" Drifting Cloud tamps a pack of Lucky Strikes on the Formica counter to square away his smokes and the woman starts opening every cabinet door in the kitchen in some frenzy.

"Relax."

"I beg your pardon."

"Relax," says Dubecheck. "Watch the correspondent. These guys made contact." He points at the little TV. The muted "chatter" of small arms fire in the background sounds somewhat comforting to him. He looks out the window and sees traffic moving in slow motion across a floating bridge in the gray distance and thinks of bringing down mortar fire on it, raking it from nine hundred yards with .50 cal, maybe calling in some air. Good God, that would fuck up rush hour. A few Phantoms in low transition over the span, cutting in their afterburners, would mess up radio reception and maybe, for garnish, a gunship manned by some hung-over screaming nineteen-year-old assholes on full auto running the length of the bridge. That would give every body-and-fender man within a hundred miles a lifetime commission.

Alas, no deal. Some woman is asking him if he likes eggs. As if he just landed from another planet.

"Yes, I like eggs. But I don't want any. Thank you very much anyway."

"Well, I just thought you might . . . I mean if you're all hungry . . ."

"I'm hungry, but I need a match."

The "correspondent" is gone and some perky girl is flacking

toilet bowl cleaner on the TV. Dubecheck wonders what happened to the "element" of some regiment or battalion for a moment, then realizes the "element" does not exist except for those momentary electrodes or whatever bombarded upon a cathode ray tube. He should know, as a leader of an "element" himself. Feels kind of good about it for a moment. It has a good chemical ring to it. Like something grounded in the universe. He liked the "correspondent's" heavy breathing. Nifty. Like Marlin Perkins running through the brush, chasing a lion bitch somewhere in Botswanaland for Mutual of Omaha. The thought he should just shoot everybody in this kitchen, plus the dogs, enters his mind for a brief instant. Of late, he is finding the dark side of his mind far more entertaining than the rest of it. But he is also so tired he thinks maybe he'll just fall down somewhere and go to sleep. He feels safe here. He knows this woman won't hurt him. He wonders what she does all day and what she did to deserve this plush prison. Some guy bought it for her. Like her husband, who must be working somewhere.

Lulu comes into the kitchen with a turban on her head made out of a towel and a huge purple bathrobe beneath which, Dubecheck knows, she's naked and somehow the realization makes him feel all the more exhausted. And duped. Christ, he's been duped forever. Really. He walks into the living room and falls into a large leather sofa as if free-falling into a cloud thousands of feet below, and so ends this day.

o   o   o

Someone is kicking the soles of his shower shoes. He is being rudely awakened, as they say.

"Who in the hell are you? What are you doing in my house?" A fire-hydrant-type guy. Salt and pepper brush cut with a dark brown suit, the jacket unbuttoned to show off his flat fifty-year-old stomach, which he is obviously proud of, setting it off with buttons, belt buckle and fly in a gig line as straight as a plumb bob. He puts his hands on his hips and spreads his legs like a drill instructor.

"Me? I'm a house guest." Dubecheck rises on his elbows.

"Christ's sake." He looks around the dusk-darkened den and shouts, "Virginia! Virginia!" He crosses to a wet bar, pulls a bottle of Chivas Regal from a cabinet, slams it on the counter and starts to build himself a drink, but can't find any ice cubes in the tiny built-in refrigerator. "No ice."

"That stuff's better without it."

"Say again?"

"That's good scotch. It's better straight."

"Oh, *really?* Maybe you want me to make *you* one while I'm at it?"

"Sure. Thanks."

Dubecheck sits up and rubs his eyes.

The guy gazes at Dubecheck for a moment with a blank look. "Which one of my shit-for-brains, dope-sucking kids dragged you in?"

"The one her mother calls 'Jane.'"

"Ah, yes. Plain Jane. Daddy's sweet little girl."

"Insane Jane."

"Bubble Brain Jane. At least you're not black. You're not black, are you? Is she pregnant? You're not Chad, are you? Come get your drink, I'm not going to bring the goddamn thing to you. Virginia! Where the hell is that—that *woman?*"

"I don't know. I've been resting. And relaxing." Dubecheck crosses to the wet bar and picks up his drink.

The man pours one for himself and hoists it. "No ice. I'll take your word for it."

Virginia enters the room and from ten feet Dubecheck can pick up the reek of gin. The man raises his glass to her.

"Ah, the 'Better Half.'" The man points to Dubecheck. "Who's this flower child with his dirty feet on my fifteen-hundred-dollar couch?"

She squints at Dubecheck, as if trying to remember where she might have seen him before.

"I'm Lieutenant (junior grade) John Paul Dubecheck."

"Right. I'm Generalissimo Chiang Kai-shek." He takes Dubecheck's hand and gives it the virile, nutcracker squeeze. He has to look up to Dubecheck, allowing for that subliminal respect men have for size regardless of anything else. He releases his grip. "You're out of uniform, though, aren't you? I thought JGs wore Navy uniforms, but what do I know? These are changing times. Maybe you're on a secret mission." He turns to his wife. "Before you fall down, maybe you could get me some ice cubes."

Virginia walks unsteadily out of the room. "And what do you do, Lieutenant, besides sleep in strange houses? Everybody else around here drinks all day or gets stoned while I work twenty-five hours a day to fund it."

"Where do you work, sir?"

"I work at the Boeing Aircraft Company. Please don't call me 'sir.' I was only an enlisted man. You're the officer, right?"

"What did you enlist in?"

"The Marines. Semper Fi." He slaps his stomach. "Korea. We learned to shoot off the stern of the troop transport going across the Pacific, crash course, real swell, but I'm sure you don't care, let alone know anything, about that stuff. All you know and care about is peace and love, right?"

"Right."

Virginia enters with a little phony oaken bucket of ice cubes in one hand and a tall, half-empty drink in the other.

"And all she cares about is her loving husband. Right, dearest?"

"If you say so, darling." She talks in a hoarse whisper. "My husband is always right, John. I've often wondered how comforting it must be, to always be right."

Dubecheck can see this is one of those great marriages where nobody really talks to each other. They just say self-serving things when there's an audience available. He doesn't feel like being their audience and wonders where Lulu and the Indian are. "Where's Lulu and the Indian?"

"An *Indian*. Jesus H. Christ."

"They left several hours ago."

"Yeah, well then, I better be going myself."

"No. Please stay," says the husband. "You can have dinner with us and we can pretend to be one big happy family. You can be my kid for the night. A boy. Three girls I've got, Lieutenant. Not a raised toilet seat in the house, and it's got four and a half baths."

"Mr. Keever wanted a son very badly, John. Unfortunately I was incapable of providing him with one. Just another one of my many shortcomings. Would you like to tell him some of my others, Harold?"

"She calls me Harold when she's being sarcastic, John. You can call me Hal, just like my pals."

"What pals? Hal doesn't have any pals, because he's a pompous ass, if you'll pardon my French. Did he tell you he works for Boeing?"

Dubecheck nods.

"He acts like he *owns* Boeing. He is very successful, though. Look at his house. Tell us how many square feet, Hal."

"Five thousand, and it's *our* house. I bought it for my family, kids. I worked hard for nearly twenty years so they could all have the things I didn't have and I'd like to go on record now as saying how pleased and grateful I am they now kindly acknowledge it. Three girls, John. Think of it. Twenty years I've busted my ass so I can live in an ungrateful sea of female hormones. Pollen? Allergies? Nothing compared to a sea of female hormones. When their month-lies come, four of 'em, count 'em, one-two-three-four, it's like the siege of the Alamo." He pours himself another drink. "Did you make anything for dinner, dear, or are you too exhausted from changing outfits all day?"

"I think that is rude and uncalled for, Harold. Especially when John here doesn't know us. Do you think he's being rude and un-called for, I mean rude and . . . ?"

"I want to get out of here."

"Smart boy, Lieutenant. So do I," says the husband.

"Well, nothing is stopping you." She looks at him for the first time, her eyelids half closed. She takes a quick sip of her drink for support. He stares back at her as if he didn't know who she was.

"I think I'd better go now. Thanks for the hospitality."

The man and woman remain staring at each other, the woman swaying like a drunken cobra. Ice cubes shift and collapse in her glass.

Dubecheck walks through the darkness of the den and out into the unlit living room, across the soft mosslike texture of the carpet. He exits the front door and stands by the pretty twisted tree. The two dogs quietly come up to him, nuzzling him for affection. The sound of glass shattering is followed by a woman's scream. The dogs whine and look at the door.

Dubecheck hears muffled shouting inside, furniture scraping across tile. The phrase "domestic violence" enters his mind and he wonders if he should go in and try to do something about it. Maybe if he just went in and watched they would calm down. He walks around to a picture window and looks in to see they are now in the living room and Harold is holding her by the wrists as she struggles to release herself, shaking her head back and forth like she's insane. Harold looks over to see Dubecheck and shakes his head at him as if totally confused, impotent, dejected . . . mainly embarrassed. He lets go of the woman. She runs out of the room.

Harold comes toward Dubecheck through some french doors and stops beside him; he looks across the flat, inky lake to the swath of dotted lights of Seattle.

Perpendicular to a wooden dock, a thirty-foot fiberglass sailboat sleeps in a slip, glowing like a Clorox bottle in the darkness. A small lawn slopes to a riprap rock bulkhead. The boat's halyard "bings" off the aluminum mainmast like a lethargic wind chime in the slight onshore breeze.

"The lake looks like glass, doesn't it?" Harold lights a cigarette and blows out a smoke ring. A guy who's really upset doesn't blow smoke rings, but Harold seems upset.

"A hundred years ago, nobody was here. It was all black and dark and quiet. Maybe all you could hear was an Indian foot tread a wet path." Then he doesn't say anything more, leading Dubecheck to wonder whether that was one of those odd things a guy says that is supposed to lead into something meaningful.

It does. Harold swirls his little cocktail glass around and ice cubes rattle. "Ice. You don't mind, do you?"

"No, sir."

"You're a nice kid. I'll tell you something. I love my wife, but if I didn't love her I'd love somebody else. I am forty-eight years old and the only thing that truly nags at me, as time flies by, is the grounder I let through my legs when I was seventeen years old that lost my last high school baseball game. That may sound silly to you in the vast scheme of things, but when you get to be forty-eight you will find that things like that are as important as glaciers."

The guy is twice as old as Dubecheck, which means he might as well have been born on Neptune. Nevertheless, they stand side by side, in silence, looking at water and sky like Lewis and Clark.

"The night my wife and I got married we made love eleven times. I was a lance corporal and on our honeymoon we ate nothing but watermelon. My buddies gave us a pot, so we couldn't say we didn't have one to pee in." He chuckles and flicks his cigarette into the black lake with his forefinger. "This is all by way of saying nothing, Admiral. Except I'd trade that house"—he tosses his head back—"for thirty years and a 1937 Chev in a second."

Oh, really, Dubecheck thinks. Fellow Americans can drive you nuts. They just live in this *vacuum*. Probably the one nature is supposed to abhor.

"How old are you, Jay?"

"John."

"How old are you, John?"

"I'm about twenty-four."

"That is a wonderful age. In many respects, it doesn't get any better than that, yet your whole life is in front of you. But enjoy these precious times."

Dubecheck is wondering how he is going to get away from this sage and his wise pronouncements which Dubecheck hopes are untrue when he sees Virginia quickly crossing the living room, rifling a purse like she has just stolen it and pulling out a ring of keys.

Dubecheck eases off a bit while Harold, his back to him, orates to the water about how unbelievably fast time goes by. He sees Virginia hustling toward the garage and he quickly runs toward her. She can't get the key into the Porsche's ignition and mutters, "Shit!" at the jingling bracelet of keys in her hand.

"I'll drive."

Virginia looks up. Her face has put on about ten years since the morning. She sniffles.

"All right."

While he's trying to find reverse, he expects his pal Hal to come running out with a shotgun, which heightens the excitement. But Hal doesn't come and he's off with the car, slowly snaking up the steep, switchback driveway to wherever.

The engine whines up the grade like a pride of purring ocelots, its tiny little Nazi valves and tappets and pistons torquing out with Germanic assurance. He swings onto a dark, undulating, twisting boulevard passing through what seems to be a forest, tiny clearings off to the sides lit with happy little homes full of wonderful families sitting down to dinner with Walter Cronkite intoning seriously on TVs that flicker ice-blue light upon the ceilings. Virginia's chin bounces off her sternum with each jolting shift of the gears.

"Virginia? You with me?"

She nods. Her eyes are like guys' he's seen hit too hard on the head.

"Then I'd like to know where the headlights are on this baby."

She reaches over and turns them on. She smells very nice. She's not wearing vanilla. A combination of gin and . . .

"Is that, that a—a—*Fabergé* you're wearing?"

"Why, yes. Yes, it is." She tries to smile but her face just slackens like she's got lips full of novocaine. Dubecheck hopes she doesn't start talking to him about her problems. Or start talking to him about *anything* and ruin this great affair he is about to have with the Porsche.

Seattle is across the floating bridge to the left but a turn to the right, he recalls, leads to a cross-continental strip of highway where he can give this baby its head all the way to Chicago if he wants. A hundred and twelve's been the fastest for him so far and that was in a '55 Ford convertible that sounded as if it was coming apart at the welds as he climbed past a hundred. These things, he's heard, are only yawning and stretching at a hundred.

He slips down an on ramp and hits the four-lane that leads east, becoming I-90, merging into the thinning rush-hour traffic heading to the suburbs east of Seattle, feeling like a wolf slipping into a herd of sheep with a shit-eating grin on its face.

Virginia still appears to be very drunk. If he cranks up the heater on high she might fall asleep and give him the peace and tranquillity he needs to enjoy this experience.

Speed and the open American West. Counties as large as Eastern states or European federations, flat-out jackrabbit lunar-landscape American West, moonlit rolling foothills, desert and sage, prairie and night-black forests growing out of cavernous canyons, mountains that block out the sun and the wide-open God Bless America Western race tracks blasted through them by men with vision and four-fifty-cubic-centimeter V-8 souls. *That's* what's worth fighting for, worth slogging around with a rifle and a pack in a swamp eight thousand miles away from the greatest merry-go-round on the planet—the West. To be able to mash Detroit iron into the wind and scream through the American West with a 6000 rpm radio tuner laying a sound track down on your rootless, can't-stop-me, flying American, cheap-gas romance ass, and although Dubecheck isn't sitting on top of a V-8 hog plunging and floating down on its feather-bed shocks as it cleaves the night with its dual Hollywood Glass-pak muffler purr, this little Nazi import isn't bad. A little shrill, a little effeminate if you think of some cigar-chomping Caddy or bourbon-on-the-rocks Buick, or some basic blue-collar three-fifty Chevy, cars built to go one-twenty as you drive with a beer in one hand and a cigarette in the other, punching AM buttons to catch KOMA coming out of the dark night fifteen hundred miles away, cars built to go twice the legal speed limit, a Detroit bone toss to the snarling scofflaw Western Yankee driver out where the only other traffic you see is a laser coming the other way, red dots in the night, racing the goddamn dawn, cocooned, encapsulated in the faint glow of silver-dollar-size gauges telling you all you ever need to know . . . oil pressure, engine temperature, amperage and E or F. As he climbs past eighty, slipping by the thinning traffic, he contemplates the near future. I-90, a billion tons of cement placed over a slightly widened, twelve-thousand-year-old Indian trail, gradually climbs to slice through the Cascade Mountains, rises gently to about three thousand feet at the summit before descending into the eastern Washington scrubland and desert, where a guy can really haul ass, where distant lights appear as stars across the vast, soulful prairie.

"Where do you think you're going?"

She didn't go under. In fact, for the first time in a long time, Virginia seems alert and, by the tone of her voice, a little miffed. "Don't you think you should slow down?"

"I don't know where I'm going. Did you have any plans?"

"I want a drink."

An overhead arc light floods the inside of the car for a microsecond, illuminating her tired face, and then they are into the dark foothills beyond the night light of the suburbs. Distant red taillights and a few oncoming headlights decorate the darkness ahead.

"Where are we?"

"Heading east."

"Oh." She leans her head against her window and looks out. Somehow she makes Dubecheck sad. And makes him wonder about his own mother, although this mother is about fifteen years, twenty years younger than his. It only takes hanging around other people for a little bit to find out that your own aren't as bad as you sometimes think. In fact, everyone he's met in a long time makes him feel guilty about not calling his mother or the Girl Who Thinks She's His Girlfriend. Mary. He'd almost forgotten her name. She's not that bad, but that's a lousy recommendation.

Dubecheck could see that this woman was very pretty once. Still is, he guesses. She's old enough she could be his mother. But she isn't and she has a very nice figure.

"How fast *are* you going?" She talks into her reflection.

"Ninety."

"Go faster."

"Faster than ninety. Like maybe one hundred?"

"Or more. I've often wondered what this thing could do. It's a birthday present."

Nice present. He remembers his mother once getting a frying pan for her birthday, and a pot holder he made in Cub Scouts. He made her a cake once, one with a rakish tilt to it, pink frosting with colorful sugar sprinkles on it looking weird in the flickering tiny birthday candlelight in the darkened kitchen, dirty dishes in the shadows on the sink counter. Once she got a checkered coat from his father. Nice lady. He'll have to sit down and write her a nice long letter someday. About the . . . weather. End it by telling her to be careful. Maybe bring Mary home and introduce them. Sit in the kitchen over coffee waiting for the strained silences to ease into a conversation. About the weather. It would be real swell. Jesus.

He punches down on the throttle and feels like he is flying in the dark as the needle wiggles slowly past the 110 mark. He also feels the woman's hand land on his thigh, which gives him a little start. He looks over to see her mouth open, her eyes staring straight ahead in a sort of wonder. Speed. The province of the wealthy of the Western world. For the first time in the history of the world a select group of people get to career about in steel chariots of mythic speed. With impunity. One hundred and twenty. A Carnation milk truck, a semi, is lugging up a slight grade. He passes it like it was a billboard. Its headlights suck back into the distance in the rear-view like contracting pupils and are replaced by a distant flashing red, ever so slowly closing. But not for long. Dubecheck floors the Porsche and watches the tachometer needle waver near the red line. The engine whines and Dubecheck imagines sitting astride a machine with huge legs galloping over the concrete, reaching out and pulling quarter-mile chunks of road beneath them with each fluid stride. Luminescent stakes and signs alongside the interstate fly by his peripheral vision like tracers. Virginia's nails dig through his pants into his thigh, heightening his sense of fear and excitement. This is what he is good at: driving in the night with no particular place to go and feeling deeply at home. Alone.

Vaguely familiar with the place names subliminally registering in his mind from the road signs, he dips down an off ramp, downshifting as the Porsche fishtails wildly into a dark two-lane blacktop that after a mile or so turns into a gravel logging road. He passes through a couple of fluorescent-eyed deer frozen in the headlights on the road, then turns into a small dirt cul-de-sac picketed by some huge firs that black out the already murky night. He shuts off the lights and engine and sits in the darkness. The wind hisses through the swaying conifers, which fling ropes of rain from their wet needles onto the roof of the car. Virginia's grip relaxes a bit, then slides softly over his thigh as his heart thumps and the familiar heavy loading between his legs starts. She slides her hand over the thickening bulge in his Hawaiian slacks and leans over and kisses him and it is like the soft kiss of a sixteen-year-old, her warm pliant lips barely parted, her tongue making tiny, tentative flicks into his mouth while her hand softly kneads, then grips at him. She lifts her hand off him and puts her arms around his neck and begins to grind her mouth into his, almost snorting out of her nose, nearly climbing onto his lap, her cashmere breast softly pressing into his PFC blouse as she whimpers, then stops with a deep gasp, falling back to her seat with her face in her hands. For a long time Dubecheck listens to the rain hit the roof.

"God, I'm old enough to be your mother."

"No, you're not. She's much older."

"I've . . . I've never done anything like that before. I just . . . I don't know what happened. I just . . ." She doesn't look at Dubecheck and begins to smooth back her hair and shake some imaginary cobwebs out of her now sober mind. "You'd better take me home, young man." She looks to him and chews her lips, a bit frightened. He wonders if her husband is sitting in the dark looking into his drink and thinking back to the time he was shooting his M-1 Garand off the stern of a pitching olive-drab troop transport into the dirty gray cold swells of the North Pacific on his way to fight the yellows. He wonders if Chip and Dale are sitting on a fir branch and looking down into the Porsche with smarmy smiles and big tears welling up in their big Disneyesque eyes.

"I really must be going." She talks like someone in a play.

"Where do you have to go?"

She looks at the fingernails on her left hand. "I'm a married woman."

"Yeah . . . sure, I'll take you back. Just drop me off somewhere."

"Of course. Where would you like to be dropped off?"

"Somewhere." He starts the car and slowly drives back out the logging road, wishing he was a Hamm's Bear, out in the woods bowling with the other bears, shooting the breeze about where they're going to hibernate next winter. He looks over to Virginia, envisioning her in an old folks' home someday, sitting in a wheelchair, staring out a window into the rain, white desiccated skin hanging from a bony frame, a broken hip, palsied lips quivering, dull eyes, wormy veined hands blotched with liver spots, a vague memory of going one hundred and forty miles an hour through the night at one point in her all too fast life. People were born to be driven fucking nuts.

On the way to Seattle she tells him her life story like they're the best of friends or something. Knock out the place names and it's the same story as a lot of other people's. Most other people's. She keeps saying she wishes she could write a book about it.

"Why don't you?"

"I've tried. It's very difficult. I've started several times, but I just kind of . . . stop. My book was going to be about just ordinary-type people. Nothing special."

"Well, most people are ordinary. Aren't there some good books about ordinary people?" He thinks. *Silas Marner*, for instance.

They made him try to read that book in high school and after that he almost quit reading forever. Then there was the guy in *Moby-Dick* who was normal, but the guy he talked about was nuts. Good book. Too long, it took him forever, but somewhere along the line he built up a grudging respect for Captain Ahab. But not Captain Veere. Billy Budd really took it in the shorts from that guy. Poor Billy, just before they hang his ass he says, "God bless Captain Veere." Billy Budd wasn't ordinary. Dubecheck would have liked to go out drinking with Billy Budd. But not with Silas Marner. He wouldn't mind going out drinking with Virginia, because she is awfully nice, really. Or maybe she's a bitch. But anyway, he likes her more when she tells him about how she took the test to see if she could come up to snuff for the Famous Writers' School and how she submitted some work and it came back and they were very complimentary about it. Marked it with red pencil and everything. She had written about the time they got a flat tire coming back from skiing. It was snowing and they didn't have a spare. Night was falling and she and Hal had all three of the girls with them. Back when they were all under ten, all dressed in their mittens and caps with flaps and scarfs and drinking hot chocolate from a plaid thermos bottle and too hot tin cups and they had that old '50 Chevy with the windshield wipers that went faster when you pressed on the accelerator and slower when you backed off, or maybe the other way around. That's when Virginia starts crying, real quietly, and Dubecheck can't think of anything to say except, "That's the start of a really good story, Virginia. I like it."

"I'm sorry." She sniffs and starts to laugh, a pretend laugh, and wipes her eyes.

"You haven't done anything to be sorry for."

"Ohhhhhhhh." She heaves a big sigh. "I don't know."

"Well. I don't know either," hoping that would cheer her up.

He finds himself on Aurora Avenue, a junky-looking arterial going through the city where it turns into a jumble of one-story houses, storefronts and car lots. At a stoplight, the windshield wipers spread a drizzle across the window and Dubecheck sees a warped plywood sign above a string of little bungalows set off the street. ACE MOTEL. Perfect. That's where he belongs. He passes through the green light and pulls into the narrow asphalt parking lot that separates two rows of a half dozen tiny houses that look like Monopoly pieces.

"This is it."

"What do you mean?"

"I'll get out here."

"Here? It's a . . . a motel."

"A crummy one, too. I like it. Especially the name."

He wonders if he should ask her in. If it would be good manners. If she wants to spend the night. But then she might say yes. The parking lot lights don't do her any favors and, as if she's aware of that, she veils her face with her left hand.

He may only be imagining that, but what a guy imagines people might be doing becomes what a guy thinks they're doing, whether that's what they're doing or not, and a guy acts upon it and that's where the trouble starts.

If he asks her, it would be a gesture, maybe of kindness, but like all gestures of kindliness, a little selfish. He thinks he might be lonely and it's dark out. He likes her because he feels a little sorry for her, but he doesn't know why. There are a lot more people in the world to feel sorrier for than her, but then again he isn't with any other people now and if he doesn't stop thinking so much about it, with the dark night and dreary weather, he's going to start feeling sorry for himself.

"I'm going to get a room. If you don't want to go home right away, you can come in for a while."

"Oh. I . . . I don't think I could do that. I've . . . I've never done anything like that—like this before."

He really does want to get into a room. And pull the shades and lie on the bed and stare up at the ceiling. What else is there to do? Go to a *movie?* He wonders what other people do to fill their lives. What would any normal kid his age be out doing now? Chasing chicks? He doesn't feel like chasing chicks. He's not very good at it and, anyway, they chase you when it gets right down to it. He doesn't have the energy to sit and listen to a chick talk and pretend it means something to him.

"I'm going to get a room. You can think about it." He gets out of the Porsche and walks over to the office, thinking about how all the fun goes out of things if you don't care.

The manager comes out of a door behind the check-in desk, which sits in a foyer the size of a three-hole outhouse. He wears a wife-beater undershirt, straps over the shoulders and more hair on his back than some guys have on their heads. He's fat and dark-eyed, and chewing food. A smell comes out of the door behind him. Dinnertime. A junior high school cafeteria smell, the cloying aroma of a casserole for five hundred. TV on. The sound of tires squealing, gunshots and the dippy music that goes with those scenes.

"I want a room."

"No fuckin' hippies."

"I'm not a hippie, I'm a naval officer."

"Oh. Well, why didn't you say so? No sailors."

Dubecheck plops his roll of money on the counter.

"One night, please. I'm cold and tired. You look like a nice guy. Be a pal."

The manager turns and pulls down a key from a rack.

"Fifty dollars. Number 7. Checkout eleven." He slides a registration card across toward Dubecheck.

"What's with the fifty dollars? Is that where the President stays when he comes here? You got a sign says twelve dollars. Twelve means twelve, even in Chinese."

"Take it or leave it."

"I take it for fifty dollars, I'll destroy the place. I take it for what's fair, I might flush the toilet before I leave."

"Okay. Twenny bucks. Fill out the card. It's a double. Nice room. Wanna see it?"

"I'll take your word for it."

Dubecheck leaves the office with the key to 7. The guy in Hawaii with the Marine was right. Fucking civilians are dog breath. The Porsche is gone. He walks to 7 and opens it up. Cars drone by on Aurora Avenue, their tires squishing on the wet pavement. Inside it's dark, save for the parking lot lights filtering through the gauzy curtains like clouded moonlight.

He flops down on the bed and looks up at the ceiling. Perfect. A truck downshifts out on the main arterial and begins a gradual climb to somewhere, hauling a load, taking Dubecheck's mind with it, into a long silence as the traffic ceases to be noticed or heard, just the way a noisy stream at a campsite eventually becomes absorbed into nothingness.

He wakes in the early morning after fitful dreams about Virginia. Just another person he would never again see in his life, like the little girl who scowled out a Greyhound bus window at him as it flew past while he stood hitchhiking in the drab flat snow of southern Idaho back in another lifetime.

The room is a bummer; a cold, cracked linoleum floor, a few wire hangers in an empty alcove closet. He gets up and looks out the window. White sky and drizzle, one of those black and white days in the Pacific Northwest when people take numbers to line up and jump off the suspension bridges.

He checks out of the Ace Motel and stands on the sidewalk wondering where to go. A nearby sign indicates a zoo in the near distance and, having his fill of humans for the time being, he decides to check out the animals.

The zoo is deserted. It's cold and the drizzle has built into a persistent needlelike rain that makes tiny puddles in the undulating asphalt paths between the penal-looking cages and grottoes of the rocky, shrub-enclosed park.

The only animal he can see is a Malaysian sun bear that sits on its haunches, a furry round yellow target on its chest. It rolls its head around on its neck, begging for something to eat. Pigeons huddled underneath benches wait out a rain delay. He appears to be the only human in sight, and it's as if the animals have taken the day off, relaxing in their private rooms watching TV. The rain feels good, bathing him with a cold humidity as he sits on a wet wooden bench in front of a semicircle of hopping, panhandling crows that look at him, impatiently expectant, through eyes like bright beads.

He hears laughter, vigorous, optimistic, genuine laughter, *carefree* laughter, and turns to see a girl and two slender guys sort of his age walking toward his bench along the wet asphalt pathway. Dressed in denim and swathed in scarves of somber tones, they look like angry students. Hiking boots. Wild hair, the young men's black and bushy, the girl's cascading down over her maroon serape like a huge wet pom-pom. They all walk with that loping, knee-buckling gait that you'd never find in an athlete, an awkward, flailing traverse of the earth beneath them that's good for neither fleeing nor chasing. Dubecheck thinks that in the olden days they'd be easy prey for some of the angrier animals now locked up in this chilly damp zoo, and if they were forced to hunt some of the more benign species, they'd starve. Except for the chick. She'd never starve. She leaps off the page with a fresh, beautiful, baby pink plumpness, an overall appeal that would make guys want to feed her. In return for certain considerations. For laughing that great round laugh.

They come closer, crashing gaily through the drizzle, bringing a slight smile to Dubecheck's face in spite of his feeling invaded. Kids. And for the first time he sees the placard the girl is carrying shift into view so he can read it. NOT ONE MORE DEAD! The sign is the size strikers carry around when they're on picket lines and she twirls it by its handle like a parasol as she laughs, bright teeth guarding a big pink mouth, laughing raucously with the two guys on either side of her as they pass by his bench, scattering the crows, who fly up and quickly land a few feet away.

Their laughter seems so incongruous with the sign. Dubecheck wonders what it means. NOT ONE MORE DEAD!

Not one more dead what? He gets up and decides to follow them. At a discreet distance. So they won't know it. As if they might even care. He jogs across the open lawn from tree to tree in the company of two fat gray squirrels with plumed tails, confused squirrels that look at him with suspicion as they bound over the grass like furry Slinkies. He hides behind a tree, catching his breath, and peers toward the jovial trio, thinking Drifty Cloud's grandfather would be very proud of him, stealthily tracking white men and their chick.

He looks over into a dark cement grotto surrounded by a concrete moat and sees a reclined leopard yawn. Christ, this is great! He feels like he could stay here forever, bounding around the nearly deserted zoological garden with a pocket full of money and another pocket full of an automatic Chicom pistol, a broken watch and a picture of some dead guy's wife. Only to return at dusk to his lair at the Ace Motel, to lie on his back and stare at the ceiling, which looks like a sky of gray cottage cheese.

But the three happy people are leaving the zoo grounds. They stand at an intersection at the border of the park, waiting for a stoplight to turn green.

NOT ONE MORE DEAD! Maybe it's the name of a band. He continues to follow the three and soon he sees other kids fill the street like filings to a magnet and a crowd is forming and he finds himself at the end of a growing throng moving up Forty-fifth Street toward the University District. They all start to chant, swarming together like lemmings from every side street and alley, coagulating in the street to where the foot traffic begins to slow and block honking autos, a battalion of kids waving placards and swirling a few North

Vietnamese flags and chanting, "Ho! Ho! Ho Chi Minh is going to win!" like it was a football cheer.

Now he knows. NOT ONE MORE DEAD! All these kids want to stop the *war*. What a groovy idea. Really. He wants to stop it too. He'll join this mob and help stop the war. He didn't have anything else to do today anyway.

A certain sense of jovial delirium hangs in the air but subsides as they get closer to the campus of the University of Washington. The whole crowd becomes a bit somber, the laughter and joyousness come to a momentary halt for the apparently sober business at hand. Dubecheck moves along, slowly jostled in the throng like someone heading toward the turnstiles of a big game.

Dubecheck doesn't like crowds. Or large organizations. Or group activity. And the meandering cattle drive he finds himself in is becoming unpleasant. He begins to ease his way out of the sluggish sloganeering crowd so as to give himself a bit of slack, odd man out so to speak, even though he is all in favor of NOT ONE MORE DEAD! Although he is not sure if these people mean not one more dead American or one more dead Asian, because there is some apparent confusion here. If they want Ho-Ho Ho Chi Minh to win, there will be lots more dead Asians and dead Americans. And Koreans and Australians. And water buffalo. And birds. And tank treads over God knows how many field mice. He's back to square one. Not one more dead what? These people seem to be pretty sure of themselves on that matter, however, and, as usual, what does he know?

Dubecheck skirts the periphery of the shuffling, relatively quiet mass of young men and women. A few older people are scattered throughout the crowd and Dubecheck is impressed by their stern sobriety, their faces set in rigid, no-nonsense propriety, like acolytes he used to know trying not to laugh during the Eucharist.

And he is struck with a dreadful familiarity. All these people are so *sure* of themselves. Just like the ones trying to get him killed seem so *sure* of themselves, and the overwhelming uncertainty and loneliness of his own ignorance falls over him with a pall like a bad hangover.

All the young people his age in this throng look like all the young people he knows in Asia but with more hair. And none of the women have teeth stained black with betel nut juice.

He pushes ahead through people who give him angry looks as if he is trying to crash a line for a better seat. Which is what he is doing. He wants to be up on point to see if he can get the Big Picture.

The incendiary, white phosphorous glow of television lights appears a short distance away over a field of bobbing heads, an odd artificial brightness in the gray day. Through a break in the bobbing heads, Dubecheck sees a small plywood platform with a standing microphone on it. A young man leaps to the stage and shoots his fist up into the air and the crowd roars. The noise reverberates off beautiful dead-ivy-covered buildings that enclose the area like a stadium.

"WADDA WE WANT?" the kid screams into the microphone. His voice streaks around the quad like incoming.

"PEACE!" the crowd chants back in a heavy dull roar that bludgeons the air.

"WHEN DO WE WANNIT?" Feedback shrieks like a wounded pig.

"Nowwwww!" The crowd does its Mormon Tabernacle best to burst the sky with a single voice.

The kid sort of reminds Dubecheck of someone who comes out and warms up the audience for a Bob Hope troop show. He wonders how long Bob Hope would last up on this platform with his golf club and his smile. "But seriously, folks . . ." They might tear him apart like string cheese and wreck every instrument in Les Brown's Band of Renown. Rip the clothes off whatever big-breasted bimbo he's brought along for the troops to impotently lust after. "Hey! You hear the one about the . . ." And all the brass up in the front row, sitting on chairs grinning like gargoyles, ready to laugh at anything he says, *anything*.

Different crowd here. The kid on the platform has an artery on the side of his neck the size of a garter snake. Dubecheck fears it might burst all over the front row if he keeps up his screaming. "WADDA WE WANT?"

What Dubecheck can't figure is that the kid already *asked* that question and everybody already *answered* him, yet he and the crowd persist in repeating themselves as if no one had heard or that this playground chant might actually bring about peace by sheer persistence, any minute now.

The kaleidoscopeic mass of faces look up toward their leader with a rapt attentiveness, a passion, faces full of a gullible willingness to *believe*. Like a pep rally. A willingness to believe in the team, in imminent victory, in concepts. For a rally for peace, a menacing whiff of violence hangs in the air.

Another young man jumps up on the plywood platform waving an American flag, a skinny kid in Levi's and a field jacket with a dirty smear of a Fu Manchu. He wears little rimless glasses that reflect the bright television lights and flash about like mirrors, making him look robotic. The guy at the microphone pulls out a Bic lighter.

"U. S. Army government issue!" he screams and the crowd roars like troops at a Bob Hope show when the chick with tits squeezes her cleavage together with her naked arms.

He puts the whooshing lighter's flame to the tip of the flag and the flag catches fire, to the mixed reaction of the delirious crowd, which has reached some sort of critical mass between confusion and release, and when the leader leaps down from the platform, waving his arms in a "Follow me!" gesture and strides off over a wide brick walkway toward a gap in the buildings, the throng seems of one mind and surges after him, the fired American flag waving in the sky like a burning candy cane, flecks of black ash swirling into the gray sky, and the chanting, roaring crowd moving like lava, building speed, ready to cascade out to who knows where. Dubecheck thinks that you could take a hill with this crowd . . . San Juan, Suribachi, Pork Chop, Hamburger, but as with all mindless frontal assaults, he figures, this one's going to create some casualties.

The crowd's pace has picked up and Dubecheck finds himself riding the front of a cresting wave, jogging to keep up or keep from being trampled from behind in the mass, thinly veiled hysteria of a forced march at double time, full packs. Dubecheck thinks this is how Bastilles fall. He huffs along. This is how evil dies, in the shuffling, one-minded frontal assault of righteousness and human will molded to simple vision. Everywhere around him are chicks. Bosoms bouncing under their heavy cable knit sweaters, corn-fed, husky-looking honeys like Lulu, pink cheeks and long healthy hair, thick strong Wonder Bread thighs and broad white butts churning and heaving under long denim skirts. And the boys, all the young 1A selective-service-rated young men, striding along in the throng shouting, "Hell no, we won't go!" some of them maybe one D-minus away from getting to spend the next six weeks chanting slogans in boot camp with a more rigorously enforced vigor. NOT ONE MORE DEAD!

But hey, what the hell? A crowd's a crowd and he finds himself moving along, sort of like what he imagines it must be like to run before the bulls in Pamplona or wherever, ready to go over the top with this dizzy group that apparently dislikes violence in any form and wants the war to end and NOT ONE MORE DEAD! but they're really crack troops and Dubecheck would give even money that if you put them in uniform, slapped a rifle in their hands, cranked up the John Philip Sousa to ten, gave 'em a "Pass in review," and a goddamn good "Eyes right!" they'd swivel their necks in unison and snap their beadies into space like a frog tongue snapping off some dumb fuck mosquito and with their backbones so goddamn straight and their guts sucked in so tight you'd think every goddamn one of them had a Burpee's Golden Bantam corncob one foot up their tight asses. *Crack troops.* The world's full of them.

And everybody around him is *white.* Actually not white, but variations on pink, like animals he has skinned. It took the Orient to make him kind of realize how ugly most of his race is. And it is also maybe the Orient that is making him realize white people don't know shit. Otherwise they wouldn't be so willing to believe anything they hear all the time. Then again the gooks don't have their shit entirely together either. A guy could get the inkling that human beings don't know shit. Just enough shit, though. Like that poor coyote.

People want to like each other. The concept drops onto his brain like bird shit. He watches his flipflop shower shoes plod over the concrete behind the person in front of him with a monotonous energy. Of a sudden he feels among friends. *America.* He'd almost forgotten he was in America, because when you are an American you take *everything* for granted. Americanness. Free lunch. The throng makes him feel like when he was in a chorus as a fifth grader. A grade school chorus for Thanksgiving songs. He had a lousy voice and he and one other guy, Warren Badger, weren't allowed in the fourth- and fifth-grade chorus because of that, and at the last moment someone decided to let them in and there, in the back row, singing, " 'Over the river and through the woods to Grandmother's house we go . . .' " he thrilled to the wonder. How imperfection blends to music. And his tiny voice became a full song and the sound came out of his body and, standing in his white shirt and damp boys' bathroom combed hair in front of the parents and teachers, he sang a *melody.* He feels sort of like a kid in this crowd. A fourth grader in a world that uses up men, and he wonders when he is going to become a *man.* If you can become a *man* here. Inside this *joke.* With all these people who really think they're putting something on the line. Like this silly old woman next to him, with a bathing cap of stringy salt and pepper hair. She wears a black turtleneck sweater under an open parka, a long skirt that stops just above her hiking boots, a large turquoise pendant on her chest, and looks up to Dubecheck with a pleased smile. She's older than his mother. What's his mother doing today? Is she wondering about him? If he is safe? If he is wearing his rubbers in the rain? Is she staring out the window, wondering what ever happened to that eight-pound pile of woe she squeezed from her gut nearly a quarter of a century ago?

"Isn't this just *thrilling?*" the woman smiles up to Dubecheck. "Huh?"

"Isn't this thrilling? I mean, to know that we can do something. To be a force." She never loses her smile, like some chick waving from a float in a parade.

Her eyes remind him of the guy who was shouting at the crowd before. Shiny, bright, glistening. Like they were wired to something, plugged into a mindless socket.

"Really."

She locks her arm in the crook of his left elbow and they fall into step, she infused with some psychic intensity and he with fatigued delirium starting to cave in on him.

He has fallen back some from the leaders, distanced himself, which is always a safe thing to do. The woman next to him, clamped to his arm with a proprietary assumption he finds a bit pushy, is humming some tune that probably has no name and it aimlessly grates on his ears. She seems to be one of those endlessly cheerful people who apparently don't really understand things. She disengages her arm and takes Dubecheck's hand and swings it to and fro between them as if they were a couple of bluebirds. Dubecheck doesn't figure her so much an indomitable spirit as a probable pain in the ass and he tries to withdraw his hand but she clamps down on it and says, "Solidarity!" The thought that he could snap her arm up behind her back and have her on her tiptoes gaping like a beached fish, wondering what the fuck, before he sent her flying forward to stomp on her neck and pin her to the ground enters his mind briefly and pleasurably. Violence. The occasional thought of its application has a calming effect upon him. He wonders if that's unhealthy. What the hell. He's beginning to think the world's sick anyway, or at least not feeling its best.

Chicks start screaming farther up front like it's a rock and roll concert but when a large, fearsome, guttural roar washes back toward where he stands, Dubecheck realizes something not good is shaping up. The throng in front of him seems to shrink back and cringe in upon itself and he is tightly packed in people as the crowd bunches up and compresses like schooling fish, a skittish, probable panic heightened by the screaming, shouting and confusion. An unintelligible voice resonates through a bullhorn, the electric amplification of authority, a cacophonous shrieking belligerence that charges the place with anger. The woman squeezes Dubecheck's hand and with her lobotomized smile looks up to him and shouts, "Courage." Boy, that's a word he's had a lot of wrestling with lately, though he's not sure it's a word you say with a shit eater on your face if you think about it.

Ranks begin to break and the mass of humans in front of him almost turns as one and breaks into an awkward trot constricted by human traffic. Wild looks on young faces, like kids being chased by *bigger* kids and that overall *chick screaming* that seems to be the sound track for the event pierces his ears. Signs are being dropped and Dubecheck sees tennis shoes running over NOT ONE MORE DEAD! while he holds his ground, either out of curiosity or because he is anchored to Mother Courage, who squeezes his hand in hers hard enough to make it ache.

It's a pell-mell retreat, one of those "every man for himself" gigs which are usually ugly to watch. Dubecheck stands, mesmerized, virtually paralyzed by the spectacle, he and Mother Courage standing like park statuary, retreating troops in full rout bouncing off them, and it dawns upon Dubecheck that a rout like this means FORCE is chasing it and it must be coming hard on these folks' ass. He gently pulls his hand away from the old woman but she won't allow it and snatches it back. The fleeing crowd in front of him is thinning and Dubecheck realizes he'll soon be in the very front row with a very good seat to see what's causing this full-on fear. And it appears just like he suspected it would. POLICE. Police in their *Man from Planet X* getups, helmets and visors and truncheons, and you can't see their eyes because of the black visors and they have leather boots up to their knees like the Nazi-faggot motorcycle cops on overtime they probably are. They're in a broad line, almost company strength, a tall insect-looking cretin out front with his bullhorn shouting, "You *will* disperse. You *will* disperse or face arrest!"

Dropped placards lie upon the damp brick plaza like fifty-two pickup and are crunched and muddied by the feet of the cops, a relentlessly approaching chorus line in black leather. Off to the side are twenty or so guys in suits and sunglasses and some other guys in dark government-issue windbreakers and baseball caps, their heads darting around like they're protecting the President or something, pretending to be real alert, vigilant, hard-ass and competent. But they don't fool Dubecheck. They work for the same company he does. Nevertheless, he figures it's about time to didi. Then Mother

Courage loses her smile and mutters, "The fuckers!" Spit comes out of her mouth. "Fuckers!"

Well, she's right. They are. Every goddamn one of them, and Dubecheck, with that gratification you must get when you've gone completely nuts, decides if she's going to hold ground he is. He looks down at her, her chin lifted up with just enough contempt to get it knocked off, but at least the manic homecoming-queen grin is gone. A quick glance at the front line shows only about forty scattered people holding the fort and most of them, as far as Dubecheck can tell, are chicks. But chicks are nuts. They think these guys might give them a break, like in "How dare you mess with women," but, like most chicks, they probably don't believe most guys really don't like women and will happily cleave open some of these noggins and are probably just sick that they can't hose down this wimpy skirmish line of pickets like they could in *Honduras* or *Botswana* or someplace neat like that.

The glare of television lights zigzags in the grayness as if the sun was tumbling from the sky and Dubecheck sees the local news crews stumbling backward and the leader, his garter-snake-size carotid artery ready to burst, screaming unintelligibly and giving the police the finger but sort of walking backward as he does it. Dubecheck feels his own heart thumping and for some reason his mind does that strange stupid thing it always does to him when reality intrudes upon his life: it fragments, and he momentarily envisions these guys as redcoats, truncheons where their muskets should be, and he's standing in a field without *anything* and they're going to club him into the dirt like a goddamn rabbit in a corner.

He glances behind him. The huge mass of people who have fled have stopped and are now screaming and waving wildly a hundred yards to the rear. "NOT ONE MORE DEAD!" *"Moral support,"* Dubecheck thinks. He turns to see the police and their friends close to within sixty feet and put on gas masks as a canister comes rolling across the bricks toward him and the old woman. "If you see the fockers comink, yust run." Why doesn't he ever listen? But run where? They're always coming. Snaky little white fumes curl up from the grenade. They didn't need to do that, but if you give them stuff, they're going to use it. He has to run before the gas really ruins his day, but the woman seems determined to stand there and get sick and go through pain, not knowing that they don't care about her, and he realizes she may not even be doing this for an idea, she might just be another selfish person pretending, doing it for *herself.* The roar of the crowd behind him sounds like a crowd in a stadium after someone has fumbled.

If they turn to run now these guys will club them, so Dubecheck stays still and is mildly surprised by the anticlimatic nature of his apprehension. The chorus line of cops moves right through him and the woman, and two guys in slickers and baseball caps grab them, him by his arm above his elbow, and walk them off behind enemy lines, a little briskly, a little rough. "Gently but firmly" is the phrase, he thinks.

"Where we goin'?"

"Shut the fuck up." A red-faced guy, maybe mid-thirties with a shiny shave, sunglasses for the gray day; he doesn't bother to look at Dubecheck, now in a single file with the people he recognizes as those who stood their ground out of either belligerence or fright. Each one has an escort who holds them by the crook of the arm and they seem to be headed on a little hike across a busy arterial where a traffic cop stands next to his motorcycle and halts traffic.

They put Dubecheck and about fifteen others inside an enclosure surrounded by a cyclone fence. Fifteen guys in navy-blue windbreakers, black shoes, Haggar slacks and sunglasses mill about on the other side. One of them occasionally speaks into a hand-held walkie-talkie. The woman who got him into this is shouting at one of the guys on the other side of the fence. Dubecheck can't understand her but he understands the guy. He says, "Lady? Hey, lady? Stick it up your ass."

Outside on the street, cars go by in both directions like normal, women out shopping, windshield wipers going back and forth across their barely curious faces as they wait for the stoplight to change outside this compound Dubecheck finds himself milling in like a slaughterhouse hog.

Some more gangsters are being led into the makeshift pen and they are shouting and screaming and being handled a little bit more roughly than Dubecheck's unit. The compound is getting crowded, and a little dangerous, like a drunk tank on Friday night, and Dubecheck can see the head jerk who appears to run the show is getting a little nervous because he's talking into his handset more vigorously and shoving guys on the shoulders toward leaks in the gate. Some radicals have put their claws through the fence and begin to rock it back and forth, threatening to pull down one side of the enclosure.

"Everybody down!" A very large, shiny-shaven man enters the compound with three men who hold nightsticks. "I said *down!* You will *all* fall down on your faces and *will all* refrain from uttering a single word. You are all *mine.* I am a United States marshal and you *will* do as I say." His deep voice resonates as if he were shouting into an empty fifty-five-gallon drum.

People do as he says. "I want hands on the back of heads. Now!" The gravelly asphalt is damp from the misty drizzle. Dubecheck puts his cheek onto the ground and sees the woman next to him, her face a foot away. She's not smiling. "You can't do this, you —you—you—you swine." A black shoe, raindrops beading off its spit-shined toe, rests upon the nape of the woman's neck. "The man says to shut the fuck up, lady. So shut the fuck up." Dubecheck recognizes the voice as his escort's, a guy not to mess with. Dubecheck's seen the type before, the ones that chew gum with their mouths closed. The foot moves on.

"Silence!" Guys are walking through the prone crowd getting people who don't believe they mean it to believe it. Soon all you can hear is occasional coughing, like an audience waiting for the second act, cars going by on the street outside the pen, a horn honking in the distance, United States marshals telling some pedestrians to mind their own business and move along, feedback, white noise and radio sets breaking squelch.

"The only way evil can triumph is for good men to do nothing," the woman whispers to Dubecheck. Her face a foot from his, as if they were lovers in bed, dark bags under her eyes, wrinkles that race out across her face like cracked glass, gravity pulls her skin toward earth. Again she whispers, "The only way evil can triumph is for good men to do nothing." Dubecheck often wonders when hearing things like that if the person wants a guy to do something right now or maybe wait a bit. Platitudes, that's what he recalls they are. Real neat things, things that look good on paper, "Easier said than done" things, "You go first and I'll be right behind you" things.

He's transfixed by her face, wondering what it looked like long ago; what thoughts floated through the brain behind it; how many days it has seen fade to night; what makes it think this is important? Because it's not important. There's nothing on the line here except inconvenience, bluffs have been called, but nobody has bet the ranch, they're all playing with match sticks. Nobody is going to get killed here, blindfolded, arms jerked behind their back and tied with rags at the elbows and told to kneel and get shot dead, killed next to your best friend and several other strangers. Shot dead so quick your neurons can still probably process the smell of cordite as you jet your way to dreamland.

"Do you want to know what's wrong with America?" she whispers.

"Sure."

"Shut the fuck up!"

One shiny black shoe looms before Dubecheck's eyes. It's his escort again. Everybody must still have a personal escort. Dubecheck's is getting on his nerves. After you've spent months playing hide and seek in the Asian night for big stakes, American cops don't frighten a guy. They can *inconvenience* a guy, but what doesn't? So roll with it.

"The man says shut the fuck up, but you just can't shut the fuck up, can you?"

Trick question. Dubecheck wonders why a guy is always having to choose sides. He could have gone to school with this guy. After work they'd go drink beer together. You just gotta know the other guy. That's all. Get personal. He's not going to answer.

"You talk to everybody else, why can't you talk to me?"

"I don't know you."

"Smart ass. You're a smart ass. Know how I can tell?"

Dubecheck turns up his head to ask but gets kicked in the face. Just a kiss, but he can feel the leak in his nose already.

"You didn't have to do that! That's despicable." The woman sits up and the guy slams her back down with a palm shot between her shoulder blades.

"You didn't have to do that either," says Dubecheck. He wipes some blood from his nose and whips it to the ground.

The guy sighs. "I get no respect. I tell you both to shut the fuck up and now it's Debate 101. That makes me unhappy."

Dubecheck sneezes and speckles the guy's shoe with blood.

"Fuck!" He pulls out a handkerchief, bends, and starts to wipe off his shoes, his sunglassed insect face a foot from Dubecheck's, redder than usual. "If . . . I . . . wasn't in here I'd rip your goddamn head off so fast that . . . shit! My shoe! Look what you did to my shoe!"

Dubecheck can see people around them lift up their heads at the minor commotion like little kids who won't take their naps. When the guy with the fifty-five-gallon drum voice shouts, "Down!" they go to sleep again. Dubecheck kneels and tries to stop the blood coming from his nostrils with the sleeve of the PFC blouse, wondering who the jacket belonged to. It's probably got a story for sure, other people's clothes always do.

"What's the problem here?" The guy with the fifty-five-gallon drum voice stands over Dubecheck and his squatting escort. He holds a walkie-talkie. He slides his sunglasses up on his forehead.

"Asshole. I've got a asshole here."

The big guy regards Dubecheck with a sigh that comes from his beer-keg chest. A sigh of exasperation, chagrin and paternal petulance.

"It was uncalled for what that man did to . . ."

"Lady . . . shut the fuck up."

"Son . . . get up."

"Me?" In that swimming miasma of fear that spins a guy's mind, Dubecheck recalls the last person who called him "son" was a drunken chaplain.

"Yes, son. You!" He grabs Dubecheck by the lapels of his PFC blouse. The guy's breath smells like a hot dog. "This is not funny. This is serious." The guy talks through clenched teeth as if he doesn't want anyone around them to hear.

Dubecheck's hands are at his side and he can feel blood sliding down his upper lip, tickling him. Behind the guy's shoulder he sees the cyclone fence and, beyond, traffic going by on the street like nothing is happening.

"He's a real smart ass, Ken."

"Well, Mr. *Smart Ass,* maybe you're not as smart as you think you are." The guy sounds fatherly. His sunglasses fall back down over his eyes and Dubecheck can see his fun-house-mirror face staring back at him, frightened.

They pull Dubecheck over to a corner of the compound and shove him up against the fence.

"Turn around, asshole! Hands high and spread 'em!" Dubecheck knows what to do from watching TV but doesn't.

"You don't need to do this."

"We make the decisions here, punk."

Dubecheck puts his back to the fence and feels it sag behind him with a teasing spring of freedom. He slowly raises his arms and they accept that.

His escort pats under his armpits, down his side and over his hips and stops. He slaps at Dubecheck's pocket. "What's in there, smart ass?" Dubecheck doesn't move. The guy reaches in Dubecheck's pocket and pulls out a wad of cash the size of a baseball.

"Well, what do we have *here?*" He holds up the cash before his eyes. Big fifty-five smiles without showing his teeth. Their faces are a foot from Dubecheck's and he can smell their Mennen Skin

Bracer through the blood that runs slowly out his nostrils like thin snot. He lowers his hands while they smile at each other like they know something, a joke they alone can understand. About inconvenience. Aggravation. Pressure. Cruelty. Obscene, what the fuck, give me a break, *inconvenience.*

A world of shit. That's what he figures he's in. And as usual it doesn't feel very good. He's sort of nauseous with a hot fear fever on top of it.

"Where'd you get this cash? You holdin'? Empty out, punk. Let's have a little inventory."

"What are you doing to this young man? I demand to know!" The old woman shoves her way between the marshals and puts her face right up into Dubecheck's escort's shiny round face. "Don't you tell them anything, young man. Have you read him 'Miranda'? He has a right to a lawyer. Do you know that? Do you know you have a right to a lawyer? Do you know a lawyer?"

"Ahh, no."

"The court will appoint you one."

"He hasn't been arrested, lady."

"Then what"—Dubecheck clears his throat and continues—"am I doing here? Ahh, sir."

"What *are* we doing here? I demand to—"

"Lady, shut the fuck up."

"How dare you talk to me that way! I'm a United States citizen."

"Great. Now would you go lay back down like a good fucking citizen and let us frisk this dealer so I *can* arrest his ass and then you can visit him in jail and give him all the free advice you want."

"I don't want to be frisked. Is there something you know about that that will make them . . . ah, maybe stop?"

Amazingly, both the men turn to look down at the lady as if waiting for her to say something on that matter.

That's when Dubecheck does the only thing a guy can do when it gets to be a real tight fit. Run. He shoves the big guy over his leg and sends him sprawling into the people taking their naps, and leaps up and pulls himself over the cyclone fence as shouting and screaming break out behind him. He kicks his feet loose from his escort's clawing grasp, losing his shower shoes, and starts running barefoot up the street, glancing over his shoulder to see his beady-eyed escort clambering up over the fence after him, the woman beating on his back with her idealistic little fists.

He dodges traffic as he zigzags across a busy arterial and finds the other side. He runs down the sidewalk, his bare feet slapping against the concrete, broken field running through pedestrians, shoving them out of the way. He's in so deep now that it's full-on flight. He looks over his shoulder and sees the U. S. marshal doing the same, fifty yards astern. The guy's good. Just his luck to get someone just out of Quantico, probably the second battalion obstacle course champion.

"Stop that sonofabitch!" He hears the guy shout but he knows nobody is going to try. *He* wouldn't. Nearly two hundred pounds of wild-eyed elbows and asshole flying down the sidewalk, his black fright wig flying out behind him like a tangle of angry snakes. And he doesn't know where he is going. His chest is beginning to burn, his gums ache and spit coagulates in his mouth like warm glue.

The campus is on his left, which he wants to avoid. Vague crowds and dull noise. Six blocks or so down a slight grade he sees water, low buildings, Quonset huts, all a half a mile away, and the guy is still behind him, falling into a good steady stride like he's into it, like he chases deer down for breakfast. Dubecheck's feet begin to scuff and bleed a bit as he cuts in front of traffic just going on a green, putting a few cars between him and the marshal, who is sort of *gaining.* He runs down a side street, ducking behind cars parked alongside the curb, and makes for a narrow alley bisecting the block, breaking into a crouch behind the cars and sprinting down the alley where he slams into a brick door well behind a dumpster. He slides down, trying to make himself small, lungs going from the size of pears to footballs and back in triple time, spitting thick spit, his temples throbbing, nose bleeding, speckling his Hawaiian shirt and losing itself in the pattern.

He wonders what he'll do if the guy comes right down on him. What will he do if he keeps smoking two packs of cigarettes a day and gets cancer and dies? Well, he'll just cross that bridge when he comes to it. Cross it, then burn the fucker. He doesn't like getting kicked in the face, running, being afraid, confused, in trouble. He hears running footsteps stop, then pace, then come trotting down the alley and slow to a stop, the guy pirouetting as he thinks. Dubecheck can hear the guy breathing hard, spitting. The guy is giving Dubecheck absolutely no options. The black shoe pokes out from the edge of the dumpster, still shiny-beaded with rain, and takes a step forward.

The man looks down to Dubecheck, but more likely into the small, endless black hole at the tip of a Tokarev pistol.

"Oh, fuck." The guy speaks flatly. He puts his little pink paws palms up in front of his stomach. "Hey . . . easy, easy a . . ."

"Shhhhhh!"

"What are you going to do?"

"Get down behind this thing, shut your eyes." They switch positions.

"Hey, c'mon. Christ, I got two kids."

"Aw, shut the fuck up! Move! I'm scared. I don't really like doing this. Turn around, kneel down and put your hands up against the door. Where're your handcuffs?"

"I don't have any."

"Whaddaya mean, you don't have any? Where's my money?"

"Ken's got it. Ken. The other guy. Honest. Honest to God, mister."

He wonders what the hell he is going to do with this guy.

"What in the hell am I going to do with you? Jesus! Take your goddamn clothes off."

"What? I mean . . ."

"Hurry up, goddamnit! Hurry!"

"Sure! Sure! That piece loaded?"

"Of course it's loaded, asshole! This isn't amateur night. Keep your face to the wall."

The guy starts taking off his shoes. "That's a nice piece. Is it what I think it is? You don't see those much. I read a magazine article about—"

"Yeah, yes, and shut up and *hurry!*"

"You sure you wanna be doing this? I mean—"

"No! No, I don't want to be *doing* this and *hurry up* before anybody comes down this alley and everything goes to shit."

"I don't think you'd do anything stupid, would you?"

"I don't know. Move it!" Dubecheck takes the guy's wallet out of the slacks curled on the ground. A ten, a Lincoln and two ones. "Seventeen *bucks?*" Dubecheck groans. He catches a brief glimpse of the guy's wife and kids behind a cloudy plastic wallet window. She looks just like the wife he has in his pocket. The kids look like kids. "Don't forget the shorts."

"C'mon. C'mon. Please?"

"Naked. Nude. Bare ass, Steve." Dubecheck's curiosity has him quickly perusing the wallet. It belongs to Steven O'Bradovich, who was born, according to his driver's license, four years before Dubecheck. Dubecheck also curiously notes that people are walking by at each end of the alley, oblivious to him and Steve. Christ sake.

Nothing means anything. This is just a little TV show nobody is watching in a drizzly alley and he's still scared shitless; feeling drifty, in that lightheaded dream state full-on reality can slam a guy into. "Roll them up in a ball and wrap 'em in your jacket."

"No."

"No? Whaddaya *mean,* no? And face the *wall!*"

"I don't think you got the balls to use that thing. I'm calling your bluff, kid." Steve talks to bricks a foot in front of his face.

The guy's pissing Dubecheck off. What the hell. He flicks off the safety with his thumb and lets one off into the empty dumpster. The roar is boggling. The guy screams and curls into a fetal position on the bricks, his little unit shrunk up to the size of a Ping-Pong ball, squirting a jerky stream of piss he tries to block with his hands when he realizes he's not dead. "Aw, shit!" He wipes his hands on his thighs.

"In the dumpster, Steve."

Steve the naked U. S. marshal jumps into the nearly empty dumpster, his eyes wide, his teeth clicking.

"Watch your fingers." Dubecheck slams the lid down. "Stay in there till I come back." Dubecheck sprints out of the alley with the bundle of clothes under his arm, quickly noting the size nines won't do, and tosses them aside as he flees down University Way. He sticks the pistol in his front pocket and after four blocks slows to a walk, looking for another alley, another dumpster. Feeling like seventeen lousy bucks.

22 This is serious. He sits on a trolley heading downtown, wondering how he is going to get to Hawaii on seventeen dollars. Sixteen and change actually, after wolfing down two tacos he bought at the drive-in where he dumped his wig, PFC blouse, Hawaiian shirt and Steven's fart-scorched Jockey shorts. He begins to quiver from nerves. Easy does it. He's seen guys literally shake apart and never get back together again. Still barefoot, in a tight FBI white shirt, his plaid pants, blue windbreaker, and Steven's sunglasses, he looks out the window at the gray city, trying to figure out why it is here. People and traffic move about among what people built as if they really had a *plan*. He wonders what he is doing here. A guy who really *needs* a plan. He's just robbed a United States marshal with a gun. *Armed* robbery. The tacos churn around in his stomach like they're planning a break and he's about to be asphyxiated by the lady in front of him, who smells like she had herself crop-dusted with talcum. Christ, the bus is such a bummer. No matter where it goes. It skirts a gray, calm lake surrounded by a huge hill of houses and the junk of half-ass industry: old ships, rusted wrecks alongside rotten piers, ramshackle marinas, sunken pontoons with houseboats rafted alongside fingering out into the oily, rain-pocked water. Thin cigarette coils of smoke rise from their little chimneys. In front of a parked car a wet cat sits in the rain staring at its front feet. And then, several blocks ahead, out the window, Dubecheck can see St. Vincent DePaul's, a large Catholic Charity secondhand emporium. He gets up and pounds on the door to get out.

o   o   o

Saddle shoes. Why not? Dump the government windbreaker and put on this fifty-five-cent green sport coat, forty-cent slacks, a little porkpie hat, throw in a pair of socks and walk out of St. Vinnie's with fourteen and change and warm feet for the first time since they stood on CONUS. Who says life's not just but a dream? And the gun. Of course, the gun. Always the gun.

Dubecheck needs one hundred and seventy-nine dollars (according to the United Airlines billboard across the street) to buy a ticket to paradise. Panic tiptoes over the tacos that still sulk in his nearly empty gut.

Suddenly he feels all alone. More so than usual. The naked marshal is still probably bent a bit out of shape. Maybe they're looking for him. Probably. It's not some sort of prank they're likely to overlook. He feels all alone, running on empty. This is the kind of time a guy wants his mommy.

He calls her collect, from a pay phone, but she isn't home or maybe she's just not answering. He hasn't seen her in months, talked to her maybe twice. "No . . . I won't be home for Thanksgiving." No canned cranberry slush, marshmallows melted over the sweet potatoes, a dish he'd eat out of consideration for his near senile Aunt Marylu's feelings. "No . . . I won't be home for Christmas." Or ever again for anything really.

The girl who thinks she loves him doesn't answer either and he listens to the phone buzz at the other end of the line over and over and over, even as the operator interrupts to ask if she should let it ring more. "Yeah. Let it ring some more." Somehow the sound, the monotonous buzz . . . buzz . . . buzz, brings him into the little room she lives in, or where she did, where he would lie in bed as she stood in her slip, ironing her blouse on a board that pulled out of the wall of the kitchenette. Mary would hum lightly as she ironed and hang up her work after looking at it closely to see if she got it all, frowning, her tongue circling her lips. The airline would check little things like that. And weigh her and examine her nails. She had to be sharp in her little paramilitary outfit with wings on her garrison cap and lapels so she could serve food and drinks to salesmen jetting high above the weather of America.

He hangs up. All his friends are in Asia.

o   o   o

This is a *bind* he's in. He's been in them before but this one wracks his brain. A passing Seattle police car causes a barely endurable rush of paranoia. He wishes it would get dark. There's a half a million people around here, but he still feels like he stands out. Guilt. The belief that this is all some horrible mistake overcomes him like it always does. According to television and the movies, they will be staking out the bus stations and airports and train stations. Do they really do that or do they just say they do? They just say they do. All *they're* really good at is spreading horse shit and fear. He stands in front of Central Loan, looking into the window through a wire mesh at an arsenal of weapons, cameras and saxophones pawned by somewhat desperate people like himself.

But it wouldn't be wise to waltz in there and hock the Cong pistol, because Steven of the Mounties was right. The gun is a rare-looking item in the land of the brave and it might set off bells and whistles from the baldheaded fat guy standing behind the counter paring his nails, peering over his horn rims through the smoke of the stogie clenched between his teeth. He wears a tattered brown vest over a white shirt that looks like to burst at the belly and to cover a real cold heart. But he's in it for the money, these guys don't care if the shit they buy comes from baby graves, wheedling and whining over the value of some tearstained son of a bitch's *heirloom*. Really.

Nevertheless. Caution to the wind. Isn't that what he was always telling his boys? Even the intrepid McDowell who, Dubecheck recalls, pointed out a verse in his ubiquitous New Testament after being chewed out over some military trifle, for having his head up his ass.

"It's right here, Mr. Dubecheck. Matthew 6:3. 'Let not thy left hand know what thy right hand doeth.' Right there. See?"

He saw. A wino comes down the sidewalk. Nothing special. A Mark I wino with a tan gabardine topcoat that looks like he found it under a parked car, the sole of his left brogan flopping loose, a purple T-shirt and relatively nice tennis hat. He strolls right by Dubecheck reeking sweetly of fortified wine, his eyes glazed, submerged in maraschino cherry juice, deep in thought. Dubecheck hooks him by the collar of his topcoat with one finger and tilts the skinny fellow backward to a halt.

"Whoa, Captain. You want a job?"

"No, I don't." A three-day growth of silver beard crusts his skinny face like rime. Two blind drunk Indians crash into Dubecheck and the wino, then zigzag down the sidewalk as if they were blind. The wino fixes Dubecheck with a confused frown.

"I want you to hock something for me." Dubecheck wonders how all the sores got on the guy's mouth. Would he kiss him for money?

"Is it stolen?"

"Of course it's stolen or I'd do it myself. You game? There's plenty of Nawico in it for you."

"I'd prefer Thunderbird if you don't mind."

"Two fifths. It's your lucky day."

"Well, yes, it seems to be." He clears his throat and spits into the wind.

Dubecheck flashes the wino a glimpse of the pistol.

"Oh my."

"Yeah. Take it in there and bring out money. Many, many dollars." He slips out the clip and hands him the piece.

"Sounds simple enough."

The wino enters Central Loan with Dubecheck's pistol in his hand like he's going to stick up the place.

The horn-rimmed broker behind the counter holds the pistol in his hands, hefts it, sights down the barrel, then *sniffs* it, the recent firing stinking up the barrel and raising the guy's eyebrows as he looks around as if to see if anyone might be watching, and then he shouts out a name Dubecheck can't quite hear and another equally disgusting-looking man appears wearing a green eyeshade, smoking a cigarette. He waddles out toward the transaction in his shiny blue suit, jacket open, and Dubecheck watches with horror through slung rifles hanging in the window as he realizes he *didn't tell the guy how much to get* and he is about to run in there and kill the deal because everybody on the buying side is looking real suspicious and the wino is looking toward the door like he might bolt when the guy in the suit rolls out a wad of bills and starts licking them off and placing them in the shaking hands of the wino. Dubecheck counts . . . one, two, three, four, five, this is going to be salvation and maybe lunch too because for a moment he has the luxury of realizing he's hungry. His nose is pressed against the pawnshop window; he rolls his forehead against the cold glass, soothingly telling himself he'll never do stupid things again, from now on it's full-on *maturity*. He's getting to the age where a guy should start thinking about acting his age and goddamnit the time is now. He closes his eyes, imagining the plump guy in the greasy suit still shuffling out Franklins and Hamiltons into the paw of the grimy wino, who better be ready to give a full accounting even if Dubecheck has to give him a strip search in the nearest alley.

The wino taps Dubecheck on the shoulder.

"Here. I did it."

"Hey. Not here. Around the corner." Dubecheck takes the wino by the elbow and firmly but gently marches him down the block and around the corner next to a water fountain. A half dozen pigeons coo and waddle at their feet.

"Give it to me."

The wino hands Dubecheck eighty-five dollars.

"Where's the rest of it?"

"That's all. That's—"

"Where's the rest of the money? Where's all the money the guy counted out into your goddamn dirty hands, ace?"

The wino starts looking around for an escape route. He starts hyperventilating.

"Eighty-five *bucks?* The guy gives you only eighty-five bucks?" Dubecheck's head starts feeling dizzy. People walk by on the street and pretend not to look at him. "Oh, Jesus H. Christ, man. That's *all?*"

The wino nods, gasping, looking down on Dubecheck, who has him hoisted up against the wall of a building by his lapels. Dubecheck lets him down, feeling as miserable as he can remember feeling for at least a week.

"How about my Thunderbird?"

"Your Thunderbird? Oh . . . yeah. Sure. Your Thunderbird." Dubecheck absently hands the guy a five-dollar bill. "Thanks. You were okay." He grabs the man again, thinking he should turn him inside out. "Show me your pockets!"

The man turns his pockets out. Nothing but snowflakes of lint drift toward the sidewalk. A pigeon runs over to peck. Bummer.

"This is it? Eighty-five? I don't believe it." Dubecheck's head feels so light it might fall off. Good. Settle things once and for all. Let it roll down the gutter until it stops and let the winos piss on it, the pigeons peck at it.

"Well . . . you can go now. Thanks. It wasn't your fault."

"That's true. But I feel bad. How much did you want for it? You never told me. I mean—"

"I know I never told you. I wanted two-fifty. Bottom. Minimum."

"Maybe you could get it back."

"It's not your problem."

"That's true. See you later." The wino ambles on down the street. A trolley comes to a halt next to Dubecheck and he looks up to see a mural of people looking out at him, as dead-fish-faced as folks must look in the grave.

Seething, that's the word he recalls that describes his state. He walks up the sidewalk, like a spawning salmon against a current of misfits, drunks and idlers and turns into Central Loan in a white, blind, mindless shaking rage.

"I'd like to see something in a . . . a pistol."

The fat man behind the counter peers over his horn rims, the short cigar resting on his wet lower lip. He holds Dubecheck's pistol in his hand and polishes it with a rag smelling of gun oil.

"You need a permit. You got a permit? You don't have a permit, you fill out a form says you don't have no felonies committed with a weapon, you wait three days and they give you a permit."

"What's that in your hand there?"

"It's a work o' art, kid."

"How much something like that go for?"

"Plenty."

"How much is plenty?" Dubecheck is so nervous he feels like he might throw up.

"Five . . . six . . . maybe seven hundred." The guy looks at the gun and fondles it with his loving hand like it's his dick.

"Can I look at it?"

"You are lookin' at it."

"No. I mean, like, look at it. *Hold* it."

The guy gives Dubecheck a quizzical cant of his head, squinting through the cigar smoke curling up under his glasses.

"No."

"Why not?"

"I don't like your looks. You look like you're a crazy fuckin' nut to me, kid."

"Yeah. You're right." Dubecheck sighs and leans against the glass counter top, staring down into a bunch of knives sleeping on a bed of velvet.

"I don't hear you."

"I said I've got a problem. That's what I said." He turns his back to the man and looks around the pawnshop. There's more rifles, shotguns and weaponry than an NVA battalion stacked in racks along the floor and hanging from the walls. He can hear the man sucking on his cigar and wheezing from the exertion of polishing the pistol.

What the fuck . . . He whirls and buries his fist in the man's beach-ball stomach. The man looks very surprised and the cigar falls from his mouth and he sags to his knees but he won't let go of the gun he clenches in his fat hand. Dubecheck is around the counter trying to pry the man's fingers off *his* pistol. They grip it like a tiny white octopus.

"I don't like *doing* this! Gimme the gun!"

The man is gasping, his glasses cattywampus on his face. *Vision.* The guy can identify Dubecheck. Forever. He flicks off the guy's glasses as a stupid afterthought and in sheer flat panic stomps on the man's wrist with his saddle-shoed left foot. The gun springs loose and Dubecheck with it, running out the door into the street, giddy, almost ready to laugh, wondering what in the fuck is going *on?* He stuffs the pistol into his coat pocket and realizes he's got to get out of town. Now. And he can't run all the way. It might be nice to stop somewhere and think for a change. But he's not sure he wants to think about what's transpired so far today. Ever. He slows to a hyperventilating walk near the Mission of Holy Light and sees the wino loitering out front with a covey of friends huddled together smoking inch-long cigarettes.

"Hey, you! It's me."

The guy looks like he might run but Dubecheck waves him away from his crowd with a jerk of his head and the guy follows him down the street and into a dumpster-filled alley.

"Let's trade coats."

"Who *are* you? I go years without a new face and now you loom large in my life."

Dubecheck takes off his sport coat and puts his porkpie on the wino's head and the tennis hat on his. "You don't have a need to know, do you?"

"No. I don't have a choice either, do I?"

"Not really." Dubecheck puts on the spotted topcoat and helps the wino into the green sport coat. "Shoes. We both look elevenish."

"Ten D."

"That'll do."

The wino sits on the bricks and takes off his brogans as Dubecheck rips off his saddle shoes. They both sit in the alley and put on each other's shoes. "There's another five in this for you, friend. You might want to forget what I look like and go to your room till this blows over a bit."

"What blows over a bit?"

"You don't have—"

"—a need to know." The wino stands up and looks down at his saddle shoes and does a little shuffle. "Well! Clothes do make the man, don't they?" He pats his chest. "You'll be wanting this, I suppose." He pulls out the pistol and hands it to Dubecheck.

"Yes. Yes, yes, yes, yes. You're a good troop." Dubecheck pulls out the eighty dollars and gives the guy a tenner, because he doesn't have a five, gives him a salute and trips down the alley on the tight, floppy-soled brogans, breaks into the light of the waterfront, crosses the train tracks under the concrete viaduct and runs across the street and catches a ferry just about to depart for Bremerton.

He stands on the stern of the passenger deck, hands stuffed in the pockets of his new overcoat, and watches the churning wake froth away from the hull, Seattle receding at fifteen knots in the gray drizzle, sea gulls swooping and diving and crying in the air above. A mother jerks the hand of a little child who looks at him and drags him off as he twists his neck, looking back over his shoulder at Dubecheck. Dusk settles with a slow dimming and, with luck, by the time he gets to Bremerton it will be dark and so will end this day.

o   o   o

He lies on his back in a hotel room in Hawaii, staring at the ceiling, thinking, Is this really it? Life itself? The Beeeg Time? and trying not to think of the demeaning way he got here. It could have been worse. He could have robbed the mom and pop grocery store that he stood across the street from for about an hour seriously thinking about, counting the six-packs and half-racks the jerks from the Naval Shipyard day shift kept hauling out in production-line plenty, knowing the joint had more money in it than a bank.

Bremerton was crawling with sailors from the ships undergoing refit, clogging up the streets just off the ferry landing where the bars and tattoo parlors were, bell-bottomed boys with Dixie cup caps heading for the locker clubs so they could change into civvies and get drunk and be hassled by the Shore Patrol which leisurely strolled the streets in pairs like lovers with billy clubs. He was about one hundred American short of getting a lei back around his neck and making the R and R rig back to Asia where he obviously belonged.

So he had to think, and he realized he'd have to hit up some people for money, sympathetic people. He knew sympathetic people with money don't take up much space on the planet, but he figured the only guys that come close are chiefs, so he set out to find their hangout and hissed down a couple on their way to the Chiefs' Club at the Bremerton Naval Shipyard after getting past the lunkhead Marine at the gate by flashing his military ID, which sure enough had the same face on it as the guy holding it, even though he looked like a wino.

He was honest with them. Told them he really fucked up and lied a little too, but told them he knew he couldn't trust any officer, but he knew he could trust them, and he really could, because chiefs understand that men fuck up and fucking up comes with the pair between your legs and guys that fuck up gotta stick together, and the chiefs were as always kind of sympathetic to scams, larceny and the camaraderie that makes guys want to have you around in case the wagons ever have to circle. Come see, come saw and, for all they knew, Dubecheck might be their commanding officer someday and a chief was born to hedge his bets and stash his markers.

Dubecheck told them he was in CONUS because of a chick and things got worse from there on out, and right away he had them commiserating and comprehending because sailors intuitively, instinctively and communally know that chicks are worse than storms at sea, that if "they didn't have cunts there'd be a bounty on them," HAW HAW HAW. And yet it was a chief who once told Dubecheck, as they stood on the bow of a liberty launch cruising into the harbor of some foggy oriental port of call, that the beauty of the whole thing (not knowing what the "whole thing" was that he was referring to) was to come into a port of call, "And look at 'em up there, Mr. Dubecheck!" The chief pointed off toward the smoky horizon at a swarm of humanity squashed down upon the shore. "See 'em? See 'em?"

"See what, Chief?"

"Wimmen, sir! See 'em up there on the ridgetop! All bare naked 'n wavin' whiskey bottles in their hands! They're happy to have us! And we're happy to *be* here!" And the roly-poly little chief laughed and slugged Mr. Dubecheck on the shoulder.

"Yeah, you're right, Chief. I see 'em. Hundreds of 'em."

"Wavin' whiskey bottles like semaphore with shit eaters on their faces because *the fleet is in!* Sir."

The three chiefs Dubecheck accosted in the shadows of the Chiefs' Club told him to clean his ass up and come on back and come on in. He cleaned his ass up with ten bucks' worth of new clothes from a five-and-dime outside the gate and came back and they got him drunk and loaded him down with names and numbers and "be sure to look ups" and were genuinely proud of him because he was over there in the shit and they all chipped in a bunch of money and stashed it in Dubecheck's shirt pocket and pants pockets. At the end of the night he didn't have any idea how much they gave him but he remembers they closed the place and he stood outside with a half dozen of them, arms over shoulders, and they all sang "Anchors Aweigh" and to top it off the goddamn "Navy Hymn" and, maudlin drunk or just the finest bunch of men he'd ever met in his life, he had tears rolling down his face as they slapped his back and waved each other away into the night as if he were a ship going off to the vast, undulating sea.

Wandering out of Bremerton on foot, convinced of the brilliance of the idea that he shouldn't try to depart from Seattle-Tacoma International Airport, which might be swarming with every law enforcement officer in the Pacific Northwest, he cleverly decided to hitchhike to Portland, Oregon, a mere hundred and seventy miles or so through the harmless rain. That idea seemed good at the time, but in retrospect he feels bad about the carful of black guys now.

He should have known better than to get in that car but, infused with the good will of hail fellows well met, full of one for all and all for one, proud, in control, self-assured for the first time in a long, long time, he climbed in, over the objections of the hall monitors screaming in his brain not to do it. Especially when they all claimed that the only place he should sit was between two in the back seat, which he had to get to by pulling the front passenger seat forward. A two-door coupe. It was real dark in that car and nobody talked, like "Where you goin'?" and "What the hell you doin' wanderin' 'round in the rain for?" He remembers starting to sober up faster than he wanted to when the driver pulled over and stopped the car and turned out the lights. It was as dark on that road as Asia. They wanted all his mothafuckin' money. He figured them for a bunch of angry PFCs from Fort Lewis, which wasn't too far away.

"My money is in my pocket."

"Well then, pull it *out*, mothafuckah!"

And Dubecheck pulled his pistol out of his pocket and with one of the better ideas he'd had lately fired a round off through the windshield, between the two bug-eyed guys looking at him from the front. The windshield exploded like white ice and the car emptied faster than he thought could ever happen and the five musty-smelling guys left Dubecheck alone in the car, his ears ringing, the two doors swinging wide on their hinges. They disappeared into the dark wild hedgerows alongside the deserted two-lane highway. Dubecheck got out of the car with the pistol dangling in his hand and apologized into the darkness, and told them he wasn't going to hurt them, but he just couldn't give up the fresh green he had groveled so hard to get. Not a peep from the people. Just the pitpat of the monotonous rain upon the huckleberry and salal leaf and the budding alders. Dubecheck could smell the heavy wet pollen in the cold spring night. He couldn't be out walking alone on a dark night with these guys rushing off to say, "There's some clown out there with a loaded piece." No, Dubecheck didn't need that crap on his wet head, so he laid a few of Czechoslovakia's finest into the tires on the right side of the car and listened to the air whistle out of them with a high-pitched sigh.

o　　　　o　　　　o

Dawn found him at a deserted wide spot in the road, smoking a cigarette in a gas station lobby, waiting for a Greyhound bus trunk line to move him through the soggy, empty-looking stump farms clinging to the slow-moving, rain-swollen, spring melt-flooded tributaries of the Columbia River. Lowlands where he couldn't tell where the light rain stopped and the fine mist began.

He had walked along the road for hours in the dark with the mist and clouds engulfing him like wet smoke as distant dogs barked cautiously. He easily covered fifteen miles, wondering at one point whatever happened to the Lone Ranger pedometer he used to have. Twenty-five cents and a Cheerios box top. It didn't work. He strapped it to his ankle and tromped all over the place. Stomped his foot down more than once to get it going. Maybe it's down in the basement of his mother's house in a sagging cardboard box with its friends, the junk of his existence: a Cub Scout Wolf badge, a souvenir bar of motel soap in its wrapper, a church key, rubber bands, the fender of a plastic Stutz Bearcat model, a few torn baseball cards, a cocktail napkin, a high school letter, papers, scraps, stuff, the stuff to prove you were here.

Rainy mornings with a cigarette for breakfast get a guy thinking. Usually about the past and about the future.

He was shivering cold when he got on the bus; the night march had decided to collect payment, and he fell into a fitful sleep, where the dreams were angry, quick and noisy, and he awoke constantly, aware of his aching neck and the cold hard window on his sticky, spit-stained cheek. No matter where a guy goes, he's trapped in his own mind. Forever.

o   o   o

He had slept the whole flight from Portland to Honolulu after spending a fitful time between consciousness and ruptured sleep in a hard chair beneath a newspaper tent to keep out the fluorescent light of the airport waiting area.

He apparently snored and smelled, for he found the small, apprehensive older couple he had sat beside on boarding gone upon his being awakened for landing in Hawaii. Dubecheck vaguely remembers drowsing off as the man smilingly discussed his pharmacy in Orem or Ogden, Utah, the weird pink of his false teeth gums the same color as his thin-haired wife's scalp. The two held hands as the jet built up speed for take-off. Soft, pudgy little white things tensing with fear and dread anticipation and Dubecheck wondered if the jet crashed if he'd end up in Mormon heaven with his seat mates by some sort of theological default.

But the plane did not crash. And he is alive in paradise, locked in a cheap Honolulu hotel room staring up at the ceiling, flat on his back, waiting for a plane ride back to Asia. It is not a safe thing to say, but things could be worse. For three days he hasn't been sure whether he has been asleep or awake. More than one rendition of "The Star-Spangled Banner" wafted weakly from the television, signaling either the beginning of an unwatched ball game or the official end of another certified American day. There were the aural hallucinations of Hawaiian weather reports and one memorable, pleasant dream.

He had rented the whole high school gymnasium at some small high school not far from Fort Wayne, Indiana. The crepe paper decorations had been hung with care. The sextet with two dreamy saxophones, a bald-headed drummer soft on the brushes and high hat, bass, piano and a smooth crooner played a lovely, hokey tune. They all wore powder-blue "dinner" jackets. Dubecheck, too, wore a powder-blue "dinner" jacket, a flouncy-breasted white shirt and black bow tie. Co Lan wore a white strapless formal and rested the side of her head on his chest. He could smell the gardenia in her hair, his nose was pressed into the gardenia in her hair, and they danced, swayed slowly from side to side as they glided beneath the basketball nets. He and Co Lan were the only people besides the sextet in the darkened gymnasium. A long covered table near the bleachers had a full punch bowl on it and only two crystal cups. The punch ladle stuck out of his back pocket. He kissed the pencil-thin artery on her neck, pressed his lips to it until he could feel the beat of her heart. He kissed the slope of her shoulder and then the beer-cap-size polyp on her shoulder where an AK-47 bullet ripped through on her tenth birthday.

And then there was the memory that was just like a dream, as so many memories often are. It was a memory of feeling foolish and vulnerable: his preinduction physical.

He stood in a line with twenty other fellows, all dressed—undressed really—in their undershorts, shoes and stockings. Opposite them, across the narrow, stuffy, pea-green room with exposed pipe on the ceiling, shuffled in another row of bowlegged, splayfooted, potbellied, flabby-assed, skinny-pimpled, fish-faced, mouth-breathing fellows to mirror the line he stood in. The two rows stood facing each other in the dumb silence new confusion brings to strangers. Dubecheck was struck by the variation in the human form and found it no great feat that no two sets of fingerprints are the same. Just like snowflakes; no two the same, although he also wondered who in the hell could check them all out to prove it. He came to the conclusion that human beings really were just like snowflakes . . . they melt and go away. That their brains were more mysterious than their strange and varied bodies was an even deeper enigma. Smart guys didn't even really know how brains work, let alone why.

Even Aristotle, the wise guy, thought it was used only to cool the blood.

Dubecheck was in this goofy reverie, staring at the walnut-size navel protruding from the hairy white beach-ball belly of some obese kid across from him, when the guy in the horn rims and white smock entered the room holding a flashlight. Behind him was an aide, a two-thirds-size scale-model clone holding a clipboard and pen. The boss stopped, looked at his watch, then commanded the row opposite to face the wall and drop their underwear. Boxers, jockeys and BVDs circled their shoed and stockinged feet in fart-scorched, come-stained, piss-speckled puddles of cloth, underwear to give mothers nightmares of embarrassment. Snickering from Dubecheck's row greeted the sight of two dozen guys looking all the more naked for having their shoes on as they faced the wall, and when they were told to bend over and grab their ankles, an explosion of laughter shot out from the spectators across the room. Dubecheck too was caught up in the contagion of absurdity and tears rolled down his face in delirium as he and his fellow strangers watched the man in the white smock bend over and examine with his flashlight the spread-cheeked rectum of each and every young man as if it was the gauge of some vast machine to be dutifully checked and recorded on the clipboard by the assistant trailing behind in ramrod-straight, expressionless efficiency.

When the other row was finished, Dubecheck's row dropped their shorts and bent to grab their ankles and the other row exploded in laughter, a spontaneous eruption of derision, and Dubecheck remembers the blood rushing to his head and his temples pounding as he bent over, clutching his ankles and thinking: Maybe all the brain really does do is cool the blood. That's all it felt like it was doing then when he felt vulnerable and foolish. And now too, as he rolls over on the bed of his Honolulu hotel room and looks at an imitation painting of a Venetian gondolier, a long, long way from home, hanging upon the wall. Tomorrow he has to go back to that dreadful place that feels more like home than home.

3

PART

23 It is like the first time he ever arrived at the place. No one seems to care he is there, or even where he's been.

He arrived back via the same route by which he had originally come many, many months ago; the last short, southern leg on a noisy, rattling, empty airplane, ear-popping landing with a barrel-over-the-falls descent, a controlled crash; then into the furnace heat of day, then thumbing a ride the rest of the way into the town that appeared out of the dismal swamps like a stinking mirage, feeling that his arrival presaged nothing but a petty purgatory of monotony, the continual daily accidents of his misspent youth.

As he walks along the narrow dirt road through the hovels on the north side of the town, heading toward the support base, nearly dizzy from the smells of the Orient, his senses inverted, sensory textures a hundred and eighty degrees out from those of the Ace Motel, he sees a Jeep approach. It is loaded to the gunwales with a few sickly-looking, bile-faced locals and two Anglos in sackcloth and ashes, one of whom is Anastasion, who without a change of expression gives Dubecheck the finger as the Jeep bounces by with its load of grief, physical pain and general bad luck.

Whatever warmth Dubecheck can draw from the world seems to be located in either pocket of his Polynesian plaid pants, where the Tokarev pistol and Thiel's watch reside like cheap talismans. Where he is and what he is doing is a tedious predicament, no more and no less. Little comfort comes from the sight of the pathetic human hoving into view: Dupree, the forlorn, who begins to frisk him for a cigarette and after finding a Pall Mall asks, "How was your trip?"

"Interesting."

"Yeah. Well, enough about you. I have big problems, Dubecheck. The problem is the impending visit of Congressman Phillip 'Phil' Kealy, who has been deemed an important man. Or so rumor has it, which makes it so."

Important? Dubecheck is not sure he knows what an important man is. But he has an inkling it has to do with relativity. The President is important, but he is not really real, so to speak. That is, he is no more real than Millard Fillmore, or Franklin Pierce or James K. Polk, who were probably as important as ancient Roman generals at one time, of whom Dubecheck knows not one by name; as important as Mr. Ming of the long-gone lonesome Ming Dynasty, as important as some Egyptian buried beneath a pyramid of stone as high as a small foothill. They're just dust.

But Recore—he is a powerful and important man, because he is in the *here* and *now*. Right *here* where he has a real hands-on, tangible effect on living humans. Like the enemy. Recore is very important in the immediate scheme of things, because an important man is one who can kill you and is roaming the neighborhood. Any lip service to the contrary is a dilution of the word.

And Recore and his small squad of well-trained young men, who like their work and are very good at it because they are interested in it, interested in killing people, are important men to the man.

It's all relative. You could ask the dead gook Recore killed about three weeks ago and he'd tell you the same if he could.

Approaching a little coconut-treed island the size of a football field, Dubecheck, Scoog, Recore and half his squad surprised a group of six men who started running. One of the men ran up a little bank about forty yards away from the boat and Recore shot him. The bullet appeared to hit him in the leg and the man cartwheeled when the bullet tore through and through. He seemed to come to earth in an awkward half gainer; he had already "passed away" from the shock, and slid slowly down the muddy bank, as relaxed as a dead snake. He was carrying a rifle, the dead guy in the mud, and he wasn't an important man anymore. Recore was. And Recore smiled, spit on his finger, wiped the end of the barrel and said, *"Uno más."*

There it was. That clean black and white sense of mission which Dubecheck both held in awe and envied and was the reason Recore seemed so much more comfortable in the world than he. *That* thing was done, now let's go to the *next* thing, moving through life like marching a peg down a crib board, and don't dwell on anything because, what the hell, it's all just farewell and adios to each swiftly passing day.

So Dubecheck wonders how "important" the congressman can really be. He certainly seems to have Dupree in some consternation because the impending visit of Congressman Phillip "Phil" Kealy and his entourage of courtiers, Navy brass, Potomac flunkies, syco-phantic news pimps and other assorted cheeseburgers will require some well-orchestrated planning. Protocol is raising its narcissistic, fag queen head and Tuta had put Dupree in charge of making sure it is paid homage.

Inside his Quonset hut, Dupree sits staring at his desk, smoking feverishly as he anticipates the crisis that will assuredly arise in the shark frenzy of paranoid ass kissing which promises to materialize tomorrow.

The only resource on protocol he has to draw upon is a volume from the United States Naval Academy published in 1916, back when, as far as he knew, the Navy routinely flogged sailors with bullwhips the size of giant kelp.

" 'Gun salutes as military honors.' Hmmm. Fortunately, nobody showing up deserves a welcome barrage, but I see a committee of Congress gets seventeen guns at departure and four ruffles and flour-ishes. Nowhere in the General Index can I find out what a 'ruffle' is, let alone a 'flourish.' " Dupree flips the pages of the musty old book.

"You're taking this pretty seriously," says Dubecheck.

"Yeah. Well, some of these guys take this stuff very, very pretty seriously, man. They really, really do. And I for one am not taking the chance that the clowns showing up for this dog and pony show are the humble, shy, retiring type. It'll probably be some anal retentive, who if we stick a ruffle in where a flourish was due, will have us keelhauled. I'm just covering our asses, since you don't seem to care. It's your breeding, Dubecheck. Your ignorance. These guys live for protocol. It compensates for the low pay."

"How come we don't have a guest list?"

"Very good question. Another crack example of naval intelligence. If a rear admiral shows up, and chances are good one will, I mean I can't see some admiral passing up a chance to show his stuff, a little soft shoe, song and patter in the combat zone for the benefit of his career. He'll need thirteen guns and two ruffles and flourishes."

Dubecheck can see at least a half dozen rear admirals and at least as many brigadiers up in Saigon right now lying under their sun lamps getting the proper weathered look in case they might get tapped to baby-sit the "no-nonsense" congressman from the "powerful" Armed Services Committee. The congressman's press release and the accompanying blurb from *Time* magazine, photostated and paper-clipped to it, continuously refer to him as the "no-nonsense" congressman.

"That means he starts drinking at five in the afternoon instead of four." Dupree shuffles through the small dossier.

"What's he look like?"

"No picture, but I can tell by the horseshit they write about him what he probably looks like. 'Young Turk' . . . 'New Breed.' He'll have razor-cut hair on the longish side like the last President that got shot and he'll pretend to be listening to you when you talk to him when all he is doing is staring at a spot on your forehead. A real look of deep concern while he's wondering how to stop keeping his balls from sticking to his thighs."

"Here he is." Dubecheck pulls out a piece of paper which appears to be a photostat of a campaign brochure.

Dupree snatches it. "Ah, yes, look at him talk on the telephone, which shows us how busy he's working. He could be ordering a pizza, but the voters think he's busy because he's using a telephone. Aha! And here's a picture of him with his wife and family who he sees every two years when he's up for reelection."

The woman standing next to Congressman Kealy is smiling as if under the threat of bodily harm. Her hairdo is swept up in a Republican matron pompadour.

Four children, two girls and two boys, ranging in age from about ten to fifteen, stand party-frocked and blue-blazered next to Mom and Dad, looking like backup vocalists in a sugar-white gospel group.

"Here's a picture of him relating to poor people, workers and colored folk. See, he's pretending to listen to them and you can tell he's just one of them because his tie is loosened around his neck, his collar's unbuttoned and he holds his jacket over his shoulder."

"Ruffles and flourishes. They don't do those in a combat zone, do they?"

"I dunno. I'll call Saigon. Why, I dunno. They're just moving colored pins around maps as meaningless to them as brain scans, sending messages to each other about the weather and shining their shoes."

Which is how Kooseman is preparing for this costume party. Shining his shoes. He was also seen in Phu Duc's tailor shop with his arms out like a scarecrow while Phu Duc walked around him in a crouch with his mouth full of pins, taking in Kooseman's fatigues in an attempt to give Kooseman the jaunty tapered look the SEALS and other local luminaries step into combat with. Kooseman is to be liaison for the "real combat operation" the congressman is to be taken on by Dubecheck and Recore. But Kooseman is merely wagging his tail like a puppy in anticipation of parlaying the event into a post-discharge job as a bright, ambitious congressional aide. And then, who knows? As he's told Dubecheck, "If we play our cards right, this could really open up some avenues of opportunity, Dubecheck."

Kooseman even had one of the Filipino messmates clean his unused M-16 for him. Dubecheck saw the jockey-size servant cleaning the barrel with a straightened coat hanger and a Tampax that he bought from one of the scullery hooch maids.

The little messmate would ram the clothes hanger up and down the barrel like he was churning butter, then hold the muzzle up to his eye and squint through it, then lay the weapon down and tear off another swab from the Tampax and place it on the tip of the hanger like he was getting ready to toast a marshmallow, dip it in government-issue cooking oil and churn away.

Dubecheck watched all this for two cigarettes while he stood in the shade and wondered whether Kooseman thought the congressman would actually grab Kooseman's M-16 and peer up through the barrel and, seeing nothing but an ice-white sheen in the lands and grooves, slap Kooseman on the back, shake his hand and offer him a job in the highest levels of government, fulfilling all his petty ambition and greed. Stranger things have happened.

"An 'envoy extraordinary' gets fifteen guns at departure and three ruffles and flourishes," Dupree says. "What in God's green asshole is an 'envoy extraordinary?' "

"Me. I'm an envoy extraordinary."

Dubecheck yawns. "I'm departing."

"Well, hang on, you're just the guy I want to see. I've got your battle plan for tomorrow. Are you interested?"

"Yeah. That's why I think I came over here."

"Well, after thorough research, I figure you can go over here." He points to a spot on the huge map that hangs on the wall over his desk like a mural. "The only thing out there, to my knowledge, are enemy water buffalo or a monkey or two. You claim, to our visiting dignitary, it is an 'enemy strongbed,' a heavily suspected concentration of blah, blah, blah and et cetera. You drop off Recore and a few of his homicidally inclined men over here, drift down to here." Dupree points at the map and silently regards it as if it is the first time he's *really* looked at it, which is highly possible.

Well, Dubecheck wouldn't exactly tar all of Recore's men with that same homicidal brush. A man's gotta do what a man's gotta do, whatever that means. They do like to kill people but, like anybody else, you scratch 'em and there's those sedimentary layers of endless surprise.

Dubecheck has found everybody seems to be able to do something you'd never expect of them. The one certifiably homicidal man of Recore's, young Mr. Van Buskirk, plays the fucking harp, for God's sake. One of those big ones like you see around the heavenly hosts on high. He carries a picture of himself and it in his wallet, in a foldout next to a picture of a girl with a pink bow in her hair like a poodle, and an expired library card from the Harrisburg, Pennsylvania, Public Library. The only drawback to the harp, he says, is that you always have to find a place to live on the ground floor because they're a bitch to haul around.

"Where and why do you haul around your harp, Van Buskirk?" Dubecheck asked.

"Department stores, mainly, at Christmastime. Your harp is not yet a year-round instrument to the fucking unwashed, sir. And they aren't cheap. You could buy a nice car or a boat for what a good harp goes for."

A regular Renaissance man. Like one of those Marines in their dress blues, who resembles some dude in the *Nutcracker* with a full Rolodex of ribbons for heroism and havoc beyond comprehension, fifteen Purple Hearts hanging from his barrel chest, a nice guy who stands in front of a cardboard bin collecting "Toys for Tots" at Christmastime. In front of a department store where in the background, on the first floor, Van Buskirk, in a powder-blue dinner jacket, plucks his big harp. Go figure some guys.

Dupree turns from his crash course in the lay of the land and presses his forefinger against the map. "Recore and his men will have a nice quiet lunch and then call you up to drop a few mortars on some fix about here, call in some Huey gunships when it gets heavy . . ."

"Seawolves? You got them in on this too? What a production. Do we have an environmental impact statement?"

"In triplicate. Then you pick up Recore here. They'll be dragging out a shot-up sampan drenched in chicken blood with a few Chicom mortars on board and your AK-47. Captured weapons, et cetera, et cetera, obviously heavily wounded scum-sucking Commies out in the bush. Claim two, three VC KIA, then it's back to the base, flushed with victory, drinks all around."

"Two KIA and no bodies? You sure you don't want to grab a couple of teenagers off the street and shoot them? We could keep them on ice and the Seawolves could drop them off when Recore's on the beach."

"That's a hell of an idea, Dubecheck. I'm beginning to think you might go places."

"Did you say chicken blood?"

"Yeah, nice touch, eh? It's red, just like people blood. Recore's down at the market now buying some chickens with U. S. Government money. His boys are out stealing a sampan now. They'll fill it with holes and stash it tonight."

"What if someone steals it?"

"We'll chain it to a tree with a 'Private Property' sign on it. Who cares? We've got more options on this gig than rats in a maze. Recore's got a bagful of souvenirs and artifacts to bring back too. Bloodstained watches, Commie campaign literature, letters from home, Christ, he's probably got Ho Chi Minh bubble gum cards. I, for one, am impressed with how I've arranged to make you look good. The Seawolves at Bihn Thuy are expecting your call about fifteen hundred. They want to be back before sixteen hundred because they have a basketball game with the Seabees scheduled at sixteen-thirty."

"You sure nobody's out there?"

"So what if there is? It's your job, isn't it, to kill them if they are? Pretend it's for real."

"Pretend-it's-for-real. I do that every day."

"Tuta wants the carpet rolled out for these twits and I'm trying to figure how to roll it out. They arrive at zero eight hundred tomorrow. I've got them locked into a schedule tighter than fourteen-year-old pussy, but I need a finishing touch. A color guard at arrival. A line of clean sailors. You got any clean sailors that can stand in a straight row without scratching their asses for five minutes?"

"No."

"Christ. I just gotta do everything around here."

"Why don't you just let me mortar the soccer field near the landing pad when they arrive? You can run around screaming, 'Incoming, incoming!' while they scatter and you can jump on the congressman and shield him with your body and win a medal. After that they won't want to do anything. They can be shot at and missed and then go drink."

"You couldn't just hit the soccer field. That would demand accuracy."

"So what if I miss? Veer left when you flee and I'll veer right with the bombs. It'd be worth it to see those assholes hit the dust, especially if they're in dress whites."

"This is serious, Dubecheck. Get serious. Just pretend it's all for real."

 Dubecheck wakes in the morning with his elbows throbbing like toothaches. They've swollen to the size of baseballs. He hurt them during the mortar attack last night. The biggest one he could remember. They must have been big ones, 122 mm mothers, because the explosions came down with the same huge roar he heard once while watching a movie about calving ice-

bergs. They jiggled the earth like it was pudding. And they were all very close. The building across the street from the hotel was hit and some people came running over asking for Recore's corpsman, the one who liked to put on a fright wig and scare Mamma-san, the hooch maid, until she cried.

Dubecheck ran down the stairs and across the street into jagged spears of wood and shards of glass that glistened in the flickering flames crackling like scattered campfires in the rubble. Heaps of plaster lay in chunks and the powdery white silt rose like steam through the flashlight beams trying to pinpoint the location of the screaming and wailing cries of bewildered babies and stunned, moaning grown-ups.

Dubecheck came running into the crazily tilting building with the corpsman and slipped in a large slick pool of blood and fell on his elbows with a crack. A wave of nausea overcame him, like being hit in the nuts, but he just had to lie there and know it would go away. Just like everything else goes away. And he lay there thinking that if everything just goes away, why does it happen in the first place? He was lying on the stairs trying not to vomit, unable to move, paralyzed by nausea, and looked over and saw the corpsman stuffing compresses into a little person who was thrashing its legs and snapping its head back and forth. Dubecheck couldn't hear it scream, because everyone else was making a ruckus. He was thinking humans are funny. They always make a ruckus and think it will help. It never helps to make a ruckus. It is the only thing he thinks he has learned in his life, the only thing of value, other than Thiel's watch, which lay in his pocket like a thick quarter, and the Tokarev pistol, which lay in the other pocket with the plump, heavy, meaningful weight of one of God's good ideas.

So starts this day as the phone next to him rings.

"They're coming. The empire's finest. They'll be here in about fifteen minutes. Sneak fucking attack and you won't even begin to believe what I have going on down here! I need help! There's a troop of goddamn jugglers down here! A fucking oriental vaudeville group that some laughing, as in 'haw-haw,' helicopter pilots from the United States Army dropped off here. There's a fucking accordion right next to me now . . . on the floor, an accordion and this oriental, whorish vision, who's pissed I don't have a place for her to plug in her hair dryer!"

Dubecheck puts his hand over the receiver to muffle Dupree's outrage. "An accordion?" But Dupree doesn't answer; he makes a sound as if he is being strangled. Dubecheck hangs up and takes a deep breath. This day, he suspects, will be more mystic than most.

o   o   o

A crowd like a Halloween party in front of a bus station mills around Dupree. Every creep, jerk, junky and kamikaze floozy in the Eastern Hemisphere seems to be swirling and hopping around Dupree in a frenzy. A Korean USO outfit has been dropped in by horrible mistake. They hold trumpets, guitars, speakers, microphones and busted suitcases with flamboyant costumes leaking out like wild flowers, and are all shouting at once while the rich kid from Louisiana tries to speak to them.

A covey of sailors in dress whites, Dupree's color guard, stand to the side, slouching and smoking in the shade of a dead palm, a few of them leaning on their rifles like a bunch of guys waiting to putt out. As Dubecheck walks by they half-ass rise to attention like the hairs on the back of a dog's neck.

A short, squatty, sweaty Korean, a diminutive guy dressed like a jive-assed pimp, green velveteen jacket and elevator shoes, shouts into Dupree's ear as he holds a sombrero in one hand while clutching a candy-apple-red accordion by its strap in the other. The little guy looks exhausted as two women with green eyelids, black vinyl wigs and pink lipstick scream at him in what Dubecheck imagines to be irate Korean. One of the women's eyelashes has fallen off like a broken awning. She wears a red fringe dress and spike heels that sink into the oily dirt. She beats a tambourine against her cocked hip. The man flinches every time the tambourine hits her hip. He looks over to Dubecheck like he knows him and shrugs.

Dupree spots Dubecheck and races to him. "Boy, am I glad to see you." He snatches the accordion from the little man and hands it to Dubecheck. "Hold this accordion. Don't play it, don't drop it. Just hold it. It's a bone of contention."

Dubecheck takes the accordion. "Who *are* these guys?"

"Hey. You got a mind like a steel trap, Dubecheck. I was wondering the same thing myself. And I'll tell you. It's Rocky Akoka's Happytime Hollywood Review, from Pusan. You've no doubt heard of them."

A horrible argument breaks out between two little men standing by a drum kit set up in the dirt. One man has a tremendous advantage: he holds the drumsticks and punctuates his range with periodic rim shots. The girl's tambourine is still ringing, giving the compound the sound of a preschool rhythm band.

"What's the problem?"

Dupree whines. "They're hungry. They're three hundred miles from their gig and they haven't been paid for two months, according to Rocky Akoka himself, who is this guy standing next to me dressed like the magic midget Pimp of Pusan."

"Really?"

"Really. Mr. Akoka, would you hide these people in a Quonset hut for the day, please? I can't feed them. *You* feed them. I've got VIPs coming here in about ten minutes. They aren't going to want to see this despicable gang of rabble hanging around a U.S. military installation."

"We can put on a show."

"We're going to put on our own, Mr. Akoka. Now go away with these people or I'll have Mr. Dubecheck here shoot them."

Akoka regards Dubecheck as if mulling the possibility.

"Please, please, Mr. Akoka. Let me be as politic as possible. You have all come at a terrible time and I wish you would all go away and die. If you can't do that, vanish and I'll make it up to you. Dubecheck, come with me." Dupree pulls Dubecheck over toward the color guard.

"Look. Dong My's finest. Do a few numbers with them. I'll ah, critique."

Dubecheck stands before the honor guard with the accordion strapped over his shoulders.

"Ten-hut! Dress right! Dress! . . . Two!" He turns to Dupree and smiles smugly. Dupree strokes his chin and nods.

"Muy military, man. I like it. Do some more."

"Preeeeezent . . . harms!"

"Hubba-hubba! Major League! Dr. Dubecheck!"

"As you were, men." Dubecheck surveys the eight teenagers under his command. Not a bright-eyed, bushy-tailed one in the bunch. Just a frowning, impotent firing squad. "Let's try it again. Preeezent . . . harms!"

Clack, clack, slap, slap. The row of sailors hold their rifles vertically in front of them. They stare straight ahead at the barrels so intently their eyes cross.

"That's goddamn beautiful, Lieutenant. Bravo Zulu. Smart. Smart lads." Dupree looks quizzically to Dubecheck. "What are you doing with that accordion on your chest? Can you play it?"

"No. You just squeeze the suckers and 'Lady of Spain' comes

out, though. Doesn't it?" Dubecheck squeezes the accordion. "Whose is it?"

"That's the bone of contention."

A crash of cymbals turns their heads toward the drummer and his rival rolling around on the ground in an angry embrace while Rocky Akoka circles them, yapping like a Pekingese.

Several sullen doxies sit on their luggage, barefoot, staring into the dirt, making patterns with their polished toes.

"How long you gonna keep these guys at freeze?" Dubecheck turns to see the color guard frozen at present arms. The compound dog sits before them scratching a flea.

"Oh. Oh yeah. Ready . . . Two . . . At ease."

"Okay, Dubecheck. You take these guys with you to the helo pad and meet the swells. They're going to be here in fifteen minutes."

"Me! Hey, wait a minute!"

"Wish I could. But no can do. You take these guys and meet Tuta out there. He doesn't want to be alone."

"What the hell's Kooseman doing? Isn't this *his* op?"

"He's off somewhere brushing his teeth with Brasso and, oh yeah, Tuta wants you to bring him some sunglasses. He left his at his dolly's last night."

"Jesus!" Dubecheck spits at the dog.

"Oh, stop sulking and give that accordion back to Rocky Akoka."

Dubecheck takes off the accordion and tosses it to the little man as if it were a beach ball. The guy staggers under it.

"What am I supposed to do out there?"

"Well you should ask. Just . . . Isn't that fight over with yet?" They see a cloud of dust moving down toward the pier along the ground like a dust devil. "You salute for openers. Just mimic Tuta and make sure these guys stay in a straight line. When the Big Kahuna gets close have these twits present arms. When the last sycophant of the entourage passes by—I mean, like, they'll all pass by like they're reviewing the troops or something—say 'Two!' And keep these imbeciles at attention until everyone is gone. I'm in charge of the caravan back to here. You guys'll walk back."

"Can't we jog?"

"Good idea. Because you gotta get back here and meet with Recore and tidy up your operation for the day. You got that all down, Kemo Sabe?"

"Why am I taking orders from you? I've every right to go back and sleep through this whole thing."

"That's true. You're doing me a favor. I'll be forever grateful. I'll never forget it and, while you're at it, try and round up some teenage whores for these guys. I'm sure they'll want chicks."

"Pimp. Lieutenant (jg). Pimp. Is that what I look like?" He snatches the sombrero off Rocky Akoka's head and puts it on his. "Huh, do I?"

"Yes, you do. Now run off, but give Mr. Akoka his headpiece back."

"You guys come with me." The color guard trudges off after Dubecheck. He sails the sombrero back to Rocky Akoka like a Frisbee. Akoka catches it and gives Dubecheck the finger.

Dubecheck has never seen a real live admiral before. A couple of years ago, while on the bow of an anchored destroyer, he heard there was one in the back of a motor launch that was cruising across Pearl Harbor. The launch had tassles and fringe on it, a water surrey with a white fringe on top, and the sailors driving it and the rest of the crew were at attention, looking more like part of the decorations than people. He thought he saw a shadow of a person behind some curtains but wasn't sure.

He's never seen a congressman before either. To him, congressmen and admirals were just people you read about in the paper and saw on television and had as much reality as electrons gunned upon cathode ray tubes. Their names weren't important, because it really didn't matter who the admiral or congressman was, just the fact the position seemed the only significant reality. It was almost like what Dupree once said of Kooseman as the latter rapturously watched the news on television. "Kooseman actually thinks the news is real."

So now Dubecheck is standing in the dust next to a circle of dead grass the size of a corral that is the local helo pad. The flight tower is a structure no bigger than a phone booth, made out of chicken wire and sandbags, with a sleepy local inside smoking a Salem and listening for a phone connected to nowhere to ring. Flies dance on the muzzle of his gun.

The helo pad, on the outskirts of town, sits across a small bridge spanning a narrow orange-colored slough, the color of which Dubecheck has never become curious enough about to investigate. It just seems logical that the water should be orange.

Tuta stands next to him, wearing sunglasses, distraught over something, pale, chewing his lower lip, looking like someone at a movie star's funeral.

Kooseman stands there too, reeking of Aramis after-shave and Crest toothpaste, encased in tailored camo fatigues and carrying, for purposes Dubecheck can't figure but nevertheless admires, a clipboard. Smart move. A man with a clipboard is an obvious mover and shaker. Dubecheck wishes he had thought of that. People try and avoid people carrying clipboards, and should.

The color guard lean on the butts of their rifles and smoke nervously. A pall of white smoke hangs above them.

Not much talk. Kooseman tries to make small chitchat about the weather, but Tuta quietly says, "Shut up, Kooseman."

Kooseman looks to Dubecheck to record his dismay but gets nothing but a quick, puckered kiss through the air for his trouble. Kooseman leafs through the papers on his clipboard.

Dubecheck begins to squirm like a little kid dragged along on an adult affair.

"Tuta?"

"Yes?"

"What's all this about, anyway?"

"What's all what about?"

Dubecheck waves his hand at the sky in the direction they expect the helos to come from.

Tuta pulls his shades down on the bridge of his nose and peers up at Dubecheck. "Atoms, Dubecheck. Atoms. It's all about atoms." He pushes his sunglasses back up and rocks on his heels.

"Atoms, sir?" Kooseman is quizzical.

"Yes, atoms, Mr. Kooseman. Write that down on your clipboard."

"Sir?"

"What's on that clipboard?" He peers over to look at it.

"Yeah, what's on that thing, Koose?"

"Shut up, Mr. Dubecheck."

"Yes, sir."

"I thought I might be of assistance with it, sir. Reminders and such."

"Write down on it to remind yourself to shut up."

"Here they come!"

They all squint into the white sky, hands bridged over their eyes. Eight little fly specks move slowly in the distance.

"Jesus, sir. Eight. Eight helos. Jesus, lock up the liquor, Koose. This is gonna be trouble."

"See to your men, Lieutenant."

"*Sí*, sir."

Dubecheck has a tactical decision to make: where to place the color guard now that the pad seems like it is about to be overrun. He'll put them on the bridge and the dignitaries will have to stroll past them like trolls. He has the color guard double-time to the bridge just as Dupree, sitting in a Jeep at the head of a convoy, comes roaring onto the bridge, scattering the guard, sending one man sliding down the bank into the orange-colored slough. He comes up gasping, dripping orange slime. He spits and screams. "What kinda water is this! How can they call this water!" He throws his rifle against the bank and wipes his eyes with both hands. "They can't even have real water around here!"

The convoy, consisting of several Jeeps and two half-tons, flies by and swings in behind the flight tower. Dupree comes running back. "Hide that sailor." He stands breathless before Dubecheck and looks down at the orange sailor, who is struggling up the bank, muttering and whining, spitting and coughing.

"What's that man's name, Dubecheck?"

"I dunno."

"What's he doing? Why is he orange? Who is he?"

A sailor, laughing so hard he can barely speak, utters, "Musgrove, sir."

Musgrove looks up, white eyes in a rust-colored head.

"Where do you think you're going, Musgrove? You wanna get your picture taken with the admiral and the congressman? Get back in the water. Dubecheck, make that guy go away. He'll ruin everything. Get him back in the water."

There is no place to hide Musgrove except under the bridge.

"Back in the water, Musgrove. Camo time." The helos are clattering in descent.

"But . . ."

"Come on, Musgrove. You know about 'Buts' in this man's Navy."

"Sheeit."

"That's a good fellow. I know you don't see the Big Picture but this is for the greater good."

Musgrove backs down on his hands and knees and reenters the slough.

"Under the bridge. I'll see you get a commendation. Dubecheck, see to it. Bronze Star. We're talking Bronze Star here." Dupree jogs off into the dust storm of the descending helos.

"Fall in." Dubecheck gets his ducks in a row.

A half dozen little children, their forebellies stuck out, dirty shorts and bare feet, stare down at Musgrove.

"Shoo! Shoo! Didi." Dubecheck chases them off a few steps. The color guard space themselves with extended left arms and sideways shuffling feet as the deafening roar of copters blankets the area.

Dubecheck is always amazed how a group of foul-mouthed, usually hung-over, quasi-cretinous teenagers snap to under ancient commands, how their clean whites can transform them back into mother's little boys, Dixie Cup hats, dickeys, bell-bottom trousers, all wedding-cake white, looking sharp at parade rest like something in a department store window. Then the first huge cloud of dust from prop wash descends upon them, coating them in red silt, which turns mud brown on the sweaty semicircles under their arms.

"Ah, shit," screams Dubecheck as he squints into the dust storm.

A squad of Air Force Special Forces, in their purple berets, ascots and pearl-handled .38s, leap from the lead helo and duckwalk out from under the blades, weapons at the ready. They set up a small defensive perimeter around the helos that bounce lightly, then land in a perfectly straight line for no apparent reason other than to make a straight line.

The Air Force guys crouch and look around uneasily.

"Those cats are really on their toes." Recore appears next to Dubecheck. "They're real cute, too. Why don't we get to wear pretty clothes like that?"

"Lookit my color guard, man. I mean, I'm the captain of this ship here. I'm responsible for this sinking mess, and I got a guy named Musgrove . . ."

Kooseman approaches. "The commander sent me here to help. Jesus Christ! Dubecheck! What happened?"

Kooseman, Recore and Dubecheck regard the once white color guard, now speckled like English setters, standing at parade rest, blinking in the subsiding dust storm. Kooseman gapes at them as if they had their dicks hanging out.

"Dubecheck. I'll get you for this."

"Dubecheck didn't do anything, Koose. The helicopters did. Whose stupid idea was it to put people in whites anyway? This is a combat zone."

"Mr. Recore. While I respect your command and—"

"Eat my bagonga, Koose."

"Yeah, Mr. Kooseman, eat my bagonga too." The whole affair is making Dubecheck giddy. He's noticed when you get giddy you become powerful.

He sees figures emerge from the helicopters. Squatting under the whistling blades. They all wear new combat fatigues and the several older men among the twenty or so people appear more relaxed and move slower than the younger men, and the younger men all carry attaché cases and form up around a tall older man and the congressman, who is readily distinguished by his longish hair, and they all group around the two big shots, the other older large man an admiral or captain by his bearing; silver-gray hair at the temples, carrying himself as if oblivious to all the attendant activity around him, used to it. The group moves en masse like a large football huddle toward Tuta and Dupree, who salute, and some people salute back and shake hands and then Tuta points toward Dubecheck, the color guard and the waiting convoy.

Dubecheck feels like he has taken some kind of drug. A good one at that, one elevating him above the lunacy he thinks is taking place. These are all the guys of his worst nightmares come to visit. And there are the "Special Forces," stylishly ready to shoot who knows who? Perhaps a crowd of curious nose-picking kids and flies.

All the clean-shaven American chins and cheeks glisten in the now bright morning sun, dead serious slits where their mouths should be, and Dubecheck can't believe them at all. They could have emerged from the helos with false noses and funny glasses and been no more or less valid. They could have emerged wearing false mustaches like a villain in a grade school play or come tumbling out like clowns and it would not have made any difference. He wonders if he is the only guy thinking this. He hears the soft thudding of some bombs in the distance. A couple of marauding jets cruise the horizon. What's going on there? Does it have anything to do with this? And what if it did? Does it make any difference what's happening over there when one is here? And vice versa. Dubecheck likes the concept of vice versa. Say, this *is* a good drug. Maybe he's part of an experiment they didn't tell him about. Some new war chemical. The kind that can make you lay down your gun and walk off into the forest and start making faces at the shrubs and vegetation. Examine lichens. Talk to them. Ask them where the weasels are. Where they hide all their money. A drug that makes you perfectly inconsequential and symbolically dead.

For some reason several of the men start exchanging attaché cases as if they've picked up the wrong luggage. What are they saying? "Excuse me, it seems I've got your attaché case full of pure drivel. Would you mind?"

"Of course not. I believe this is your drivel. May I have mine?"

Dubecheck wouldn't be surprised if the last helo in line in the settling dust was Cinderella's pumpkin. Mice and horses and footmen.

Now the picture taking starts. Cameras appear from nowhere, moving and stills. The movie man walks backward in front of the entourage as it heads toward the bridge.

"Get ready, boys." Dubecheck gets that edgy adrenalin rush that accompanies the fear of wondering whether human beings under your command can come to attention and hold guns in front of their faces without fucking up and what the big deal about fucking up something like that is anyway.

The movie man can't see where he is going, he has an assistant holding him by the back of his shirt to guide him so he won't miss getting all these people walking filmed for posterity and maybe the "Nightly News."

An admiral. Dubecheck sees two stars on the big man's baseball cap where a ball team's initials should be. And scrambled eggs on the bill, just like the one they gave the congressman so he wouldn't have to feel inferior to the admiral. The scene seems to want a Greek Orthodox bishop out front sprinkling holy water on the dust from a fish and chip vinegar bottle.

The admiral and the congressman walk abreast with a practiced indifference to being filmed, pretending the camera is not there as they look around and pretend to be interested in the lay of the land. The congressman is better at it than the admiral, though. The admiral occasionally glances over to see if he's still "on," a confused look on his face somewhere between a stern visage and saying "Cheese."

Flunkies surround each chieftain like remoras, importance and rank diminishing and spreading outward from each man like circles from a stone dropped in a pond. To a man, they all look nervous. For all their seriousness and imagined sagacity, not one of them, Dubecheck thinks, knows Musgrove is standing beneath the bridge up to his chest in orange water. They approach in a clumsy triangle with the admiral, congressman and Tuta at point.

"Ten-hut!" Dubecheck stands beside his men. Out of the corner of his eye he can see the little kids laughing and pointing at Musgrove beneath them. His color guard goes rigid. "Preeee-zent . . .

HARMS!" It's fun to talk that way when it's expected of you. You don't feel like a complete ass.

For looking like fry cooks, the boys aren't bad. They move as one. Always something a little sharp and snappy about military drill. Sets man above all the other beasts when you really think about it. One doesn't see chipmunks out and about on the forest floor, for instance, smartly doing a little close-order drill, even though they look perfectly able.

Dubecheck snaps up his hand and cants it over his eyebrow, blocking out the sun. He sees a flurry of salutes as the congressman cruises by with a beauty pageant smile, perusing the boys in the color guard, who gaze with frozen stares off through their vertical rifles into the distance at a tree or cloud, scared stiff they might fuck up or, worse, be asked a question by one of these guys. Dubecheck knows these guys like to ask the lowest form of military life where they're from and if the chow is good to show they care for the little guy without whom the war couldn't be blah, blah, blah.

The admiral stands next to the congressman, a pained, confused look on his face, as if he doesn't know if it would be all right to go apoplectic. His face seems to redden as he looks at the color guard, speckled as if they were in the wrong place when the shit hit the fan. Tuta is expressionless behind his sunglasses. Duprec is biting his tongue, making faces at Dubecheck.

Dubecheck can hear the movie camera whir and the 35mm SLRs click and he has the urge to jump up and down and wave like some kid in a home movie. The congressman seems to be wearing makeup, some orange-brown paint. His face is caught between middle age and irretrievable youth, creases and cracks around the eyes and mouth, right on the cusp between plum and prune. His eyes are clear and watery and half-lidded as if he's had about three drinks. . . . Sweat lies on his upper lip like a smear of Vaseline.

"And where are you from, son?"

The kid's still at "Present arms" and doesn't know what to do. So he says nothing.

"Speak, sailor!" The admiral speaks in a hoarse voice.

"America, sir." The kid is so nervous his teeth start to chatter.

"Great. Great place. You getting enough to eat?"

"Yessir."

"Great. Outstanding."

The congressman moves on while the admiral lingers a microsecond to sear Dubecheck with a gaze he can see out of the corner of his eye. Admiral Le Guinn, a confirmed asshole by rumor, a certified smoldering shithead by fact. He rose to admiral, so the rumor goes, because of an ancient but now forgotten reputation as a wunder-kind at Annapolis. Arrested development set in at age nineteen and apparently went unnoticed for twenty-five years. For, in addition to the often misguided impression that size gives dimension to a man (he was large, therefore good), he was quiet by nature. Quiet men often give the erroneous impression that they are thoughtful, intelligent, taciturn, sage, choosing well their words, when in fact they are often merely at a loss for them. Dumb, as they say.

Surrounded by an aura of strength and wisdom, he rose as silently as a bubble up through the ranks with the help of the one and only attribute common to all officers of general rank: vanity.

His thick silver hair undulates atop his head in waves as smooth as sand dunes and he often strives to show it, taking off his cap to wipe his brow whenever the mercury reaches 45 degrees Fahrenheit.

He is mopping his brow now, because it's nearly twice that hot. His hair gleams like a powdered aluminum wig in the sun, perhaps raising havoc with the light meters, since the cameras stop whirring and clicking.

Which causes the congressman to start, imperceptibly, like a deer hearing a twig snap in the forest, and cast an eye toward the cameramen. They start up again and the congressman seems to relax, smiling as he seeks out another sailor, take two, to show the world or whoever cares that he can mingle with hoi polloi with utmost concern. He stops in front of Seaman Deuce Drury, a good choice. "Where you hail from, son?"

Drury is a guy who probably doesn't even know when he was born.

"I yuh, I yuh, I yuh . . ."

Dubecheck leans out and sees Drury look like he's got a golf ball in his throat. Another case of stage fright.

"Your hometown, son."

"A-a-a-a . . ."

"Mars." Seaman Deuce Marsh whispers next to Dubecheck, causing the sailor next to him to burst, spray blasting from his mouth in a sneeze of restrained hysteria.

"Two!" Dubecheck tries to salvage the disaster.

The color guard bring their rifles down and stand at attention. If the congressman wants to chat, Dubecheck figures to loosen things up a bit.

The congressman is puzzled by Drury, who stands soundlessly gaping, like a goldfish, and moves to the next kid.

"And you. Where are you from?"

"Manila, sir."

"Huh? I mean where . . . ?"

"Manila. Philippines."

"Oh yeah, yeah. Helluva place."

Dubecheck sees that he's hit up Third Class Petty Officer Gomez, the pecan-colored little steward Kooseman used to clean his rifle. He also sees Admiral Le Guinn giving him the eagle-eye fleegle, as if attempting to sear the sight of Dubecheck's face into his mind for all time.

"And how's the chow? You getting plenty of chow?"

"Sure, sir."

The congressman looks at the admiral and they both smile at each other and nod, both of them beaming like idiots, pleased as fucking punch the little monkey from Manila—Christ sake, they *eat* monkeys in Manila, don't they?—is getting enough to eat. The admiral and congressman look at their entourage, backed up behind them like guys waiting in line to piss at a ball game, and nod and smile. All those guys start smiling and nodding to one another and Dubecheck figures if they don't stop pretty soon there'll be a break-out of backslapping.

All through this, Tuta stares into the admiral's back as if he were staring into a wall, going through the motions of the reception line as if in a trance. Kooseman has cut in behind him, pleased to be fourth in line, smiling beatifically in the train of power. The line trails off into the helo pad with the guys in the back craning their necks up toward the front wondering what the hang-up is.

"Where you from, sailor?" The congressman tries another white kid who might be able to talk.

"Centralia, Illinois, sir."

"Illinois."

"Right, sir. Illinois."

"Wonderful state. I know hundreds of people in Illinois. I have many friends from the great state of Illinois."

"I only have a couple friends there now. But I haven't been back there in some time. My grandmother still lives there, though. She's lived there all her life. She has a big garden out back. Keeps her young, I guess. . . ."

The congressman has hit a gusher. Some clown from the Midwest. Dubecheck has found that those guys can *talk*.

"Well, that's very nice. Very nice."

The congressman maintains a glazed smile, giving away nothing.

He steps back from the color guard and for some reason known only to himself salutes the sailor. He about-faces and decides to speak to the multitudes.

"I'd like to personally say . . ."

"You *are* saying it," the sailor next to Dubecheck whispers.

". . . that I am proud to personally acquaint myself with the wonderful youth whose sacrifice touches not only my heart but the heart of a grateful nation, a great nation, America, which has produced these wonderful young men."

"Except for the Flip," whispers Marsh.

The congressman turns and throws another textbook salute at the color guard, his hand snapping off at the end as if he burned it on the bill of his cap. He walks off toward the waiting Jeeps, smiling and waving at a cluster of curious, dirty kids. He stops, bends down and picks one up.

He sits the kid in the crook of his arm and smiles and waves and the cameras whir and click like locusts. The kid begins to cry and struggle to get out of the congressman's clutch.

"There, there."

Everyone smiles and chuckles and nods and Dubecheck is infused with the warm feeling that permeates this pleasant interlude in an otherwise rusty chain of events of no order, logic or meaning. The congressman puts the little kid down and strides toward the convoy with the admiral at his side. The entourage follows like a huge litter of clumsy puppies.

"At ease, guys."

25 Clean-cut, serious-looking people. The whole entourage. Healthy young white men from the capital of the empire and a few hand-picked military aides with bland good looks and clean, starched fatigues, eager beaver no-nonsense spring in their step, a goddamn veritable chorus line of The Best and The Brightest, guys with "unflagging spirit," full of "vim," strong chins, mesomorphs, 42 regular, born leaders, sophomore class treasurers, debate and track, assholes.

They briskly traipse by with quick sidelong glances, as if Dube- check, Recore and the seven sailors are, if not invisible, nothing more than dull scenery.

Dubecheck remembers these guys. They'd always have their pictures in the paper doing something with vigor when vigor became fashionable and politic. They took fifty-mile hikes when the Kennedys made that stupidity seem like a good idea. Serious people would "like the cut of these guys' jibs," but then they were always cut of a different cloth than Dubecheck. If they didn't go into meaningful government service, they went into the Peace Corps. Real neat people. Dubecheck remembers sitting at his kitchen table late one night in a beery fit of altruism, filling out an application for the Peace Corps. It was the thing to do. Take all his American expertise to some country buried deep in the bush of some less benign continent and help some poor, ignorant native grow rutabagas where previously a bug-infested bog lay. Tell his mud-stained wife to wash their scruffy kids' faces and inoculate them against dying too soon and hurting everyone's feelings. The application form impressed upon him that he was sorely unqualified to join the Peace Corps. He didn't have a talent, a field of expertise. The only foreign language he knew was Canadian. How do you convey on a form that you are nothing but a born leader? Anyway, it turned out that he *was* in a Peace Corps of sorts. Keeping the peace. Fighting for peace. He turned out to be a sort of American policeman in Southeast Asia. A U.S. marshal. A deputy sheriff. Right on the time-honored cusp between cop and crook.

He wonders how he got such a low opinion of everybody.

"You don't think much of people, do you?" Anastasion had once asked him.

"I did, until I started meeting so many of them."

"That just means you really have a low opinion of yourself."

"Yes. Yes, I do have a low opinion of myself. As a moral eunuch, what do you expect?"

"But then you must be under terrible strain."

"Not at all. I just have no idea what's going on."

"Here?"

"Everywhere."

"Really?"

"Really."

"Hmmmm."

"Not an inkling. And maybe I'll never know, even if I think I do. You could just sink in a sea of clues if you don't learn to float."

Was that two days, two weeks or months ago?

And isn't there something he's forgotten? Yes. Musgrove, bawling like a stuck calf, standing knee deep at the edge of the slough in a coat of many colors, mainly orange.

"Musgrove, come on up." Dubecheck starts the trek back into town with his color guard as Musgrove emerges from the slough, dripping like a creature in a science fiction movie, whining about poison, heavy metals and disease.

"A medal. You're going to get a medal, Musgrove, so shut up. We've all got problems."

He was going to add, "Don'tcha know there's a war going on?" like all the other assholes say when you want to complain and tell them you'd rather not die, or get hurt that you'd rather just go home and go to bed. "Don't you know there's a war going on?" What a catchall. There's always a war going on somewhere. It shouldn't be an excuse anymore.

He can hear some erratic faint thumping in the distance where people are lethargically dropping bombs or firing off some H and I artillery to break the monotony or, more likely, fill some quota. Keep the merchandise moving, rotate the stock. They're not building these bombs and projectiles and pouring out these bullets like pennies in a mint just so folks can count them like their money. There are silos of gunpowder somewhere that have to be emptied and moved, projectiles piled to the ceilings of warehouses the size of stadiums, blocking out shafts of sunlight. Quiet forklifts, in dark shadows, move the stuff around on pallets. Shipping and receiving. It goes off to war and gets used in a little battle or skirmish Dubecheck can skim over in *Stars and Stripes*, something as pointless as an old weather report.

Speaking of the weather, the natives are getting restless. Mamma-san, the hooch maid, has told him the monsoon is late, which means the rice crop is "in a world of shit, Diwi." She told him the government radio station has asked everyone to pray for rain, for the Catholics to go to their churches, the Buddhists to their temples and every other sect to wherever, but to go for sure, to get that message through to God, Who's apparently not been taking calls.

And the weather, the imminent change or lack of it, has the boys in intelligence up to their succinct, cogent assessments. The enemy is either preparing for an all-out attack or they are not. Or they're waiting for the monsoon, in which case "planners," short range and long range, Mark I and Mark II, get to use words like "broad contingencies, relevant countermeasures and viable alternatives." Essentially, to Dubecheck, it means he'll have to go to work in a raincoat. As for the others, he imagines a long file of infantry trudging along holding umbrellas over their heads. He wonders what the command would be to open them. There'd have to be a command. You just couldn't have every dolt opening his umbrella any time he felt like it. It would have to be something snappy, along the lines of "Fix bayonets!" When you were issued your olive-drab umbrella they'd give you a sixty-five-page khaki-colored booklet entitled, "The Care and Maintenance of the Mark I Bumbershoot." There would be a training film about it that put you to sleep faster than most. You'd nod off, right after the stentorian voice said, "The Mark I 'Rainbender' is the finest combat bumbershoot known to exist at this time." And everyone thinking, as they drowse off, that that means the Russians probably have a better one. It wouldn't leak in the rain.

Dubecheck has time to ponder as he walks back into town, watching his scuffed combat boots move one in front of the other over the red dirt. He's gonna have to change his attitude. Like it's really starting to get him down.

o   o   o

Word of the congressman's arrival had apparently spread up and down the river like an oil slick, bringing every 0-5 and above with nothing to do down to Dong My to press the flesh and show the flag out of a mixture of courtesy and narcissism. There were several colonels from Dong Tam, some Air Force deep thinkers from Bihn Thuy, some Brown Water Navy from Vihn Long and all their Vietnamese counterparts, two thirds scale, hovering a half step behind the Americans like caddies, aping every gesture of stern, no-nonsense competent concern like diminutive mimes.

Dupree's briefing had to be moved to a larger venue, so it was held in the mess hall, where everyone sat at the little round dining tables with condiments in the middle of the red-checked oilcloths, giving the scene the appearance of a small lounge act.

Dubecheck stood at the back by the door, watching Dupree go through his spiel just like guys he's seen on the TV and in war movies; his pointer pointing at a map that could just as well have been Yosemite National Park, the statistics some numerical jumble from some partisan activity in Yugoslavia thirty years ago. Yet the rapt audience appeared to hang on his every word like a high school boys club listening to an inspirational Friday afternoon assembly pep talk from the head of the local Chamber of Commerce. Except for Tuta, who, as the nominal host, sat at the front table with Admiral Le Guinn and Congressman Kealy, and seemed to stare at the mustard and ketchup as if they made more sense. Kooseman diligently took notes on his clipboard. Recore rolled his eyes and Dubecheck went away.

o   o   o

Rocky Akoka's accordion has a lot of holes in it because one of Recore's men shot it with a twelve-gauge Remington shotgun for good reason. Akoka and "his people," none of whom gave the slightest indication they remotely revered him, had been down at the base eating free United States Government rations and making a general nuisance of themselves when Rocky started playing "Lady of Spain" over and over and over again to the annoyance of the people who had to put in a full day. A contract was put out on Akoka's accordion and it was taken out for a pack of cigarettes. When Dubecheck shows up, Akoka sits against the side of a Quonset hut staring at his accordion with a look of stunned resignation.

"I'm sorry about your accordion."

Rocky Akoka looks up to Dubecheck with a semi-pained face. "No problem. I'll just make it by in this shithole on my looks."

Dubecheck sits down in the dirt next to Akoka, his back against the solid sand dune corrugation of the Quonset hut, and lights up a cigarette, blowing smoke into the five-thousand-degree heat and humidity. "Bummer."

"A bummer. Life is a bummer and then you die."

"That sounds like something people could tape on their refrigerators."

"What?"

"Nothing. I was just thinking about how words, the more you use them and stuff, don't mean shit."

"No shit." Akoka fingers the holes in the bellows of his accordion. There are nearly as many holes as all the little black buttons set like geometric polka dots along the ersatz ivory side.

Dubecheck gets a roll of magic green tape and helps Akoka patch the holes in his accordion as Akoka tells him of the first Americans he ever saw in his life, back when he was a little kid living near Pusan. The Americans had rags wrapped around their heads, blindfolding them, and their wrists were tied behind their backs with rags too, and they were lying in a gravel road, face down, eight of them in their olive-drab uniforms with big boots with welts on the bottoms, and some Chinese guys with quilted jackets shot them all in the back of the head, except they didn't get one guy just right and after he was shot near the nape of his neck, between the neck and the shoulder, he writhed around on the ground like a burned worm until they shot him about fifteen more times and some dogs came up and started to lick the blood that was steaming off the gravel because it was cold. Rocky took the guy's shoes off and ran until his lungs burned.

"Well. I think your accordion's fixed, Rocky."

"Oklahoma."

"What?"

"The guy they had to shoot a lot kept screaming, 'Oklahoma.' It's the first word in English I ever heard and never forgot. You ever been there?"

"No, I haven't."

"Later I looked it up on a map. I worked at the Seattle World's Fair in '62 for a couple of months, making kimchee in the Food Circus. I always wanted to go there, Oklahoma. I wonder what it's like."

"It's in the middle of nowhere, Rocky."

"Yeah . . . well, what isn't?"

o o o

A guy's "home" isn't in the middle of nowhere, but Dubecheck isn't certain what "home" is anymore unless it's that vague area between all the places you've been and all the places you want to go to. "Home," at least, is not here. An ache prevails.

The truth of the matter is that Dubecheck has lost all confidence in how he is to address the world. Is it to be one skirmish after another? Forever? Only one thing seems clear, and that is he will get no help from his fellow man on the matter. They try tripping him from the sidelines, and as he runs down the path of life through that gauntlet of jeering, malevolent well-wishers, all he seems to be doing is running out of breath. And it's not that he's a pessimist or any of those things it's not proper to be, but down at the end of the road, according to all he's seen, are these people older than he who are in total disarray. Either you get the Big Picture or you don't get the Big Picture and the thing is, it doesn't seem to matter either way. Now what kind of predicament is that? Is it something of value?

According to his new friend Rocky Akoka, the only thing of value is food. But that's to be expected from some guy who spent his youth wiping with his greedy fingers the moldy scum from empty tin cans in the garbage dump.

"Soldiers were out there to shoot at all the rats, but they thought it was pretty funny to shoot at us too. It was worth it if you could make off with a dead rat."

"You ate dead rats?"

"Well, we cooked 'em first. After all, we were civilized."

"What does a cooked rat taste like, Rocky?"

"It tastes like food, Lieutenant."

The remnants of Rocky's command sit across the compound in the shade cleaning their instruments, painting their toenails, smoking, yawning, scratching and snoozing, looking like any raggedy-ass platoon of humans waiting for the next incident in life to alight upon them like a housefly.

"What's going to become of you and your people?"

"Well, we ate today. I consider that a triumph. We were booked to Nha Be and haven't been paid by the USO in a month, but hey! It's great to be here and you're really a wonderful audience and as long as we're near where an American shits we'll never go hungry."

One of the earlier sullen and outraged women paints her toenails with an intense delicacy. She sits in the shade on an overturned oil drum in her tight slip of a red dress. Its fringes shimmer in the gust of a merciful off-river breeze that smells of diesel and cologne.

"That's Tiger. She studied opera in Inchon for ten years. What a bitch. But, what the hell, she's got her story. It's a long way from *La Bohème* to 'I Left My Heart in San Francisco.' "

She reminds Dubecheck of a sleek, short-haired cat cleaning itself. The feeling that there are far more people in the world than one can ever come to grips with lies upon him with the same heavy weight as the heat and humidity. The thought of Lamont Shay and Tiger, she sitting cross-legged upon his Honolulu piano singing "People" in a dark lounge duet overwhelms him with woe. He is sinking fast, focusing on Akoka's accordion to see if the geometric solidity of it, the essence of it, can ground him like an anchor in the brown mayonnaise mud of a dirty Delta slough.

Not hardly. He is sinking.

Congressman Kealy's chin juts into the breeze like the wooden fig-
urehead on the prow of a ship going in harm's way. Dressed in a
helmet, flak jacket, brand-new jungle boots and a camouflaged face
to go with his camouflaged fatigues, the guy looks somewhat lethal.
As he was dressed to the nines, everyone else had to dress to the
nines, so Dubecheck's boat is filled up and decked out to a defense
contractor's dream with the congressman, two congressional aides
(whatever that meant), a Naval Special Warfare Group Pacific Lieutenant Commander from Saigon (NAVSPECWARGRUPAC
LTCMDR KELLY), Recore and a half dozen of his highly skilled
assassins, Dubecheck and his crew and Lieutenant Kooseman in lieu
of Tuta.

Consequently, not bothering to check the whole manifest,
Dubecheck estimates eighteen souls on board his boat, their heads
cooking under steel pots, armed to the teeth, overqualified for the
job at hand.

This is a no-nonsense operation because, after Dupree's briefing,
Lieutenant Commander Kelly from Saigon took over, much to
Dupree's dismay, his well-organized flimflam operation shit canned
for something relatively real, leaving Dupree to sulk about, wondering aloud what the difference between a fake operation and a real
one was anyway, a distinction Dubecheck could not make for him
even if he tried.

Lieutenant Commander Kelly is very tan and pretty with a Kirk
Douglas chin and straw blond hair that lies as flat and sleek as the
grass where a deer has lain. He has a huge, broad forehead which to
Dubecheck looks to encase a brain at least six slices of Wonder
Bread thick.

After the picture taking, handshaking and attendant obsequent
ceremonies revolving around the congressman were finished, all the
visiting powerful men left as if they had something absolutely pressing to do elsewhere, and the group became a bit more manageable
and under the apparent guidance of Kelly—who, it was discovered
through Dupree's quick snooping, is some naval movie star on a fast
track, a specialist on the COMNAVFORV staff being "groomed" for
bigger, better things.

He held a briefing in the death row atmosphere of the ammo
hut, presumably to give a dramatic solemnity to the event at hand.
The operation is to be nothing more than what Recore and Dubecheck have done a hundred times before—go look for a little trou-

ble, maybe kill a couple guys, and hope it stays little. The big difference in this one is that "Intelligence" is absolutely certain two enemy superstars on their own fast track are thought to be in transit at a certain set of coordinates at a given time. At this bit of information, Dupree, deep in the shadows behind some mortar crates, crosses his eyes and jams a finger up his nose in an expression of mild derision if not sheer disbelief.

Another difference is that a United States congressman is coming to watch, albeit from a goodly distance, like it's a spectator sport, and it's gotta be done sorta quick because the congressman's ETD is 1830, so we gotta get movin', so let's roll and good hunting. Jesus.

Fortunately, Admiral Le Guinn will be elsewhere. He'll be in his own helicopter in case he's needed. Le Guinn's hobby is archery and, either from some longing for another time or from a real desire to personally and vigorously prosecute the war, he likes to fire flaming arrows from his compound bow into the highly flammable local housing while hovering at several hundred feet.

Like practically everyone else in the world Dubecheck has met, once he got to *know* the person, the congressman doesn't seem like such a bad guy. The fawning deference paid to him by those of high military rank was fun to watch. Grown men, whose power was based on fear, did everything but curtsy before the civilian as if he were some potentate. His awkward performance at the reception by the helo pad aside, Congressman Kealy came across more like a genial grocery clerk, earnest and intelligent, eager to please and totally competent in his field. But he still scared the shit out of Dubecheck, and when Kealy approached him, after the ammo hut briefing, he felt like running.

And then the rap happened. As Dubecheck and the United States congressman strolled in a little tight circle, off by themselves, under the shade of a huge dusty tree, Dubecheck got to find out the man had his own problem.

"I was too young for World War II and in law school for the Korean conflict and I feel, as . . . a, a, man, as an American, I've missed something." Congressman Phillip "Phil" Kealy stood in his camouflage combat fatigues, hands deep in his pockets, and stared into the oily dirt deep in thought, or so Dubecheck imagined, and continued, eyes dulled, staring off into memory.

"I used to play with P-38s and P-51s, little toy airplanes that came in boxes of Kix, tanks, what have you, and I'll never forget when the war ended, the Big One. We went down to the train station and all the troop trains would come thundering in, billowing steam, loud, noisy, and soldiers just flooding off, running into the arms of their wives and mothers and fathers, sons and daughters with smiles on their faces, that sea of khaki . . . I just missed it in '45 and then . . . well, then the Korean War just sort of came and went while I was in law school . . . and public service."

Across the compound Dubecheck saw Rocky Akoka trying to take care of his ill-tempered crew, pacing like some guy in front of ladders with pissed-off lions squatting on them. The Korean "conflict" just sort of came and went for him too.

"Do you know what I'm talking about?" The congressman stopped walking and looked up to Dubecheck with a mild, quizzical look on his face. It wasn't a test question, it was just one of those things people say when they're sure they're not getting their thought across.

"Yes, sir. I do," Dubecheck said. The guy was talking nonsense and Dubecheck was beginning to understand nonsense perfectly. As for the *drift* Congressman Kealy was taking, Dubecheck didn't care to venture a guess.

"It has to do with what we feel about being a man. A man in the generative sense. We're not all that far from the . . . well, our ancestors, from the cave. Hobbesian society or lack of society, if you will. Where life without the constraint of civilization would be nothing but brutal, painful and short."

Like right here, in little old Hobbesville Corners, Dubecheck thought. He looked over at the congressional aides, Kelly, Kooseman and an assortment of people he'd never seen before pining over toward him and his buddy the congressman like they wanted to cut in on their dance.

But the dance was apparently to be all his. There was a little time to kill as Scoog took care of logistics. And the operation was to take place in a familiar area only about an hour downriver in the middle of a desolate, prehistoric-looking wasteland uninhabited by man or beast, a place left to the rotting, defoliating fauna, sinister insects, macabre birds and toxic reptiles.

The congressman put his hands behind his back like some statesman Dubecheck had seen strolling in a documentary somewhere. Dubecheck did the same and immediately felt immeasurably more important and wise and, stride for stride with the congressman, felt some sort of epiphany begin to course through his body like the first wash of Lulu Turrentine's lysergic acid. And the epiphany came with what the congressman said.

"A rite of passage. I feel I have missed a rite of passage as a man. . . . I think all men wonder . . . think . . . question deeply how they would measure up in combat. I feel empty in a sense, Lieutenant. I have not had that rite of passage." He stopped his stride and, with a lobotomized visage that reminded Dubecheck of his dipshit Bible-bearing crewman McDowell, the congressman asked Dubecheck once again if he knew what he was talking about. And Dubecheck was nearly ecstatic with relief. He *did* know what he was talking about. He was saying what Dubecheck thought he was always too dumb to truly believe. And that was that the whole fucking human race is probably very seriously out to lunch.

Dubecheck looked into the congressman's eyes. They had yellow in the irises and were red rimmed. The man looked older than he was supposed to be and his combat fatigues looked as silly on him as a baseball uniform on an old man. He looked so weak, it scared the shit out of Dubecheck. Mercifully, Lieutenant Commander Kelly arrived to tell the man it was time to get himself dressed.

When Recore came out from the ammo hut, camouflaged face, web gear with grenades, barefooted and toting his M-16, he poked Dubecheck in the chest with his finger. "Dubecheck, we pull this one off, believe me . . . lifetime passes from the commissioner of baseball."

26 Now Recore jumps off the bow of Dubecheck's boat as it noses into the riverbank and seven of his men follow him like little lethal ballet dancers, descending upon the soggy shore, rifles high to balance their landing as they tippy-toe off behind some shrubbery, down some thousand-year-old path to set up an L-shaped or U-shaped ambush in the middle of nowhere as everyone on board Dubecheck's boat watches like touring Sea Scouts.

Recore is to go in several hundred yards and set up in a tree line and look for "three huts," which are the honest-to-God horseshit words the guy Kelly from Saigon used. Dubecheck will drift down to coordinate suppressing fire, communication, blah, blah, blah, and the congressman and his entourage will get an inkling of what the fuck is going on out in the combat zone.

You can feel it. You can feel when something ugly is going to happen, when you're not as dumb as you usually feel and you become like a dog before an earthquake, a canary in a mine shaft; maybe it's an epiphany of fear. It is not long after Recore and his squad disappear that Dubecheck feels something is wrong with the whole basic alignment of everything. His men seem normal, but it is the luggage: Kealy, Kelly, Kooseman, et al and their shadows, looking as ruthless as Hollywood pirates, waiting for some goddamn *movie* to unfold. It is then Dubecheck realizes that his fellow Americans are so enamored of warfare because for the most part they have never really been in it. That war to America for over a hundred years has always been a movie, a newsreel, a TV clip.

Rites of passage. Well, let's have a rite of passage then. It's his boat. They gave it to him and they gave him the whole miraculous monster of the techno-arsenal. Just pick up the phone and he can bring the wrath of Jehovah down upon any acre of the planet he approaches.

Normally, Recore never talks to Dubecheck over the little PRC 10, but this little chicken shit gig is nothing to grind one's teeth over, so Recore comes up on the net like he's in a phone booth. "Ah, Dark Singer, this is me. *Cómo está?*"

"*Muy bien. Gracias. Qué pasa?*"

"We're set. Out."

The day is as pretty and calm as a watercolor. Clouds jumble up against each other in puffy confusion and the declining sun has set off their edges like gold neon. On shore, incredible variations of green run amok in dead, dying and struggling surreal vegetation tortured beyond recognition by poison and drought.

Kooseman and the congressman peer shoreward with the intensity of bird dogs. Lieutenant Commander Kelly scans the flat expanse with his binoculars. People are quiet. Sisler idles the boat on the brown current. Dubecheck looks at the radio set and wonders what is happening. Everybody melts in the heat. The dead flat water ticks against the hull of the boat like a metronome.

You do this shit long enough and the shit eventually hits the fan. A shot goes off in the distance and Lieutenant Commander Kelly from Saigon whips down his binoculars and looks to Dubecheck with a grim visage. The congressman also gets a grim visage, then Kooseman gets a grim visage and they all tense like erections, questioning each other with narrowed eyes which eventually all land on Dubecheck with expectant longing.

"Lieutenant?" Kelly regards Dubecheck.

"Yes, sir?"

"Aren't you going to do something?"

Dubecheck sees the congressman slowly slide off the safety on the M-16 he was issued, lick his lips and peer forward in the direction of the distant pop.

"Well, Lieutenant? Do I have to take charge here?" Kelly is actually serious.

"Take charge of what, sir?"

"Goddamn it, Lieutenant! Don't get smart with me. This isn't a *game*. Those men in there are our responsibility and I want you to see to it that they get some goddamn *air cover*. Do you understand that, mister?"

This is embarrassing. Dubecheck feels his face flush as the congressman looks at him like a vice-principal.

"Do as you're told, Dubecheck!" Kooseman says.

"I wasn't told to do anything, Koose. Relax—"

"Don't call me Koose! I'm a full lieutenant and you are to address me as such. *Do you understand?*"

"Commander Kelly, sir. Mr. Recore will ask for air if he needs it. He hasn't indicated—"

"What if he can't? Have you ever thought of that?"

"Have you, Dubecheck? Those are our men in there." Kooseman points off into the scabland where nothing can be seen except for a few birds zigzagging like gnats in the far distance.

"Okay. I'll call up some air. What shall I do with it when it gets here?"

"Use it, goddamnit. This isn't a *drill*, this is a goddamn *war*, and you get some air in here right now, sailor, or I'll have your ass!" Kelly's carotid artery tumesces at the side of his neck. He turns from Dubecheck and peers through his binoculars.

"Aye, aye, sir." And Dubecheck decides to call in some air. There will be a half dozen Zoomies sitting around playing acey-deucey in their pressurized suits down in Bihn Thuy he can roust up here in their big, noisy Phantom jets, some Huey gunships, or an OV-10 bomber or two. Every one of them can be on scene in about five minutes and he could have them churn up and rearrange the landscape for as far as the eye can see. Dubecheck decides to bring every one of them and, as he hangs up from the last radio communication, he visualizes all the fit young men running to their various craft across the tarmac of various airfields spread out over an area of fifty square miles. A mad rush of adrenal power brings a smile to his face, a flutter of insanity passes over him like the shadow of a gliding hawk. This is it. Sheer madness.

Thousands of tons of Americana are on the way, screaming through the air laden with projectiles, bullets of a half dozen different calibers, rockets, bombs and explosives of every hue, color and stench in the universe, a mad chemist's inventory of jellied naphtha, kerosene and phosphorus, expanding gases, gyroscopic infrared, gravity-pressurized air-to-surface honest-to-God hell-fire. One pass from a Phantom could turn a whole ancient Roman legion into a five-acre, knee-deep slick of humanity, like a tanker spill of Franco-American spaghetti. Bring in some air! Well, Dubecheck did and pretty shortly they're all going to be on his net asking him "What the fuck?" and "Where do we do it?" and he realizes he doesn't have a clue. He can't even bring up Recore because his radio is off.

Three Huey gunships, Seawolves, appear as dots on the horizon from the northwest against the pale yellow cauliflower clouds and almost simultaneously two OV-10 Broncos, "Black Ponies," streak astern down the river, rocking their wings, the pilots' crash-helmeted insect heads visible through the canopies, hard penile rockets slung underneath, ready to come.

Everyone on board swivels his head to follow the aircraft as they streak downriver, awed and excited by machines eating up time and space with the roar of a thousand snare drums. And that's nothing. The home run hitters haven't shown up yet, the fast movers, ten million dollars' worth of titanium, aluminum and hydraulics being flown by some United States senator-nominated hometown-hero Air Force Academy graduate with nuts the size of brass baseballs. But they show up in seconds, two Phantom jets burrowing a supersonic cone in the air like forty-foot bullets, outracing their own sound, leaving it five football fields behind, and when it does come, everyone's hands go to his ears to muffle the screaming thunder that vibrates the body.

All the toys are now here and locked into Dubecheck's net, but to what perverse purpose he has no idea.

"They're here, sir," Dubecheck shouts over the roar to Lieutenant Commander Kelly and slugs Kooseman on the shoulder for effect. "How about that, Koose? You want 'em, I got 'em."

The congressman turns to Dubecheck and gives him a thumbs up and what he supposes is a wry grin.

The trouble is, Dubecheck now has two jet pilots, two recip

pilots and three copter pilots wanting to know what to do. He sends them all up in little holding patterns from one to ten miles.

A Huey pilot calls up Dubecheck to tell him he's got "a little activity" in the tree line about four hundred yards inland and Dubecheck asks him if there are "three huts," very loudly. There are no huts but there are some old bunkers and what appears to be a pig tethered to a stake.

"A . . . say all after 'what appears to be . . .' "

"I say again . . . a pig tethered to a stake."

"One pig? Over."

"A, that's an affirmative, Dark Singer. One large pig. Over."

"Roger. Out." Dubecheck looks over to see Kooseman, Kelly and Kealy with frowns of consternation, mulling the news with those grim visages meant to convey deep, seriouser-than-thou, no-nonsense concern. They stare at the radio set as if the guy was trapped inside.

Sisler, at the helm, looks to Dubecheck. "Is it a sow or a boar, sir?"

"Ah, Dark Singer, this is Black Pony Alpha. Roger, your hog. Please advise." Someone up there doesn't know a United States congressman is having a rite of passage down below. Levity is beginning to raise its funny face and ruin everything.

The Phantoms are doing slow figure eights in the distance.

"Hey, it's me. What's the Air Fair about? Something you're not telling me?" Recore pops up on the Prick 10 net.

Lieutenant Commander Kelly snatches the handset from Dubecheck. "This is Red Dragon Two. Seawolves have activity your sector. Over." The guy is actually breathing heavily. Christ almighty, *Red Dragon.* They could just as easily name these guys Pink Carnation or Water Lily.

"Well, I've got a real large pig surrounded. But maybe it's a trap. Over."

"Is it a sow or a boar?" Sisler asks of no one in particular.

"What's the difference between a boar and a hog?" Dubecheck asks Sisler. Sisler shrugs. Dubecheck sees that the congressman is looking at him like maybe the heat is starting to take effect. He looks pale and confused. Hey, welcome aboard.

Lieutenant Commander Kelly has got a problem. Millions of dollars' worth of aircraft are cruising around with the guys driving them ready to go on overtime and somebody somewhere is going to want to know how come some enemy *regiment* isn't being shit on by the boys in the wild blue yonder.

"Dark Singer, this is Bow Constrictor. Over."

"Who the fuck is Bow Constrictor?" Dubecheck snatches the handset back from Kelly, who looks like the inside of his head houses five thousand Chinese actuaries computing the odds for him getting out of this one with his shit smelling like the ice cream he thinks it does.

"Boa Constrictor, this is Dark Singer. Over."

"This is *Bow* Constrictor. What's going on down there? Over."

"Nothing. Over."

"Tell him about the pig," Sisler whispers to Dubecheck.

"What do you mean, *nothing!* My ETA is 1435 and it looks like a bees' nest over there! Over."

"Who the hell's Boa Constrictor, for Christ sake?" Dubecheck asks.

"It's Admiral Le Guinn," Kelly whispers with hoarse desperation.

"Oh, *Bow* Constrictor. I *get* it. Like a *bow.*" He feels a little faint. It's all coming down. The drill for the Armageddon Day picnic. To prove it, McDowell has appeared out of nowhere to peer through his thick glasses into the wheelhouse like a Mormon elder at the gates of Mary Kay's cosmetic heaven. "What do you want, McDowell?"

"Sir, one of Congressman Kealy's aides is throwing up near the bow. I believe he's seasick."

"Seasick?"

"There's vomit all over the mortar tube, Mr. Dubecheck, and Scoog is telling the man he better clean it up most skosh or he'll throw his ass into the river. Pardon my language, your honor." McDowell looks apologetically toward the congressman, who nods contritely and then looks to Lieutenant Commander Kelly very quizzically.

"Lieutenant Kooseman, could you see to the congressman's man? Here's a rag." Dubecheck hands Kooseman an oil rag providentially lying atop a radar console.

Kooseman takes the rag, nose up, as if it were already drenched in vomit, and leaves the wheelhouse with a petulant look back to Dubecheck.

"Dark Singer, this is Bow Constrictor. Over."

"This is Dark Singer. Over."

"Give me Red Dragon ASAP! Do you read me?"

Do you read me? Everyone has gone Hollywood on Dubecheck. He tosses the handset to Lieutenant Commander Kelly.

"Red Dragon here. Over."

"What's going on down there? I want to see some action!"

"I think a hog is a boar with his nuts cut off. Like a pig steer or somethin'." Sisler looks at Dubecheck and pulls at his chin. "But I'm not sure. I'd have to look it up."

"Well, there's activity in the tree line, sir, and—"

"They lay some *heat* in there, Red Dragon! Is that understood?"

"Ah, Roger, Bow Constrictor. But, but . . . but, sir, I—"

"Lay some heat in *where?*" Recore screams into the circuit. *"We're* here. Us and the fucking pig!"

The congressman's head swivels like he's watching a Chinese Ping-Pong match inside the wheelhouse.

"Who is that? Who is that talking like that on the net?" Admiral Le Guinn shouts.

"You need heat, we got it," Black Pony Alpha chips in.

Dubecheck's brain is suddenly short-circuited by the sudden roar of Bow Constrictor's helo hovering fifty feet over his boat.

"I got movement by the bunkers. The pig is really agitated. I'm goin' in to draw some fire." It's one of the Seawolves deciding to flash his résumé and the Huey dips down toward the tree line three football fields away as the other Huey covers him from above, riding shotgun, then swooping down as the door gunners hose down the earth to cover their ass and swoop up and away. Dubecheck can see Recore and his squad running toward the shore, running for their lives in a broken field retreat.

"They're under fire! There must be a million of them in there!" The lead Huey gunship has seen Recore and his squad running wildly across the dry rice paddies toward the shore. "We're taking fire!"

Taking fire from one of Recore's men, who is so pissed off he wants to kill them and stands in the distance spraying up at a helicopter with his M-16 before he is pulled off by Recore to continue their escape from the tree line.

"I want fire and thunder in there!" Admiral Le Guinn screams into the circuit.

The two OV-10s come in on a low pass and release their rockets, creating thunderclaps, dirt geysers rising quickly and falling slowly like black rain. They pull up as deftly as swallows and curl off to make room for the Phantoms, which come in low, tumbling napalm into the tree line, leaving ten-story-tall tumbleweeds of roiling orange and black in their wake. Everyone on board cheers as if they were watching a ball game.

Except Dubecheck: he's scanning the ugly, olive-drab playing field with his glasses. He sees Recore and his men flat on the ground with their arms over their heads, probably feeling the gusts of heat and concussion, and that's when Dubecheck notices the little girl running across the dead rice paddy toward Recore. She has her hands over her ears and is stumbling as she runs. Her mouth is wide open and she is screaming but there is so much noise Dubecheck can't hear her. Behind her is an old man in dirty white pajamas, hobbling like a cripple over a broken dike. Grandpa. They are running toward Recore and his men, who don't see them because they are hiding like ostriches as the Hueys make another pass, chattering and clattering and spitting bullets into the earth, the red tracers stretching down in slow motion. It seems like the little girl and the old man will never make it to wherever they are going as a Phantom jet comes in from another quarter, releasing with a giant hiss two rockets that sidewind toward the earth and die in an inferno that tears into and shatters a copse of trees like lightning.

The little girl and the old man seem about to overrun Recore and, amazingly, no one has looked up to open fire and shoot them. They make it and fall down among Recore's startled squad.

But the pig doesn't. It comes staggering into the open, running and falling, slipping, scorched and singed, terrified, dragging its peg at the end of a long rope. It gets a lot of laughs as it staggers around, bleating, falling, getting up, smoking and screeching, and then everyone on shore starts shooting at it . . . thunk, thunk, punt, punt, thwap, thwat! until the pig falls on its side in the dirt, bleating and honking and jerking with each bullet that slams into it as if it had a twitch, bleating like a broken horn until it stops and everything is oddly quiet for a moment.

Lieutenant Commander Kelly stands transfixed, holding the handset, staring at the dead pig a hundred and fifty yards away.

The congressman, like everyone else, is flush-faced from the excitement. Man's instinct to commit murder has been somewhat sated.

Dubecheck has Sisler close the shoreline to extract Recore's squad. They are all standing now and the old man is crying and trying to talk at the same time, turning to point at the pig as he weeps and blathers. The little girl walks to the pig and kneels down to pat it.

The Phantoms want to make one more pass for drill and to dump some leftover ordnance. Whatever was in that tree line has either been vaporized or fried.

Whatever was in there. People probably were in there.

"We're talkin' Crispy Critter City," says one of the Huey pilots.

Dubecheck sees Recore loom over the little old man, then point toward the boat, apparently referring the man's problem elsewhere.

Dubecheck takes the handset from the mesmerized Kelly and sends all the air home with a thank you and a job well done and a blah, blah, blah. "Bow Constrictor" adds a few accolades and signs off with a quaint little bit of business about "heading for the barn" and an order for Recore to go in and get a verified body count for the SPOTREP.

Admiral Le Guinn's helo lands just ashore, the prop wash beating the grass flat, creating a din that overwhelms the congressman's heartfelt congratulations. He moves through the boat slapping backs, shaking hands and winking, and two of his aides and Lieutenant Commander Kelly help him off the bow and then they all duckwalk under the prop and climb aboard Le Guinn's helo and are up and away with no room for Kooseman, who is left beneath the ascending helo, standing in the noisome wind, waving an oil rag full of vomit.

o   o   o

In the peace and quiet the only sound that can be heard is the old man shrieking at Recore, who is marching off toward the tree line with his squad.

Dubecheck takes off his helmet and flak jacket, feeling instantly cooler in the hundred-degree heat, and looks off toward Admiral Le Guinn's quickly receding helicopter. He feels as rotten about something unnameable as if he was getting away with a dirty little lie—as ashamed and impotent as one of Anastasion's moral eunuchs, everything seething inside his head like a pile of worms: fear, cowardice, duty, honor, capitulation and petty despair. But then again, fuck it. There is no way in the world he was prepared for any of this and he knows it was never supposed to be easy to make one's way in a world one's poorly equipped to be in in the first place, that great place of glacial indifference where one must often find the third option in a world of sink or swim.

"Dubecheck? I suppose you thought that vomit business was funny." Kooseman is in the wheelhouse, still holding the oil rag.

"No, sir, I didn't. I was busy."

"Your Scoog should have handled that mess. I think you deliberately tried to—"

"I didn't do anything deliberately. Scoog is a gunner's mate first class with responsibility for the weapons on board this vessel. He can't have vomit on his mortar tube."

"I'm warning you, Dubecheck. One of these days you're going to get it."

Dubecheck regards Kooseman's sweat-greased, cretinous gaze, thinking the only reason Kooseman exists is because there is room for him.

"I already get it, Lieutenant."

Dubecheck can still see the little girl, a couple hundred yards away, kneeling over her dead pig, petting its scorched hide as if that might bring it back to life.

"We should pay for that pig, sir," Sisler says.

"Yeah, we probably should."

"Why should we?" says Kooseman.

"I dunno," Dubecheck says. "Maybe because it's the right thing to do."

Three clicks come over the Prick Ten net. Dubecheck answers with two.

"Come on over here. You gotta see this." Recore's voice sounds grim.

Dubecheck walks across the scruffy, premonsoon rice paddy, the M-16 the congressman left leaning against the bulkhead of the wheelhouse hanging in his left hand. He stops at the pig and squats down next to the little girl, who won't look at him, her face canted away, her body trembling. He puts his hand on her shoulder and she goes rigid. He wants to put her in his pocket and take her away but wonders, to where? He gets up and looks down at the flyblown wide-open eyes of the pig which have begun to glaze with the dull film of death, then continues on toward the demolished little tree line.

"We got one," Recore says. He stands with his seven camouflage-faced guys in the smoking, stinking, charred remnants of a little stand of trees. A couple of little fires crackle in black dirt. "Right there." He points and Dubecheck sees an eviscerated dead monkey, twisted and contorted like a piece of charred driftwood. "The other one's wounded."

Dubecheck follows Recore for about twenty feet and they look down upon another monkey that writhes on its back, pounding its stomach, trying to tear at it with its hands. It stops and lolls its head over, looking at Dubecheck with its wild brown eyes, and bares its teeth and tries to hiss but blood gushes from its mouth and it tries to spit through its ketchup-colored teeth.

"Jesus, Recore."

"No shit. Activity. This is an insult to our profession."

The monkey tries to tear at its guts again, pounding in primal rage.

"What's he doing?"

"I dunno. He's got a bullet in there is my guess. He wants to pull it out."

"Whaddaya want *me* for?" Dubecheck finally notices the old man, who points to the monkey, then starts chattering in an unfathomable singsong, looking to anyone who might listen.

"J.P." Recore squats down on the ground with a sigh, steadying himself with his M-16.

"For the record and off the record, what we've got here is a body count. We got one KIA. But it's a *monkey*. A dead, killed-in-action monkey, but I'm in no fucking mood to split hairs. I wanna know what to do with *this* monkey."

"You got me over here to ask that? *Me?* Like what? Maybe we bring it in an' interrogate it? You think it can march down to the boat with its hands on top of its head?"

"I can't just leave it here."

"Well, put it out of its misery, for Christ sake!" Dubecheck notices the little old man has finally shut up and become a spectator totally consumed by curiosity about what Americans might do next.

"I can't. Nobody can. *Look* at him."

Dubecheck does. The monkey stares straight up into the Technicolor sky as if waiting for everything to be over with so he can go back to reality, his lips working like big rubber bands over his grimace.

"Whaddaya mean, *nobody* can? You guys kill people for breakfast."

"This ain't a person, J.P."

"So what about first aid or something? This the fucking Humane Society?"

"The monkey won't let nobody near him," Recore's corpsman says. "They bite you, you can get a disease."

"I don't believe this." Dubecheck looks at the monkey, which turns on its stomach and tries doing the breast stroke over the smoldering earth, then stops to cough blood.

The little old man starts chattering again and, since Dubecheck is the only one who seems to listen to him, the man grabs him by his

shirt and Dubecheck looks down into his eyes, which seem submerged in tears. The little ninety-pound man jerks at Dubecheck's
fatigues and pleads an unintelligible case as Dubecheck looks behind him to see the monkey roll over and raise itself on one elbow.
Little fleas or parasites can be seen scurrying in panic in the thin
hairs near its armpit as if the word is out.

"I'll kill it," says Dubecheck.

With that, Recore gets up and walks out of the smoldering slash
burn with his squad following. The old man releases his grip on
Dubecheck's fatigues and hobbles off after them and Dubecheck
finds himself alone with the monkey, whose eyes longingly meet
Dubecheck's.

The monkey begins to make a noise Dubecheck has never before
heard on the planet. A guttural, manic growl rising to an octave
beyond hope, as if monkeys had hope, Dubecheck thinks, but if you
can have fear you can have hope and the monkey is afraid, afraid of
dying and afraid of pain, and it lies in the dirt in a spasm of terror
. . . and it's oh, so fucking hot and humid and it stinks because the
monkey starts to shit, snapping its head back and forth, embarrassed and virtually paralyzed, so Dubecheck pulls the Tokarev pistol from his baggy pocket, slides off the safety with his opposable
thumb and stands over the monkey and fires a Czechoslovakian
bullet into the monkey's wondrous face, just above its confused
watery brown eyes.

He walks out of the shattered copse, which crackles behind him
like a cozy fireplace. Cozy, with a dead monkey sprawled on the
hearth like a tiny bearskin rug.

Halfway to the shoreline, he sees Recore and his squad standing
around the dead pig while the old man pisses and moans, pointing to
the pig, the sky, the river, Recore and eventually toward Dubecheck. The little barefoot girl squats next to the pig and stares
down at it. Dubecheck stops and watches the distant scene. An odd,
goofy tableau with so little movement it could be a watercolor. The
pastels of the pale grasses, the now dead-calm, mile-wide river in the
background reflecting the huge, voluminous, pus-colored cumulus
clouds banked against the thin blue sky. An idyllic oil entitled, *Old
Man Fruitlessly Complaining to Young Men About Unfortunate Turn
of Events.*

Dubecheck trudges toward the scene, the Tokarev dangling in
his hand, the warm stink from its firing still lingering. He hears the
old man's voice pause more as his argument and pleadings reach the
point of futility and exhaustion.

"Ah. Mr. Dubecheck, I presume." Recore looks up with a glazed Chiclet smile, all the flashier for the mess of dark camouflage on his face. Dubecheck wonders who in the hell makes camouflage for soldiers' faces and what they might be doing now. Probably teeing it up at Pebble Beach. Standing in the winner's circle at Santa Anita.

"It's me. What's the international incident about?"

"Nguyen here, although we speak a different tongue, he has been quite eloquent. He's bummed about the pig."

With that, everyone regards the dead pig as if observing a dignitary lying in state. It is quiet except for the little girl, who is crying like she has the hiccups. Dubecheck feels dizzy.

"I wonder if this is the same pig?"

"What same pig?" Recore asks.

"Remember? That pig that blocked the road when we went to that party?"

"What party?"

"The party, I dunno. Two weeks, two months, two years ago. The old lady who beat the shit out of you?"

"Oh, yeah. *That* pig. You think so? Nah."

"It looks a lot like that pig, Recore. On its side. Put 'em in a lineup together . . . I dunno."

Dubecheck looks at the old man. If you look at someone long enough he stops being an "old man" and becomes a real person who just happens to be old. Like a friend's father or something. His face is shiny because the skin is so taut over his bones. The wrinkles are deep crevices and he has a dozen dark moles. His wispy billy-goat beard drifts in the onshore breeze like a tell tale. Dubecheck figures the old man listening to him and Recore talk is under the delusion they are maybe discussing his best interest.

The Mark I standard issue little peasant girl continues to sniffle. Dubecheck realizes he will never see these two people again anywhere. Ever. The temptation to walk away, as if the whole event was just a stupid dream, is overwhelming.

"We gotta fix this up."

"You think that could be the same pig?"

"I wouldn't be surprised to have a pig shadow me throughout the Orient."

"You kill the monkey?" Recore's corpsman asks with belligerent suspicion.

"Yeah, I killed the monkey." Dubecheck looks around into a semicircle of smirks. "So give the guy some money for the pig." He remembers something that crazy chaplain told him in what seems another lifetime ago. "Money answereth all things. Ecclesiastes 10:19."

"Well, I don't have a cent," Recore says. "We don't carry cash after dark. Or before, either."

Dubecheck looks toward the river at his boat and his crew standing aboard, looking shoreward, wondering what's going on.

"Maybe Kooseman's got some money," says Recore, following Dubecheck's gaze.

"I say we gut the sucker and roast its ass," one of Recore's men says. One of those guys Dubecheck wouldn't want anything to do with unless he was in trouble.

"Any way you cut it, we ought to dress it out," Recore says, and the guy who wants to roast the pig pulls out his K-bar knife, one of those eight-inch, semidouble-edged jobs that would scare the shit out of a Turk.

Dubecheck picks up the little girl, who squirms in his arms, smelling like dirt. He turns his back to the pig and hears the knife puncture the underbelly. It sounds like a dull saw going through canvas as the guy opens it up.

The girl thrashes in his arms and he lets her down and she runs back toward the smoldering tree line, shrieking, stumbling, not looking back.

The pig's gut pile gives off a thick, warm stench.

"You shoulda left the guts in, man. Cook it Flip style." One of Recore's guys is a gourmet.

Dubecheck's had roast pig Filipino style before himself. They just bury the whole dead thing, guts and all, in the ground with hot rocks for a day. The hide has the consistency of peanut brittle and the chef recommends you dip a chunk of it in the liver, which has the consistency of oatmeal when it's been cooked inside a carcass for eight hours. It's a delicacy. Dubecheck thinks foreigners come up with the worst thing they can imagine and say it's a delicacy. They'll be affronted about it if you don't eat. Revenge.

At the bottom of the slippery gut pile a tubeful of thumb-sized fetuses roll out. And that sets the old man off again.

"Pork belly futures," says Recore.

"I wonder if he had his pig insured."

"That's stupid, Dubecheck."

"With Allstate or something. Can't you see some guy in a suit and tie with a briefcase handing this guy a check?"

"The heat is getting to you, Diwi."

One of Recore's men grabs the pig's front legs and another grabs the back ones and they haul the sow toward the shore. The rest of the squad follows, leaving Recore and Dubecheck alone with the old man.

Flies have materialized out of nowhere and swarm upon the gut pile.

"I'd like to quit my job."

"Hey, when the goin' gets tough, the tough get goin'."

"Where do they go?"

"They shuffle off to Buffalo."

"Maybe they go crazy. What can we give this guy? You went to college, you're smart. What do you think?"

"We gave him two monkeys. Those babies'll be on the grill before we're two klicks down the road. Don't feel bad, Dubecheck."

"Why should I? It's God's will." He walks toward the boat and motions the confused old man to follow. Somewhat reluctantly he does. Atonement is just another word for shoveling sand against the tide.

 "Jesus, Dubecheck. Sorry about the monkey." Dupree's bourbon breath blasts into Dubecheck's face as his arm falls heavily over Dubecheck's shoulder in deep commiseration.

Rocky Akoka is playing "Lady of Spain" on his accordion in the compound outside the O Club as Tiger, the opera singer, dances on the cracked concrete, imitating a flamenco dancer, red bangles swirling up her honey-colored thighs.

In the several hours after the congressman and his entourage had arrived, and before Dubecheck returned, Dupree had arranged for Rocky and his troupe to perform and a "light buffet" was put out but then the congressman's entourage left for wherever it is Very Important People go after stuff happens.

"You know what Recore told me about you? Do you?"

"No, I don't, Norman." Dubecheck hasn't talked to Recore

since they decided to give the old man and the little girl two cases of C rations to make up for the death of their pig.

"No, what did he say about me, Norman?"

"He said he didn't think you had it in you."

"Have what?"

"I dunno."

o   o   o

Dubecheck walks out of the compound down the curfew-deserted streets. The heavy nighttime shadows of the huge plane trees block out the sky like thunderclouds. He had left the forced hilarity of drunken, tired man-boys, tiring of Dupree's analysis of the events of the day and how the congressman and his aides, Admiral Le Guinn and Lieutenant Commander Kelly had all knelt before a photographer like some Little League baseball team and held weapons in their hands and smiled out from their camouflaged faces for a portfolio's worth of photos, then left with little fanfare other than the joyous camaraderie attendant on such occasions.

He walks down Tu Do Street into the darkness toward the little house on a dirt street where an old lady has four or five fifteen-year-old girls who sit around in baby-blue baby dolls or their underwear and play cards and drink Coca-Cola until some drunken Americans show up with hair dryers, electric fans, Gleem, Salems or money and then they'll lie on their backs for them, behind bed-sheet curtains, on beds as narrow as shelves. He figures to go get a little peace.

He plays cards in a room the size of a sandbox with two of the girls and one of their six-year-old brothers, beneath a naked light bulb. A seventy-five-pound girl who calls herself Marilyn is upstairs with some agricultural expert attached to AID who is a friend of Snazzy's from Washington, D.C.

The card game is "fish" and the little fat-faced, black crew-cut boy is beating Dubecheck real bad, grinning mischievously, saying, "Go fish, sucker," when the first mortar hits.

It is very close. The shock wave rocks the little house, and the next one is closer and the noise makes his ears ring, and just as the electric power goes off he sees one of the little prostitutes scrambling on her hands and knees in front of him, her bare little pale ass mooning out her baby doll pajamas and her thighs damp with a little piss that splashes down on them as she awkwardly claws across the floor, tossing her cards away as an afterthought. The little boy pulls a crouching Dubecheck by the hand and everybody is choking on the dust that fills the air with a thickness that coats the tongue with dirt.

They all end up in a little bunker beneath the floor; the little boy pulls the trapdoor hatch down over them. It is dark and close, sweaty bodies scrunched next to one another in a space the size of an outhouse. A match is lit and Dubecheck sees the old woman lighting a candle stub. She holds a naked little baby to her dirty white tunic. The prostitutes smell sweet, like lilacs, in the cramped heat, motes of dust stream in the candlelight and another two rounds of incoming smash into the neighborhood. The old woman starts to moan, eyes closed, trying to sway, and the baby cries and one of the little prostitutes starts to whimper, then cry, and the little boy chews his lower lip and looks into his feet on the dirt floor. The other little prostitute squats, her mat of black pubic hair damp and scraggly, her inner thigh damp.

There is a pounding on the hatch and Dubecheck opens it and Marilyn jumps in on top of him and pulls the hatch down as another mortar shell goes off, sending shrapnel spitting through the air and into the walls above.

She smells of coppery seaweed, her slick crotch straddles his thigh, her baby doll pajamas stick against her sweaty skin and she sits on Dubecheck's lap and his penis swells as she puts her arms around his neck. She is breathing hard from running and fear and the heat beats against his ear. She feels his erection and puts her hand on it and squeezes, kneading it, as the baby continues to cry and the old woman rocks and clutches and fingers her rosary and Dubecheck clutches and fingers his dog tags, and the little boy starts to sneeze in the dust and the candle goes out and everyone is quiet and Marilyn starts to kiss Dubecheck, her lips grinding into his as if she wants to hurt herself, and Dubecheck lets her and it feels good and he is as aroused as he's ever been in his life, his hand on her tennis-ball-size tit with its nipple burrowing into his palm like a soft nail, and she is whimpering and he tastes blood from her lips, then she begins to suck his neck, hitting his shoulders with her fist, and just as suddenly stops and curls up in his lap. The candle is relit and Dubecheck sees around the little prehistoric-looking cave, sad, strange, foreign faces looking at him through the veil of golden dust that hangs suspended in the close air. They all sit quietly, no one speaking, for ten minutes or so, just breathing, occasionally coughing, wiping the sweat from their faces, making mud stains, waiting for a nonexistent "all clear" to sound.

After the attack Dubecheck crawls out of the bunker, his fa-

tigues clinging to him with a glue of sweat and dust. He goes
through a curtain into a darkened room to find some water and sees
mosquito netting, a mesh tent suspended over a pallet covered with
squirming baby humans, a half dozen or more squirming in the
dark, like puppies, gurgling and cooing, and one is twitching and
Dubecheck peers down closer to part the net, to view this bizarre
litter, the fruits of fucking, and one lies twitching in a puddle upon
the wooden pallet, twitching like a little tadpole in a puddle, and
then Dubecheck sees the little jagged triangle of shrapnel protruding from its back, a perfect little dorsal fin, and the little baby stops
twitching and a Tommy Tippy cupful of blood surges out of its little
mouth to join the pool it lies in.

Tired. That is the emotion he feels. Just tired. Nothing else.

●   ●   ●

He makes the mistake of stopping back by the O Club and has been
cornered for a long time by the flamenco-dancing opera singer from
Inchon, who calls herself Tiger. She is wearing a bright red dress,
bangled with fringes, and she has Dubecheck backed up against the
wall and is talking to him as if she's known him for a long time,
telling him aspects of her life that are tragic enough to bring copious tears to her eyes, which miraculously never manage to fall out.
Going on in a quiet, thoughtful tone about how her husband, a
captain in the ROK Army, was killed two years ago in Tay Ninh.
How her American lover, a captain, was killed a year ago in Dak To,
and how her new lover, a captain of course, had lost his foot in
Pleiku and was now in Japan getting a plastic one. He had just
written her saying he would probably be unable to return but of
course still loved her very much. But probably not as much as his
wife and three kids back in Boise, Dubecheck thinks. And certainly
not as much as his foot.

The feeling she is one of those people close proximity to whom
brings grief crosses his mind and he doesn't quite know what to do,
torn between his concern for her and the vague feeling he is being
hit up for something. Over her shoulder, he sees Dupree and Rocky
Akoka head to head in maudlin whispering. It is late, the time of
night when, if he finds himself awake, he gets to see the curtain
drawn back on the Big Picture and it makes him feel closer to other
people than he thought could happen.

To top all this off, Anastasion stands glaring at him from across
the tiny room as if she is his wife or something.

Tiger starts to sob in great whoops, which Dubecheck thinks sort of operatic, and she buries her face in her hands. He leans over and pats her on her back, which is heaving and damp from sweat, and wishes he could do something. He wonders why people always seem to take him into their confidence and realizes that is the price one often pays for being taller than most. When you're bummed out, go talk to a tall person. It must be the looking up that does it. Like you're talking to a grown-up and somehow the grown-up will make it better. And it also helps if the tall person doesn't talk much. It's hard to piss and moan if you can't get in a word edgewise.

Dubecheck tries to sneak out before Anastasion can attach herself to him like an angry limpet.

"You didn't tell anybody, did you?"

"Tell anybody what?"

She talks through clenched teeth as she looks around for eavesdroppers. "What I did."

"What did you do?"

"Don't give me that shit, Dubecheck. If I find out you told everybody what I did, I'll tell everybody you couldn't get it up."

"Oh . . . oh, that."

"Yeah, that. You didn't tell anybody, did you?"

"No."

"Really?"

"Really."

That's another thing. The world could be burning up or crumbling beneath the feet, but all that people really seem to care about is what other people might think of them. It's hard to tell people that everyone else is so consumed by what other people think of themselves, they don't think of other people.

He decides to take Tiger away from everything and, because of her high heels, ends up carrying her like a newlywed over the threshold of the dark, empty, chuckholed, garbage-strewn street leading to the old hotel.

He carries her piggyback up the three-story stairway, her head gently bouncing off his back, her arms loose around his neck, her high-heeled shoes dangling from her hands and resting against his chest, her warm thighs getting sticky as they rest on his forearms. She hums sleepily and he has to admit his feeling for her at the moment is as close to love as he has ever felt for any woman and it is a feeling he wants to keep.

In the darkness she undresses and drapes her clothes neatly from a cord stretched across the room, then bends over, picks a fatigue blouse off the floor and puts it on. She comes to Dubecheck and puts her arms around him and he feels her tiny teacup breasts flatten against his tacky skin.

"Recore say you take me to America. You have big band, play at Disneyland on New Year's Eve."

"Really?"

"Really."

"Sing for me, Tiger."

"What?" She lifts her head off his chest and looks up at him wonderingly. The room is close, dark, quiet, and smells of rotten water.

"A song. Like a song for Disneyland on New Year's Eve."

She smiles and backs to the center of the floor. In Dubecheck's fatigue blouse she looks like a little kid in her daddy's pajama tops. She purses her lips as she thinks of a number, bends down to pick up a shower shoe and holds it before her as if it is a microphone and begins to sing in a small, shaky voice.

" 'I left my heart . . . in San Francisco, High on a hill . . .' " She knows all the words and sounds as if she does indeed miss the place. He gets up to dance with her, holding her slender softness close to him.

"Keep singing."

She does and puts her head against his chest as they do what he imagines is a slow fox trot beneath the skeins of her lingerie that hang in the darkness like Spanish moss, his nose pressed into her crunchy vanilla-smelling hair, listening to the words cease and drift into a humming lullaby that resonates against his slowly thumping heart.

Tiger and he decide to make love. Not out of passion, friendship, need or want. Just because they feel they are supposed to or something. She, perhaps, out of the realization that is what she has to do to get her job at Disneyland and he because she seems set enough on it that he doesn't want to hurt her feelings. But instead a little fire fight in the suburbs several hundred yards away has them looking out the window and over the balcony at the pretty tracers and flares. After the brief skirmish, Dubecheck can hear voices shouting in the night, sounding like a playground mob around a fist fight, ultimately rising in pitch and intensity to indicate someone probably got hurt bad. The interlude seemed to take whatever inclination they had out of them, and they go to sleep in each other's arms like children.

**F
L
O
A
T**

Recore and Dubecheck have gone to Saigon for two days to attend a "Lessons Learned" seminar for people like themselves who apparently just keep fucking up enough to ensure the continual holding of such conclaves. The "Lessons Learned" were actually nothing but horror stories of incompetence and bad luck that could no more have been avoided, anticipated or foretold than natural disasters. But one and all were admonished to, in the future, have both a lot of common sense and a crystal ball. Lieutenant Commander Kelly was master of ceremonies and Dubecheck observed some of the newer guys actually taking notes.

After the last "Lesson Learned" confab, they were invited to a staff "cocktail" hour, a postgraduate soiree that was to be attended by some admiral who'd just had his wife flown in from the Philippines. A lieutenant commander accosted them in the hallway outside the meeting room and told both of them if they even thought about coming to get their hair cut and if they might be thinking of attending the "reception" to "titivate ship" and he gave Dubecheck's fatigues a few quick tugs. The lieutenant commander wore his summer dress khakis and looked sharp. A Bing-cherry-size stone in his class ring. Some Annapolis ring knocker.

Dubecheck stood behind Recore and noticed the dried pig blood on the hem of his pale, sun-bleached fatigue blouse, the red Delta mud encrusted on his combat boot heels, and heard him say, "Yes, sir. And ASAP. We were just on our way," and they walked out of the building and made for Tu Do Street and the first sleazy bar they could find.

"Our *hair*. We're going to get our *horns* trimmed is what we're going to do."

They rode a cab through the cycle- and scooter-clogged streets, the traffic swirling in centrifugal chaos in the roundabouts, horns constantly bleating in the dusty din of confusion.

"You ever met a guy from the Academy that didn't have his head up his ass?"

Dubecheck thought on it.

"One or two."

"They graduate a thousand every year. Those are good odds. They lock them up for four years like monks or somethin'. Soon as they graduate, most of 'em marry some chick they met on a blind date after the Army-Navy game. They get married for two reasons: the first chick they meet they think it's heaven on earth, or the second is it's a prudent career move. But you, Dubecheck, I can see aren't interested in prudent career moves, so do I have a girl for you!"

Recore, in a touching display of affection, flashed a huge wad of piastres and with his arm around Dubecheck's shoulder pulled him into the Black Cat Nite Club and was soon buying gasoline-colored Kool-Aid cocktails for a half dozen mini-skirted, raccoon-eyed, black-bubble-bouffant-hairdoed, eighty-pound Asian chicks who sat on their laps, giggled, pouted and dragged them up to dance on the empty precocktail-hour dance floor to a 110-decibel jukebox.

It was wonderful and with Recore's roll they were treated like visiting dignitaries. They should never have left.

They left because Recore is one of those people who really shouldn't drink.

They emerged from the Black Cat into the Saigon dusk, lights twinkling, the traffic thinned with the bar girls waving, jammed up at the door, several in mock throes of tearful despair, waiting for them to come back for "beaucoup boom-boom." Great girls. Great country. Great evening full of delight and promise and joy.

That's when Recore said they had to go to the reception for the admiral and his wife. Dubecheck waffled. Recore, as a full lieutenant, "ordered" him to come with him. But not before Dubecheck dug into his kit to put on his polyester plaid slacks and St. Vincent de Paul sport coat.

They entered the reception reeking of bar girl, swiveling the heads of the thirty or so officers.

French doors opened on a garden and several tables were covered with thick linen tablecloths and had tiny Vietnamese men in white tunics standing quietly behind them at near attention, waiting to mix cocktails or lift the shiny silver lids of the chafing dish trays full of egg rolls and grilled chicken livers.

Clumps of officers in starched tropical khakis stood holding their cocktail glasses wrapped in paper napkins, and none of them knew what to say because nobody was about to make a command decision.

Like most gatherings of that sort, ensigns stood with ensigns, jg's stood in clumps with jg's, lieutenants stood with lieutenants, out on the perimeters of rank that emanated outward from the thermal center of the reception—an admiral from Staff at Fleet in Pearl.

That was how Recore and Dubecheck were able to make it all the way to the crystal punch bowl full of pink liquid with lemon slices floating on the top. They had walked in through an outer perimeter of guys of their own rank who weren't about to stop them, staff guys, a glorified secretarial pool.

Dubecheck held out a plate for some chicken livers and looked about the room, which had the soft ambiance of a country club, and spotted what he thought must be the admiral, a tall gray man dressed in tropical whites, next to a huge woman in a flamboyant muu-muu and a black beehive hairdo. They were surrounded by an audience of subflag rank. That was when Dubecheck heard the gargling. He turned to see Recore gargling into the punch bowl to the awestruck, mouth-gaping horror of everyone near the table except for the waiters, who looked stoically into space.

"Blurrrrrrrrr." Recore fluted his lips into the punch bowl. "Jesus, I'm drunk!" He cupped the punch in his hands and splashed his face, trying to wake himself up. Then he passed out, pulling the tablecloth down, covering himself with several hundred chicken livers and three gallons of lemonade punch.

The admiral calmly wanted "that man's name," and he got it from Dubecheck, who was being held at the arms by a khaki lynch mob.

"Lieutenant *Recore?*"

"Yes, Sir Admiral." The room swirled before Dubecheck. It was utterly silent except for punch dripping on the rug and it smelled like chicken livers.

"I know *him*. Of him. This man's Navy would be a damn sight better if we had a thousand more like him."

Recore and Dubecheck were locked up for the night in an office where Dubecheck spent the night on the floor while Recore snored on a couch, but the admiral saw to it they had a big breakfast on him the next morning, on white linen, served by three of his Filipino messmates.

O   O   O

On his return, sweating to death in his St. Vincent de Paul sport coat and Polynesian plaid pants, Dubecheck barges into Dupree's Quonset hut.

"Hey, Norman. Is Tiger still here?"

"Yeah, and am I glad to see you."

"Well, I'm glad to see you too, Norman. My respect and admiration for you, while negligible at best—"

"Hush. First things first. It's about Tuta."

"Oh. Go on."

"He's naked and won't come out of his room."

"That's okay. That's a very good idea. I wish I'd thought of that."

"Yeah, but for almost three straight days it is bad management practice and this is where you come in."

"Surprise me."

"You are the only one he says he'll talk to."

"And I've been gone. I'd say the man has his shit together, Dupree."

"Please go over to his little hut and talk to him."

"What's his problem?"

"Grief. Utter grief. The enemy, in their constant pursuit of the best of all possible worlds, shot the back of her head off and set her on fire, or vice versa, it being impossible to tell really the exact order of damage."

"Who?"

"Who? Madame Phong. Tush. The man's reason for being."

"Oh . . . no."

"Oh, yes. The fortunes of war, and she really wasn't in it."

"When?"

"Three nights ago. Say, Dubecheck. You look awful. Didn't you have a good time?"

"I don't know yet. . . . I don't think so."

Dubecheck meanders out the compound gate and wanders slowly into town, wondering where he was three nights ago. With Tiger, probably, watching it happen out the window in the tracer-streaked night.

And what is one to make of something like that?

Lulu, with her hippie dippy bullshit on the way to her parents' house, would have said Tush chose to get the back of her head shot off and her body set on fire, that everything in life is a choice, that everyone chooses what happens to them. If such is the case, people are worse off than Dubecheck imagined. Tush was okay.

A small covey of people loiter about Tuta's front door. The OD in his schoolboy patrol bandolier and armband, a couple of cigarette-smoking sailors and Dubecheck's good friend Lieutenant Kooseman.

Dubecheck decides to salute Kooseman.

"You're out of uniform, Dubecheck. That's neither necessary nor proper."

"How's Tuta?"

"How would you be? How would you be if someone you not only loved but respected died brutally and senselessly?"

Dubecheck regards Kooseman for a long moment, the weight of the heat over his head like a wet bag.

"Is this a test? Is that a test question, Kooseman? Is this some fucking pop quiz you're giving me? Is it? Is it . . . you, you—"

"Watch it, Dubecheck. You're asking for it again. You're dismissed." Kooseman flicks the two sailors and the OD away with his thin white hand. They leave with the reluctance of the morbidly curious.

"You shouldn't talk to me like that in front of enlisted men."

"I'm sorry."

"No, you're not."

"Honest. I really am . . . really."

"Are you all right, Dubecheck?"

"What do you mean?"

"You . . . you look . . . you don't look very well."

"Well, no, I'm not all right. Why should I be all right? Can I go in and get this over with? Dupree says he wants to talk to me."

"Yes. I don't know why he only wants to talk to you."

"Don't feel bad, Kooseman. I don't either. I'm sure it's nothing personal. Do you want to knock or should I? What's the protocol here?"

Kooseman gently raps his knuckles against the door.

"Sir? . . . Sir?"

"Don't whisper."

"Sir! . . . Sir!"

"What now?" Tuta's voice barely works its way through the door.

"It's Lieutenant Kooseman, sir . . . I've brought Mr. Dubecheck." Kooseman turns to smile.

Presently the door opens a crack. Tuta's nose appears. A hot locker-room stench wafts out.

"Come in. Come in, Lieutenant."

Dubecheck edges sideways through the slight opening as Kooseman cranes his neck to peek in. "Don't look, Kooseman. He's naked." Dubecheck shuts the door behind him. He can barely breathe in the sauna of b.o.

Tuta slumps in his chair, his plump nakedness the color of cold bacon fat. The pouches of his breasts sag on his hairless chest as he slumps in a state of woe so deep he looks deboned. Or pithed.

The desk in front of him is covered with message traffic, a few fresh fried chicken bones and the open book of Hieronymus Bosch.

"Have you ever noticed how hot it is here?"

"Yes, sir. I have."

"I'm surprised everyone doesn't go naked." He puts on his glasses, which somehow make him look more naked.

Dubecheck swelters in his sport coat from St. Vincent de Paul's; the thought he could conceivably melt enters his mind.

He wonders if he should tell Tuta he's sorry about Tush, but he's not sure he is or can be. It's like telling someone you're sorry they broke their leg. Other people's pain is essentially meaningless. You can't really feel it or assuage it. It exists only in a word that doesn't do it justice.

"I'm sorry."

"Sorry? Sorry about what, Lieutenant?"

Good question. Where does a guy start? He shrugs.

"I've found a few more things in this triptych I thought I'd share with you. Look here." His pudgy finger points to some quasi-human monkey business going on in the black shadows of a fearsome conflagration. "Human suffering and degradation. Absolutely no end to it. As Casey Stengel said, 'You can look it up,' and have you noticed how this eggshell fellow looks a bit like the old Perfessor himself?"

"Yes. He looks like Casey Stengel must have looked as a young man."

"What's that in your hand?"

Dubecheck is surprised to see he is flipping the picture of Duwayne from Wayne's wife over and over in his hands like a playing card. It was in the sport coat.

"Is that a baseball card?"

"No. It's a picture of Duwayne from Wayne's wife. Duwayne's dead now."

"So, now she's your wife?"

"No, sir. I'm not married."

"Let me see her."

Dubecheck flashes him the picture.

"She looks like my wife. But . . . all cats are gray in the dark, so they say. I've got a problem, Lieutenant."

"Really?"

"Yes. It's about Madame Phong. See, she's not buried yet."

"I see."

"And her body . . . the supply officer . . . ah, what's his name?"

"I don't know. He's new, sir, and I haven't—"

"Well, he's been kind enough to let me keep the remains in his freezer next to the various concentrated juices, but his kindness and indulgence—" Tuta waffles his hand. "She had no family, I was surprised to find. I thought she was related to the President."

"And she wasn't?"

"No. She wasn't. A pity."

Dubecheck wonders why it's a pity. He wonders about the word itself. Maybe it's as empty a word as "sorry."

For a long time Tuta looks at a detail of Hieronymus Bosch's triptych about life on earth.

Dubecheck busies himself studying the moons of his fingernails until the buzz of a fly draws his dazed attention toward a wall three feet away. A fat winged creature the size of a pea struts back and forth on the ledge of the sill where the idle, broken air conditioner rests. The bug looks like it wants to jump but is hesitant and it's looking down and Dubecheck follows its "gaze" and sees a half dozen similar bugs milling around in a circle on the floor beneath the sill. And they're looking up. And, in the stifling heat, they're screaming, "Don't jump! Don't jump! Please! Please!" and some are crying and hugging each other and there's a newspaper reporter bug and Dubecheck looks up to see a bug crawl along the ledge of the sill toward the other bug and it's a *priest* bug saying, "Easy. Easy does it. Reach out. Reach out and take my leg. I've got six of them. I'm an insect too. I know how it feels."

The bug jumps. It hits the deck with a barely perceptible "click" and then joins the formation of bugs on the floor as they march toward Tuta's foot. They stop and seem to observe it as if it were a gigantic, ancient ruin of great archaeological interest. Tuta suddenly rises, takes one step to nowhere and unknowingly crushes them. He doesn't feel a thing. Then he takes another step and turns. Dubecheck looks from the flattened squad of bugs to the back of Tuta's ample ass, which looms before his face.

"She wasn't a Christian."

"Bummer."

"I beg your pardon?"

"I said, that's too bad."

"No, it's not. She was Cao Dai. You know the sect, Lieutenant?"

"Not well, sir." Dubecheck hopes Tuta doesn't decide to turn around. He feels like he's in a septic tank and he's about to make a break for it when Tuta turns around and starts to cry. He covers his face with his hands and his cold bacon-fat-colored belly quivers and Dubecheck finds himself staring into the folds of flesh that roll down to the curly brown rat's nest of Tuta's pubic hair, his penis showing pink, like a poorly hidden Easter egg. Nothing in life really prepares a guy for stuff like this. Dubecheck averts his eyes toward the Bosch detail and then drops his gaze to stare at the bugs squashed on the floor like crushed chocolate chips. Tuta sniffs, chokes and hyperventilates, and Dubecheck figures if he doesn't stop soon he too will begin to cry. He's found crying is sort of contagious, like yawning.

383

"Sir, could you . . . could you, like, get ahold of yourself, sir?" Maybe he should slap his face. Maybe he should leave. He stands up. He's sopping wet from sweat and his clothes hang on him like weights.

"Sit down!" Tuta wipes his eyes with both hands. Dubecheck slides down the wall and sits on the floor. "I've got to get dressed. We'll go pick up the remains. We'll get a flag and bury her at sea. We'll take one of your little boats. You and me. I'll say some words. The Cao Dai are very eclectic people, Lieutenant. Victor Hugo. Charles Dickens. All Saints. Honest Abe too. Mohammed. Christ. Gautama."

"Bosch?"

"I'd hope so. Let me get decent." Tuta waddles through the Taiwan whorehouse bead curtain into his boudoir.

"Tuta, sir. I'm not sure about this."

"What do you mean, Lieutenant?"

"Is . . . maybe this isn't legal or something."

"Who cares?"

He's got Dubecheck there.

"You mean, we get . . . her body and get the little boat and sort of . . . ?"

"Roger. . . . I think that would be nice."

Dubecheck can hear Tuta on the other side of the curtain huffing and puffing into his clothes. He puts his head in his hands and stares through the bars of his fingers at a vision of the wide, brown, slow-moving river. "Ah . . . can I bring some beer?"

"Sure."

Dubecheck wishes Tuta had let him change clothes. Somehow a burial at sea, even if it was a dirty brown river, seemed to call for a spiffing up. But Tuta took command and Dubecheck is content to have another guy tell him what to do for a while, for he has no idea what to do on his own anymore.

The "remains," as they are euphemistically referred to in military and other violent circles, were in a Conex box some boy wonder had converted into a freezer. It sat across the compound from Dupree's Quonset hut, not too far from the ammo hut and beneath a palm tree near the dock. The compound, deserted in afternoon siesta, seemed an isolated make-believe outpost distant from itself. Dubecheck could hear the interrupted strains of "Lady of Spain" from some hidden corner of the compound, as if Rocky Akoka, the Korean virtuoso, was trying to get a certain passage "just right" or had gone off the deep end once and for all. He wondered where Tiger was, as if that vagabond neurotic could even his keel.

While Tuta went to get the key to unlock the freezer, Dubecheck stood thinking how much he didn't want to be involved in the event. And when the man returns he'll say so.

"Tuta, sir. I'd really rather not . . . you know, *do* this. It's sort of a private, religious thing between you two."

"See that flag on that boat down there? Old Glory limp on the staff?"

"Yes, sir. It's one of my boats, so to speak."

"Well, get it. We'll wrap the remains in it."

"Doesn't she have to be an American citizen? I mean to . . . ?"

"She couldn't help it she wasn't an American. Suffice to say, she was in her heart."

"I don't think the flag's large enough."

"You haven't seen what's left of her."

"I don't want to either."

"There's a lot of things, as we hump through this veil of tears, we don't want to do, Lieutenant."

Madame Phong lies on a couple of cardboard cases of frozen orange juice concentrate from the Sunshine State, covered by a frozen poncho liner that looks like a battered piece of sheet metal.

Tuta lifts it off. She's like a small charred log, something he's seen smoldering on the beach at dawn after the bonfire of the night, unrecognizable as a human, really. But the thing was a human. He remembers once seeing it asleep on a bed, maybe dreaming in absolute ignorance. He turns away to lean his still sweaty forehead against the wall, and before he realizes his mistake, it freezes to the metal. He snaps his head back, tearing his forehead off the wall like tape, leaving a frosty swatch of skin. "Jesus Christ!"

385

"Give me the flag, Lieutenant." He hands it over his shoulder and listens to Tuta wrap the charred corpse as he wheezes through his nose.

"I'll go get the boat ready."

o   o   o

Somehow, Kooseman's gotten the word and comes running down the dock ramp, apoplectic.

"You can't do that! That's . . . that's . . . You can't do that. That's American property, Dubecheck! Where's Tuta?"

"He went to take a leak. Then we were going to bury his baby at sea." He points to the flag-draped bundle sitting in the bulge of the Boston Whaler next to a six-pack of Hamm's.

"The man's incompetent, Dubecheck. They're coming to get him. *I'm* going to be in command. Even *now* I could order you not to do this, because I outrank you."

"Order me not to do it, then."

"I order you not to do this! It's obscene! You are not to under-take this travesty, this desecration of the flag of your country. Do-you-understand, mister?"

"Yes."

Kooseman hyperventilates in free-form rage. His shrieking has drawn the attention of previously idle people now poking their heads out from behind trees and the several Quonset huts. Dube-check sees Scoog as one of them and waves hello.

Tuta comes down the ramp buttoning his fly. Dubecheck gets into the Whaler and starts undoing the lines.

"Didn't you understand me?" Kooseman screams.

"Yes, I did." Dubecheck wishes he had paid more attention in school. His head is a jumble of memories about Huckleberry Finn or somebody who felt his allegiance wasn't to the law but to some higher order or something; he can't quite remember who or when or what but he recalls why.

"I ordered you not to do this!"

Now it comes back to him. "I take my orders from a higher authority."

"Who is that?"

"Anybody but you," says Dubecheck and he helps Tuta into the boat and they drive away. Just another day at the beach.

o   o   o

He remembers little of the burial at sea as he makes way for the hotel and "home" through the dusk-shaded streets, lanterns and colored lights twinkling in the day's settling dust like concussion spots before his eyes.

The burial detail was a quiet trip for the most part, Tuta mentioning that at one time there used to be millions of mummies in Egypt, but then they decided to use them for fuel to run the locomotives. Really. And that the Japanese soldiers used real humans, civilians, for bayonet practice after they conquered Singapore during W. W. Deuce. And whereas they used the mummies to fuel locomotives in the nineteenth century and the Japanese soldiers bayonetted folks in the twentieth, one century seems to be much the same as another, year in, year out.

Dubecheck took the little Boston Whaler downriver for over an hour, to where the shoreline appeared remote, uninhabited, chartreuse, vermilion, fungicidal, a place where he would not be surprised to see dinosaurs grazing like cattle.

"This looks good to me." Tuta came out of what Dubecheck imagined a deep reverie.

"You think so?"

"Sure."

"I brought a Bible along. Cao Dais believe in the Holy Scriptures . . . among other things. Do you have any thoughts? I mean, what might be appropriate?"

"Let not the right hand know what the left hand doeth."

"Come again?"

"I really don't know much about the Bible, sir. Open it anywhere. A lot of it all sounds the same to me and I can't understand the rest."

"Yes. I see what you mean. . . ."

"Whosoevereths and thees and thines and thous."

Tuta leafed through the Bible with his hands shaking, a frown on his face, inhaling a few false starts before finally shutting it with a defeated sigh. He got up and, cradling the flag-draped remains, leaned overboard and gently placed the colorful red, white and blue bundle upon the mud-colored water. They stood and watched the ebb tide draw Tush's floating body down toward the South China

Sea. Tuta said, "I love you," then sat down, rocking the boat. Dubecheck drove the boat back in semisolitude.

o   o   o

Upon his return, Dubecheck is informed by Dupree of Scoog's arrest. Kooseman had apparently become very angry and screamed to one and all and everyone else within range of his rage-cracked voice that Dubecheck was finally going to get it. Kooseman was going to file the proper papers leading to a full-on court-martial and was striding toward the Com Hut to send messages and do whatever must be done to do the right thing when he ran into Scoog's grime-encrusted fist.

Dupree continues, "I believe Scoog only meant to convey his mental anguish over what Kooseman meant to do to you, the injustice of it all, but in his best Billy Budd manner he could only stammer, eventually giving vent to his anger by breaking the full lieutenant's nasal passage with his fist."

"Yikes!"

"Precisely. Mr. Recore, however, indicated to the offended officer, should he continue to seriously consider pressing charges against you, that he, Mr. Recore, being of sound body and unsound mind, would kill the aggrieved lieutenant and put his body into the blender generally used by galley personnel to grind meat."

"And?"

"The local military contingent awaits the outcome of all this with bated breath. You may help by coercing a written apology from Scoog, who has claimed he'll go to the gallows first. You have always inspired great loyalty in your men, Dubecheck. It's a pity your talents are wasted."

o   o   o

It did not take Tuta, weighted down with woe, long to cave.

As Dubecheck arrived back at the hotel, Dupree called with the news.

"The noblest of us all attempted to commit suicide. His unfamiliarity with the weapon of choice caused it to discharge as he was loading it, blowing off parts of two fingers on his left hand. As usual, he made a small spectacle of himself, hopping up and down, naked, clutching his wounded hand and screaming in pain and anger, spewing blood about the mess hall. Hooch maids screaming, cooks shouting. You may visualize. They are coming to take him away."

Dubecheck runs down to see the man off, which is only natural, being that he is the man's only friend, and he sees they have Tuta sedated, morphined and wrapped up as they load him like a drugged, rubber-legged nincompoop into the front of an Army two-ton from Dong Tam. Simultaneously, Rocky Akoka's Happytime Hollywood Review from Pusan is being loaded into the back of the truck like a honking gaggle of unruly geese.

Tiger doesn't even give Dubecheck a glance as he stands beside Dupree at the back edge of a curious crowd.

She sits on a side bench in her shiny red dress with the bangles and fringes, staring down at the floor, looking as if she's been captured.

Dubecheck edges his way through the crowd to try and get another look at Tuta and is met by Rocky Akoka.

Akoka hands Dubecheck the accordion. "Take it. It don't work too good. I figure, in the whole Orient, it's got a good home with you." Akoka smiles.

Dubecheck never remembers Akoka smiling.

"Sure. I'll learn to play it."

"No, you won't." Akoka laughs and runs to leap up into the truck, which makes a slow U-turn that brings Tuta into view. He sits between two sullen-looking, mouth-breathing GIs. His eyes meet Dubecheck's and then the truck goes away down the dusty tree-lined street forever. And the crowd breaks up and everyone wanders off to do whatever it is they do. As if they have a purpose.

Dubecheck turns to Dupree. "I think people who commit suicide don't want to die, they just want to stop the pain."

"You know what Recore said about you?"

"Yeah. That he didn't think I had 'it' in me."

"Yeah. And that you just look stupid, you really aren't."

"What's Recore know?"

"He knows how the meat gets on the end of the fork for one thing. And you don't see him standing around with a broken accordion strapped to his chest."

Dubecheck looks down at all the black buttons. "You know, Norman, all in all I have done nothing of which to either be proud or ashamed of. So far, life in Asia has been a wash."

"I have noticed a tendency you have, Dubecheck. It's a fruitless one."

"Really?"

"Yeah, really. You are mistaken. You think there are lessons to be learned from things. There aren't. Stuff happens. Like Rocky Akoka and his Happytime Hollywood Review. They were just here. One day they won't be anywhere and that's that."

"Are we here?"

"Yes. We are here. Someday we won't be here and that's that too."

"And nothing makes any difference. Right?"

"Right. Stuff happens and nothing makes any difference. And what if it did? Who's to tell?"

"And there are no lessons to be learned."

"Right. Take Kooseman for example. He really believes in life's linearity. He thinks after he is done here is he going to go home to America and become a businessman. No, he's not. He's going to go home to America and constantly become Kooseman. He will remain Kooseman until he is dead."

"Somewhere along the line I had hoped to do something of value, maybe even something courageous. Not heroic. Just courageous enough to be able to *know*. To know *something*. But I'm beginning to think there's just a tunnel at the end of the light, Norman."

"There's a place in the New World for you, Dubecheck."

o   o   o

Scoog had been confined to quarters, house arrest, but since Lieutenant Kooseman had to visit his physician and would be out of town for most of the day, Dubecheck has decided to take his leading petty officer out on his leash for a few hours of fresh air and convivial banter. It's not that he intends to fraternize with an enlisted man, he just thinks it the decent thing to do since the fellow stands a good chance of doing hard time unless everyone can get deep enough into Kooseman's febrile mind to make him let bygones be bygones.

Take Scoog out in the Boston Whaler with a couple of Cokes and the accordion for a cruise under the benign blue sky.

He steers the Whaler off the main river up a tributary past skinny fish stakes jiggling in the current, cruising close by a small island with a deserted six-shack hamlet. A Sunday ride into the country. The narrow waterway opens up to reveal a labyrinth of waterways snaking off from a muddy brown half-moon bay.

Dubecheck cuts the engine and lets the boat drift, listening to the incessant, soft patter of the river chop against the hull.

He watches a mosquito alight upon the back of Scoog's sweaty, acne-textured neck as the sailor squats in front of him, repatching the accordion.

Dubecheck watches the mosquito engorge itself on Scoog's neck, calculating its probable life span. The insect doesn't know it has blundered upon the king of beasts, the top of the chain.

Scoog slaps the back of his neck and regards the squashed black snowflake in his palm. "Fuckin' skeeters!"

Dubecheck feels the heat getting to him. He is suddenly dizzy and the dizziness washes over him into a buzz of noise. Through his clouded vision he sees in the distance the main river carry people upon it, borne upon its murky current, gliding through the daily accident; breathing, watching, listening, lives idling like two-stroke engines.

He feels dizzy with a free-floating emptiness he now realizes he has no particular right or obligation to fill. At one point he would have wished to fill it with heroics . . . nobility . . . a good deed well done . . . integrity. Something to do with fine-sounding words such as those.

Several more mosquitoes land among the welter of pimples, nicks and previous bites speckled on Scoog's back, which curves so that his spine appears like a long row of knuckles. The sight makes Dubecheck keenly aware of life, as if he could reach in and wrap his hand around Scoog's spine like the grip of a suitcase, like the spine on the body of a dead gook whose lower half had been blown off. The spine lay dangling out of his torso like a frayed white cord, the bone still shiny and moist as flies drank from it.

Dubecheck picks a mosquito off Scoog's back between his thumb and forefinger and holds it up to the sun and flicks it away.

He and Scoog dangle their bare feet over the sides of the Whaler into the water, sip Cokes and smoke Scoog's Lucky Strikes. "It isn't respect for authority that makes things work, Scoog. It's manners. See, you don't have to respect a guy like Kooseman. Not even his authority. But see, good manners say you don't bust a guy in his chops."

"Yessir. I agree. Manners make the world go round. I don't got 'em. My upbringin', I'm sure."

"You had a rough childhood, Scoog. Not that I care or it's any of my business, but your defense attorney might use that, you know." Dubecheck watches a smoke ring roll out, warp and vanish in the breeze. "I appreciate what you tried to do for me, Scoog. But we can't have it . . . sailors going around belting officers, even if they got it coming. It's bad manners."

"Will Mr. Recore kill him?"

"I don't know. Mr. Recore has killed many people for lesser reasons than he has to kill Mr. Kooseman."

"But those was gooks . . . gooks. I don't see how the gooks take it, sir."

"I think how it works is they have to sort of take it whether they like it or not. Just like everybody else." Dubecheck leans back over the gunwale, the top of his head inches above the water, taking in the gently rocking world topsy-turvy: pretending the gray-brown water is the sky, the huge cumulus reflections of another world shimmering in his vision, and then walking out of the green brush of the new sky is a human being. A man.

He swings up his head in a dizzying swoop. They have drifted close to shore in the drowsy warmth and, no more than twenty yards away, walking along a path paralleling the shore, is a healthy Asian male—out in the middle of nowhere, acting totally oblivious.

The guy is an obvious gangster. He is ignoring Scoog and Dube-check with such tunnel-vision intensity that Dubecheck *knows* the guy *knows* he's waltzed into deep, deep shit. He knows the guy wants to scream, "Who in the hell are *those* guys and what are they doing *there?*" He wears blue pants and a short-sleeved white shirt and he is out in the dead open staring dead ahead, putting one foot after another, and Dubecheck can almost see the guy throb with fear. He doesn't even dare swipe at the mosquito that is homing in on his cheek. He is fit and sleek and he must be thinking his number is up.

"Jesus Christ," Scoog whispers.

Dubecheck gropes for the M-16 he brought along. He shoved a clip in it before they left and he remembered the clip felt light and thought it was probably empty. He raises the M-16 and watches the guy continue his trancelike stroll, crossing the T, right down the end of Dubecheck's barrel.

"Grease the fucker, sir." The man takes a right-angle turn as the invisible path must have taken through the knee-deep grasses that dance in the wind.

"The guy's gotta be hard core, sir."

"Tell him to stop."

"LA DEY MOTHERFUCKER!" Scoog screams.

The guy keeps walking away, steady, presenting his broad white back, shirttails waving in the wind, the back of his head black, the skull beneath full of gray, electric pudding. Dubecheck fires off a round, aiming four feet over his head. Ice. The guy is ice. He maintains his steady gait, slowly receding yet still locked in for at least another hundred yards of near point-blank range where even a lousy shot like Dubecheck could send one through the back of his head and take his face off.

Dubecheck drops his aim and fires one a foot over the guy's head. Nothing.

"I said, 'LA DEY!' you sonofabitchin' bastard!" Scoog stands in the boat with his hands on his hips as if he is miffed. He looks down to Dubecheck.

"Well, how in the hell you like that, Mr. Dubecheck?" Scoog sounds hurt, seething through the cigarette clenched in his teeth.

Dubecheck rests the sight upon the huge white target of the man's back, sees the shirt flutter, and beneath he envisions the shaded crevice of his spinal column and with the gun sight moves up along the spine, following the circuitry up to the dark-haired skull housing the madcap mystery. The back of the man's head wavers in the sight like a small black rubber ball.

"Fuck it." Dubecheck tosses the rifle down into the corner of the stern and never looks at the guy again.

He closes his eyes, straps on the accordion and dangles his feet in the water. A shift in the current, now ebb tide, drags them through the water and he can feel his toes leaving little eddies in their wake.

After a long time Scoog heaves a sigh. "That guy sure had a pair, didn't he, sir?"

"He sure did."

"You think he was hard core?"

"Harder than me, Scoog. Harder than me."

"What if he was the guy who did the Goofy cartoon, Mr. Dubecheck?"

"There will always be someone who will do a Goofy cartoon, Scoog. But to tell the truth, I don't know how to answer that."

"Really?"

"Really."

The soft brown water slurps against the hull of the Whaler and Dubecheck gazes through the haze of his eyelashes up into God's great sky. This wasn't *all* for naught. Out of this will come some good, for surely God did not make the planet so pretty that it must be a sewer of rage, stupidity and chaos. For himself, Dubecheck intends to do good. Dupree is wrong. There is a meaning to things that transcend the incalculable. Now what it is, he doesn't have a clue, but he has decided that a certain resolve is incumbent upon a guy.

The womblike warmth of the Mekong Delta breeze caresses his cheek and envelops his skull.

He idly fingers the black buttons and piano keys of the worthless accordion and stares off toward the wide main river and imagines looking as far away as he can: to where the river enters the sea, to where the sea becomes the vast ocean, to where the horizon endlessly falls away to become the curvature of the earth.

"Nice day."

"Yeah, really."

ABOUT THE AUTHOR

David Eyre was born in Seattle in 1941 and graduated from the University of Washington in 1965 after interrupting his studies to hitchhike around Europe and the Middle East.

Mr. Eyre served as an officer in the United States Navy in the Western Pacific and Southeast Asia in the late 1960s.

After his discharge, David Eyre moved to Venice, California, and then to Aspen, Colorado, before returning to the Pacific Northwest. Mr. Eyre now lives in Winthrop, Washington, about thirty miles south of the Canadian border.